The Fractured Road

Part I: East and West

Britt Holewinski

ISBN 978-1-4810617-1-1

For Patrick and Thomas

And for Katrina,
who gave me the confidence to keep going.

Prologue

They move quickly under the cover of night, the summer air thick with humidity. Sweat trickles down their foreheads and spines as they scurry like frightened rabbits through the trees, with only the single beam of a flashlight to guide them. A new moon makes the darkness complete—a rare advantage for them.

There are two of them, boys barely old enough to be called "men" in an age long gone and mostly forgotten. A year separates the older from the younger, but they both run at the same speed, the elder taking longer strides while the younger keeps up with a quicker gait. Armed, they each carry loaded M4 rifles. The younger one presses the button on his watch to activate the light; the green glow reveals thirty seconds left on the clock. Twenty-nine…twenty-eight…

They are fugitives, but revenge is worth the risk.

In less than thirty seconds it will be done. All that remains is to drive away—to somewhere they will never be found.

Twenty...nineteen…eighteen…

The truck is just a hundred yards away now. They couldn't park close at the risk of being seen by the guards while masking their getaway. Both are out of breath, but they press on as fast as they can.

Nine…eight…seven…

They finally clear the trees as their feet leave the grass and hit the pavement, the truck now in sight. The older one reaches into his back pocket and manages to grab the key while maintaining his speed.

Three…two…one…

The explosion is loud, and the resulting fire lights up the night sky to their left; they pause only a second to look. It is done, and there is nothing left to do except drive—and drive fast.

They reach the truck and scramble inside. The ignition mercifully fires up on the first try, and a moment later, they are gone. The headlights of the truck remain off. Darkness is their ally.

The old pickup disappears onto I-270 South as they continue to distance themselves from New York.

Chapter I

My name is Andrea Christensen. I am one of the oldest people in the world.

Every story has a beginning; for me, this one began on the twenty-fifth of June, 2020, exactly three days before my nineteenth birthday. That day is forever burned in my mind as the day my best friend was raped. Everything before then was little more than a precursor of what was to come, although I would never have guessed it at the time.

This is the story of the human race's return to humanity…

I grew up in the suburbs of Philadelphia, an only child to two wonderful parents. When I was thirteen, my mother and I suffered a horrific car accident. I escaped with a few bruised ribs and minor scrapes and scratches, but my mother wasn't so lucky. The oncoming SUV slammed into our car, striking the driver's side directly, crushing the entire left side of her body. The paramedics did their best to revive her, but less than thirty minutes after the accident, she was pronounced dead. It was two weeks before Christmas.

I stumbled through the remainder of the school year, walking the corridors like a zombie, while my father had all but abandoned his private medical practice. He canceled more appointments than he kept, and I often wondered if he felt partially to blame for the accident. He was supposed to be in the car with us that day but work delayed him. My mother still would have been behind the wheel, for she loved to drive as much as my father hated it. But—in his mind—had he been in the car with us, he would have been able to save her. He would have been able to pull her back from the brink.

* * *

25 May 2015

Both my father and I needed a change; we needed an escape from the emptiness and from the memories.

My father had an old college friend who owned a house in Bermuda, and he offered to let us stay there—the entire summer if we wanted. The tiny, secluded island was the perfect place for us to abandon the pain that had suddenly entered our lives. In that house, which sat less than a hundred yards from the ocean, my father and I found refuge. While he spent most of his days fishing and reading in a beach chair before sunset, I wandered the island seeking any adventure of interest to a thirteen-year-old. It wasn't difficult to convince the locals to let me rent a motor scooter, despite the fact that I was clearly underage. All that was required was a few extra dollars and a winning smile. My mother had always said that I had a bright, beautiful smile. Personally, I always thought it looked slightly crooked—at least whenever I looked in the mirror.

It was while riding a scooter in downtown Hamilton that I first ran into Morgan and Charlie…literally. They were crossing at an intersection when the brakes on my scooter seized up, causing a horrible skid. The scooter hit a newspaper stand, knocking it over and pushing Morgan off her feet. She then collided into Charlie, who fell hard to the ground. Fortunately, neither had been seriously injured, and I'd somehow managed to remain seated on the scooter throughout the entire incident, the first of many escapes in years to come. Once the chaos was over and my father examined all three of us, we were all properly introduced.

Morgan and Charlie Pemberton were born and raised in England, although their parents were Scottish. They lived in Oxford—their father a history professor at the famous university, while their mother worked as a nurse. They had rented a house on the beach for the entire summer, which made me very happy. Just a few months younger than I, Morgan was tall and willowy with wavy, chestnut hair and pale skin. She was a delicate creature, and I wasn't surprised to discover she had studied ballet for ten years. "Not long after I learned to walk, I was already twirling around in a tutu," she'd remarked. I liked Morgan immediately. She was soft-spoken and polite, not loud and obnoxious like most of the silly girls I went to school with. From the very beginning we were kindred spirits.

My first impression of Charlie was that he was a genius in the very literal sense of the word. His mind was simply a wonder to observe. Words like "magnanimous," "exacerbate," and "contemptuous" wove through his sentences with remarkable ease, and I often felt like I was speaking to an adult, at least on an intellectual level. At the time, those words meant nothing to me, and I often had to ask Charlie what they meant. Thankfully, conceit was not one of Charlie's other qualities, and he would happily translate anything into a vocabulary that my mind could comprehend. Like his sister, Charlie was wiry and pale with brown hair and light brown eyes. He was tall as well; though I was three years older, I barely edged him in height.

The three of us quickly became inseparable. Luckily, my father and their parents gave us the freedom to roam the island to our hearts' content. We spent hours wandering the beaches and swimming along nearly every inch of shoreline. When we weren't traveling on the ferries that shuttled tourists around the island, we bummed rides from locals on motor scooters from the capital city of Hamilton to St. George and back, which, in hindsight was probably a foolish thing for three children to do. But, like most children, we were invincible.

Being the tomboy that I was, I tried anything—from diving off cliffs to swimming with sea turtles. Charlie, being nearly as fearless, followed me off the cliffs and alongside the turtles. But Morgan was more timid. Often she would just sit on the shore and watch, hoping we wouldn't hurt ourselves. Not that I thought Morgan was a coward; it's just that I was daring to the point of recklessness. And Charlie wouldn't dare let a girl outdo him.

As these sun-soaked days passed, the sting of my mother's death slowly began to wane. When I wasn't wandering off with Morgan and Charlie, I would join my father for a few peaceful moments fishing off the pier near our house. We didn't say much. Every so often he would give me pointers on the "fine art of fishing" while I pretended to be interested. One day, about a few weeks after our arrival, my father caught a large grey snapper, and as I watched the smile spread across his face as he reeled the hapless fish in, I realized that it had been months since I'd seen my father look so happy. Then I realized something else, something that made me very sad: my father would never again be as he'd been when my mother was alive. Before the accident, I had many friends whose parents were either separated or divorced, and they would often tell me how lucky I was that my parents were still together. In my mind, I didn't think of it as luck. My parents were more likely to be separated by death than by divorce, which unfortunately became the truth. As I viewed them, they were soul mates. Not once in my thirteen years did I ever hear my mother and father fight. They were simply happy together, always joking around and showing each other affection. I used to roll my eyes at how they would always hold hands in public like two teenagers on a date, and then tell them how embarrassing they were. But deep down, it was comforting to see them so happy, which is why I felt so much more than sadness for my father after my mother died. Though I knew he loved me, I knew I could never fill the hole that my mother's death had left behind, and because of that, I felt helpless.

Maybe it was this helplessness that made what happened only days later seem like a blessing, at least for my father. For everyone else on the island, it was to become the beginning of something no one could have ever imagined.

* * *

24 June 2015

Our thirty-first day on the island, I woke up much later than usual. I could tell immediately that it was late by the angle of the sun streaming through the blinds in my room. I quickly rose out of bed to check the time. It was 9:47 a.m. Judging by the silence in the house, I assumed my father was already out fishing. Heading downstairs to the kitchen, I heard Morgan and Charlie talking. There was a strange edge in their voices.

Still groggy from sleep, I rubbed my eyes as I looked at my friends, and noticed that both had been crying.

"What's the matter?" I asked, not sure of what to expect.

Neither Morgan nor Charlie answered or made a move to do so. Their silence was disturbing, but their stillness made my heart pound.

"What's happened?" I demanded. I looked at Morgan with desperation, but she could only shake her head as she began to sob. I turned to Charlie for some kind of response. He stared back at me with weeping eyes for what seemed like an

eternity when his mouth opened to speak.

"They're sick…they have that virus…the one on the news," he gasped.

"Who's sick?!"

Charlie's lips parted once more. The words barely made it out.

"Mum and dad…people are dying from it," he whispered before collapsing into a chair at the kitchen table.

We'd heard about it on the news the past few days: a virus that had accidentally been released somewhere on the East Coast of the United States. But listening with the ears of children, the details of the situation were quickly forgotten once we stepped outside and into the ocean. With so many problems in the world, the virus seemed to blend in with everything else. And if my father—a doctor —wasn't concerned, then I wasn't going to be concerned.

But the look on my friends' faces changed that.

Without a word, I bolted out the front door, leaving Morgan and Charlie in my wake. The bottom of my feet pounded so hard against the ground that I could not feel them make contact. I ran to the beach, toward the pier where my father normally sat fishing as the sun rose in front of him.

The pier was about a hundred yards away from the house. Without a single cloud to shadow it, the sun, already strong and steady, forced me to squint my eyes. I tried desperately to see if my father was at the end of the pier, but my vision was further blurred by my running. A rush of relief flowed through me when I saw him sitting at the edge of the pier, and I lunged toward him. But my relief would be short-lived.

My father turned to me, his face incredibly pale despite all the hours of sunshine during the weeks prior.

"Andy, honey…I'm not feeling so well…"

He could barely stand up, and I had to help him to his feet as my heart sank.

Two days later, my father was dead.

Chapter II

The days that followed were the most terrifying of Andrea's young life. The once-tranquil island of Bermuda rapidly transformed into an isolated prison of chaos and fear. The virus that had been reported on the news was far more serious than anyone could have imagined…and far more deadly. It was an airborne contagion with an incubation period of ten to fourteen days. An infected person could be walking around for two weeks without showing any signs of being sick, while spreading the virus to people in their neighborhood or strangers across the globe. Once the symptoms appeared, however, certain death occurred between two and four days. There was no vaccine. Before the televisions went silent, the last news reports suggested that the release of the virus was accidental and had occurred at the Center for Disease Control in Georgia. The origin of the virus, however, remained a mystery. Within several weeks, over six billion people were dead.

Despite its virulence, there was one particular group who was completely immune to the virus: children and young teenagers who had not yet completed puberty. Based upon existing levels of hormones in the body, the virus was either one hundred percent deadly or entirely harmless. Since they were both thirteen, Andrea—or Andy as she was called—and Morgan, were among the oldest survivors on the island. Their late development into adulthood was the only thing that saved them. On average, girls completed puberty before boys, so the oldest survivors tended to be male.

Of the seventy thousand people who'd been living on the island before the virus, about thirteen thousand, including tourists, had survived, most of them younger than fourteen. The majority of these survivors lingered in or around Hamilton, the centrally-located capital of Bermuda, or in the northeastern town of St. George. Andy's vacation home, where she now lived with Morgan and Charlie, was located on the southwestern end of the main island, and as far as possible from both Hamilton and St. George. This physical distance from the surviving population was a welcome separation, for more than fifty thousand corpses littered every house, street, and building across the island. Within days of the last death, the stench of rotting flesh had become unbearable; the trio removed as many bodies as they could off the streets near their home and inside the neighboring houses. The thought of dead bodies rotting away in houses within view of their own home was too much to bear. The mere sight of death itself had become maddening. At first they buried each body in the ground, but after a week, digging fresh graves became too exhausting. Cremation was the only sane solution, although creating a human bonfire seemed to approach a new level of depravity. In the beginning, Andy wondered about every person she threw onto the fire and what their lives had been like, but after forty or fifty bodies, her curiosity waned. The emotional detachment was disturbing, but the efficiency was undeniable. Soon the smell of decaying flesh ceased, along with any reminders of death.

Their parents received far better and more thoughtful treatment. Morgan and Charlie chose to bury their mother and father under a large, flowering tree that lined the 15th hole of the Port Royal Golf Course, not far from their new home. Regarded as one of the finest courses in the world, it was an appropriate resting place, considering their parents had not only loved golf, but were both from Scotland where the game originated. For her father, Andy chose the ocean as his final resting place. Using a small motorboat, she laid his body inside with a daisy-chain of Bermuda Easter Lilies around his neck, then turned on the motor, and let the boat head out to sea. She watched the boat as it disappeared over the horizon.

Food quickly became an issue once all the grocery stores and markets were emptied. Initially, Andy, Morgan, and Charlie had gathered enough food to completely cover their kitchen floor with boxes and cans, but this stash lasted only a few months, so they became skilled at fishing and gardening to survive. It turned out that Andy was a natural at fishing; her newfound talent, seemingly inherited from her father, kept her and her friends alive during the first year on the island. Growing vegetables, however, was much harder to master, but fortunately the soil beneath the same golf course where Morgan and Charlie's parents were buried proved to be fertile and forgiving to novice gardeners. By the time the canned vegetables ran out, their garden had yielded just enough to get by.

That first year was the most difficult. When not guarding their home and food from the thousands of other survivors scattered throughout the island, there were storms to contend with. Three hurricanes pummeled Bermuda in August and September, each one destroying whatever repairs had been done to fix the home's roof after the previous storm. After the third hurricane, they gave up trying to keep the roof intact until hurricane season was over as both sun and rain entered the home uninvited. Illness plagued all three of them at some point—everything from the common cold to dysentery. On Christmas day, Andy vomited so much from a stomach virus that she half-expected her insides to come out. Children were, for the most part, resilient—physically and emotionally—but the trauma of being orphaned and stranded on a remote island made it seem as though God was playing a cruel joke on them.

Fortunately, the distance of the beach house from Hamilton and St. George isolated them from the chaos infecting the rest of Bermuda. The survivors were starving, and vicious fights broke out every day over a couple of cans of food. Inevitably, the older survivors formed what could only be described as gangs that quickly multiplied throughout the island. Controlled by older children, much of the heavy lifting was carried out by the younger survivors who stole food and supplies from other gangs and hapless survivors to maintain strength and power. Luckily, these gangs kept to their own neighborhoods and rarely roamed toward the west end of the island. On the rare occasions when they strayed too close, Andy, Morgan, and Charlie would fortify themselves inside their home until the threat moved on. Andy ensured the house was armed with a sufficient stock of guns and ammunition, which were found after extensive scavenging of neighboring homes and buildings, as well as the local police station in Somerset Village at the west end. She and Charlie would often practice their firing skills by targeting sea gulls on the beach, and anything they killed usually became supper. At first, the power of a gun was intimidating, but over time their comfort with the weapons increased. For mild amusement, Andy and Charlie would race to see who could dismantle, then reassemble their weapon faster, and though Andy usually won, Charlie wasn't far behind. Morgan on the other hand, hated guns, but she forced herself to learn to use one just in case.

When they weren't busy trying to stay alive and out of danger, the three each found their own way to pass the time.

* * *

How does one measure time?

Adults often measured time by their accomplishments, either personal or financial, while children would count the days they would have to wait between one exciting event to another—like the two excruciatingly long months between Halloween and Christmas. The elderly, meanwhile, measured time by how much things had changed over the course of their lifetime, like the exponential rise in the cost of a movie ticket from their distant youth to the present.

Andy measured the passage of time by how many different medical books she read, and how many procedures, however simple, she learned. Along with fishing, she had acquired a passion for her father's profession, and after more than a dozen dangerous trips to the King Edward Memorial Hospital in gang-infested Hamilton, she had all the reading material necessary to gain a rudimentary understanding of a variety of ailments and the drugs required to treat them.

At first, Andy's studies merely centered on keeping her and her two friends as healthy as possible. Without the normal volume of patients to practice on, her knowledge remained limited to merely the theoretical application of medicine. She learned everything she could about human anatomy; how each part worked and interacted with one another, and what happened if one part became broken or damaged. She memorized symptoms for even more obscure illnesses and diseases until her brain ached. During the second year on the island, Charlie suffered an unexpected bout of gangrene in his left foot, and suddenly, out of necessity, her interest in medicine accelerated.

It was an ingrown toenail that became infected to such a degree that his big toe became grossly discolored. Afraid that it would spread further, Andy tried to treat the infection with every remedy she could think of, save amputation. There was no way she could ever gather the courage to perform such a procedure, even for something as small as a toe. Instead, Andy bombarded Charlie's system with antibiotics from the local hospital, had him breathe pure oxygen from tanks for a full week to slow the growth of the bacteria in his foot, and even prescribed an herbal regimen of dried ginger, garlic, and ginkgo biloba to improve circulation. Whether by medicine or miracle, Charlie's infection cleared up, and soon after, a handful of trustworthy survivors living nearby began to seek Andy's help for their minor aches and ailments. Though happy to offer her skills, both for the experience and for the satisfaction of helping other human beings, Andy knew she was merely a novice, an inexperienced nurse at best.

Meanwhile, Morgan and Charlie found their own ways to pass the time.

Charlie was indeed intelligent, but after playing around with some old IQ tests found at a nearby school, he proved it on paper. His mind simply thirsted for knowledge. He could spend hours at one sitting doing nothing but reading book after book on subjects ranging from the origins of the Universe to the history of Australia. He even read some of Andy's medical books, at her encouragement. A good doctor always knows that a second opinion is important to the patient, and Charlie was more than willing to let Andy take advantage of his brainpower.

Morgan continued to practice ballet, her lifelong passion. One of the spare bedrooms in the beach house had been converted into a dance studio, complete with mirrors on three sides and even a makeshift barre for stretching and warming up. Morgan spent at least two hours in that room every day, wishing that she still lived in a world where she could one day be a prima ballerina. When she wasn't practicing tour jetés or pirouettes, she loved to draw. The evenings were her favorite time, sitting on the porch during the sunset, painting anything that came to mind. Andy often observed how Morgan sketched as effortlessly as she breathed. The movements of her hand were as graceful as the movements she performed while dancing.

A warm yet delicate creature, it was difficult to imagine Morgan surviving this strange and chaotic world without her tomboyish friend or brother to protect her.

* * *

Spring 2020

Five years passed.

Andy and Morgan grew into young women of eighteen. One day Andy looked in the mirror and suddenly realized that she was no longer a child. Her long blond hair, nearly white from years in the sun, framed a face that had become more oval in shape over time. Her eyes, green as emeralds, sparkled not with the carefree air of youth, but with the wisdom of age beyond her years. And despite the years of living on a meager diet, Andy's hips and chest had swelled just enough to create an hourglass figure. These changes, however, were imperceptible to her. She only saw the muscles in her shoulders and arms from swimming in the ocean, and the calluses on her hands from fishing and climbing trees.

Morgan, meanwhile, grew both taller and more beautiful. With her delicate features, pale skin, and high cheekbones, she resembled the models plastered on the pages of the tattered women's magazines that she and Andy had skimmed through millions of times.

"With your looks, you could've been one of these women," Andy often told her friend, who in turn would laugh and say, "Why would I want to be one of them? All they do is stand there with big pouts on their faces."

"I know that. I'm just saying that you're as pretty as these women."

"Well, so are you."

As usual, Andy would scoff at this and quickly change the subject. The truth was that both girls had become attractive women in their own right, but while Morgan understood that she was beautiful and merely shrugged it off, Andy was blind to the truth about her own appearance. She was a tomboy, and tomboys weren't supposed to be pretty.

Charlie grew an average of two-and-a-half inches per year, and his voice deepened with the onset of adolescence. Now a good-looking young man of fifteen, Charlie emerged from the typical awkward phases of a boy's early teens, to a teenager full of confidence and a passion for adventure. He proved to be a terrific athlete, and over the years he and Andy continued their good-natured swimming and running competitions along the shoreline. During the first three years, Andy remained victorious. Around Charlie's fourteenth birthday, however, he finally caught up to her, and by the fifth year, Andy was the one trying to keep up.

"I gotta face it. You finally have enough testosterone to beat me," she said breathlessly one morning after another defeat in the ocean.

"I'm afraid I'll never be able to beat you again."

"Aw, you're fast, Andy…for a girl," Charlie teased, provoking a large splash of saltwater in his face.

"Oh, yeah? Well, if I *were* a boy, I'd beat you every time!"

Along with his athletic skill, Charlie's mental knowledge expanded enormously over the years. Books, however, no longer took up all of his time. Instead, the majority of his days were spent learning practical things like how car engines worked or hooking up a generator to their home. But it was sailing that became Charlie's passion. Using an abandoned sailboat left at a nearby pier, and combining his love of the ocean with his desire to learn, he became as close to an expert sailor as anyone could tell.

Charlie's love of sailing secretly pleased Andy, for in her heart she knew the day would come when leaving Bermuda would no longer be a possibility, but a necessity. Although they had managed to stay alive for five years, she could see changes taking place on the island that gave cause to her increasing worries and sleepless nights. Children were increasingly becoming ill from lack of food and clean water, resulting in serious disease and even death. Desperation to survive resulted in violence that had begun to creep dangerously close to their home in recent months. More than once Andy was forced to use her gun to scare away trespassers threatening to attack or vandalize their home. It was no longer a matter of *if,* but *when* extreme measures would need to be taken.

* * *

04 June 2020

The night everything changed, Andy was busy mending a boy's bloody leg. He'd taken a nasty spill down a rocky slope near his home and needed a few stitches on his kneecap to close the gash. Just as she was finishing the last stitch, Andy was interrupted by Charlie. His face, like Andy's, glistened with sweat from the humidity.

"Have you seen Morgan? I can't find her anywhere, and I need to ask her something."

"She went to the school for English class," Andy replied as she dabbed the boy's leg with disinfectant. "She should be back soon."

Charlie merely nodded and left Andy alone with her patient.

Morgan had been teaching English to survivors for the past two years. She viewed it as a way to give the children she taught some structure and sense of accomplishment in their otherwise chaotic lives. As much as she loved dancing and drawing, teaching English had given Morgan a sense of value as her adoring students evolved from illiteracy to reading Shakespeare.

While Andy and Charlie appreciated Morgan's efforts, both had begun to worry about the increasing lateness of her teaching hours. It was often dark when Morgan finished class, and the school sat nearly a mile away from the house. Once safe for nighttime travel, the road between had grown more and more dangerous as people continued to migrate to the west end of the island. But when Andy expressed her concerns to her friend, Morgan had simply waved them off. Her students needed her, she argued, and they were living in more treacherous areas than she. Andy eventually left the issue alone.

But this night, a full hour after Morgan normally returned from class, she still had not returned. Outside, the darkness of a moonless sky enveloped the island. In the kitchen, Andy paced aimlessly back and forth across the floor while Charlie sat huddled in his chair with his knees hugged to his chest, making him look ten years old again. Neither spoke; both were consumed with worry.

In a sudden flurry of movement, Andy grabbed a flashlight from underneath the sink before dashing upstairs to retrieve a pistol from the lockbox in her bedroom. When she returned to the kitchen, she began loading the gun.

"I'm gonna go look for her. Stay here and if anyone comes, grab the shotgun."

Charlie looked back and forth from Andy to her pistol and stood up.

"I'll get it now," he said unevenly and headed to the coat closet by the front door where the shotgun was kept. Andy despised the shotgun because of the large bruise it left on her arm every time she fired it, but Charlie was now strong enough to suppress its fierce recoil.

"I should be the one to go look for her," Charlie said as he returned to the kitchen, gun in hand. "She's my sister."

"That's precisely why I should go look for her. I'll be thinking more clearly than you."

Charlie opened his mouth to protest, but stopped before any words came out. "All right," he ultimately relented. "I'll stay and guard the house."

Moments later, Andy began making her way toward the school. Even with the flashlight's wide beam, the road was pitch-black. She moved as quickly as possible, both out of concern for her own safety and the urgency to find her friend.

There was no sign of anyone when Andy approached the school. The classroom Morgan most often used was empty, except for a young girl sitting on the dingy floor in the back corner. No more than six or seven years old, she was curled up in a terrified ball of gangly arms and legs. Slowly, Andy tucked the pistol behind her back so as not to frighten the girl. As she approached, Andy could see the glistening streaks of tears running down the girl's cheeks.

"Hey, sweetheart," Andy said in her most gentle tone, despite her increasing concern. "What are you crying about?"

At first the girl merely whimpered but finally managed to say, "They took Miss Morgan!"

Andy felt her stomach plunge.

"Who…who took Miss Morgan?" Her voice trembled.

The girl could only shake her head as her face began to crumple. Tears returned and streamed down her face as Andy tried her best to remain patient.

"Please, honey, you have to tell me where they took her. I need to help her."

The girl remained silent and Andy was about to give up when the girl began wailing.

"They—they took—her to—the bathroom. And then—and then they—locked the door!"

The girl took two sobbing chokes as the blood in Andy's ears began to pound.

"Some—some of the older boys try—tried to open the door—but they—couldn't!"

With that, the girl's body began to shake with uncontrollable sobs. Andy jumped to her feet and bolted outside into the hallway. She raced down the hall and found the bathrooms.

The door to the women's room was somehow locked. Andy withdrew her gun, racked a bullet into the chamber, aimed at the keyhole and fired, praying to God that the bullet wouldn't hit anyone inside. The bullet ripped through the lock, and Andy kicked the door open. The room was dark, so she turned on her flashlight.

It took a moment to register what she saw, and when she did, Andy became nauseous and vomited in the nearby sink.

Morgan lie on her side in a crumpled heap on the bathroom floor. Naked from the waist down, her thighs and torso were covered in fresh bruises. Her left eye had already swollen shut, and blood ran from her nose to her mouth. Through the intense beam of light, Andy could see that she was unconscious but still breathing. Despite the horror of witnessing her best friend in such a ghastly state, Andy gathered the strength to examine her properly as she would any patient. When she lifted Morgan's T-shirt, she discovered more bruises on her back and ribs.

God, what have they done to you?

Opposite the door were two windows with their panes missing, providing a clear indication of how the assailants managed to leave the school while keeping the bathroom locked. It wasn't enough for them to beat Morgan within an inch of her life, but they had to make it difficult for anyone to find her.

Andy gingerly rolled Morgan onto her back to check for other injuries, and she began to silently cry as she realized that Morgan had also been violently raped. The physical damage between her thighs was extensive.

Dazed, Andy attempted to put Morgan's underwear back on but they had been torn to shreds. Stifling another wave of nausea, Andy reached for Morgan's jean shorts laying a few feet away and carefully slid them on her friend. Then, with every ounce of strength she had, Andy hoisted Morgan off the bathroom floor and flung her over her shoulder.

Outside again, Andy carried her near-lifeless friend in near-darkness back to the beach house, all one hundred and ten pounds of her.

* * *

Morgan's rape left an emptiness that could never be filled. Her physical condition, though horrific to behold at first, slowly healed. A few stitches and antibiotics ensured a full recovery while sleep took care of the rest. And sleep Morgan did, thanks to hearty doses of sedatives. Soon her bruises lightened from purple to yellow, and the swelling receded.

But the physical wounds were nothing compared to the emotional turmoil Morgan suffered. She would cry for hours on end, then suddenly stop and stare out her bedroom window toward the endless ocean for another hour or two. Her appetite had vanished, and Andy and Charlie's mutual urgings for her to eat went ignored. Her once tranquil and generous nature had transformed into one of heavy silence.

For weeks, neither Andy nor Charlie knew how to act around her. They tried being supportive, but that only seemed to irritate her. When they tried to pretend as though nothing had happened, it only compounded her silence. At fifteen years old, the last five of which had been spent in relative isolation, Charlie knew almost nothing about sex except from a scientific point of view. To him, the act of sex itself was another frontier yet to be discovered. Nevertheless, when Andy had carried his broken sister home on her back and tearfully explained what happened, Charlie's initial revulsion turned to anger. He simply could not comprehend how anyone could do something so heinous to someone as kind-hearted as Morgan. Charlie vowed revenge, but the identities of the two rapists were unknown to Morgan, thereby denying any possibility of retribution.

One night, about three weeks after the rape, Andy and Charlie had a serious discussion alone in the kitchen. It was Charlie who suggested leaving Bermuda, and Andy came to agree that it was time to go. What had happened to Morgan had forever tainted their home in such a way that even the little joys, like watching the sun set beyond the ocean or swimming among the fish or telling stories by a moonlit fire, had lost their splendor.

When Andy brought up their idea to Morgan, tears emerged in her eyes and splashed her cheeks. Choking back sobs of relief, she nodded weakly but said nothing more. It was a start.

One day, she'll get through this, Andy would tell herself.

* * *

The United States was the only realistic destination. At a distance of six hundred miles from the shores of North Carolina, Bermuda's remote location offered little choice in that regard. Though Charlie was confident in his skills as a sailor, he admitted that navigating across several hundred miles of water would challenge the limit of his abilities.

"I'm just warning you that I may overshoot Cape Hatteras by more than a few kilometers. And if the weather's bad, we may land somewhere north of Nags Head or somewhere south into Cape Lookout."

"Charlie, I'll just be glad if we hit land that's somehow connected to America," Andy replied with amusement as she followed along with a map.

Charlie shrugged. "Okay, I just wanted you to know that I may not be accurate with my calculations."

"I'm sure we'll be fine."

Andy and Charlie did most of the packing. Morgan continued to recover physically, but her mental condition remained fragile, and Andy worried how she would handle the voyage. Would she have the strength to save either her brother or Andy if one of them fell overboard? What if she fell overboard herself? Would she have the will to swim and save her own life?

When Andy cautiously voiced these concerns, Morgan's brusque reply was, "I was raped. If I can live through that, I can live through anything. I just want to leave this island forever and never return."

After that, Andy said nothing more on the subject.

Few items were taken for the journey. Besides sufficient supplies of food, water, clothing, and medicine, Andy brought along her collection of medical journals and her pistol. Charlie took his favorite books, sailing tools, and the shotgun. And Morgan brought only a single painting and her ballet shoes. The painting, one of the first she'd completed five years earlier, depicted the house where she and her brother had grown up in Oxford. It was the only painting that wouldn't remind her of Bermuda.

Amazed how five years of living could be condensed into a few hours of packing, they closed the beach house for the last time only three days after their decision to leave, and coincidentally, the fifth anniversary of the death of Andy's father.

The sky was beautiful that morning and the wind perfect for sailing. The sailboat, equipped with two beds and a small kitchen below deck, got off to a quick start. Two hours after leaving the dock, Bermuda disappeared over the horizon.

Andy knew they would never return. The only question was how unrecognizable her homeland, her country, would be.

Chapter III

01 July 2020

Despite overwhelming odds, they reached the outer shores of North Carolina after six days and nights at sea. Dehydrated, seasick, and exhausted from restless sleep, all three collapsed onto the sand under the sun until their equilibrium stabilized and their stomachs stopped churning. Once their balance returned, they turned their focus inland.

With the sailboat securely anchored, they walked north along the shore to determine where exactly they had landed. After a mile, buildings materialized to their left a few hundred feet from the shoreline. Leading the way, Andy turned her back to the ocean and headed toward the buildings until reaching what appeared to be the main road dividing a small beach town. Derelict homes and storefronts just one bad storm away from crumbling to the ground were scattered along this road. Another quarter-mile further, they approached a tilting sign that read 'Salvo'.

Charlie retrieved a folded map labeled 'Cape Hatteras National Seashore' from his back pocket and found the town of Salvo. After a quick mental calculation, he pointed out their location for his sister and Andy.

"We're here, about fifty kilometers south of Nags Head, which is…" Charlie traced the map with his finger, "…here. From there we can take the bridge on this road…I-64…over to the mainland. Or this road…158." Charlie shrugged. "I guess it all depends on where we want to go from here. But we're still technically on an island and have to go north regardless."

Andy squinted at the map, shading her eyes from the summer sun. "Fifty kilometers? That's what, roughly thirty miles? We're not walking thirty miles." Her tone left no room for argument, but no one disagreed. The journey at sea had taken its toll on Morgan. The yellow bruising around her eye on her otherwise pallid face gave her a rather deathlike appearance.

"We can either hope to find a car in town or go back to the boat and sail north along the coast."

"Andy, I don't think I can spend another minute on that boat," Morgan mumbled weakly, pleading with her eyes. "I know I'll get sick again. I'm sorry."

"Okay, then we'll just have to find a car," Andy said in her most reassuring voice. She placed a hand on Morgan's shoulder and nodded over toward a rickety wooden bench on the other side of the road. "Why don't you go sit there while Charlie and I find a car? It shouldn't take us long."

Andy looked over at Charlie, who nodded in agreement. Morgan gave a faint smile and moved rather slowly across the road. Andy couldn't help but notice how frail she looked. Already a thin girl, her weight had clearly dropped since the attack.

"She looks awful," Charlie muttered once Morgan was out of earshot.

"She just needs food and rest," Andy quickly replied to hide her own concern. She gave Charlie's shoulder a little nudge. "C'mon, the sooner we find a car and get some shelter, the better for all of us."

Salvo was a nothing more than a hollowed-out ghost town swept away by wind, sand, and time. The beach homes and restaurants that had once received care and attention from their adoring owners now showed all the obvious signs of abandonment: peeling paint, broken windows, and cracked sideboards. After a few blocks, they stumbled across two human skeletons lying on the sidewalk, partially covered in tattered clothing. Andy skirted around them, followed closely behind by Charlie.

"No cars anywhere. How did people get around?" Charlie remarked after a dozen blocks of fruitless searching. "I thought Americans loved their cars. That's what my dad always used to say."

"I'm sure there were once plenty of cars, but anyone passing through this place in the last five years probably snatched them up long ago. If we do find a car, it probably wouldn't have any gas in it."

"Then maybe we should head back to the boat," Charlie suggested wearily. "I know Morgan's not feeling well, but we don't really have another choice."

Andy stopped walking and placed her hands on her hips. She let out a deep sigh as her eyes desperately panned across the immediate area once more, hoping to spot at least one car.

"I'm afraid you're right. There's nothing here."

The two headed back and met up with Morgan, who was still sitting on the bench. Though hardly excited by the idea of returning to the boat, she understood there was no other option.

Unfortunately, an uncooperative wind worked against their sails, and it took more than half a day to reach Nags Head. By sundown, they finally anchored the boat and chose to forego their search for a car until morning. They grabbed a few cans of food, water, and their weapons before heading into town to find shelter for the night. Stumbling across an abandoned three-bedroom house near the edge of town that was corpse-free and somewhat less dilapidated than those around it, they settled in for a long night's rest.

On a musty king-sized bed in the largest bedroom, Morgan and Charlie slept soundly. Andy, meanwhile, took the twin bed in the smaller bedroom. Her sleep was restless and uncomfortable.

* * *

The sun rose to a clear sky the following morning. Groggy, Andy crawled out of bed and checked on her friends. Morgan was snoring like a log, but Charlie was beginning to stir, and Andy crept toward his side of the bed.

"Wake up, sleepyhead," she whispered.

"Err…nooo," Charlie groaned and rolled away from her. Andy gave his shoulder a gentle nudge.

"C'mon…time to find a car."

Charlie rubbed his eyes open and looked over at his comatose sister. "Probably just as well. She keeps kicking me."

"You didn't sleep well?"

"I slept fine until about an hour ago when the ballerina here decided to practice in her sleep." Charlie rolled out of bed. His short brown hair stuck up in the back like feathers. "I told her we were too big to share a bed."

Andy laughed lightly at the sight of Charlie's hair as he climbed out of bed and followed her into the hall.

"Well, you're probably right about that," she whispered. "But I'm just glad she's getting some rest."

"I know. That's the only thing that stopped me from kicking her back." Charlie stopped in the hallway and looked back toward the bedroom. "Should we wake her and tell her we're going out for a bit?"

Andy thought a moment before nodding. "Yeah, just in case we're gone awhile. The last thing she needs is to go wandering off looking for us." She reached behind her back and retrieved the pistol tucked into her belt. "Here, put this beside her bed."

After waking Morgan just long enough to explain where they were going, Andy and Charlie each ate a can of peaches before heading outside to a beautiful morning. Like Salvo, there was not a soul in sight. After zigzagging though several empty streets, Charlie spotted an SUV sitting in an otherwise empty parking lot.

"It's an older model, so it should be easier to hot-wire," he remarked before scurrying ahead of Andy to check out the vehicle.

"Careful!" she warned him in case its owners suddenly returned.

The SUV was unlocked but there was no key. Undiscouraged,

Charlie managed to start the engine in under a minute.

"There's half a tank!" Charlie exclaimed.

"Are you serious?!" Andy cried in disbelief as she hopped into the passenger's seat. "Amazing! Let's head to the house."

Charlie obeyed, but the moment he put the car into drive, the sound of a gunshot shattered the air off in the distance. Startled, Andy and Charlie looked at each other, eyes wide.

"Morgan," Andy whispered hoarsely.

Without a word, Charlie floored the gas pedal, the tires squealing in response. Pulling up beside their borrowed house, Andy was already leaping out of the SUV before Charlie had fully applied the brakes. Heart pounding, she dashed inside the house and sprinted up the stairs two at a time. With Charlie closely behind, Andy burst into Morgan's bedroom, then stopped and stared.

Sitting upright in bed, Morgan was holding the pistol in her shaking hands. Andy's eyes darted from the gun to the foot of the bed. On the floor lay a large, black dog. It wasn't moving.

Andy slowly approached the side of the bed and carefully retrieved the pistol from Morgan's trembling grip.

"It's okay," she whispered gently.

Charlie moved over to the animal and quickly realized that his sister had indeed killed the creature.

"Christ, what happened?"

"Morgan?"

Andy gently shook her friend's shoulder. Visibly still in shock, Morgan opened her mouth to speak.

"I'm sorry. That thing just…it came in here…I was sleeping…"

"It's okay, you don't have to explain," Andy assured. "Nice shot, by the way."

Morgan managed a smile as Charlie took a closer look at the animal now that the gun was out of his sister's hands.

"It's a Rottweiler," he remarked

Andy recognized the breed as the same dog owned by a neighbor during her childhood. That dog had been playful and gentle, quite the opposite of the breed's reputation as a savage, wild beast. This particular dog, however, had obviously become rabid, as was evident by the thick white foam around his mouth.

Charlie spotted the bullet hole through the animal's chest.

"Blimey, you got him right through the heart!" he exclaimed. "Nice shot, indeed!"

Following the incident, the three wasted no time leaving the house. After making a quick stop by the sailboat to pick up the remainder of their personal items, they headed north, opting to take Route 158 instead of the Interstate.

As the SUV drove out of view of the sailboat, Andy heard Charlie mutter, "She was a good boat."

* * *

"Where are we going?" Morgan asked Andy, who'd been driving for an hour.

"Philadelphia," she replied. "Some of my school friends might still be there. But we'll go by Washington DC on the way. Maybe we'll have luck picking up some extra food and water there too."

Morgan merely nodded. Since neither she nor Charlie had ever been to America, anywhere they went would be unfamiliar, so they left the navigating to Andy.

Still miles away from I-95, the SUV ran out of gas on Route 158 as they headed farther inland. Andy had hoped to make it all the way to the Interstate, where she believed they were more likely to find more gas or another car, but the SUV sputtered to a stop on a lonely stretch of road. Fortunately, Charlie had spotted a few abandoned bicycles along the way from Nags Head, and they'd decided to take them along for precisely this reason. However, it also meant that they would have to abandon most of their personal belongings.

"I can leave behind the painting," said Morgan. "I can carry my ballet shoes, though it seems rather silly at a time like this."

"It's not silly," Andy corrected as she stuffed her pistol into her back pocket. "You'll use them again. Besides, they're easy to carry."

But the books treasured by Andy and Charlie would have to

remain behind. They solemnly emptied their backpacks of the books and added food, bottled water, and ammunition. Andy managed to squeeze her favorite medical book into the bag, but she could not help but look back at the SUV with regret as they cycled away. It was at that moment that she realized life would be like this—living nomadically and taking only what could be carried.

Luck appeared after a mile of pedaling when they came across an abandoned pickup truck. Charlie reached the car first and yanked on the driver's side handle. Unfortunately, a grisly surprise awaited him inside.

"Bloody hell!"

Charlie jumped back and covered his nose. Andy and Morgan dropped their bikes to the ground and ran towards Charlie. Arriving first, Andy took one look inside the truck and recoiled backward. She tried to warn Morgan but was a moment too late; her friend had already peered inside. Seconds later Morgan was on the opposite side of the road, bent over retching into the grass. Andy rushed over to her and pulled her long hair away from her face. Meanwhile, Charlie regained his composure and inched toward the truck, his face contorted in an expression of horror. With one hand, he covered his nose.

A horrendously decomposed body sat in the driver's seat, the seatbelt still buckled over what remained of the person's lap. It wasn't a virus victim; there would have been nothing but the dry bones of a skeleton. This was a recent death, and with the windows rolled up and the car sitting in the hot summer sun, the body had been baking unnaturally as the flesh melted into jelly. Maggots crawled in and out of the mouth, nostrils, and other orifices. The corpse was in such a state of decay that Charlie could not determine its sex.

Andy rejoined Charlie by the door while Morgan remained where she was with her back facing the truck. Her vomiting had stopped, and she now focused on breathing in fresh air.

After getting past the shock of the ghastly sight, Andy began breathing through her mouth and noted a rifle trapped between the body's legs, its barrel pointed up to the sky.

"My cousin had a weapon like that in Iraq when he was in the Army. I saw pictures of him with it."

Scrunching up her nose, Andy reached inside the truck, grabbed at the barrel, and pulled the weapon outside while careful to avoid brushing it against the fleshy goo of its former owner. She took a moment to inspect the weapon. It seemed to be in working order, complete with a sturdy shoulder strap. Andy carefully removed the magazine and emptied the chamber.

"It's an M4," Charlie remarked as he watched with interest. "How did you know how to unload it?"

"I didn't, but I guess when you know how to unload one weapon, you can figure out how to unload others."

Charlie nodded. "I wonder what it was doing there just sitting between his legs."

Frowning, Andy looked around before handing Charlie the weapon and magazine. She then jogged a few yards away and bent down to retrieve a stick and returned to the truck.

"What's that for?" Charlie asked.

"I'm gonna check the head. I think he, uh…it…blew its brains out."

Charlie's face paled.

"And why do we need to verify that?"

Andy ignored him. Leaning inside the truck while maneuvering her torso away from the body, she poked around the neck and skull with the stick. It was a macabre effort, but moments later, she verified her theory.

"I was right. There's a bullet hole under his chin and the entire top half of his skull is missing." Then, with a look of satisfaction, Andy leaned back and said, "I could've been a criminologist. Or a detective."

Charlie made a face.

"More like a coroner. I think you were right to choose medicine. You certainly have the stomach for it." Charlie continued to pinch his nose. "Can we get out of here? The smell is repugnant!"

Wearing a smirk, Andy slammed the driver's side door shut.

"Hang on, you big wuss. I'm gonna check the back first." Then she grabbed the M4 out of Charlie's hand as she passed him on the way to the rear of the truck. "Finders keepers."

In the truck bed, she found something even more valuable: three two-gallon containers of gasoline.

"We're not driving this truck," Charlie called back with insistence. "I'm not sitting anywhere near that human jelly monster. He's practically melted all over the front seat!"

Andy laughed at the 'jelly monster' comment.

"No, we aren't driving the truck. The battery's dead. I tried the ignition when I checked the skull. Maybe that's why he…or she…killed themselves. They finally gave up."

"So we're heading back to the other car?"

This was Morgan. She had regained her senses and now stood beside her brother, though her eyes carefully avoided the driver's seat of the truck.

"Yeah, but we need to haul back these containers," Andy replied as she picked up a heavy-looking plastic jug.

"Is that petrol?" Morgan asked.

"Looks like it. We'll have to prop them on top of the handlebars. Do you think you can manage that?" Andy was speaking directly to Morgan. She had no concerns about Charlie's strength or agility.

Morgan nodded firmly, determined not to hold them back.

"I'll manage."

Andy gave her friend an encouraging smile.

"Don't worry. If we have to, Charlie will go on ahead and pour his gas into the SUV, then drive back to pick us up. Sound good, Charlie?"

Charlie nodded as he slung his backpack over his shoulders. "Brilliant."

In the end, Morgan managed to bike the mile back to the SUV without issue. After pouring all the gasoline into the tank, they stopped for a quick meal before continuing on their journey. Morgan offered to drive as Charlie navigated from the passenger's seat. Andy, meanwhile, spread out in the back seat and soon fell asleep.

* * *

After crossing the Virginia-North Carolina border, Andy felt her confidence swell. The SUV had enough gas to get them at least another hundred miles. Washington DC was less than two hundred miles away, and Philadelphia was another one hundred and fifty more. If they managed to find a bit more gas, they'd reach the city by nightfall.

Unfortunately, the SUV suffered a flat tire a mere fifteen miles into Virginia, and as expected, the spare was completely flat. Stranded between two small towns named Emporia and Jarratt, they had no choice but to find another car or bike all the way to DC. Going through the same routine they had earlier that day, the three discouraged souls carried their necessities on their backs and biked north on I-95.

After a few miles, Morgan became short of breath. She was running on empty.

"I can't go anymore," she gasped. "I'm sorry."

Andy examined her friend with concern. There was no doubt that she had pushed herself as far as she could go and needed to stop and rest. Charlie shuffled through his bag and pulled out the map. In the waning sunlight, he made out exactly where they were standing.

"Can you see those train tracks up ahead?" Charlie pointed off into the distance. Andy and Morgan squinted until they could make out the rails.

"Yeah, I see them," Andy replied as Morgan nodded.

"Okay, well, just a little beyond that there's an exit. Maybe we can find a place there to stay tonight."

Andy looked at Morgan. In spite of her tremendous fatigue, she remained reassuring.

"I'll make it."

Charlie's prediction was correct. They found a vacant hotel with only a few skeletons scattered about, and ate a small meal before going to sleep. This time, Charlie took his own room and bed.

"I refuse to get karate-kicked in my sleep again," he mumbled before saying goodnight.

* * *

03 July 2020

Though the next day proved no less exhausting than the previous one, the trio came within twenty miles of Washington DC by midday. After leaving the hotel that morning, they made their way to a neighboring gas station where they discovered both a twenty-year-old minivan with a working battery, and a few more containers of gas hidden away in the garage.

"It's probably been sitting here forever. Petrol does expire, you know," said Charlie as he poured the stale gas into the minivan.

"As long as it gets us to DC, I don't care how old it is," Andy replied as she climbed into the driver's seat.

Living on a tiny island for five years made it easy to forget the importance of things like gasoline. They'd never needed it in Bermuda, but now it was imperative. And as long as oil refineries remained inactive, finding gasoline would be almost impossible until the supply finally vanished. It all seemed hopeless until Andy had an epiphany.

"I'm getting off at the next exit. I just thought of something."

"What is it?"

"I wanna find a liquor store."

In the rearview mirror, Andy could see the confusion on Charlie's face.

"What, you want to get pissed?" he called back to her.

Andy just shook her head, smiled, and waited for Charlie's brain to catch on. Like a light switch, his face brightened.

"Andy, that's brilliant. I can't believe I didn't think of it myself."

"Me neither. You're supposed to be the genius around here."

"Okay, someone please explain what's going on," Morgan said

irritably from the passenger's seat.

"Cars can run off of alcohol, especially pure-grain alcohol."

"Really? Is that true?" Morgan replied, turning to her brother.

"It's true," he nodded. "It's bad for the engine, but do we really care?"

Andy patted the steering wheel. "Not about this piece of junk."

Laughter filled the van. It was a welcome sound.

* * *

After ransacking five liquor stores and finding nearly two dozen illegally-kept bottles of 190-proof Everclear, they reached the outskirts of Washington DC.

They didn't need the map or highway signs to tell them that the city was approaching. At first, there were just a few cars stranded in the middle of the highway. Soon, however, they increased to such a number that Morgan, who was now behind the wheel, was forced to weave between the vehicles as though the highway were an obstacle course. At one point, the road was completely blocked. After considerable encouragement from Andy and Charlie, she rammed her way through the vehicles. Some of the cars, Andy noticed, housed a skeleton or two, while others sat empty. The congestion worsened as they approached the on-ramp for the outer loop of I-495—but the Beltway was impassible. It was as though the virus had struck every driver dead at the exact same moment during the peak of rush hour traffic. Five years later, the cars remained where they had stopped that fateful day.

Things improved once they reached I-395 heading north toward downtown DC. Abandoned cars were still an issue, but the minivan managed to move forward, albeit very slowly. Andy had a map of Washington DC open on her lap, one she'd managed to find during their many stops in search of gasoline.

"Just stay on this road. It'll take us right into the city."

"All right," Morgan responded as she continued to maneuver skillfully around yet more abandoned vehicles.

"You know, Morgan, between shooting that dog yesterday and

ramming through all these cars, my opinion of you is improving every day," Charlie teased, to which Morgan responded with a roll of her eyes.

"Oh, just shut it, Charlie," she replied though secretly enjoying his comment.

They passed the southern end of Arlington National Cemetery and the Pentagon, though these landmarks weren't visible from the highway. Soon after, Morgan drove across the Potomac River, still swerving to avoid an astonishing amount of vehicles, which only made Andy more apprehensive. A functioning city, even semi-functional, would never allow its roads to remain so impassable.

"Where to now?" Morgan asked.

Andy leaned in closer to the map. "Um, hang on a sec…okay, follow the signs to Route 1. That turns into 14th Street, which goes directly north into the city." She leaned back in her seat before adding, almost as an afterthought, "We'll pass right by the Washington Monument."

Morgan craned her neck and looked at Charlie. Both were thinking the same thing.

"Oh, let's stop there to see it," Morgan remarked with keen interest. "Just for a moment, and then we'll keep moving."

Andy shrugged her shoulders. "Sure, why not. I'd be interested to know if it's still standing," she said half-jokingly.

Indeed, it was still standing. As the highest point in the District, the Washington Monument was impossible to miss. The ivory-white obelisk had always dominated the capital skyline, and Morgan noted the signs that once directed millions of flocking tourists to the monument every year. They easily found a place to park before crossing the sadly-overgrown lawn surrounding the front of the monument. The entire area was disturbingly quiet; not a soul or sign of life in sight.

Andy came within fifty yards of the entrance before stopping dead in her tracks.

"Jesus Christ. What the—?"

Where there had once been a proud display of fifty raised American flags encircling the monument, now there was nothing but shredded remnants of the once-beautiful banners strewn all over the ground, and flag poles bent askew—some nearly horizontal. But even worse, graffiti covered most of the bottom forty or fifty feet of the monument's surface. As Andy got close enough to decipher some of the words, phrases that read "America is dead", "In God We No Longer Trust", and especially "Fuck the USA" stood out. Though the rest of the monument was devoid of graffiti, being too high for anyone to reach, the once-pure marble was now a dull, yellowish-brown hue despite undergoing a massive cleaning effort just prior to the new century.

And without realizing it, tears sprung in Andy's eyes.

"How could they…?" she whispered inaudibly.

Morgan and Charlie moved behind her. Though not as affected by the sight as Andy, they were nonetheless saddened by what they saw. The damage represented a lack of civility and respect. After traveling a thousand miles by land and sea to flee violence and chaos, they seemed to have stepped right back into it.

Morgan moved beside Andy and placed a hand on her shoulder.

"Come on, Andy. Let's go."

But Andy did not move. She could only stare back at the monument with a mixture of shock and disgust.

"I thought if any place could pull itself together, it would be here," she said hoarsely. "I thought Americans, even young Americans, would never stoop so low."

She looked down at her feet and shook her head. A wave of sadness overwhelmed her.

A moment later, however, her thoughts were interrupted by the harsh crack of gunshots in the distance. All three of them frantically looked around, but Charlie was the first to see it.

Across the Mall toward the Capitol Building, a cluster of people were running about and apparently shooting off guns, either at one another or others hiding elsewhere. As though in a dream, Andy and her friends remained rooted to the ground and watched in disbelief. Only when the far-off figures began to grow larger did Andy shout, "Get back in the car…now!"

They ran back to the minivan and sped off along 14th Street, heading north. In the back seat, Morgan glanced anxiously behind her. Despite being in a moving vehicle, the figures seemed to be getting closer. When the crowd suddenly turned north onto 14th Street, she let out a scream.

"They're following us! Move faster!"

"I can't!" Andy shouted back as she experienced firsthand the ordeal of driving between, and sometimes through, yet another parking lot of deserted vehicles.

"How many are there?!" Charlie asked fearfully.

"I don't know…maybe thirty?" Morgan yelled back.

Another series of gunshots rang out. When a bullet struck the rear windshield of the minivan, causing Morgan to scream once again, Andy slammed on the brakes and threw the car into park.

"That's it!" she yelled. Within seconds, she reached over the back seat, retrieved the M4 rifle, and loaded the magazine before removing the Glock secured in her belt. She thrust the pistol at Charlie.

"Roll down the window and fire back, but stay close to the car. Morgan, get down!"

With that, Andy opened the door, aimed, and sprayed a round of bullets at the pursuers. Dazed, Charlie hesitated a moment until he realized that this was actually happening. After Andy released a burst of ten or so rounds from her rifle, Charlie responded with several shots from the Glock.

The zealous crowd quickly stopped their forward pursuit after several had been hit in the legs. A few sustained blows to their upper body, most of them fatal. The remainder of the crowd immediately turned back, sprinting away like scared cats. When satisfied that the threat was over, Andy and Charlie jumped back in the minivan and drove off, though still at a snail's pace.

Stunned, Morgan slowly rose up in her seat as her eyes darted wildly until they fixated on the bullet hole in the rear windshield. *Just a few inches to the right,* she thought with a chill.

Andy reached back and grabbed Morgan's arm.

"You okay?"

Shaken, Morgan could only nod in response.

"You're not hurt?"

Morgan shook her head before finally responding, "I'm fine."

Charlie handed the pistol back to Andy and said, "I thought you said you never fired that rifle before."

"Yeah, well…sometimes," Andy began breathlessly, "adrenaline is enough."

After their pounding hearts settled, Andy turned the car around to face the direction they'd come from and stopped. Charlie turned to her.

"Now what?"

But Andy couldn't answer right away because she didn't know. With the engine still running, she glanced ahead and saw three fresh corpses lying in the street mere yards away. Her stomach turned uncomfortably.

I've killed someone…more than one. I am a killer…

She forced her eyes to look away.

"Can you hand me the map of the entire country?" she asked Charlie.

After rummaging through the pile of maps on the floor at his feet, Charlie found the correct one and handed it to Andy. She unfolded the map and stared at it for almost a minute while her friends waited anxiously.

"We're going back south," Andy finally announced.

"What?" Morgan and Charlie said simultaneously.

"What about Philadelphia?" Morgan continued.

Andy shook her head fiercely. "No. DC is the southern-most point of the Northeastern Corridor. Between here and Boston are half a dozen cities all mashed up together, including Philly and New York. It's like one gigantic city. If things are this bad here, they'll probably be just as bad or worse the farther north we go. And if it *is* that bad, any friends I knew years ago are probably long gone. "

"But we're so close. Are you sure?" said Morgan.

But Andy was already heading south on 14th Street.

"I'm not risking us getting shot at again. At least we know what to expect by going south."

"But we have to have some idea of where we're going if we turn back," Morgan argued.

"I know, but we can't stay here. It's filthy, there are cars *everywhere*, and we just nearly got killed…call me crazy, but I don't think this place may be any better than Bermuda. In five years there, I never killed anyone, but in less than an hour here, I've killed at least three people."

The car fell silent as it swerved across the Potomac. The thought of backtracking a few hundred miles was less than appealing.

"Look," Andy began, her tone softening, "we'll head down I-95 until we pass Richmond, then we'll get on I-85 until we reach I-40. That will take us west and away from the big cities on the East Coast." She passed the map back to Charlie. "Here, show Morgan what I'm talking about. Maybe we can find a small town to settle in for a while until we get our bearings. A small town in the middle of nowhere can't be worse than this. We might even meet some people who won't shoot at us before even seeing our faces."

It was all Andy could do to reassure the others, and though her logic was sound, it would take more than words to spark any hope of finding Utopia somewhere within the enormous country they had fought so hard to get to.

Worse still, they were once again running out of gas. And food.

* * *

Ben Kelly tapped his fingers impatiently against the driver's side doorframe of his old pickup truck as he waited for his cousin Jim to exit the convenience store—the fifth one they had stopped at that day. An ancient minivan sat parked outside the store—an expected sight in the city, but not on a lonely stretch of Virginia's I-85. If the previous four stores had not been vacant, they would have passed this one entirely, especially with another vehicle parked out front. But they were desperate enough for food and water to risk fighting strangers for it.

Ben checked his watch. Nearly seven o'clock. The sun was beginning to set behind him, and he cursed under his breath. They should have been in Tennessee by now.

The day had been a complete disaster. After zigzagging their way southwest from Fredrick, Maryland into Virginia late the night before, they stopped to rest in the small town of Front Royal, seventy miles west of Washington DC. Had they not been so exhausted after the previous evening's activities, they could have made it all the way to Tennessee by early morning before stopping. Though they got off to a quick start this morning, a random passerby informed them that I-81 just north of Harrisonburg had been blocked off by the very people they were running from. This hiccup forced them to backtrack nearly a hundred miles to I-95, which ran south toward North Carolina instead of southwest toward Tennessee. Hours of precious time had been wasted when time was against them. Worse still, he was starving when not a scrap of food could be found anywhere.

While stewing in frustration, Ben suddenly heard the front door of the convenience store burst open, followed by the sound of people shouting. Jim was the first to appear, his right hand grasping for the pistol in his holster. Ben stood up in alarm, but what happened next startled him even more.

There was a girl arguing with Jim, which alone was an unusual sight. But even more alarming was the M4 rifle she was carrying, secured across her torso by a strap over her right shoulder. And by the way she handled the weapon, Ben could tell that she knew how to use it. Seconds after she appeared, another young woman emerged from the doorway and ran after the first.

"Andy! Wait!" the second woman yelled. Ben jumped out of the truck and jogged over to Jim after quickly grabbing his own shotgun out of habit.

"What's going on?"

His cousin turned to him, clearly aggravated.

"They're taking all the food!" he yelled and made a gesture toward the two women.

Without a word, Ben turned and gave each of them a long look. The unarmed girl was tall, about 5'8" and wiry. Ben thought her rather pretty, though a bit pale with a bruised eye in the latter stages of healing. She had delicate features and beautiful dark, wavy hair. But it was the first girl that intrigued him more. Shorter than her friend, trim and athletic, she had sharper features. Her long, unruly blond hair hung over her muscular shoulders, but it was her eyes that caught Ben's attention; they were green, like emeralds, and were filled with the intensity of a wild animal. She didn't just look at you; she leveled you with those eyes. And right now her eyes were looking at Jim as though she were ready to attack. But instead, she opened her mouth.

"We were here first. This food is ours," she declared unapologetically. Her tone left little room for argument.

"Just because you got here first doesn't mean you can take everything that's in there," Jim countered. "Just take what you can carry and leave us the rest."

This only angered the blond further, but her friend stopped her before she could protest any further.

"Andy, we can share. There's plenty in there for all of us."

Moments later a boy, probably younger than the two girls, appeared from inside the store carrying four or five plastic bags full of food. He stopped as soon as he noticed the commotion.

"Morgan?" he called out. "What's going on?" His voice carried the same accent as the brunette.

Morgan, the brunette, turned around.

"Nothing. Just put the bags in the car."

The boy cautiously obeyed. At the same time, Ben drew closer to the group. He looked over the three strangers carefully.

"What are two girls doing out here alone?"

"They aren't alone!" the boy called out as he slammed the car door behind him once the bags were inside.

Ben's eyes squinted on the boy's face. The resemblance to the brunette was undeniable. "You two related?" he asked.

The boy gave a faint nod. "She's my sister. Who are you?"

"Ben…this is my cousin, Jim."

Ben had looked directly at Andy as he spoke. She didn't flinch. Instead, her eyes narrowed on him.

"What do you mean, 'what are two girls doing out here alone'? You trying to scare us?"

Ben titled his head to the side. "You guys aren't from around here, are you?"

"So? What's that got to do with taking our food?" she retorted as her hands inched dangerously close to the trigger.

"It was just a question. You obviously aren't from around here or you wouldn't need to ask. And *you* two…" Ben gestured toward the brother and sister, "I've heard a lot of accents these last few years, but not yours…not so much."

"Charlie and I are from England…Oxford, actually," Morgan replied gently in an attempt to ease the tension. "I'm Morgan. And Andy here is American."

Ben scoffed at the word.

"American? There's really no America anymore."

"Yeah, we kinda noticed after seeing the Washington Monument," Andy replied with biting sarcasm. "Now, we're taking our food, and we're getting out of here."

Without another word, she turned away and headed toward Charlie, who was about to climb into the minivan.

Ben gave Jim a look as if to say, *what do you want to do now?* But Jim shook his head in reply. *Let it go.*

Despite his hunger, Ben surrendered and headed back to his truck. But after a few steps he stopped and turned back.

"You know, I wasn't trying to be an asshole when I asked what you were doing out here alone. In my experience, girls on their own usually end up in trouble…you know, getting kidnapped, beaten…even raped." Ben gave Andy a thoughtful look, unaware of the anger he was about to spark. "Well, maybe not girls like you, but definitely girls like her."

Ben nodded toward Morgan, and instantly her eyes grew wide and full of panic. But before he could take another breath, Andy charged toward him, enraged, and sucker-punched him squarely in the chin.

"Fuck you!" she growled through clenched teeth.

By the time Ben regained his senses, the two girls were already piling into their minivan. However, when Charlie went to start the engine, it refused to ignite. After multiple attempts, all three reluctantly climbed out of the car. Charlie opened the hood while Andy searched the trunk, presumably for jumper cables. Morgan, meanwhile, stood by looking helpless.

Massaging his chin and wondering what he'd done to deserve the punch, Ben watched as Jim walked toward them.

"You guys need any help?" he called out.

Andy ignored him, but Morgan seemed relieved by the offer.

"Well, probably…if you wait a minute, please." She hurried over to her brother, and the two spoke inaudibly for a moment before rounding the minivan where Jim stood.

"This old battery is dead," Charlie concluded before craning his neck toward Andy. "Any luck finding cables?"

Andy emerged from the trunk and slammed it shut.

"No cables," she announced, clearly irritated.

"We've got some. We can jump your car for you," Jim offered, looking directly at Morgan, who returned a smile.

"That would be fantastic."

Jim passed Ben as he jogged back to their truck and slid into the driver's seat before realizing Ben still had the keys.

"Hey, throw me the keys," he shouted through the window

But Ben only stared back at his cousin with a look of utter

confusion.

"Wait, we're helping them? They just punched me in the face, took all the food, and now we're gonna jump their car?"

"First of all, *they* didn't punch you, only the blond punched you. And they didn't take all the food. There's still plenty in the store…trust me. And after all that genuine concern you showed about two girls being alone with only a younger brother to help 'em out, don't you think we can at least get their car started?"

Ben hated when his cousin manipulated him, but he wasn't a fool either, and he gave Jim a knowing look as he hopped into the passenger's seat.

"Jesus, you're so obvious. I realize she is very pretty, but we gotta keep moving."

"I don't know what you're talking about," Jim replied calmly, but his attempt to appear completely objective was less than convincing. "It'll take five minutes, at most. We can spare five minutes."

"We can't spare five *seconds*…but go. Go and help them. I won't stop you." Ben fished the keys from his pocket and handed them over.

Two minutes later, Jim had the truck facing the minivan with the jumper cables properly connected between the two batteries. Morgan and Charlie watched him work quickly, but Ben and Andy maintained their distance from everyone as well as each other. When Ben sneaked a glance, it was obvious from her expression and body language that she just wanted to get out of there. His gaze lingered a moment too long, and when she caught his eyes on her, he quickly turned away. He could feel his face flush.

"When I turn on the car, wait a second before trying to turn yours on," Jim instructed Charlie.

"Okay."

A minute later, the minivan was running again. Still, Jim warned that the battery probably wouldn't function much longer.

"It's on its last legs. I bet it won't turn over the next time you try starting it."

"That's fine," the blond piped up, plainly eager to get underway. "This is the third car we've driven today. We're not exactly married to it."

"So when the battery dies, you'll just find another car?"

"Yep, or when the gas runs out."

Jim gave Ben a look, but Ben shook his head slowly yet firmly. *We don't have time for that.* Jim, however, ignored his cousin.

"Where are you guys headed?"

"Well…" Morgan began until Andy interrupted.

"No, Morgan…let's just go."

Then after a grudging 'thank you' to Jim, Andy marched straight to the driver's seat of the minivan and got in.

"Charlie…Morgan…let's go!"

"Wait a second!" Morgan snapped back before softening her face and voice to address Jim. "We're going south, then west on I-40. But we don't really have a destination in mind."

"Well, that's the same direction we're headed. If you want, you can follow us until you need a new car, and then we'll help you find another one. After that, we'll part ways."

Naturally, both Andy and Ben began to protest this plan, but before either could utter another sentence on the matter, Morgan turned to her brother and said, "Sound good to you, Charlie?"

Unprepared to make the decision, Charlie looked back and forth between his sister and Andy, weighing not only the options but the consequences of vexing one over the other.

"Uh, I think we should take the offer."

Charlie braced himself for Andy's reaction, but to his surprise, she merely rolled her eyes and got back inside the car. Morgan, however, smiled warmly.

"We accept," she said to Jim, putting an end to the argument. "We'll follow you, and when we flash the lights, it means we're out of petrol."

"Uh, okay…by petrol, you mean gas, right?" Jim asked, embarrassed for not being familiar with the word.

But Morgan blushed as well.

"Oh, yes…sorry. In England, we called it petrol."

Jim nodded slowly, suddenly reminded of how big the planet actually was.

"All right, sounds like a plan. Just give us a few minutes."

Morgan and Charlie headed back to the minivan as Jim headed back to the store. Ben was already inside and had quickly filled his arms with foodstuffs. When he saw Jim enter, he didn't bother to hide his annoyance.

"Congratulations…guess you're the big hero, huh?"

"Oh, c'mon…we're far south of their reach. There's no way they'll track us."

"You don't know that. I think you're forgetting what they're capable of."

"Man, I remember. What I think you're forgetting is what it's like to worry about someone other than yourself. You wouldn't be so callous if it was Karen stranded out there instead of three strangers."

Jim regretted the words as soon as he said them, and he literally bit down on his lip. Ben's face grew hard and his whole body tensed. His eyes narrowed on Jim.

"One hour," he warned solemnly. "You don't talk to me for one whole hour, or else I'll really make you feel like shit."

Without another word, Ben stormed past his cousin and exited the store.

"And I'm driving," he added with intentional harshness.

Moments later, the two vehicles, both filled with unfamiliar tension, set off south on the Interstate.

Chapter IV

Jim waited an hour and a half before he dared to utter a word to his cousin, and when he did, he spoke with unnatural reserve.

"I wonder what their story is. Where do you think they came from?"

When the question went ignored for longer than normal, Jim threw his hands in the air in frustration.

"Forget it…I give up. I'm sorry I said anything about Karen. I'm not perfect, but neither are you. In fact, you can be a real asshole sometimes."

The insult cracked the tension, and Ben released a chuckle.

"Yeah, I know." He gave Jim a grudging tap on the arm and added, "I can't stay mad at you long. You're the only person I have left to piss off in this world."

Smiling, Jim gave a head-nod toward the reflection of the minivan headlights in the rearview mirror.

"I dunno, I think you managed to piss off what's-her-name pretty well…the blond one."

"Andy," Ben muttered as he absently rubbed his chin where she had punched him. "I'll be damned if I know what that was about. I've never been punched by a girl before; slapped, yes—punched, never."

"I don't think she counts as a girl," Jim replied. "She'd probably rip a lion in half if she had to."

"Seriously. She looked at me as if *I* were about to rape her."

"Nah, I'm sure she thought you were charming," Jim teased before frowning. "I think something happened to the other one, though…Morgan. That bruise around her eye definitely has a story to it. And did you see her face after you said she was the type of girl who was in danger of being raped? I thought she was gonna cry."

"I was too busy being punched to notice. I see you remember *her* name, though."

Jim shrugged off the remark. "So what? She's a beautiful girl, even with the bruise. And would it be so bad to make friends with some girls? Some normal ones?"

"I wouldn't call her friend normal. I've never seen a girl carry a gun before, but she seemed to handle hers like she's fired it a few times."

"That's not exactly a bad quality, Ben. She's probably just protective of her friends." Jim paused a moment, then added, "It's strange how her friend referred to her as 'American,' and how she said she and her brother were from England. We haven't heard people talking about countries like that since…since before the virus."

"Well, they're definitely not from around here," Ben replied lightly.

"But didn't the blond one—Andy—say something about the Washington Monument? And now they're headed south?"

A mixture of concern and bewilderment slowly appeared on Ben's face. "What are you saying? That they could be working for him?" He shook his head. "No way."

But Jim continued to wonder aloud. "He knows we would never suspect two girls driving in that piece-of-shit minivan. It's the perfect cover if you think about it. We may hate the guy because he's the Devil, but he's also wickedly smart."

Ben frowned as he glanced in the rearview mirror, hoping that Jim was merely being paranoid and that the minivan following them wasn't part of a more ominous scheme.

"We'd better figure this out soon. If this is a trap, I really don't want to make a run for it in the dark. Our tank is half-empty already, and they could've been lying about how much gas they have. For all we know, they could actually have a full tank *and* a backup tank."

"I hope I'm wrong," Jim replied, "but either way, this won't turn out good." Then, with a weary sigh, "Damn, I was hoping we might make some friends."

"Sorry man, but it looks like you'll have to meet your future girlfriend some other time."

* * *

Andy looked at the knuckles of her right hand as they grasped the steering wheel. They were still throbbing more than an hour after leaving the convenience store. Despite the violence that had invaded her life over the past five years, she'd never actually punched someone, and it felt strange to hurt someone with her own hands.

Morgan sat in the passenger's seat, staring off to her right and stubbornly giving Andy the silent treatment, but Andy didn't care. She was too angry to tell her best friend how stupid it was to follow two armed strangers in a truck—a truck that was probably far more reliable than their clunker minivan. Morgan was generally too trusting of strangers, but this was complete idiocy. Still, Andy had made all the decisions so far, and since it had been her disastrous idea to go to DC, she figured it was best to let Morgan have her way, at least for now.

Poor Charlie had been thrust in the middle. It was his nature to talk through problems, regardless of the subject or circumstances. But mild-mannered as he was, as well as being the youngest, he obeyed the unspoken war of silence until he nodded off from boredom.

Several more minutes passed before Morgan finally spoke.

"Why did you have to punch him? He was only trying to warn us to be careful, and he couldn't have known about what happened to me."

Stirred by the sudden end to the quiet, Andy delayed in answering immediately.

"I don't know," she said at last. "He offended me."

"But *I* was the one who was raped, not you."

"And you're my friend. When people harass my friends, I tend to get upset."

"I know," Morgan replied, sighing. "I just wish you hadn't been so aggressive toward them. You're already intimidating enough to begin with."

"Intimidating? Why? 'Cuz I was carrying a gun?" Andy gestured toward the M4 resting in the back seat beside a sleeping Charlie.

"No, not just that. I can carry a gun, but I'm not intimidating. I suppose it's your whole demeanor; the way you walk and compose yourself."

"How do I 'compose' myself?" Andy asked, intrigued by this revelation.

Morgan took a moment to find the right words. "It's hard to explain, but just little things. Like how you move in one direction but your eyes are focused somewhere else entirely. You never seem to worry about what's in front of you, because you know that whatever you're confronted with you'll be able to handle it. It's your confidence, I suppose."

Andy simply nodded. "Isn't that a good thing?"

"Yes, it's a good thing," Morgan assured. "I wish I could appear more confident at times, but I suppose we all have to accept who we are and learn to live with it."

Andy turned to her friend with heartfelt seriousness and said, "You're a wonderful and gracious person, Morgan. And despite what happened to you and what you think, you're strong. Stronger than you know."

At this, Morgan could barely manage a smile before biting her trembling lip.

"Sorry about getting sick before." she said softly, her voice filled with shame.

Andy turned to her in confusion. "Sick when?"

"Back when we found that truck yesterday…you know, with the body?"

So much had happened since then that Andy had forgotten all about Morgan throwing up. It felt like a week had passed since then.

"Why would you be sorry about that? Even I felt my stomach turn. It was nauseating." Andy started to say something, thought better of it, but then changed her mind again. "You know, when I found you, after you were attacked…I threw up as soon as I saw you. You can't help how your body reacts in certain situations."

Morgan glanced briefly at Andy before staring down at her lap. Andy could tell that something else was weighing on her friend's mind, something beyond inconvenient nausea. After glancing behind her to make sure Charlie was still asleep, Andy gently placed a hand on Morgan's shoulder.

"What is it?" she whispered.

Looking at her delicate hands, Morgan shook her head. Her face crumpled and tears sprang from her eyes and splashed down her cheeks.

"I'm just scared," she choked. "I keep getting sick." She said nothing else; she was too scared to admit what was now apparent.

"Are you sure it's not just from having been on a boat for the past week and getting seasick?" Andy asked, her voice sounding hollow.

Morgan shook her head.

"I got sick yesterday morning, right before I shot that dog. I woke up because I felt sick, and after I went to the bathroom and got back into bed, I heard the dog come into the house. Then I got sick again this morning…and…and I'm late."

Unable to say anything, Andy only managed to give her friend's shoulder a squeeze.

"It's gonna be okay," she whispered, struggling to sound more hopeful than she actually felt. "I'll make sure everything's okay."

"Just don't tell Charlie, okay? I don't want him to know—not yet, anyway."

"Of course," Andy replied while putting on her bravest face, despite her trepidation.

What were the odds? One in a thousand? Ten thousand? A million? A small part of Andy wanted to go back to Bermuda just to find those boys and put a bullet in each of them.

They drove on in silence. Relieved of her secret, Morgan drifted off, leaving Andy alone with her thoughts. The sun disappeared over her left shoulder as the minivan continued along the Interstate. It was uncomfortably hot, and she felt like her skin couldn't breathe. Even with windows rolled down, the rushing wind offered little relief.

The events of the past two days replayed like a movie in her head. The dog Morgan killed…the rotting body in the car…the horrific state of the Washington Monument and being shot at by faceless strangers…punching the tall, good-looking but grossly insensitive guy in the chin. His voice suddenly echoed in her mind: *There's really no America anymore…*

What did that even mean? Did a country no longer exist because those who were once in power were now dead? Was a country merely a collection of cities, buildings, and the people living inside its boundaries? Or was it something more?

Her seventh-grade history teacher once said that America was not just a place where people lived, but an ideal that people believed in. It had been built on the principle that every human being had the right to pursue their own dreams and achieve personal happiness—a wonderful concept that had been a reality for so many people for more than two centuries. If there was no America anymore, did that mean that this belief had died along with its citizens? Or did all the children who grew up without parents and teachers to guide them even consider such things now? Was daily survival now something that consumed everyone's time, leaving no room for anything else?

Questions like these would not easily be answered while driving on a lonely stretch of highway with darkness approaching. In Bermuda, Andy and her friends had struggled to survive, but they still managed to fill their days with reading, thoughtful conversation, and solitary contemplation. Without this, they were little more than animals, fighting each day just to live to the next, and Andy couldn't help thinking that this was the only future she had to look forward to.

More tired than she could ever remember having been, she leaned against the open window with her elbow and cradled her head in her left hand. The temperature had fallen with the setting sun, and the air coming through the window now felt refreshing. For a few miles, her mind became mercifully blank. With both Charlie and Morgan now sound asleep, a welcome serenity enveloped her. Unfortunately, her tranquility was short-lived.

The taillights of the truck glowed bright red and suddenly there was no longer a gap between the truck and the minivan.

"What the heck," Andy muttered under her breath as she applied pressure to the brakes. As she watched the truck come to a complete stop on the shoulder of the road, a tiny voice told her that something was wrong and to keep driving, but a quick glance at Morgan gave her pause, and she reluctantly pulled over about fifty feet behind the truck. She kept the motor running just in case.

"Charlie, wake up."

Both Charlie and Morgan awakened at the sound of Andy's voice.

"What's going on?" asked Morgan. "Are we out of petrol?"

"No. They just pulled over for some reason," Andy replied as she craned her neck to face Charlie, whose eyes fluttered open and adjusted to the dark.

"Hand me the rifle and get your pistol loaded. I want you to come out with me. I don't have a good feeling about this."

"What are you talking about?" Morgan countered sharply. "All they did was stop. Maybe they're just having problems with their truck."

"Maybe, but I want to be sure," Andy replied.

"I think you're being paranoid," Morgan went on.

"And I think you're too trusting," Andy shot back as she opened the door and stepped outside. "Keep the engine running."

With his pistol secured behind his back in the waist of his jeans, Charlie followed Andy as she slowly approached the truck. Her rifle was slung around her neck, but in an effort to appease Morgan and not appear too aggressive, she let it hang by her side, using one hand to secure it against her body to prevent the barrel from banging into her thigh as she walked.

Both of the young men had stepped outside and were talking amongst themselves at the rear of their truck. Though the headlights of the minivan shadowed Andy and Charlie's faces, their silhouettes clearly showed that Andy was armed. Ben gave her a long look as she approached.

"You always carry that thing?" he said, referring to the rifle.

"Only around people I don't trust."

He laughed. "Fair enough. You know, it's funny you mention not trusting people. See, Jim and I here just figured out that you guys may not be who you say you are."

"I don't remember us saying that we were anything," was Andy's quick retort as her hand fidgeted with the rifle grip.

Sensing the increased tension, Charlie drew up next to Andy and boldly put his hands on his hips. It was moments like this that reminded her of how brave he really was.

"Why don't you ask us what you want to know?" Charlie offered sensibly. "We have nothing to hide."

"Why is she sitting in the car?" Ben nodded toward Morgan in the minivan.

"She doesn't like confrontation," Andy countered.

"That's not good enough. What is she doing in there? Reporting about us on a radio, or maybe a cell phone?"

Genuinely confused, Andy glanced back at Morgan.

"What the hell are you talking about?"

"You slipped earlier, you know…when you said you saw the Washington Monument. What were you doing in DC? That's not too far from Frederick, you…"

"Hey, enough with the interrogation!" Andy yelled, cutting him off. "We don't have to answer to you." Then to Charlie she said, "Let's get outta here."

Charlie hesitated a moment before following Andy back to their vehicle. The situation appeared to be at an impasse when Ben stopped them.

"He really should've sent better spies, you know. Too bad he's so concerned with taking us alive. It would be so much easier to just kill us here in the middle of nowhere."

Though utterly baffled by what Ben was talking about, Andy couldn't help but turn back and yell, "Don't tempt me. I've already killed three people today."

"Hey, take it easy," Jim muttered to his cousin. "She seems genuinely confused. They both do—I don't think they're spies."

"Well, she just said she killed three people today. Does that sound like someone who can be trusted?"

"I'm sure she was kidding."

"I'm pretty sure she wasn't."

"Well then it was probably self-defense. You know DC is much worse than New York. They probably ran into the wrong people."

At this point, Morgan got out of the minivan and began marching toward the truck.

"What are you doing?" Andy asked as Morgan walked passed her.

"I'm going to clear up whatever this bloody confusion is about."

"Christ, Morgan, let 'em go. We don't need them."

"No, I want to know what they think we're up to."

"You heard our conversation?"

"No, but I can tell they were accusing us of something," Morgan called back. She was already halfway to the truck.

"Jesus," Andy cursed under her breath before gesturing to Charlie to turn around once more. "C'mon, back before she gets us all killed."

As the protective brother, Charlie jogged to catch up to Morgan.

Meanwhile, Ben and Jim argued on as Morgan approached.

"Okay, let's straighten this all out, shall we?" she began with uncharacteristic assertiveness. "I have no idea who you two think we are, but until two days ago, my brother and I had never set foot upon this continent. And Andy hadn't been back here for five years."

Now it was Ben and Jim's turn to be confused.

"What do you mean? Where have you been?" Jim asked.

"Bermuda. Ever since the outbreak. Actually a few weeks before, to be precise. Our families were there on vacation when the virus came."

Ben and Jim both looked equally stunned and confused. This was beyond any explanation either of them could've expected.

"We sailed here from Bermuda," Charlie added to further explain. "We left just over a week ago and reached the Outer Banks of North Carolina two days ago."

"But you mentioned something about being in DC," Ben countered, looking squarely at Andy.

"We were there earlier today," she replied coolly. "I used to live in Philadelphia before the outbreak, so we were headed north first to see if any of my friends were still around. But then we ran into some problems in DC and turned around. We figured it wasn't gonna get any better if we continued heading north."

"What sort of problems?" Ben asked, his tone becoming less interrogative.

"Some random people starting running after us and began shooting at us near the Washington Monument. We didn't provoke them or anything, but Charlie and I had to shoot back at them to drive them off. Three of them were dead by the time the rest decided to run away."

"My shots were worthless. Andy got all three of them," Charlie added humbly. "She's bloody brilliant with a rifle."

"Where did you get it? The M4, I mean?" Ben asked.

"Inside an abandoned car on the side of the road in North Carolina. Its previous owner was literally melting away in the front seat. Bullet to the brain." Andy gave a quick tug on the magazine, but didn't remove it from the well. "Unfortunately, there's only about four or five rounds left. After that, this thing is nothing more than an awkward club."

"We've got extra ammo in the back…five-fifty-six millimeter," Ben offered, to everyone's surprise, Andy most of all. "Go ahead and take a box or two."

"Thank you," she said, hardly believing what she was saying. "That would be…helpful."

"So you two believe us?" Morgan asked with hope rising in her voice.

After an exchange of glances, Ben said, "Yeah, we believe you."

"Who did you suspect we were, or worked for?" Andy wondered aloud.

"You really don't want to know," Jim replied. "And be thankful that you don't know, trust me."

"Are you guys in trouble or something?" Morgan pressed.

"Everyone here is in trouble," Ben deflected. "Right now, we really need to keep moving. So if you all still want to follow us…"

Morgan looked at Andy, who merely shrugged her shoulders indifferently. Knowing her friend wanted more enthusiasm, however, Andy relented.

"Yeah, that would be great," she said while trying to keep her tone as neutral as possible. She hadn't made up her mind about these two new strangers, but she didn't want to keep quarreling with Morgan either. Sometimes it was best to compromise, and sometimes you just had to give in.

Andy let Charlie switch places with her in the car, and she immediately stretched out in the back seat.

"I wonder who they're running from," said Charlie.

"Lord knows," Andy mumbled absently.

"Could be anyone, I suppose," Morgan chimed in. "What exactly did they say to you before I stepped outside?"

Charlie repeated the conversation from memory to his sister.

"They thought I was using a radio to contact whoever is chasing them? Unbelievable!"

"Either that or a mobile. It was all a bit dodgy, but I think our confusion is what finally convinced them to believe us. Right, Andy?"

"Yeah, probably," Andy replied with a yawn. "I think it's interesting that cell phones are still being used, at least to some extent. Someone must be maintaining the networks somehow."

"Interesting? I think it's bloody fantastic," Morgan declared. "That means someone out there is trying to rebuild…well, something."

"Yeah, I suppose."

"Don't sound too excited, Andy, or you might hurt yourself," Morgan went on with sarcasm.

"There's nothing to get excited about. We don't know anything—if we did, we wouldn't be following strangers in the dark in the middle of nowhere." Andy closed her eyes as a long sigh escaped her lips. *Such a long day…and it's not even over…*

"Well, whoever they are, I hope they do intend to help us, because we're about to run out of petrol," Charlie reported suddenly. "The fuel light just came on."

"Great," Andy mumbled inaudibly.

As Morgan and Charlie chatted about something inconsequential, Andy's mind drifted to thoughts about the two young men inside of that truck. She meant what she'd said about their intentions likely being honorable, but there was definitely something mysterious about them, especially Ben. She guessed he often avoided personal questions and topics, preferring instead to throw the attention back on someone or something else. The other one, Jim, seemed less guarded, and ultimately more friendly. They did not look like cousins, or any blood relation for that matter, although cousins often shared little or no resemblance with each other. They were both close to Andy's age, somewhere around eighteen or nineteen. Ben was at least six-one or six-two, and looked strong enough to lift twice Andy's weight with ease. Normally Andy wouldn't consider punching a guy like that without good reason, but he had managed to give her one.

He reminded her of a younger, but rougher version of Clark Kent, with his dark brown hair and memorable blue eyes. A Superman wearing a ragged T-shirt and tattered jeans, with dirt under his nails.

Jim was shorter than Ben by only a couple of inches, and was leaner but still sturdy—a good comparison being that of a football quarterback and a soccer midfielder. His hair was sandy blond, cut short like a soldier, and his eyes were either green or hazel…Andy couldn't recall. He had a boyish charm that made him instantly likeable, in vast contrast to Ben's more reticent demeanor.

Andy hadn't thought much about boys since her mother died, and through no fault of her own, her experience with them from a romantic perspective was severely underdeveloped for a girl of nineteen. The only significant males in her life had been her father and Charlie. Before the outbreak, it was rare to find nineteen-year-old girls who were still virgins, and yet she had never even kissed a boy, not even in school as a young teenager. Morgan, meanwhile, had kissed two boys in her life: one who later broke her heart, she claimed, and one who became her boyfriend for a whole month in school—an eternity for a thirteen-year-old. But Morgan had also had her virginity stolen from her when she'd been so violently raped, and that alone had forever ruined for her the glorious memories of the adolescent thrill of kissing boys for the first time. Experiences that were embarrassingly foreign to Andy were the source of Morgan's worst nightmare.

Her thoughts fading as she began to drift off to sleep, Andy was stirred awake by the car's slow but steady decline in speed. She sat up and looked out the window. Charlie had apparently flashed the headlights, indicating they'd run out of gas, and they were slowly drifting toward the rear of the truck, which had come to a stop just a few feet ahead. They didn't bother to pull over to the shoulder—they hadn't passed a single car the entire day.

Charlie applied the parking brake after the minivan ceased to roll another inch, and both he and Morgan stepped outside. Andy paused for a moment to gaze at the area around them, but it was too dark to make anything out. The dim glare of the minivan's headlights was the only source of light in the moonless night.

Ben and Jim were already waiting outside their truck with the engine turned off.

"Well," Ben began once Andy was finally within earshot. "You guys may as well ride with us until dawn. I haven't seen another car since we left the convenience store, and in the dark, you'd have to be pretty damn lucky to find one with gas, *or* a gas station that had any. Unless you want to take your chances, you'll save a lot of time by hitching a ride with us for a while."

Of course he was right, and though they would be stupid not to take the offer, Andy wasn't going to be the one to accept. Her willfulness proved to be futile, however, because Morgan accepted, and rather quickly.

"Can we take our stuff? It's not much, I promise."

"Yeah, whatever you can fit," Jim replied happily as Ben inwardly hoped that Morgan wasn't exaggerating about the sparseness of their possessions. More stuff meant more weight which meant lower gas mileage, and three extra bodies was weight enough. But to his relief, Morgan had not been exaggerating. Two small backpacks, the food from the convenience store, and one M4 later, the minivan became an abandoned vehicle once again.

Knowing his cousin would appreciate it, Ben suggested that Morgan ride in the front of the truck with Jim, as he hopped into the truck bed in back.

"I'm tired of listening to him all the time," was his feeble excuse. "My ears need rest."

Morgan hesitated half a moment before recovering. "Um, okay." Then to her brother, "you okay riding in the back?"

But Charlie was already following Ben.

"No worries," he called out.

"The wind will feel good," Andy added, preempting the same question. She climbed in last and quickly positioned herself into a corner at the rear so she wouldn't have to face Ben. Once they were underway, she closed her eyes. Amused, Ben found himself staring at her in the dark even though he couldn't see her face, or notice that she had already fallen asleep.

Chapter V

04 July 2020

After what felt like only a few hours, Andy woke up. It was still dark, and since she never wore a watch she could only guess what time it was. The truck was driving much slower than it had been, and they were weaving through fairly treacherous terrain with many hairpin turns and altitude fluctuations. She wondered where they were when she saw a passing sign for Route 441 reflecting off the headlights—a route that meant nothing to her.

The air had grown cooler, so she pulled the bottom of her oversized sweatshirt over her knees and grabbed a blanket lying nearby. Apparently, it wasn't the first time people had slept in the back of this truck. After snuggling herself into a cozy bundle, she gazed up at the sky and let out an unexpected gasp. Thousands upon thousands of stars shone like tiny pin pricks of light in the navy sky. Within a few minutes, Andy witnessed three shooting stars. It reminded her of Bermuda at night, with the smell of moist forest trees replacing the salty sea air and the rhythm of small waves lapping at the coastline.

"Pretty, isn't it?"

Ben's voice startled Andy. She could barely discern his silhouette, making his voice seem disembodied.

"What?"

"The stars…they're beautiful out here."

"Oh, yeah. They are."

A long pause followed. Andy didn't know if the brief exchange was meant to be the start of a conversation, so she remained silent.

"So what was Bermuda like?"

Okay, a conversation it was.

"Bermuda? Well, Bermuda was a little bit of everything, I guess."

"How do you mean?"

"Well, it's tropical in the summer, but cooler in the winter…"

"Wait," Ben interrupted. "I can't hear you…hang on."

The truck had begun to pick up speed, and the passing wind made it difficult to hear. Ben slid over to the rear of the truck bed until he and Andy were sitting across from each other. Charlie, meanwhile, was asleep at the front of the bed.

"Sorry, say that again," Ben said after settling in.

Andy couldn't believe the same guy she'd given her best right hook to just hours earlier now wanted to talk civilly. Stranger still was that he appeared to be genuinely interested in what she had to say.

"I said it's tropical in the summer, but the winters are cooler."

Andy had to almost shout her words to be heard.

"I thought Bermuda was in the Caribbean."

Andy shook her head. "It's much farther north."

Off to her left, the faintest light of dawn could be seen. It suddenly struck Andy how long they'd been driving without running out of gas.

"How can you drive so long without stopping?" she asked.

"This truck has three tanks," Ben replied. "We could go about nine hundred miles without a stop if we had to."

"Three tanks? Most trucks don't have three tanks."

"No, but Jim and I modified this one."

It sounded pretty ingenious to Andy, but the darkness concealed any expression of admiration.

"How do you find more gas when you run out?"

"We have our ways."

Andy could almost *hear* the smug look on Ben's face.

"And what ways are those?"

"Well, stick with us long enough and you'll find out."

Unsure of how to respond, Andy chose silence and returned her gaze to the stars. The fast approaching dawn was fading their intensity. She tried to close her eyes again but found she was no longer sleepy; there were too many questions floating around her head.

"Where exactly are you guys headed?"

"New Mexico."

"What's in New Mexico?"

"Nothing. Just seems like a good place to hide out for a while."

"Hide from whom?"

"No one in particular. Just to get away from all the people."

Another vague answer that Andy wasn't buying.

"You know I think you're full of shit, right?" she said.

Ben laughed. "Yeah."

"You guys are running from someone, and you accused us of being a part of it."

"What's your point?"

"My point is it's hard to believe anything you're telling me."

"Well, we are going to New Mexico. It'll take another day and a half to get there, but you'll see for yourself."

"And what makes you think my friends and I will hang around that long?"

"Because I think your friend wants to, and she seems to be the one calling the shots. I'm not sure why exactly because you seem to be more of the take-charge type, but I have a feeling it's got something to do with that bruise around her eye."

That's because my best friend was raped, and now she's carrying the unborn child of one of her rapists, and I don't have the heart to refuse any of her wishes right now…

"It's complicated," was all Andy said.

"I'm sure it is. Life isn't easy anymore."

Ben accurately summarized the last five years into four little words.

"Where are you and your cousin from?" Andy asked, changing the subject.

"Virginia. The suburbs of DC to be exact. Our parents lived two miles from each other."

"You two don't look related."

Ben laughed again.

"That's because we both look like our mothers, and it's our fathers who were brothers."

"How do you know so much about cars?"

"Jim's dad was a car mechanic. We used to hang around his shop on weekends just watching him, and we picked up a lot. After the virus, we had all the time in the world to mess around with cars."

Andy nodded. It was the same for her and medicine.

"You like working on cars?"

"I do. And I'm good at it. Cars make sense to me."

Andy understood. Medicine made sense to her.

As if reading her thoughts, Ben asked, "And what do you do to pass the time…other than sailing across oceans?"

"Human anatomy and medicine. My father was a doctor."

It was odd to talk about herself with a complete stranger.

Ben let out a whistle. Apparently, he wasn't afraid to show *his* admiration.

"What kind of doctor?"

"He was a heart surgeon for a long time, but then switched to his own general medicine practice when I was nine or ten."

"Why did he switch?"

"The hours. I barely saw him when he was a surgeon. But having his own practice gave him the flexibility to set his own schedule and decide how many patients he saw."

Ben began to ask something else when the truck slowed down and then stopped. Jim and Morgan emerged from the front, both chatting about something that Andy couldn't hear.

"Hey, my butt's getting numb," Jim began, mainly addressing Ben. "Let's switch for a while."

Charlie had woken up but still looked half-asleep. "Where are we?" he asked.

"Tennessee," Jim replied. "We're in the Great Smoky Mountains, if you know where that is."

Charlie did know but said nothing. He just wanted to go back to sleep.

"Is it cold back there?" Morgan asked Andy, looking perfectly content—even happy. In fact, Andy couldn't remember the last time she looked so well. Some of the color had even returned to her face.

"Not really. There are blankets back here," Andy replied, holding hers up to show Morgan. "I guess you guys sleep back here often."

"When we have to," Ben replied before hopping down to the ground.

"Charlie, do you want to stay back here or ride in the front?" Morgan asked.

"I'll stay here. I'm tired."

Morgan reached over and tousled his hair. "Okay, but don't snore." She climbed into the back, along with Jim.

"You're the one who snores," Charlie accused with a yawn.

Morgan froze with embarrassment until Jim said, "Don't worry…you can't hear someone snoring over the engine or the wind."

"I don't snore," Morgan insisted, wanting the last word on the matter.

It suddenly dawned on Andy that she hadn't had anything to drink or gone to the bathroom in at least twelve hours. Thinking about it made her not only thirsty, but aroused the need to find a bush somewhere.

"I gotta pee," she declared in an unladylike fashion and headed directly toward the forest that lined the highway.

"I do too," Morgan echoed, following Andy into the misty trees.

Charlie looked at Jim and Ben. "Take the other side then?"

Without a word, the three young men headed to the opposite side of the road to relieve themselves. Five minutes later, everyone reconvened at the truck. After a quick bite and some water, they were ready to move again. Andy joined Ben in the front of the truck as everyone else piled into the back.

"So how much farther can we go before we run out of gas?" Andy asked Ben when they were underway.

Ben glanced down at the dials in front of him.

"Probably another two hundred miles. If we're really lucky, we'll make it to Nashville."

Andy merely nodded and turned her attention to the passing scenery. As the early morning mist began to fade, the blue-green hues of the mountains became more vivid.

"Beautiful…" Andy murmured to herself.

Indeed, it was beautiful. The air alone was like magic as the smell of spruce filled her nostrils.

"Ever been here before?" Ben asked as he maneuvered the truck around several sharp turns.

"No, never. You?"

Ben nodded. "Once, when I was about eight or nine. I mostly remember the smell."

"Yeah, it's so fresh. These trees are…potent."

Andy turned her gaze from the window and stared sideways at Ben for a long moment. She opened her mouth to speak, hesitated, then finally asked the question.

"Why are you talking to me after I punched you in the face?"

After a single laugh, Ben smiled and said, "Would it make things any better if I got mad at you for that?"

"No…but most people don't think so logically, either."

"Was that a compliment?"

Andy stifled a smile. "More of an observation."

Ben laughed freely once more and said, "I can see you and I are going to have interesting times together."

The words hung in the air with a strange heaviness that made it impossible for Andy to respond easily away. There was a certainty to them that was both unnerving and reassuring.

Who was this person sitting beside her? Andy would have described Ben as indifferent if it weren't for his dogged avoidance of personal questions. He was confident and possessed enough detachment that made it seemingly impossible for anyone to inflict a verbal attack upon him. Andy silently envied this latter quality. Unlike Ben, she responded poorly to personal insults; she either internalized them or lashed out at whoever voiced the offense. It had been that way since she was a young child.

"Something wrong?"

Ben's voiced stirred Andy from her introspection.

"No…just thinking."

"About what?"

His question was casual and merely served to continue the conversation.

"I was just thinking about the last time I took a shower," Andy lied. "It's been two days since I last rinsed off in the ocean. I'm starting to feel pretty dirty."

"Well, get used to it," Ben remarked unsympathetically. "Must've been nice living on an island and always having a place to take a bath."

Andy nodded absently. "Just a matter of stepping outside and jumping off the dock."

"Sounds like heaven," Ben remarked in earnest. "What made you guys leave?"

"Bermuda is a tiny island," she began. "We lived as far away from everyone as possible, but we couldn't stay isolated forever. Things just became too dangerous, so we left."

Though truthful, her response was purposely vague. The real reason for their departure was Morgan's secret to keep, not hers.

"Makes sense," Ben replied, seemingly satisfied. "Having your own space, your own corner of the world…it's worth everything.

Once it's gone, it's time to move on."

"Is that what you're looking for in New Mexico? Your own corner of the world?"

Ben shrugged. "Maybe."

He was being equally avoidant, but Andy pressed further.

"So why are you headed west now? Why not five years ago?"

Despite the dim morning light, Andy could clearly see Ben's body stiffen and his jaw harden, and she almost regretted asking the question. He reapplied his grip on the steering wheel and cleared his throat.

"Things weren't always so bad. Life was pretty quiet for a few years after the outbreak. It didn't get really bad until about…two years ago."

"What changed two years ago?"

Ben released one hand from the steering wheel and ruffled his hair with it. It was a gesture Andy had noticed a couple times already as a way to pause a conversation.

"Well, I'm sure pretty much the same thing that happened to you on that island, except on a much larger scale. Gangs began to grow and spread and fight one another. Things went from bad to worse for everyone. Stuff like that."

There was so much Ben wasn't saying, but Andy knew she wouldn't get anything more out of him, not now at least. Still, questions continued to fill her mind.

"New Mexico is far away. Do you have friends there?"

Ben shook his head. "No, no friends, but the farther west we can go, the better."

"But it's so dry there. Won't it be hard to find water?"

"There're lots of rivers…big ones, like the Rio Grande. 'Grande' is Spanish for big, you know."

Andy let out a chuckle. "I know."

"Sorry," said Ben with slight embarrassment and cleared his throat. "Anyway, the winters are warm there, and it's got mountains. I could never live on flat farmland like the middle of the country."

"Yeah, me neither."

Ben took his gaze off the road and turned to Andy.

"Well, since you don't seem to be too interested in New Mexico, where would you pick to live?"

She had to admit she hadn't really thought about it, especially now that Washington DC, and most of the Eastern Seaboard for that matter, were no longer options. Their only goal had been getting to America.

"I don't know, but if I could really go anywhere, I guess I'd pick somewhere by the ocean. I already miss the ocean, and it's only been a few days. But not an island. I don't want to feel that trapped again."

"Maybe a bigger island then…like Hawaii?"

"Hawaii would be big enough, but it's in the middle of the Pacific. I'd need a really big boat or be able to fly there…hardly options."

"Oh, I don't know. I'll bet there are a few people out there who can fly a plane."

Andy looked at Ben with skepticism, which he challenged.

"What, you don't think some rich parents ever gave their twelve-year-old son or daughter flying lessons? You learned about medicine from your dad. Why wouldn't flying be the same?"

Andy shrugged. He had a point.

"I guess so. It just seems very risky."

"And cutting people open isn't risky?"

"I've never cut anyone open," Andy quickly replied. "I'm nowhere close to being a surgeon. You could hardly consider me a nurse."

"Maybe, but I bet you could be a surgeon if you wanted to."

"Sure, if medical schools still existed, but not now…"

"I'm sure you could figure it out."

Andy scoffed. "Surgery is not like fixing a car. You mess up the slightest thing, and your patient is dead."

Ben nodded slowly, but countered, saying, "That's true, but aren't most people who need surgery are going to die anyway? You're just giving them a chance, even if it's a very small chance. After a while, you'd get better at it."

"Yeah, after watching several people die in the process."

"Well, isn't that part of being a doctor? Even the best surgeons lose patients."

"I know, but I'm exhausted by death and people dying," Andy replied with a shrug and stared off to her right. "Aren't you?" she added rhetorically.

"Maybe you chose the wrong profession," was Ben's painfully honest reply.

Without warning, he reached over toward the glove box, grazing the top of Andy's thigh in the process, and opened the tiny door. "Sorry," he mumbled as he fished inside a moment before pulling out a can of what appeared to be peanuts.

"Want some?"

Andy cracked a smile. Of course she wanted some.

"Thanks."

"Would you open it?" Ben asked, holding the can out to her with his right hand, his left hand on the steering wheel.

"Yeah, sure."

The smell of roasted nuts and salt filled Andy's nostrils the moment she peeled back the aluminum seal. She grabbed a large handful before holding the can out for Ben.

"Thanks," he said and helped himself.

The entire can was gone in less than ten minutes.

"There should be some water bottles behind the seat," Ben said after finishing his last mouthful. "Can you grab me one, too?"

"Okay."

The water quenched her dry, salty throat. It was the best thing she'd ever tasted.

"Oh, and by the way, now that you're back in the States..." Ben began, his right hand holding his bottle up in the air as though he were making a toast. "Happy Fourth of July."

* * *

Minutes passed into hours as Andy dozed off. As Ben had hoped, the truck managed to reach Nashville without running out of gas. Just before reaching the beltway that wrapped around the city, he took the exit for Nashville International Airport. The decrease in speed was enough to awaken Andy, and she rubbed her eyes open and looked around.

"Where are we going?"

"Getting gas," said Ben.

The airport was utterly void of any sign of life, which came as no surprise. They approached a sign that read "Airport Services" and a corresponding arrow that pointed off to the right. Ben followed the arrow and continued around the main terminal until reaching a restricted area where only airport vehicles driven by employees were once permitted.

"Airplane fuel?" Andy blurted aloud. "That works in cars too?"

"Some airplane fuel can run a car, but it's such a high octane that it'll ruin the engine," Ben replied as he weaved around airplanes and other various support vehicles.

"Then why are we here?"

"Like I said, for gas. When it became scarce, most survivors never thought to check out airports. One of the best-kept secrets Jim and I discovered was that airports always had tanks of gasoline for all the vehicles used to move luggage and stuff around. Even some of the smaller private planes use the same gas as cars."

"So that's your secret." Andy remarked, clearly impressed. "That's clever. Really smart."

Ben merely shrugged at the compliment.

"When everyone is out for themselves, it's survival of the fittest."

Andy nodded in agreement. "Darwin was right."

"Damn right," Ben added. "Now let's just hope we have a little luck, too."

They did have luck in the form of a full, untouched tanker truck of gasoline, direct from the oil refinery.

"But this has been sitting here for at least five years," Andy commented once everyone was out of the truck. "Won't the gas be stale or something?"

"Nah, these tanks are vacuum-sealed. Gas only goes bad only when it's exposed to the air," Ben replied as his cousin headed toward the rear of the enormous tank, carrying what appeared to be a small toolbox.

Andy, Morgan, and Charlie stood back and watched as Ben and Jim opened the valves at the rear of the tank and somehow managed to get the fuel moving into their own trunk's tanks. The speed and dexterity with which they performed this task was quite impressive.

"I take it you two have done this before," Morgan remarked.

"How else do you think we managed to keep driving all these years?" Jim replied, flashing Morgan a warm smile. "Gas at the pumps ran out long ago."

"Yeah, we've noticed," Andy recalled bitterly.

As the precious liquid filled the truck's tanks, Ben reached behind the front seats and retrieved three large, cylindrical plastic containers, each empty.

"How much petrol does each of those hold?" Charlie asked.

"About eight or nine gallons," Jim replied as he grabbed one of the containers from Ben and began to fill it up. "They'll give us another four hundred miles."

"Is that part of the eight hundred miles you mentioned, or is it extra?" Andy asked Ben.

"It's extra. We should make it to New Mexico without having to stop again."

Morgan glanced at Andy, her eyes filled with apprehension. She feared Andy would not agree with the idea of going to New Mexico with their new acquaintances and that she would now say something about it. But Andy remained silent. There was no better plan at the moment. Rather, there was no other plan at all. They were going to New Mexico.

Charlie, meanwhile, was scratching his head. "Gallons? Miles? Why don't you use metric measurements here?"

"Hey, don't give us hard time," Andy reprimanded him lightly. "Miles and gallons are *English* units, after all."

"Yes, but we eventually realized the silliness of it and changed to metric. You Americans should have, too."

"Yeah, well, hardly the biggest of our problems now, is it?"

Before Charlie could say anything more, Jim topped off the last container.

"Done," he happily proclaimed.

* * *

They drove…and drove.

The landscape changed. The lush foliage of Tennessee thinned out as they moved west beyond the Mississippi River. Long, pale green grass, slave to the will of the winds, dominated the landscape. The crossing streams allowed everyone to enjoy much-needed baths to remove the film of dirt that relentlessly clung to their skin. On the second night, they stopped at an abandoned motel near the Oklahoma-Texas border. The beds were old and creaky, and the rooms reeked of mildew, but everyone was too exhausted to care. Andy was asleep before her head hit the pillow. Shortly after dawn, they were driving again, across the Texas Panhandle. The green grass turned to yellow, and the trees seemed to disappear completely.

If they ever once passed another person or moving vehicle, Andy never noticed. The highway was lonely and desolate, and the random scatterings of abandoned vehicles only made it appear more so. During the silent stretches of time when she wasn't sleeping or engaged in conversation, she considered the uncertainty of the future. The endlessness of the wide open spaces around her seemed to reflect this notion, the vast emptiness surrounding them. Mostly, she thought about the recent past, about Morgan. Though they hadn't talked about what had happened since leaving Bermuda, Andy would often detect brief but unmistakable expressions of both fear and shame on her friend's face as her mind struggled to come to terms with it all. Then there was the baby, growing slowly inside her belly, currently no larger than a poppy seed. How could something that tiny and innocent so painfully represent the consequences of a single, horrifying event? Did Morgan even care that there was a potential human being relying on her to keep living and breathing for its own survival? Or did she only think of the embryo as a parasite, a leech reminding her that she'd been a battered and bloody mess on the filthy bathroom floor where Andy had found her? These were questions Andy could neither ask nor answer herself, as least not yet. Her own memories were troublesome enough: the caustic sensation of vomit coming up her throat the moment she saw her best friend lying half-naked on that floor; the heaviness of her limp body as she carried her, unconscious, back to their home, her knees nearly buckling under the strain. They would both need the passing of time before such things could be discussed.

Ben was driving when they entered New Mexico, Andy once again sitting beside him. At one point, she noticed him yawning and offered to drive. Though grateful, Ben declined the offer.

"Okay, but tell me if you change your mind."

Reaching down between her feet, Andy lifted her backpack off the floor and placed it on her lap. With most of the food and water already consumed, it was pretty light. Only her favorite medical book, three magazines—one for her Glock and the other two for the M4—and two cans of fruit remained. She unzipped the small front pocket of the bag, reached inside and fished around for one more item: the iPod her parents had given her on her thirteenth birthday. It was one of the last models Apple had made, and it was the last gift she'd received from her mother before her death. The battery was dead, but she had the car adapter. It was the only way she could recharge it.

"You mind if I plug this into your cigarette lighter?"

Ben glanced at the iPod and charger in Andy's hand and shook his head lightly.

"No, go ahead. It's under the radio."

"Thanks."

Once the battery symbol on the screen lit up, Andy plugged the distinctive white earbuds into her ears and skimmed through her playlists. She found the one she was looking for, pushed "play," leaned back in the seat, and closed her eyes.

"What are you listening to?" Ben asked just as the music got underway.

Andy opened her eyes and whirled her finger counterclockwise around the touch-sensitive wheel to decrease the volume.

"Sorry, what?"

"What are you listening to?"

Andy opened her mouth to answer, but then stopped. She tilted her head to the side and narrowed her eyes at Ben as a look of warning.

"You promise you won't laugh?"

Ben raised a hand defensively.

"Well, I can't promise I won't laugh if you say something like 'circus' or 'elevator music.'

Laughing, Andy shook her head and said simply, "It's Bach."

Expecting a look of disdain from Ben, Andy was surprised by the flicker of interest that crossed his face instead.

"Which one?" he asked.

"Which symphony?"

"No, I mean which Bach? Wasn't there more than one composer named Bach?"

Now it was Andy's turn to be surprised.

"Uh, yeah. Johann Sebastian was the father and most famous one. He had three or four sons who became composers, though some were more famous than the others."

"Oh yeah, that's right," Ben replied, as though he were scouring the depths of his memory. "Was it fifth grade? No…sixth grade. Miss…Miss…God, what was her name?"

He snapped his fingers in an effort to force it to come to him.

"Miss Johnson! That's it!"

Ben lightly smacked the top of the steering wheel upon the remembrance.

"Miss Johnson was my music teacher. God, I haven't thought

about her in forever. She was this sweet, older woman—at least sixty—and never married. But she loved music, especially Bach. She called him 'Herr Johann,' and she would go on and on about the greatness of the 'Bach musical dynasty.' Jim and I used to think she was in love with him."

Ben shook his head and smiled at the memory. "We were pretty stupid back then."

"You and Jim were in the same class?"

"No, I was a year ahead, but we had all the same teachers."

Ben combed his fingers through his hair once again, which meant that it was time to change the subject.

"So which Bach are you listening to?"

"Herr Johann," Andy replied with a light chuckle.

"Can I listen for a sec?"

Andy shrugged at the unexpected request.

"Uh, sure. Here."

She passed the earbuds to Ben and moved the iPod closer to him. As he secured the speakers in his ears, Andy resumed the music. She watched him closely as he listened, but his expression never changed and his eyes remained fixed on the road ahead.

"What's the name of this one?" he asked after more than a minute had passed.

"It's one of his cello suites…Suite Number 1 in G major, the 'Prelude,' to be exact."

Ben nodded slightly, then added after a long pause, presumably once the music ended, "It's just one instrument."

"It's the cello. It's one of the 'Six Unaccompanied Cello Suites.'"

"It's beautiful," Ben remarked genuinely and removed the earbuds before passing them back to Andy. "It's too bad it's so short. Just when you get into it, it ends."

"I know…this one's my favorite," Andy replied, amazed by Ben's interest.

"Of the six suites, you mean?"

"No, my favorite piece of classical music."

"Why is it your favorite?"

"Because my mother used to play it at concerts. She was a cellist with the New York Philharmonic before she married my dad. Then she joined the Philadelphia Orchestra once I was old enough to go to school."

Ben let out a whistle.

"Wow, that's impressive. She must've been really good."

"She was. Before she died, she was the principal cellist, which means that she was the lead cellist in the entire orchestra." Andy glanced down at the iPod in her lap. "Anyway, a few days before my thirteenth birthday, she played this piece during a concert that was being recorded. As a birthday present, she and my dad bought me this iPod with the recording already loaded onto it."

"So what I just listened to is actually your mother playing?" Ben asked with mounting astonishment.

Andy nodded and smiled proudly.

"I was in the audience when she played it. She was flawless."

"It sounded flawless," Ben agreed. "I can't believe that's your mother playing. Did you ever play?"

"What, the cello?"

"Or any instrument?"

"No." Andy shook her head. "I didn't like sitting inside and practicing. I liked being outside playing sports instead."

"So more of a tomboy then, huh? No surprise there."

"What's that supposed to mean?"

"It means that you have a pretty good right hook."

Wearing a smirk, Ben gently stroked his chin.

"You deserved it," Andy replied sharply, though she was half-smiling.

"I guess so, but I have no idea why. You ever gonna tell me what that was all about?"

Andy's smile disappeared.

"No, not now at least. Or ever, maybe."

"Really? Not ever?"

Andy thought she detected a small sound of distress in Ben's voice that was contrary to the more cool and composed demeanor that she had come to expect from him.

As to the question, she did not know how to respond, and once again, Ben brushed his hand through his hair, which Andy now realized was something he did when he was nervous.

"Sorry," he began after clearing his throat. "Whatever it was, it's obviously something personal, so I won't ask again."

"It's okay," Andy replied quickly, trying to sound reassuring.

"I guess I was just thinking that it would be cool if you guys stuck around for a while, you know? Maybe long enough that you'd tell me what I did to make you so angry."

It was then that Andy realized she'd been mistaken in her initial judgment of Ben. He *did* care what people thought about him—or, at least he wanted to understand how he'd wronged someone. Suddenly her opinion of him improved.

"But you hardly know us. How do you know that you won't get sick of us?"

Ben chuckled. "I don't know, but you three are at least smart and self-sufficient."

"And what, everyone else you meet is stupid and lazy?"

Ben raised an eyebrow, indicating she wasn't far off the mark.

"Let me ask you," he began. "Before the virus, when you were in school, did you get good grades?"

"Yeah, I did."

"And when you were in Bermuda, did you guys feed yourselves by fishing and growing your own food?"

"Yeah, we fished almost every day, and we had our own garden."

"Okay, and I suppose you all read a lot of books, right?"

"Uh, yeah…hundreds, probably."

"I rest my case. You're an exception. Most of the survivors aren't like you. They're uneducated…many can barely read. Most can't feed themselves, so they either steal food or rely on others to feed them. They're totally helpless, like infants. Meanwhile, you three managed to sail hundreds of miles from Bermuda to the coast and survive…alone."

Ben gave Andy a serious look. "Yeah, you three are *definitely* an exception."

Andy turned away and looked out the window to her right. "Shit," she muttered under her breath.

"What?"

"Well, not that any of what you just said is a surprise, but it still scares me. My dad used to say that ignorance was dangerous."

"I think your dad was right. But all that means is that you've got the upper hand."

"'Knowledge is Power,' Sir Francis Bacon."

"Okay, now you're just showing off."

Andy laughed. "Well, I have to give credit to Charlie for that one. He loves quoting famous people."

"He seems like a smart kid."

"No, I'm smart. Charlie is a genius. His I.Q. is off the charts."

"Good, 'cuz we need all the brains we can get."

"Well, I suppose we'll *have* to stick around then," she said sarcastically after feigning a sigh. "Unless a better offer comes along."

"I wouldn't hold my breath," Ben replied as he smiled broadly at her.

And at that moment, a sudden and strange warmth erupted somewhere in the lower part of her abdomen. It was like nothing she'd ever felt before, and with agitation, she recognized that it had everything to do with the person sitting beside her.

Chapter VI

06 July 2020

Eastern New Mexico was dry and hot. Andy felt like she was standing in an oven, her skin cooking under the intense sun. She wore a baseball cap and a thin white linen shirt over her T-shirt to keep from getting sunburned, though neither could ward off the heat. Even the warmest days in Bermuda had never been this hot. And it was quiet, like a void. Gone were the sounds of the ocean and the tangible feeling of moisture on her skin.

Sitting in the back of the truck with Ben and Charlie, Andy turned to Ben when the truck slowed down enough for him to hear her.

"I know this part of the country is a desert, but did you guys ever consider how hot the summers would be when you picked this state? Or did you just spin a globe and decide on the first state west of the Mississippi that your finger landed on…or maybe throw a dart at a map?"

Charlie was more polite about the matter.

"You know, Ben, after living through those cold, rainy winters in England, I'm all for warm weather, but I have to agree with Andy. This is *hot*."

Ben was unaffected by their remarks. There was a reason he and

Jim had decided on New Mexico, and it was entirely geographic. One of the most sparsely populated states in the country before the outbreak, the probability of New Mexico containing the same dangers that existed back east was extremely low. What these dangers were exactly would remain unknown to Andy for a long time, though she would ponder the possibilities more than just occasionally. Those bizarre and furiously delivered accusations they had thrown at her and her friends that first day could not easily be forgotten.

The last stretch of their journey ended a hundred miles west of the Texas–New Mexico border in the town of Santa Rosa. It was a small town and from all initial appearances, entirely deserted.

When she was ten, Andy's father bought her a book of photographs of the Grand Canyon. Young Andy scoured through its pages until the binding broke, but all she remembered were the images of brilliant reddish-orange hues that continually changed with the shifting sun. However, this eastern portion of New Mexico, with its bland, brownish plains covered with tufts of burro grass, was anything but brilliant. Both Morgan and Charlie agreed, the latter remarking that even the English moors of his childhood had more character. These sentiments, along with the climate, inspired little confidence in their decision to come to New Mexico. But for the sake of much-needed rest, they stayed in Santa Rosa for more than a week.

It wasn't difficult finding a place to stay, since the town was nearly empty. They found two modest homes across the street from each other in a quiet neighborhood. Days were spent either in the shade or at the nearby lakes in the area. Santa Rosa, as they soon discovered, was surrounded by many lakes, an unusual geographic advantage for a town situated in such an arid climate. But other than bathing and swimming in the lakes, there wasn't much else to do or see in the town, and food was nowhere to be found. Had it not been for a chance meeting with three siblings living in a house on a neighboring street, their stay would have ended much sooner.

Maria, Julio, and Carmen Rodriguez had been living in Santa

Rosa since the early months after the virus. They had come across the border from Juarez, Mexico, where life before the outbreak had been difficult but became far worse afterward. Their father had been a high-ranking member of the violent Juarez drug cartel when members of a rival cartel murdered him a mere three months before the rest of the world plunged into chaos. Due to their father's status and wealth, the three children had lived a privileged but dangerous life, often becoming targets themselves. After the virus, the children of the rival cartel responsible for Señor Rodriguez's death continued their father's legacy and attempted to kill his children. The three managed to evade death in Juarez for nearly three months until a bullet meant for Maria grazed her younger sister's arm. They left Juarez for good the following day, and Santa Rosa had been their home ever since.

Despite their father's profession, neither Maria, her brother, or sister exhibited any indication of having been raised by a man who smuggled illicit drugs into the United States using ruthless and often violent means. They were kind and warm-hearted, and each seemed genuinely happy to meet some new people. Furthermore, there was a hint of contempt in Maria's voice whenever she mentioned her father.

At eighteen, Maria was the oldest. She was very pretty, with long dark hair, hazel eyes, and a thin frame. Julio was thirteen. He was a tad shorter than Charlie, with dark hair and eyes that matched those of his two sisters. Aged ten, Carmen was a miniature version of Maria. When in one another's company, they spoke Spanish, but thanks to expensive private schools and living within miles of the Texas border, all three spoke English with barely an accent. In fact, Morgan and Charlie's British accent was more pronounced than theirs.

Upon meeting the five newcomers in their neighborhood, the Rodriguez siblings invited them to dinner one night shortly after their arrival. The group of eight sat around the dinner table to a wonderfully warm meal of chili and fresh baked cornbread, but before anyone could ask how they'd managed to prepare the meal without electricity, Maria asked where they were all from.

Charlie answered first for himself and his sister, explaining that they were from England and had met Andy in Bermuda.

"We spent five years on that island, but left just a few days ago."

"Why did you leave?" Maria asked, unaware of the agitation that particular question caused.

"The island was becoming too small and too chaotic," Andy replied quickly.

Maria nodded as if she understood.

"It was the same with Juarez. After that bullet nearly killed me and grazed Carmen's arm, there was no doubt that we had to leave. We didn't want to, but we had no choice."

Then after a spoonful of chili, Maria turned to Jim and Ben.

"What about you two?"

Andy watched the two cousins carefully as Jim answered for both of them. Unfortunately, he revealed nothing more than the fact that they had been living in Virginia at the time, which she already knew.

"Virginia? That's near Washington DC, right?" Maria continued. "I was always terrible at geography."

"Yeah, DC sits at the north of the state," Ben answered plainly.

Maria turned to her brother. "Julio, do you remember those three boys who passed through here about a year ago? They were a little older than you. I think they were from somewhere near Washington DC, right?"

Julio remembered, but he shook his head.

"It was Philadelphia. I remember because I asked them about the Liberty Bell and if it was still cracked."

Julio smiled at the joke, and everyone laughed.

"That's right, Philadelphia," Maria continued. "I think they were on their way to Phoenix. They had friends there or something. They didn't say much about where they came from, but I remember getting the feeling that it wasn't something they wanted to talk about. They seemed really anxious to get to Phoenix."

"I'm from Philadelphia," Andy remarked. "Do you remember their names? Maybe I knew them."

Maria frowned. "No, I don't." Neither did Julio or Carmen.

"Well, it's a big city. The chance of me knowing them would be slim."

Throughout the meal, Andy continued to eye Ben and Jim, watching for any sort of reaction that might give something away. It was pointless, however. Both remained entirely expressionless and said little.

Sitting at the end of the table, Morgan was the first to excuse herself. She had been quiet all evening and now looked tired and pale. After thanking Maria for the meal, she returned to the house a few blocks away where she, Andy, and her brother were staying.

After she left, Jim turned to Andy with a look of concern.

"Is she okay?"

Andy forced a smile.

"She's fine, just a little tired."

* * *

Later that night after everyone went to bed, Andy woke up to the sound of Morgan crying and crept quietly into her room to avoid waking Charlie across the hall.

"Morgan?" she whispered softly as she tiptoed toward the bed, moonlight streaming in through the window.

Morgan's back was to her, and Andy could see her body shaking. She sat down on the edge of the bed and gently stroked Morgan's hair. It was something her mother used to do when she was upset.

Morgan made no effort to sit up or move but continued to cry. It broke Andy's heart to see her friend in such a state.

"Andy…how can I raise a child in this world? A child that I don't even want."

Andy didn't say anything. She just remained still and let Morgan speak through her sobs.

"I'm so tired…so tired of feeling like there's no end to it all. Every day is such a struggle. Food…water…and now petrol? Even going to the bathroom is an effort. When does it end? When will life get easier?"

It was all well-covered territory. These woes were nothing new. The only change was that it would all soon involve a child, a helpless infant whose mother had never asked for its existence in the first place.

"We'll do what we've always done," Andy began. "We'll adapt and we'll get through it together."

Andy knew she was trying to reassure herself as much as reassure Morgan.

"But where are we gonna go? We can't stay here; this town is empty, and there's no food. No ocean to fish, no garden to grow. It's dry and dead here. And hot. I can't sleep at night. All I do is sweat, and the bigger I get, the more I'll sweat…"

"…Shh…It's gonna be okay. We don't have to stay here. It's just temporary until we come up with something better."

Morgan rubbed her moist eyes and looked up at Andy.

"I'm so sorry I'm such a burden. All of this is my fault. If I hadn't…if those boys had never—"

Andy abruptly stopped her.

"Don't ever say that, Morgan. You're not a burden, and none of this is your fault."

"But if it weren't for me, we'd still be happy in Bermuda."

"But I never wanted to stay in Bermuda forever, Morgan. I wanted to come home. I'd wanted to return for a while, but I was never going to leave you and Charlie as long as you were both happy. You guys are my family, and you always will be. You two are brother and sister I never had. The only good thing that fucking virus ever did was bring us together."

Morgan's face broke into quiet laughter.

"You should curse more. It suits you."

"Maybe I will," Andy replied, smiling. "But seriously, you're gonna be okay. And your baby is gonna be okay. I promise."

"But where are we gonna go?" Morgan asked again.

Andy had no answer.

"I don't know. I'll talk to Maria tomorrow. Maybe she has some ideas. I know we can't live off her hospitality forever."

"What about Jim and Ben?"

Andy shrugged. She hadn't thought that far ahead.

"They can do whatever they want, I guess. Stay, or come with us."

"Will you ask them to come with us?"

"Do you want me to?"

Morgan hesitated a moment before nodding.

"It's nice having other people around to talk to. Not that you and my brother aren't enough, but you know what I mean."

Andy smiled faintly. "Yeah, I do. Jim is a good guy, I think. And Ben…well, he's growing on me, I suppose. It would be nice to have a couple extra sets of hands around to help out with whatever comes along."

Morgan sniffled. "So you'll ask them, then?"

"Sure, but why don't you ask them?"

"I don't want them to think I'm asking for help because I'm pregnant and I need them to take care of me."

"But they don't know you're pregnant."

"They'll find out soon enough, if they stick around. I can only pretend so long, but my belly can't."

Andy hadn't realized until then how much Morgan had considered the matter.

"Ok, I'll ask them. But if they don't come, you'll still have me and Charlie, okay? No matter what."

Morgan grabbed Andy's hand and gave it a squeeze.

"I know…and I thank God for you both."

* * *

Andy didn't sleep much that night. Worries consumed her.

Things had been easier in Bermuda. There was never any apprehension about the future. It just came, day by day, and they'd survived—they'd adapted.

But this was different. Morgan had been right. There was no ocean to fish and no garden to grow; only dry, desert soil and heat. She wondered if they would've been better off staying back east in some beach town in North Carolina or Virginia. But it was too late to go back. They had been seduced by the offer of help from Jim and Ben when they had never needed help before. Now that they had accepted it, they seemed more off-track than ever.

All night, troublesome thoughts hounded Andy, and by five in the morning, she'd had enough. Her room was dark, but she managed to fish around for her clothes and shoes. After tiptoeing out of the house, she headed toward the Rodriguez home. They would still be sleeping, but Andy wandered that way. She just needed to clear her head.

Upon reaching their home, she was surprised to see Maria standing at the end of the driveway. Even more surprising was the presence of a mid-sized trailer truck with its engine running. There were two young men inside, and Maria was talking to the passenger at the window. A moment later, she watched as the truck drove off and didn't see Andy approach.

"Maria?"

Maria whirled around, startled.

"Jesus! Andy, you scared me!" Then catching her breath, "What are you doing here?"

"Sorry, I didn't mean to sneak up on you. I couldn't sleep, so I went for a walk and just kinda wound up here." Then, after an awkward pause, she added, "Mind if I ask what that was about? The truck, I mean."

But Maria did mind.

"I wish I could tell you, Andy, but there are certain people I have to protect. I'm sure you're trustworthy, but I just don't know you well enough."

Andy shrugged.

"Fair enough. I *am* trustworthy, but I understand the need for secrecy, too."

In the approaching daylight, Andy could see Maria nod faintly.

"I'm just trying to help out some friends from Juarez. Things are still very bad there."

"It seems like things are bad everywhere," Andy remarked heavily, and Maria readily agreed.

"It's true. You either have to live out in the middle of nowhere, like here, or in the middle of chaos with all the other survivors. You have to choose: isolation or anarchy."

"So you chose isolation?"

Maria's jaw hardened.

"We had no choice. Julio and Carmen were so young when everything happened, and they depended entirely on me. I became their mother. When Carmen was nearly shot, I had to make a choice."

"That's a lot to ask of a thirteen-year-old."

Maria's eyes narrowed as she gazed off toward the horizon.

"They're my brother and sister. I'd do anything for them. Even move to a dead town like this. I don't want to be here, but there were no other options. And I have friends depending on me."

"Will you ever leave here?"

"One day, if things get better in Juarez, we'll return. But I have a deadline: my twentieth birthday. If things aren't better by then back home, we'll go somewhere else. That's a year and a half from now. I can make it here until then."

"Where would you go?"

"Colorado," Maria replied instantaneously. "I've heard rumors from people travelling through here that some of the ski towns managed to become pretty organized in the past year or two. I've even heard that they have power and electricity in most of the homes again, and water too. But you also have to be invited by its residents to live in those towns."

"Invited? How?"

Maria shrugged.

"I don't know for certain, but like everything these days, you have to have something other than money to bargain with. Money is worthless, but if you have certain skills or supplies that people want, you have a better chance of getting invited."

Andy nodded. She wondered how valuable her skills as an amateur doctor would be.

"Which ski towns in particular did you hear about?"

Maria frowned.

"Why, you all thinking of leaving already? I was hoping you would stay awhile. So were Julio and Carmen."

"Really? Well, we would stay longer, but Morgan…well, it's complicated."

"She's pregnant, right?"

Andy looked at Maria with surprise.

"How did you know?"

"Actually, it was just a guess, but last night, before she left, I noticed her touching her stomach quite a bit. At first I thought she wasn't used to the spicy chili, but that usually causes heartburn and the pain would be much farther up than where a fetus would be."

Andy frowned.

"Your observation skills are a little scary."

"Well that comes from being the oldest daughter of a former drug lord who had multiple death threats out against him. You learn to watch your back and watch others."

"That's a good skill to have," Andy remarked. "Do you miss your parents?"

"I miss my mother," Maria replied quite easily. "And if Julio and Carmen were around, I'd say I miss my father too. But in reality, it's hard to miss someone like that. Julio and Carmen were too young to know what he was really like, but I remember. For their sake, though, I keep my feelings to myself. It's not worth ruining their memories."

"Memories are all we have now," Andy muttered before turning the conversation back to Morgan.

"Please don't say anything to the others about her being pregnant. Even Charlie doesn't know. I'm the only one she's told."

"Of course," Maria assured. "Everyone's entitled to privacy."

"Thanks."

"So when will you all leave?"

Andy shook her head. "I don't know, but probably in a few days. I'll talk with the others first."

"Well, let me know when you decide." Maria put her hands on her hips and looked off toward the east. The sun was just about to appear.

"Another day," she remarked with a heavy sigh.

Andy nodded silently and looked on as the sun emerged over the horizon. It was a beautiful sight.

"Someday, we'll leave," Maria said quietly, almost in a whisper.

* * *

Morgan awoke to the familiar sensation of nausea and hurried outside to vomit since the bathrooms had no water to flush anything down. When she finished, she saw Andy walking toward the house.

"You're awake?"

"Yeah, couldn't sleep, so I went for a stroll."

Andy looked down at the pile of dirt that Morgan had kicked over the contents of her stomach.

"You okay?"

"Just the usual morning sickness."

Andy nodded with a look of sympathy before glancing at the house across the street where Ben and Jim were sleeping.

"Any sign of them this morning?"

"No, but I just woke up…and it's early."

"I ran into Maria while walking. She was already awake."

Andy didn't mention anything about the mysterious truck, but recalled the rest of their conversation for Morgan.

"Do you believe her?"

"Why would Maria lie to us?"

"I didn't mean lie. I mean do you think she's right? Do think there are towns in Colorado that are more organized?"

"Dunno. She said it was all just rumors, but why couldn't it be true? It's not impossible to imagine that some survivors actually managed to get a whole town up and running again."

"It sounds like a bloody miracle to me," Morgan remarked dryly. "But if it's true, then sign me up."

After a laugh, Andy turned to head across the street.

"I'm gonna go get the map from them and figure out the route we'll take north."

"You'll ask them now?" Morgan called back. "To come with us, I mean?"

Andy shrugged. "Might as well."

After crossing the street, she knocked on the door once, twice, then three times. After the third knock, she suddenly realized how early it still was, but it was too late. Ben answered, his eyes half-open and wearing only his jeans.

"Oh, sorry," Andy blurted out. She averted her gaze from his bare chest. "Forgot how early it was."

"Didn't sleep?" Ben asked groggily. He rubbed his eyes with one hand and backed away from the door to let Andy inside. She hesitated a moment before entering.

"Not really. I woke up about an hour ago and went for a walk."

Ben wandered toward the kitchen and took a seat at the tiny kitchen table. Andy followed but didn't sit down. Instead, she stood in between the kitchen sink and the refrigerator, neither of which were operational. Stuck to the front of the fridge with magnets were pictures of some family who had once inhabited the house. Children possibly long gone and parents long dead.

"Where did you walk?"

"More like 'wander,' but I ended up at Maria's house."

Then as she had done for Morgan, Andy recounted her discussion with Maria to Ben. He listened carefully and refrained from speaking until she finished.

"So you want to go to Colorado."

It was a statement, not a question, but Andy responded as though he were asking.

"Maybe…yes. It's worth checking. If it doesn't work out, we can always come back here."

Ben sat back in his chair and cracked his knuckles, one at a time. He was thinking.

"By 'we,' you mean you three?"

He was going to make her ask.

"And you and Jim, if you want to come." There, she thought. Nothing more than a simple offer.

Ben looked at Andy for a long moment, which made her uneasy, and she wondered if he knew that he could affect her that way.

"I'll ask Jim when he gets up," was all he said.

Andy merely nodded. There was nothing more to say, so she asked him to see the road map.

"Yeah, it's in the truck. I'll grab it."

"No, I can get it…"

But Ben was already back on his feet and walking toward the door. He reappeared a minute later with the map. Instead of handing it to Andy, he returned to the table and laid the map out flat. He leaned over and began to study it.

"You don't have to do that," Andy insisted as she moved toward the table. "I can look at it later."

Ben shrugged.

"I was just curious," he said, then gazed at Andy with a mixture of suspicion and amusement. "Maybe you don't want to tell me where in Colorado you plan to go."

"I don't know where we're going yet."

She noticed a blue T-shirt lying in a pile on the kitchen countertop, which she picked up and threw on top of the map. Ben looked at the shirt for a second and then looked at Andy. He smiled, stood up straight, and picked up the shirt.

"This isn't mine. It's Jim's."

"I'm sure it fits."

"Am I making you uncomfortable? Not wearing a shirt?"

Andy's hand clamped around the edge of the countertop. He was enjoying this.

"You look cold," was her feeble reply.

"It's like eighty-five degrees out already."

"Well, you're making me cold just looking at you."

She knew how stupid she sounded, so she reached for the map and snatched it off the table.

"I'll bring it back later," she muttered before bolting out the front door without looking back.

Startled by her sudden departure, Ben stared after her like a statue. He then let out a laugh that even he didn't expect.

* * *

"So what'd they say?"

Not ten seconds after Andy returned was Morgan already hammering away with questions.

"Ben said he would talk to Jim after he woke up."

"Did he indicate if they would be interested in going?"

Andy threw her hands up in frustration.

"He didn't indicate anything one way or another. He never indicates *anything*. He only says the bare minimum all the time, and it's starting to piss me off. I don't know *what* could be such a damn big secret!"

Without realizing it, her voice had risen considerably, and a moment later, Charlie emerged from his bedroom and entered the living room where they were sitting. His hair was disheveled and his steps were uneven.

"Good Lord, what are you two yelling about?" he mumbled before plopping down next to Morgan.

"Sorry," Andy said before filling him in on the morning's events. When she finished, he simply blinked his eyes open and closed a few times, then stood up.

"I'm starved," he declared before stumbling into the kitchen. "I need to elevate my blood sugar levels before I can even think about Colorado."

Despite her mood, Andy began to chuckle, which provoked

Morgan to laugh as well.

"Your brother says the funniest things sometimes."

"I know, and he doesn't even realize it, which makes it funnier."

"What are you two saying about me?" Charlie called back from the kitchen. He was in the midst of wrestling with a can opener and a can of peaches. "You know, I think I need to spend less time with girls. You two are mental sometimes; I'm surrounded by too much estrogen."

This only made Andy and Morgan giggle harder. Nothing Charlie said had been particularly funny, but the two merely needed to let off steam. Stress ruled their lives, and a good fit of laughter was often their only release.

"Then convince Jim and Ben to come to Colorado with us," Morgan said after she finally calmed down enough to speak normally again. "Then you won't be surrounded by women."

Charlie returned to the worn sofa with his opened can of peaches. Without his consent, Morgan reached inside the can, plucked out a slice of peach, and put it in her mouth. After swallowing, she smiled with satisfaction.

"Get your own food. And get your own boyfriends, both of you. I'm not helping you with that."

"Boyfriend? Who said anything about a boyfriend?" Andy replied sharply, feigning understanding Charlie's meaning for Morgan's sake. "I'm not interested in those two. My mom always said to be weary of boys who were too handsome. If *Abercrombie & Fitch* ever went back into business, we could tell them where to find two more models."

"Why did she say that?" Morgan asked with surprise. "What's the matter with boys…or men…who are good-looking?"

Andy shrugged.

"She said they were too difficult to please and too hard to keep around."

"But I remember your father; he was handsome. If your mother believed that, why she did marry him?"

Andy shrugged again. "I guess she made an exception for him."

But Morgan still wasn't satisfied. "Then in her experience, it wasn't true. So why would she tell you that?"

"I don't know," Andy replied with growing exasperation. "She said it a long time ago, so I don't remember the context of the conversation. But it seems true, you know…in books and movies. The good-looking guy often ends up being a jerk and the not-as-good-looking guy who is still sort of cute and a lot nicer ends up getting the girl."

Morgan thought about that for a moment before her face transformed into a disapproving expression.

"That's not true. What about *Sixteen Candles*? Samantha ends up with the hot guy, Jake."

It was a movie that she and Andy had seen more than once in Bermuda just before the outbreak.

"That's one exception," Andy countered. "And in real life, that never happens. In real life, Jake would've stayed with the pretty blond girlfriend. Pretty people stick together. Those are laws that never change, even now."

"Molly Ringwald was pretty," Morgan argued. "Charlie, don't you think that Molly Ringwald was pretty?"

But Charlie had had enough. He abruptly stood and made a beeline to the kitchen with the rest of his can of peaches. "This is what I'm talking about. These girly arguments! Who cares about Molly-whoever? It's a movie; it's not real."

Charlie then hastily gobbled up the remaining peaches, slammed the empty can down on the kitchen table, and headed to the front door. "I'm going across the street, and I'm gonna beg Jim and Ben to come with us…for *my* sake!"

The front door slammed behind Charlie, its echo resonating throughout the house.

"Well," Morgan began after a long silence. "It took him long enough, but I think my brother is finally losing his mind. I was starting to feel like the only one who's gone mental."

"He's right, though," Andy remarked plainly. "It can't be easy growing up with two girls and no male friends." Then, with an almost motherly embarrassment, she added, "His hormones are probably…what did they used to call it? Raging? Raging hormones?"

Morgan let out a laugh.

"Oh, God, my mother used to say that about me after I turned thirteen. She would use those exact words too, 'raging hormones.'"

She sighed a bit sadly just then, and echoed Andy's maternal tone.

"You're probably right. He's just starved for male friends. All he has is his older sister to nag him, and you—no offense."

"None taken."

The two fell silent again as Andy stared through a window next to the front door. The sunlight was intensifying. It was going to be another hot day.

"I really don't understand why Ben and Jim chose to come here."

"Me neither," Morgan agreed. "It's hard to believe that just a few weeks ago we were in Bermuda. This place is so different from anything I've ever seen before. England doesn't have anything like this."

Andy nodded. "I know, it's weird…surreal even. What's even stranger to me is that in the two thousand miles we drove to get here, we never once ran into another person until we met Maria and her brother and sister. Every town we passed was like a ghost town. I know that we didn't exactly stop anywhere long enough to see much, but still..."

She turned away from the window and sank back into the sofa. "Where could everyone be?"

"Well, they aren't in this town," Morgan replied. She threw her head back against the sofa and let out a weary sigh. "I feel like we're going everywhere and nowhere at the same time. I mean, what are we doing, Andy? What is the plan, really? Go to Colorado and hope that we find a better place to live? At first I was excited by the idea, but now I'm not sure. I'm not sure about anything anymore."

"Neither am I," replied Andy in a hollow voice that sounded foreign. "You're pregnant, I'm always hungry, Charlie's moody…"

Andy shook her head. "Right now, at this moment, I actually miss Bermuda."

"So do I, which scares the hell out of me."

* * *

17 July 2020

Despite their doubts and because there were no other options, Andy and Morgan abided by their decision to go to Colorado—and Morgan finally told Charlie that she was pregnant. The news shocked and upset him.

"How did this happen?" was his initial reaction, followed by a look of fierce anger and exasperation from Morgan. After realizing the callousness of his words, Charlie sheepishly apologized, and Morgan's condition did not come up again for quite some time afterward.

Ben and Jim agreed to drive the three to Colorado and would decide later if they wanted to stay or ultimately part ways. It was a compromise that Andy understood, but was a disappointment to Morgan.

"I thought Jim and I had a connection, but I guess not."

Then after looking down at her belly and frowning, she moaned, "He won't be interested after I get fat, so I guess it's better not to get my hopes up now."

But Andy told Morgan not to get ahead of herself and reassured her that Jim alone could not decide for both himself and Ben. She did not, however, admit to Morgan that she believed Ben was typically the decision-maker of the two.

On the day of their departure, Maria came by the house with a large box of food, both canned and fresh, and Andy wondered once again how she was able to maintain a seemingly endless supply of food. Maria did have a garden in her backyard, but it certainly didn't grow fresh spaghetti with meatballs. Andy suspected it had something to do with the truck she had seen the morning Maria told her about Colorado, but she never asked. She was simply grateful for the generosity, as were the others.

Ben offered to drive the first leg of the trip north. Andy sat beside him while the others sat in the back.

"If it doesn't work out, we might be back," Andy called out to Maria through the window after Ben started the engine.

Wearing a sad smile, Maria approached the truck and reached out to give Andy's hand a squeeze.

"Well, for my sake, I hope you do. For your sake, I hope you don't. But you know where I'll be, at least for the next year and a half." She uttered this last part so that only Andy could hear.

Maria backed away from the car and waved to everyone. Julio and Carmen stood beside their sister and waved as well.

"Good luck!"

Andy looked back until Maria, Julio, and Carmen disappeared around a turn in the road and lamented that they were not coming along.

Chapter VII

21 July 2020

It turned out that Maria had been right; Colorado was the place to be. At first it seemed a mistake to venture north after stopping at eight ski towns along I-70 with no success, and having to sleep three nights in a row either in the truck or in abandoned homes. Echo, Arapahoe, Loveland, Keystone, and Copper were all utterly vacant while Breckenridge and Vail weren't interested in gaining more residents. "Not enough food," was the reason. And as explained by three male residents who gave Andy and Morgan uncomfortably long stares, Beaver Creek had a shortage of women in town and was only interested in acquiring new female residents. Any place with that kind of policy was not an option even if Charlie, Jim, and Ben had been allowed to stay.

After some coaxing by Andy to head farther away from I-70 than the previous eight towns, they reached Aspen on the fourth day. It would be the end of their arduous search which had left them exhausted, hungry, and dirty.

Upon entering the outskirts of Aspen from the north along State Highway 82, the truck was stopped by a barricade guarded by four older male teenagers, each armed. It seemed as though everyone was armed these days, and mostly with M4s, the standard-issue assault rifle of the U.S. military at the beginning of the twenty-first century.

As soon as Ben saw the guns, he wanted to turn around immediately. Andy, however, argued that they were only carrying guns for their own protection and not to attack without provocation. Still, she reloaded her own M4 just in case. Ben followed suit with his shotgun. Watching them, Morgan instinctively crouched lower and pressed her back harder against the front of the truck bed.

Two of the males approached the truck while the other two remained at their post. The two moving toward them split apart, each taking a side of the truck. The grip on their weapons remained firm but the muzzles were pointed down in a non-threatening position. Ben and Andy stood up in the truck bed to make themselves and their own rifles visible, partly as a gesture of good faith, and partly to demonstrate their own firepower. Jim, who had been driving, rolled down his window. He spoke first.

"Morning. We were looking for a place to stay for a while. You have any room here?"

It was direct and to the point. They were all too exhausted for pleasantries.

The guard on Jim's side glanced at his very expensive-looking watch.

"It's afternoon, actually. Twelve-fifteen to be exact."

"Oh, good afternoon then," Jim muttered, unsure of how he was supposed to respond, and he turned to Charlie sitting next to him with an uneasy look. Equally confused, Charlie shrugged, so Jim looked back at the guard who had yet to say anything else.

"Uh, so what do you think? Any chance we can go through?"

Instead of responding, the guard reached behind to his back pocket and unclipped a push-to-talk radio. He turned away from Jim and the truck and began communicating with someone. The conversation was out of earshot.

"What the hell is going on?" Andy whispered to Ben, who was busy studying the situation.

"Dunno."

A minute later, the guard returned and clipped the radio back onto his pocket.

"You can go through, but you have to leave your weapons here."

"Sorry, not gonna happen," Ben called out, preempting any response from Jim or the others. "Our weapons stay with us."

But the guard stood firm.

"Those are the rules. Either you leave your weapons here with us, or you turn around and head back to wherever you came from."

The increasing tension hung thick in the air, and no one dared to speak until Morgan slowly stood up to take a look at the scene for herself.

"Why don't two or three of us stay here with the weapons and the rest go through and see what the deal is?" she offered, her voice weak from fatigue but her words were resolute.

It seemed to be a reasonable compromise.

"Fine, but first I want them to tell us if there's even a possibility that we'll be able to stay, assuming we still want to," Andy replied. "I'm not sure how I feel about staying in a place that's so unwelcoming."

"I don't like it," Ben remarked plainly and with a shake of his head.

"Well, I don't care, Ben," Morgan snapped back. "We have to stay *somewhere*. And leaving our weapons behind makes sense to me from their point of view. They don't know who we are or what our intentions are. Seems like they're just trying to keep themselves safe, and who can blame them? But if you don't like it, then leave."

Andy couldn't help but appreciate Morgan's uncharacteristic obstinacy, making her argument all the more compelling. Biting his lower lip, Ben turned away. He knew this was one fight he wasn't going to win.

Jim and Charlie got out the truck to discuss the situation with the others in the rear. Eventually, they all agreed to go with Morgan's suggestion, though Ben remained reluctant. It would be Andy and Charlie going on ahead while the others stayed behind with the truck and weapons.

The guard radioed ahead to some unseen person, telling them that a male and a female were coming their way, along with a brief description of Andy and Charlie.

"Where exactly are we going and how far is it?" Andy demanded of the guard.

"Just keep going along this road for about two miles. You'll see some guards waiting there. They'll take you to where you need to go."

Andy and Charlie exchanged uneasy glances. Neither liked the thought of trusting strangers while unarmed.

Two miles…

Andy wondered if they should take the truck and just leave the others with the weapons to save time. But then if they got into some kind of trouble, their friends would be too far away to help. No, best to leave all their resources in one place.

"If we don't come back in two hours, come after us," Andy said to Jim, who was holding her M4. "We'll walk quickly, so it shouldn't take longer than that to find out what the deal is."

"All right, we'll stay in the truck just in case," Jim replied.

"Don't do anything stupid," Morgan called after her as the pair began their way down the road.

Andy glanced over her shoulder and gave her friend her most reassuring smile.

Once they had walked about half a mile, Charlie revealed to Andy that he had tucked her Glock behind his back between his belt and jeans. It was concealed by his T-shirt and an old long-sleeve dress shirt he often wore.

"Just in case," he added. "If they search us, I'll just say I forgot it was there."

"Think they'll believe that?" Andy replied, looking doubtful.

"Want me to stash it somewhere along the road here instead? We can pick it up on our way back."

Andy thought for a moment and shook her head.

"No, take it. Just in case."

* * *

Nataliya Ivanova stood watching through the enormous second floor window of her home as the two strangers approached the front gate. She had already instructed the gate to be opened, and as they passed through and headed up the long driveway, Nataliya was able to get a good look at them. The male looked to be a little younger, with the build of someone still in the midst of adolescence. The girl was older, probably the same age as her. It was difficult to tell yet if the girl was pretty, but from a distance, the possibility was there. Nataliya didn't mind pretty girls, as long as they weren't prettier than her.

Once the two strangers reached the front door, Nataliya headed toward the top of the large spiral staircase to greet them. She waited until they were let inside by her guards and were standing in the expansive foyer before she took her first step down the stairs. Making a proper entrance was very important, and Nataliya liked how people were forced to look up at her as she made her way around the staircase, as though she were on stage and everyone else was the audience.

"Hello," she began simply, her accent immediately noticeable after one word. "My name is Nataliya. Nataliya Ivanova."

She approached the two strangers and extended her hand. They each shook it as she gave them a quick once-over. Though it pleased her that they both looked dreadfully dirty and tired, she hated to admit that the girl was indeed very pretty, though a bit rough-looking at the moment. However, she would clean up well, much to Nataliya's dismay.

"Andy," the girl replied, followed by the boy saying, "Charlie."

Nataliya tilted her head to the side and gave the girl a questioning look.

"Andy? Isn't that a boy's name?"

"It's short for Andrea," the girl answered easily as though she'd heard this question many times before.

"Of course. You Americans love to shorten your names so often that people never actually know your complete name. It's funny."

"I take it you weren't born here," Andy remarked. "I'm guessing Russia or one of the former Soviet republics?"

"Russia," Nataliya relied flatly, not liking the fact that she was suddenly the one being questioned. "So, why don't you both come in and sit down."

She led them to the living room, which was large and beautifully furnished. Adjacent to the living room was a kitchen that even the pickiest gourmet chefs would have been hard-pressed to find fault with. Her father had bought the house when she was nine-years-old while still living in Moscow during a time when the American economy was in the midst of a recession, and foreign entrepreneurs began taking an interest in the nation's real estate market. The multi-million dollar home was one of the largest in Aspen, and it remained occupied by Nataliya and her younger brother Mikhail after their parents' death.

"This is a beautiful home," Andy declared honestly but without any hint of being overly impressed. Abandoned mansions were probably abundant everywhere.

"Thank you," Nataliya replied simply as she gestured for the two guests to take a seat on one of the nicest sofas Andy had ever seen.

"How long have you been living here?"

"Nine years, since we moved from Moscow."

"And it's got air conditioning," Andy remarked with interest. "Does everyone in Aspen have electricity, or just certain homes?"

Andy hadn't meant to imply that somehow Nataliya and her brother had special privileges that others didn't have, but it was interpreted that way.

"All homes that are occupied have electricity," Nataliya insisted with a defensive edge to her voice. "The solar power and hydroelectric plants that were built in Colorado just before the virus are still functioning and give us power, though I don't pretend to understand anything about it," Nataliya said with a dismissive wave of her hand. "There are other people who handle that."

Charlie, however, was interested, and Andy could tell he wanted to ask more questions about it, but she cut him off before he had a chance to open his mouth. She wanted to get to the point of their visit.

"So, Nataliya," she began in a businesslike tone. "There are five of us here. The three others are Morgan, who is my age and Charlie's older sister, and Jim and Ben, who are cousins and both about my age as well."

"And you want to come live here in Aspen?"

"Well, maybe. We'd like to have a look around first, I think. But the fact that you have electricity here makes it more appealing than anywhere else we've been."

"Yes, it's very nice here," Nataliya remarked haughtily. "But not just anyone can live here, you know? There are rules."

Charlie and Andy exchanged glances.

"What rules?" Charlie asked, speaking for the first time since introducing himself.

"Well, I'll explain," Nataliya replied before standing up. She headed toward the kitchen and opened a stainless steel refrigerator.

"Are you thirsty? Hungry? You both look like you could use some water and a good meal."

"Um, water would be nice," Charlie said, trying not to sound too eager, despite the desert his mouth had become.

"Andy?" Nataliya queried as she grabbed two glasses from one of the cabinet shelves.

"Sure, thank you."

Nataliya poured two large glasses of filtered water and returned to the living room. She placed them on two coasters on top of the Brazilian rosewood coffee table and sat back down. Andy and Charlie picked them up almost immediately, each finishing more than half the glass before stopping to take a breath. Nataliya looked on with amusement.

"Maybe I should bring the pitcher over too, no?"

When neither Andy nor Charlie declined the offer, Nataliya returned to the refrigerator to retrieve the pitcher.

"So, the rules," she started. "There are a few, but basically, if you want to live in Aspen, you have to work. Some people take care of the power and water, others take care of the food, and some take care of security—as you can see—but everyone works and we all benefit from it."

"Sounds very communist to me," Andy remarked dryly. The fact that Nataliya was Russian only made the comment more ironic.

"Well, yes. There is no other way for things to work now. Money is worthless, so the only things of value are things we all need to live and survive."

Andy nodded. The concept was pretty much how Maria had depicted.

"What if you have special skills?" Charlie asked as he poured himself another glass of water.

Nataliya raised a well-groomed eyebrow.

"Skills? Like what?"

"Well, Andy's father was a doctor, and she's been learning and practicing medicine for the past five years…"

Nataliya tried not to appear too impressed.

"…and I have an I.Q. of 188."

"And what exactly does that mean?" asked Nataliya, as though a high I.Q. was of little significance.

"It means that he's smart enough to build a spaceship and send it to Mars if he wanted to," Andy retorted defensively. "Charlie's ridiculously intelligent."

"Well, we don't need to send anything to Mars, but I guess I see your point," Nataliya responded in a passive-aggressive manner that was beginning to annoy Andy. "What about the other three…sorry, I have forgotten their names already."

"We haven't known Ben and Jim long, but from what I can tell, they are very good with cars…fixing them, modifying them…that sort of thing."

Nataliya nodded.

"That is always very useful. We don't have too many mechanics here."

"And Morgan, my sister, is very good with children," Charlie added brightly. "She's also a teacher. Reading, writing, math…"

But Nataliya pursued her lips together in a disapproving manner.

"Well, we really don't need any more babysitters. We have plenty already."

Then, sensing Andy's rising irritation as well as silently admitting that the skills the others had were indeed valuable, she quickly added, "But I suppose we don't want a bunch of idiot children running around here that cannot read or write, no?"

Andy forced a smile.

"So, are you the one who decides if we can live here?"

Nataliya slowly shook her head.

"Not entirely, no. Aspen has a council that I am a member of. There are ten of us on the council, and together we vote on who can become a resident. But because I am the leader of the council, I decide whether or not a potential new resident is offered a trial period of one month. After the month, the council votes to determine if they can stay or not."

"So what's your decision about us?" Andy inquired, getting right to the point. Her directness actually appealed to Nataliya, even if she didn't appear to care much for her otherwise.

"I'll have to meet your friends first before I make a decision."

"They won't leave our weapons behind," Charlie assured. "So unless you let them through with them, you won't meet them."

Andy reinforced Charlie's words with a nod.

"Not unless Charlie and I go back and tell them that it's okay to come here unarmed."

But Nataliya shook her head.

"That won't be necessary. I'll tell the guards to let them through with their weapons. There are plenty of others here who protect me…just in case."

"Our friends won't try anything, trust me," Andy was quick to reply.

Nataliya ignored the remark and grabbed the radio sitting on the kitchen counter. After a few exchanges with the guards at the other end, she sat back down in the living room.

"No cell phones?" Charlie asked.

"No, but we are working on it," Nataliya replied. "There have been a few problems. Things I don't understand."

"I'm sure Charlie will be able to fix it," Andy remarked as she gave Charlie an encouraging smile.

Nataliya smiled thinly. "We'll see."

A few minutes of awkward silence passed as they waited for Ben, Jim, and Morgan to arrive. Charlie finally asked a disinterested Nataliya about the solar power plant. Andy, however, blocked out the conversation as her gaze shifted back and forth from Nataliya to the expansive room around her. Nataliya seemed to fit perfectly amidst such luxury. She was impeccably clean, and her long, golden brown hair had a shine to it that Andy's hair used to have when she was younger, in the days when running water was a reality. Her complexion was milky and flawless, not dirtied and reddened by the wind and sun like Andy's. She was tall and slender, her build similar to Morgan's, and her clothes were right out of a fashion magazine. Jewelry that appeared to contain fine gemstones dangled from her ears, neck, and wrists. Although Andy really didn't understand the need to dress beyond basic functionality, she admitted that such efforts with regard to physical appearance had an intimidating effect, made more so by the fact that Nataliya was a very attractive young woman.

Andy glanced down at her own hands. Besides being dirty, they were callused by years of manual labor. Nataliya's, meanwhile, were lily-white and adorned with rings. As Andy began to surreptitiously clean the dirt from underneath her fingernails, the front door opened.

A guard entered the house first, followed by Morgan and Jim with Ben bringing up the rear. Thankful for the distraction from

Charlie's litany of questions regarding solar power plants and electricity in general, Nataliya bolted off the sofa and scurried into the grand foyer. Andy and Charlie followed but without the urgency of their host.

After waving the guard off and introducing herself to the three strangers, Nataliya gave Morgan the same judgmental inspection that she'd given Andy. Immediately disliking the looks that Morgan was blessed with, she quickly moved her attention to Jim and Ben. Here, she perked up.

"My goodness," she began, placing her hand to her chest in an overly-dramatic fashion. "Andy did not mention that you two were so handsome."

Andy rolled her eyes.

"Andy didn't think it was important," she replied sharply in the third person.

Nataliya dismissed the remark and requested that they all return to the living room. As everyone followed her, Ben pulled Andy aside.

"Who the hell is this person? And what's with the accent?"

"She's from Russia, and I'm still trying to figure that out," Andy whispered back the answers in reverse order. "Apparently, she's the leader of some council that governs Aspen."

Ben frowned.

"So she's like the chief in this town? How'd she get that job?"

"No clue. But be nice to her. She doesn't like me already."

"What, did you give her your classic first impression and try punching her in the face?"

"No, it's not just me," replied Andy with a smirk. "She wasn't friendly to Morgan either. I don't think she likes other girls stealing attention away from her."

Ben nodded slightly. "Yeah, I can see that."

Once everyone was seated in the living room, Nataliya repeated the rules for Morgan, Jim, and Ben. Andy noticed that Nataliya was looking only at Jim and Ben as she spoke, though particularly at Ben as she may have assumed something already existed between Morgan and Jim based upon the close proximity in which the two sat together on the sofa. Or maybe Nataliya simply thought Ben was more attractive than his cousin, which somehow vexed Andy more.

"So will you let us stay here for a month?" Morgan asked Nataliya when she had finished her spiel.

Andy cringed at the anxiousness of her friend's tone, while Nataliya pondered the question for an unnecessarily long time, as she had already made up her mind but didn't want to appear too eager. Had it not been for the presence of Ben and Jim, her decision would likely have been different.

"Well, we can talk about that later tonight at dinner," she answered coolly. "You will all eat here as my guests and stay for the night at least. There is an empty house just down the road from here. It's not quite as nice as my home, but it has five bedrooms and three or four bathrooms with showers, I believe. I will ask someone to make sure it's clean and that all the beds are made."

This plan was acceptable to everyone, and they agreed to return that evening at seven o'clock for dinner. Anxious to leave the house and Nataliya's presence, Andy was the first to exit, with Morgan hurrying behind her.

"Was it just me," Morgan began when they were out of earshot, "or is Nataliya sort of a bitch?"

Andy laughed heartily.

"Sort of? She's a complete bitch. She practically ignored us and Charlie. Her eyes were all over Jim and Ben."

Morgan pursed her lips together.

"Yeah, I noticed that too. Hopefully they will both see through her act and not be hypnotized by her perfect hair and clothes and sexy accent."

"I think Ben already has seen through it. And your accent is better, hers sounds too harsh."

"Thanks," replied Morgan, grateful for the compliment.

"I just wonder what her story is," Andy continued. "She says she's the leader of the council here, and she seems to have everyone wrapped around her finger. The guards were all jumping at her requests like they're her servants."

Charlie approached just then, his face clouded over.

"I think I annoyed her…Nataliya, I mean. She kept ignoring my questions about the solar power plant."

"Don't take it personally," Andy replied.

"Yeah, I don't think she likes talking about anything that doesn't involve her," Morgan added while giving her brother a half-hug over his shoulder.

When Ben and Jim were finally able to extricate themselves from Nataliya's palatial home, everyone returned to the truck. As Ben got in the driver's seat, he called out to Andy as she jumped into the back, "She was wearing perfume! Can you believe that?"

Andy laughed aloud, and as they drove down the road toward their home for the night, she glanced at her fingernails and suddenly didn't mind so much the dirt underneath.

* * *

During the first decade of the twenty-first century, Aspen had become the most expensive town in America. Average home prices reached several million dollars. Hollywood movie stars, famous athletes, and billionaire businessmen from around the world had made Aspen their second or third home, and usually inhabited the ski town for only a fraction of the year. Andy guessed that Nataliya's father had been such a businessman. His daughter had obviously grown up in a wealthy family, and now she was still living in grand luxury, even after the greatest disaster the human race had ever known.

Her description of their temporary home had been grossly understated. The house, which was just a few hundred yards from Nataliya's, was quite impressive. Though indeed smaller, it was spacious with décor that was more rustic than Nataliya's elegant yet pretentious theme. Andy preferred the exposed wood beams, stone tile, and natural hardwood floors with dark knots to a more modern, artificial interior, and was better suited to the mountains and trees that surrounded it.

Everyone had their own bedroom, and Andy and Morgan each had their own bathroom. Ben and Jim were more than willing to share a bathroom, and Charlie took ownership of the smallest bathroom down the hall from his room.

"It's not as nice as yours," he said to his sister, "but it's all mine."

And all four bathrooms had running water. It was miraculous.

There was a sense among the group that they would be staying longer than one night. Though agitated by Nataliya's attention to Ben, Andy knew it would likely result in an invitation to stay in Aspen for at least a month, and when she stepped into the shower—her first in more than five years—she decided that she could put up with almost anything if she could experience this every day. As the rainfall showerhead and jets positioned along the shower walls propelled warm water over her body, she felt as though a layer of something beyond dirt and sweat was sliding off her skin and disappearing down the drain. All worries vanished for the moment.

As she toweled off, there was a knock at the door. After wrapping the towel around her, Andy opened the door to find Ben standing there. She instinctively pulled the towel tighter above her chest.

"Sorry, I didn't know you were in the shower."

The apology was flat, and Ben seemed to hardly register Andy's lack of clothing.

"No problem, just anxious to use a shower for the first time in years. What's up?"

"Jim and I are gonna drive around for a bit. You know, check out the town. If you wanna come, we'll wait for you to get dressed."

Andy nodded. "Sure, sounds good. What about Morgan and Charlie?"

Ben shook his head. "No, they're both taking a nap." Then, as an afterthought, he added, "Morgan looks exhausted today. Is she okay?"

"Yeah, I think so," Andy said with a casual shrug in an effort to appear unconcerned. "I mean, I think we're all tired, right?"

"True," Ben answered slowly. He did not quite believe Morgan was simply fatigued, but knowing better than to question Andy when it came to her friend, he said nothing further.

"We'll be downstairs when you're ready."

"All right, I'll be down in a few."

Ben turned and headed toward the staircase while Andy shut the bedroom door and proceeded to get dressed.

Before making her way downstairs, she quietly poked her head into Morgan's room. As Ben had mentioned, she was fast asleep, her soft breath in perfect sync with the rise and fall of her chest. She looked so thin and fragile.

Minutes later, Andy emerged fully clothed with her long, wet hair pulled back into a loose French braid. At that exact moment, her stomach growled exceptionally loud, and she wondered what time it was. In recent years, she had grown accustomed to ignoring pangs of hunger out of necessity. Food was simply not available every day, three times a day. In Bermuda, eating had been more consistent, thanks to fishing and the garden. Yet in the weeks since returning to the continent, meals had become much more unpredictable, and her clothes were becoming loose. There were days when Andy consumed barely enough to sustain her, and others when there was hardly anything to eat at all.

Morgan, meanwhile, was becoming increasingly frail at a time when her body needed to be strong and well-nourished. It was a source of constant worry for Andy, but she couldn't bring herself to hope that a place with electricity and running water might also eliminate their food concerns—at least not yet.

"Okay, ready," she announced after descending the stairs.

"Where did you put your weapons?" Jim asked her.

"In my room, under the bed."

"When we get back, you should put them in my room," Ben remarked. "I found a good hiding place in the back of the closet."

"All right," Andy replied.

They set out and locked the front door behind them with the single set of keys they had been given. Ben volunteered to sit in the back of the truck while Jim drove.

"Maybe we can find another car soon," Andy said hopefully while climbing into the passenger's seat.

As they pulled out of the driveway, Jim turned to Andy and repeated the same question Ben had asked minutes earlier.

"Is Morgan okay? She looks ill."

The concern in his voice was sincere.

"She's just really tired. I am too. Remember, we're not used to this…all this moving around, I mean. We spent five years on a very tiny island, and even then, we barely left our small corner of it. And now, in less than a month, we've traveled thousands of miles by boat, bike, and car. It's been overwhelming."

Despite the recurring omission of several key components to Morgan's story, Andy voiced the honest truth. She *was* exhausted. Damn exhausted.

"I keep forgetting that," Jim admitted. "This all must be such a shock to the system for you."

Shock to the system. It was a phrase her father often used.

"Yeah, that's exactly what it is."

Though not knowing exactly where they were going, Jim managed to make his way out of the winding neighborhoods to downtown Aspen, where the streets were arranged in a grid pattern. Other vehicles were parked along the sides of the road, but no one actually seemed to be driving. Instead, people were either walking or riding bikes. Andy suggested that perhaps they should also park and walk around, and Jim agreed.

"What's up?" Ben asked after Jim pulled the truck into an available spot on Main Street.

"We decided to walk around instead since no one seems to be driving down here."

"Maybe we can check out some of these stores," Andy added. "See if they're all empty or not."

"Cool," Ben muttered as he looked around. "Maybe there's someplace to get food. I'm starving."

"Me too," both Andy and Jim said simultaneously.

As they began wandering around, Andy was struck by how clean the streets were. The people walking around looked clean as well, wearing clothes that appeared crisp and new. It was a stark contrast to the raggedy jeans and threadbare T-shirt she was wearing. Her current wardrobe was sparse in quantity and variety, and although nearly everything she owned was at least two years old, it was something she'd hardly noticed until now.

Another detail that struck Andy as interesting was the sense of purpose everyone seemed to possess. Nobody was loitering or watching time pass for the sake of watching time pass. People were bustling about as though they had things to do.

Soon after leaving the truck behind, they approached a grocery store and were shocked to find that people were inside buying food. Instead of money, people used gold tokens similar to those once used at country fairs and carnivals in exchange for going on rides and playing games like Skee-Ball.

"Too bad I haven't been to a carnival lately," said Ben sarcastically as they watched others picking out fruit, vegetables, meat, and milk—all of it was for sale. Andy could hardly believe her eyes.

"Where do they get all this?" she mumbled under her breath.

"From my brother and me."

"Huh?" Andy uttered as she looked around to find the source of the voice. "Who said that?"

"Who said what?" Ben asked, peeling his eyes away from the delicious-looking food.

"I did."

Determining that the voice came from somewhere below her waist, Andy looked down to her right. Kneeling on the floor as she tied her shoelaces was a slight girl with bright blue eyes and shoulder-length hair that was as light as Andy's. When she stood up, she was a few inches shorter than Andy and appeared to be in her early teens.

"Hi, I'm Susan. Susan Hamilton."

The girl politely extended her hand to Andy, who shook it wordlessly at first, then belatedly uttered her own name. Susan then shook hands with both Ben and Jim, who each introduced themselves in return.

"You must be new here, huh? My brother told me that some new people came in this morning."

"Your brother?"

"Yeah, his friend is one of the regular guards working at the north gate on Route 82."

Andy nodded, still waiting to hear what any of this had to do with food.

"Brian and I…that's my brother…we live on a farm right off of 82, about ten miles north of here. We raise everything: horses, bulls, cows, sheep, and chickens. Then we sell what we don't eat here, which is a lot."

"Just the two of you?" Jim said with surprise. "That's a lot of work for just two people."

Susan laughed and shook her head.

"It would be, but no. We have help from a few people who live here in town."

"What exactly do you sell?" Ben asked with interest, as he knew little to nothing about farming.

"The sheep are for meat only. We keep the cows and bulls alive for milk and breeding. Same with the chickens. We keep them for their eggs until they stop laying them, and then we kill them for meat. Well, I don't kill them. Brian and a couple of the others do all the killing. I'm too scared to do it. I take care of feeding all the animals instead, which is a whole other job. Harvesting hay is a pain, you know?"

Andy nodded as if she did know. Fishing and growing vegetables was much simpler.

"And what do you get in exchange for the food?" Ben asked,

interested in the economics of the town.

"We get the same things other people get. Electricity, running water, clothes, other food that we don't have. And security. It works out pretty well for everyone."

Andy smiled at the girl. She had a genuine and friendly demeanor.

"So are you guys going to stay here or what?"

"Well, we aren't sure yet," Andy began, glancing back and forth between Ben and Jim. "But we'll know more tonight after we have dinner with Nataliya. I guess it's up to her."

Susan made a face. "Yeah, I know."

Susan's expression and her tone with regards to Nataliya gave Andy a sinking feeling in her stomach, but before she could press further, a tall and lanky but pleasant-looking young man with scruffy blond hair approached Susan. Andy assumed this was her brother, Brian, which was confirmed after Susan introduced him to everyone.

"Hi, nice to meet you guys," Brian replied. He then handed some tokens to Andy so they could buy food. "It's not much but it'll tide you over 'til tomorrow."

Andy smiled gratefully, and Ben and Jim both thanked him.

Brian was probably Andy's age, and like his sister, he seemed just as friendly. He promised to stop by their home the following day and give them 'a local's perspective of living in post-virus Aspen'.

"I hear Nataliya is having you over for dinner. Don't worry about her. She'll let you stay for a month. She just gives the impression that Aspen is super-exclusive or something. The fact is we need all the extra hands we can get. Unless you're a thief or some psycho-killer, you won't be told to leave, not now at least."

Brian then looked at his watch and told his sister it was time to go. After a polite goodbye, they left the store. Just before stepping outside, Brian gave Andy a long look that escaped her notice.

Ben noticed, however, and he cast a sideways glance at Andy. She didn't notice that either.

Chapter VIII

Morgan was awake and sitting in the living room downstairs when Andy, Jim, and Ben returned. It was after five o'clock and the angle of sunlight had shifted considerably throughout the house.

"Where did you guys go? I was worried when I woke up and you were all gone."

Andy shot both Jim and Ben an irritated look. She had assumed that one of them had mentioned something to either Morgan or Charlie before they left. Jim quickly apologized as he took a seat next to Morgan on the sofa, Ben and Andy sitting opposite them.

"Sorry, you and Charlie were both asleep before we left and we didn't want to wake you."

"It's okay, I'm just glad you guys are back," Morgan replied with a half-smile as she delicately placed one hand on her lower abdomen, a gesture Andy had begun to recognize recently. "Charlie's still asleep, I think. So where did you go?" she repeated.

"Just downtown and wandered around a bit," Andy replied. "You won't believe what we found."

"What?" Morgan asked as her interest piqued.

Jim jumped in. "An actual grocery store that's selling food, and I mean fresh food…steak, chicken, fruit, vegetables…you name it."

"Selling food? Are you joking?" Morgan's eyes had grown wide, and Jim, Andy, and Ben all nodded simultaneously.

"But…how? And what do people use to buy the food?"

Jim recounted their brief meeting with Susan and her brother, Brian.

"That reminds me of living in Oxford," Morgan remarked after Jim had finished. "Children worked on the sheep farms almost as much as their parents." Then with an impish smile, "They were pretty cute…the sheep, I mean."

The others chuckled at this last comment, and Morgan frowned.

"What? You all grew up in big cities, but Charlie and I didn't. Oxford is surrounded by farmland, you know?"

"I guess we'll have to consider you the expert in farming now, huh?" Jim joked.

"Hardly," Morgan replied. "But maybe I can help this girl Susan and her brother from time to time. It would be nice to work outside, especially since it's so much cooler here than New Mexico."

"Well, you can ask Brian tomorrow," said Andy. "He said he would come by here sometime and hopefully tell us all the stuff that Nataliya won't."

"Good, I will."

Up to this point, Ben had said nothing since returning to the house. The food purchased at the store with Brian's charitable tokens was sitting in a bag at his feet, and he bent down to pick it up before heading to the kitchen.

"Anyone hungry?" he called out behind him. "I know I am. I could eat five dinners right now."

It was a feeling shared by all.

"Morgan, you better wake your brother," Ben went on as he grabbed a butcher knife. "Otherwise he'll miss out. God knows what that Russian chick considers 'dinner.'"

* * *

After an incredible meal of fresh steaks, potatoes, and spinach with carrots, they walked down the road to Nataliya's house for their second dinner.

"You're a good cook," Andy admitted to Ben as they made their way down the curving road lined with tall pines. They were walking behind the others.

He laughed lightly as he kicked at a stone on the ground. "It's not difficult with a decent kitchen and food that doesn't come from a can."

"Makes all the difference, doesn't it?"

"Yep."

Andy looked up at the sky during its last couple hours of daylight. She took a deep breath in through her nose and let it out, enjoying the crisp scent of the trees.

"You know, I could get used to this place. Living like this."

"I know," said Ben. "But I just have a feeling that it's not what it seems."

"Don't say that yet," Andy urged, despite the fact that she couldn't help but agree. "Not until we prove it's true."

"Sorry," Ben replied. "But when something is too good to be true, it usually is."

"I know, but let me keep the fantasy a little longer, okay?"

"Okay."

Charlie reached the front gate first and pushed the button to let them inside. The gate swung open, and moments later the front door of the house opened. Making her way up the drive, Andy saw a boy of twelve or thirteen standing in the doorway. She correctly guessed that it was Mikhail, Nataliya's brother.

"Come in," he said with a sullen expression on his face. There were no pleasantries or gestures of politeness either. He lacked the thick accent of his sister.

Great, Andy thought. *A bratty younger brother to go with his stuck-up older sister.*

They entered the house tentatively, as Mikhail had merely turned his back after uttering his two-word welcome before scurrying off somewhere inside the house. Nataliya entered the foyer moments later and gestured for everyone to come inside.

"You'll have to forgive my brother. Manners are something he lacks."

Andy and Morgan eyed each other after this understatement.

Being the last person to enter the house, Ben reached for the door to shut it, but Nataliya brazenly intercepted the door handle and brushed his outstretched arm intentionally as she moved past him.

"I'll get it," she said with a seductive smile that would've disgusted Andy had she seen it, but she and Morgan were already in the adjacent dining room.

Seven sets of dinnerware and silverware encircled three silver platters of hot food with steam rising upward, and two other plates with food that Andy could not yet identify. In between the platters were two lit candles. If Nataliya's intention was to impress her guests, she had succeeded, though Andy decided that such efforts were aimed at targeting solely Ben and Jim's attention.

It became glaringly apparent that Nataliya had not lifted a finger to prepare the meal when two young girls emerged from the direction of the kitchen, one of them approaching Nataliya.

"Everything's on the table. Is there anything else you need?"

"No, thank you, Jenny," Nataliya replied politely to the girl but with an air of authority. "Come back around ten or so. You can clean up then."

The two girls nodded and quickly left the house. Meanwhile, Morgan and Andy exchanged glances again as they read each other's minds.

"All right, let's sit down," Nataliya ordered, and everyone obeyed wordlessly. She had changed out of her clothes from the afternoon and had put on a summer dress that enhanced her slender figure.

As hostess, Nataliya took a seat at the head of the table. She gestured for Ben to sit beside her. Andy sat next to Ben on the other side followed by Charlie. Across the table, Jim and Morgan sat next to each other with Morgan sitting closer to Nataliya. The other end of the table was occupied by Mikhail, who skulked into the room minutes later.

As brother and sister, Nataliya and Mikhail looked very much alike. Their facial features, particularly their eyes, carried a strong resemblance. Though Mikhail was dressed far more casually than his sister, his clothes appeared new, like everyone else's in town.

Once everyone helped themselves to the roasted chicken, scalloped potatoes, steamed broccoli, French bread, and salad, Nataliya initiated a conversation.

"So," she began in dramatic fashion, "how do you like your home?"

After chorus of affirmatives from her guests, Nataliya smiled, looking pleased with herself.

"Yes, this is one of the nicest and most expensive neighborhoods in Aspen," she remarked as though the monetary value of a home still had meaning. But perhaps here in Aspen, it did.

Nataliya began talking to Ben, asking him if they managed to see any part of the town. He nodded in return and politely described their afternoon outing. Meanwhile, Andy became preoccupied with her potatoes, wondering where the cheese came from. Making cheese was a process that went beyond simply milking a cow. She had no clue how to make cheese, but she knew that squeezing a few udders was merely the first step of many that followed.

Everything tasted delicious, and as Ben had predicted, they all ate heartily despite having eaten just a couple hours prior. Throughout the meal, Andy said very little and then only when asked some mundane question, usually from Nataliya. She spent most of the time observing the others. Everyone spoke politely to Nataliya, careful not to offend her, and Nataliya, who controlled the conversation, seemed to enjoy that. Mikhail remained silent, however, his eyes never leaving his plate. Being the student of medicine that she was, Andy began to wonder if Mikhail possibly had some kind of social disorder, like autism. She then considered a far simpler answer: he just didn't like strangers in his house and chose to ignore them. After she caught him rolling his eyes and making faces at some of the remarks being made throughout the meal, she decided her initial instinct about him was correct: he was merely a spoiled brat. When he finished his plate, he pushed his chair back and left the table without a word. His sister didn't seem to notice or care.

There were only a few comments Nataliya made during the meal that were of actual interest to Andy. She learned that nearly eight hundred people currently lived in Aspen, ranging in age from five to nearly twenty.

"I'm not quite the oldest," Nataliya added. "But I'm close."

Andy learned that Brian, Susan's brother, was one of the ten members of the town council. She also determined by the sudden change in Nataliya's voice that she wasn't happy that he was on the council, which came as no surprise given what Brian had said about Nataliya that afternoon.

After everyone had cleared their plates, including helping themselves to seconds and thirds, Andy decided it was time to get to the point of the evening when Morgan beat her to it.

"So, Nataliya, you said this afternoon that you would let us know this evening if we could stay here or not. What's your answer?"

Andy smiled covertly at her friend's bluntness.

Taken slightly aback, Nataliya blinked once, then twice before responding.

"Getting straight to the point, I see."

She then took a long sip of water as though purposely trying to create suspense.

"Well, I have to admit, you have skills that we could use here, so for now, I do not see any problem with you staying for a month. After that, the council and I will decide if you can stay permanently. Sound good?"

Everyone nodded in agreement.

"Excellent," Nataliya concluded. "I hope you all enjoyed dinner."

Again, everyone nodded. No one stood up, however, so their hostess took the lead and pushed herself away from the table.

"Well, if you all don't mind, I have some things I need to take care of before I go to bed."

At that announcement, everyone stood and headed toward the

front door.

"I believe Brian will be coming over to your house tomorrow to talk to you all about the tasks each of you will be given, along with the rules that we all must live by here, myself included."

Andy had her doubts about that last part.

"I did not want to go over all of that tonight since you all must be tired," Nataliya continued as she escorted everyone to the front door and bid them goodnight.

Once they were through the gate and out of earshot, Charlie declared, "That was rather painless."

"Almost painless," his sister responded. "She sure has a way of making everything about her, doesn't she, Andy?"

Andy shrugged. "Honestly, I was hardly listening. I was more curious to know how the cheese got into my potatoes. That and Mikhail's behavior. What a brat he is!"

"I didn't notice him being bratty," Ben piped in.

"That's because you were too distracted by Nataliya's flirting," Andy said with an edge.

"Hey, I can't help it if she finds me irresistible."

"Then she's got strange taste," Jim teased, provoking a hard smack on the arm from his cousin.

Annoyed, Andy let out a moan and walked ahead of the others. Morgan caught up to her as the boys held back.

"I wonder what important things she has to do at this hour," she said.

"Who knows? Maybe Brian can tell us more tomorrow."

"What's this Brian like?" Morgan asked, lowering her voice.

"He seems nice enough, though we only met for a minute."

"Is he cute?"

Andy shrugged. "Yeah, I guess so. Does it matter?"

"Not really. I was just curious. I'm not asking for my sake, of course," Morgan quickly added.

This was obvious enough to Andy. "You're looking out for me, I see."

"Of course, why not? You're my best friend, and I just want you to be happy."

Happy. That was a relative term. Andy had been happy growing up with her parents. There had even been moments of happiness in Bermuda. But since Morgan's rape, Andy hardly knew what to expect from one day to the next anymore, and until life stood still for a while, happiness seemed irrelevant.

"Maybe one day I'll be happy," was all she replied.

"Maybe we'll both be happy," Morgan corrected, and she took her friend's arm as they continued down the street.

"Can you do me a favor?"

"Sure, what?"

"Can you tell them that I'm pregnant?"

"Who, Jim and Ben?"

"Yes."

Puzzled, Andy replied, "Are you sure you don't want to tell them yourself?"

"Yes. I don't think I could manage it."

Andy shrugged. "All right, I'll tell them tomorrow, but let me know if you change your mind."

"I won't."

* * *

22 July 2020

Andy slept better that first night in Aspen than she had in months. She attributed it to the cool mountain air and her wonderfully soft bed.

Connected to the living room by a glass door was a large wooden deck with a Jacuzzi, though it was presently empty of water. After rising out of bed, Andy headed downstairs to the kitchen, grabbed an apple purchased the day before, and settled into a comfortable lounge chair on the deck.

After finishing the apple, Andy closed her eyes to enjoy the warmth of the rising sun on her cheeks, only to be stirred moments later by the sound of the glass door opening from the inside. It was Ben.

"Morning," he said groggily.

"Morning. Sleep well?"

"Like a rock. You?"

"The same. I think I was asleep the second my head hit the pillow."

As Ben took a seat beside Andy, she decided it was time to get personal.

"So what do you think? Are you and Jim gonna stick around for a while?"

Ben didn't answer right away. Instead, he combed his fingers through his hair in that now-familiar way and cracked his knuckles.

"Yeah, at least for now."

"For now? What else are you looking for?"

Ben faced her, his expression stern.

"I'm not looking for anything, Andy," he said a bit defensively. "I'm just saying that this place will do for now."

Grudgingly accepting that it wouldn't do any good to press further, Andy changed the subject.

"So Morgan wants me to tell you and Jim something, but I guess I'll tell you first."

"What is it?"

"Do you remember the day we met? How I punched you in the face because you mentioned something about Morgan being a potential rape victim?"

"Yeah, how could I forget?"

"Well, the reason I hit you was because you happened to say the one thing that turned out to be horribly true. Morgan *was* raped. That's why we left Bermuda."

"What?" Ben blurted out. He was genuinely stunned.

Over the next few minutes, Andy went on to describe for Ben their last days on the island. How she'd found a bloody and unconscious Morgan that night. How they finally made the choice to leave…and how Morgan was currently pregnant and hadn't known the rapists, and therefore had no idea who the father was.

"Jesus Christ," Ben mumbled breathlessly once Andy had finished. "I mean, I knew that there was something you two were keeping from me and Jim, but I never would've guessed it was something like this. Shit, no wonder you punched me. I'm surprised you didn't shoot me." He shook his head. "Man, I was such an asshole for saying that."

"You couldn't have known then, but now you do. It's also why she looks so exhausted."

"Yeah…"

Ben's voice trailed off as he stared off beyond the mountains, and Andy decided to take another stab into his mysterious past.

"You know you can trust me, right?"

Still distracted, Ben clumsily swiveled his head to face Andy again.

"Huh?"

"Look, I know there's stuff that you and Jim aren't telling us, and I don't understand why. We've got nothing to do with whatever happened to you before we all met, so whatever it is, you can tell me. What happened to Morgan…there are images from that day that I will never be able to get out of my head as long as I live, so I can't even imagine what it's like for her, especially carrying a baby she doesn't want."

"What's your point?" Ben responded, his defenses returning.

"What's my point? My point is that nothing can be as bad as what happened to her, so why keep it a secret?"

"You have no idea what truly 'bad' is, Andy. Trust me, I've seen it."

Andy felt as though Ben had just kicked her in the gut.

"You're kidding, right? Are you honestly saying the rape isn't bad?!"

But Ben ignored her and abruptly stood up. After yanking the glass door open, he looked back at Andy with a mixture of agitation and pain.

"At least Morgan is still alive."

And with that, he slammed the glass door behind him, leaving a dumbfounded Andy alone as the pane of glass rattled in its frame.

* * *

A few hours after her altercation with Ben, Andy welcomed Brian at the front door.

"Wow, nice house you guys got," he said after stepping inside and giving it the once-over. "One of you must've done something right for Nataliya to give you guys this place."

Andy threw up her hands. "Definitely wasn't me."

Brian immediately understood her full meaning.

"No, probably not. She doesn't like most other girls her age, especially those who are pretty."

Andy wasn't sure whether or not Brian had just complimented her, but she didn't dwell on it.

"Come in," she said, closing the door behind him. "Where's your sister?"

"She's at home, though she wanted to come. She had to take care of the horses."

"How many do you have?"

"Four. They can be a pain to feed and care for, but they're helpful for transporting things into town with gas being so hard to produce."

Andy was leading Brian into the living room, and when she heard this, she looked back at him with surprise. "Gasoline is being made?"

"Yeah, although it's a work in progress, you could say. It was only six months ago when it started being produced again. But it's tricky. There's only one refinery in Colorado, and we have to share with other towns. Luckily, most people here in Aspen don't drive much. Everyone just uses their bikes or walk. Whatever gasoline we get is mostly for people who need to drive outside of town."

Andy and Brian were both sitting now in the living room. She listened with interest.

"I'm surprised gas is being made at all."

"Well, why not? The technology exists. We just had to figure out how to do it ourselves, like everything else."

Andy nodded. Everyone knew that performing brain surgery or building rockets was possible; the hard part was learning *how* when there was no one left to teach.

"I think Ben and Jim, who you met yesterday, went into town this morning with Charlie. They knew you were coming over, so they should be back soon. His sister Morgan is upstairs reading, I think. I'll go get her."

But before Andy even stood, she saw Morgan descending the stairs and heading toward the living room. She approached Brian and held out her hand.

"Hi, I'm Morgan."

"Brian. Nice to meet you."

The three of them chatted while they waited for the others to return. They discussed their backgrounds and where they'd grown up. Andy and Morgan talked about their time in Bermuda, which seemed to interest Brian. He told them how he and Susan stayed on their childhood farm and managed it nearly on their own in the recent years. They had worked the farm from an early age, so feeding themselves came easy when very few others could. This, Brian explained, is how Aspen became what it was now. Survivors began giving him and Susan things, from batteries to five-gallon tanks of gasoline in exchange for fresh meat, milk, and eggs from their farm. Knowing that batteries and gasoline would quickly run out, Brian and a few others realized that if the survivors could learn how to make things and perform the same jobs that adults had, they would be better off. So they convinced Aspen to begin working together to do just that.

"Is that how you became a member of the town council?" Morgan asked. "Because you helped to organize this effort?"

"Yeah, plus I was one of the oldest survivors, so others were willing to listen to me, I guess. Age and experience were everything back then."

"Who are the others on the council?" Andy asked.

"Five of them are friends that I went to school with. Two of them work as mechanics and repairmen. The other three have farms like me, two for agriculture and one for livestock."

"And the other four council members? Actually, three, since Nataliya is one?"

Brian hesitated before answering, indicating there was a story involved. Just as he was about to answer, however, the front door opened and Jim, Charlie, and Ben entered. After seeing that Brian was there, they came into the living room. Jim and Ben extended their greetings and Charlie introduced himself.

"We were just talking about how the council here was formed," Andy explained before repeating Brian's account of the town's evolution from the early days to the present and the origins of the town council.

"Five of them were old school friends of Brian's. Two of them are now repairmen and the other three have farms."

"And the others?" asked Ben.

"That's as far we got before you guys came in," Andy answered, her tone icy. She hadn't forgotten his earlier behavior.

Unaware of any hostility between Andy and Ben, Brian picked up where she'd left off.

"I'm sure you all guessed that Nataliya's family was insanely wealthy. Her father had to have been a billionaire to afford a house like that. They came here from Russia a few years before the outbreak; she probably told you. I didn't know her or her brother before then, but afterwards, she and her equally privileged friends tried to control everything in Aspen. They stole most of the food in the supermarkets, most of the gas that was left at the pumps, and took control of all the power facilities that serve Aspen—although none of them had any idea how to actually get the power back on. It took some of my friends to figure it out. Only after food and gas ran out did people start to turn against them, and they were finally forced to compromise with others. Things got better after that, but unfortunately, Nataliya and her friends still have a lot of influence because they live in enormous houses and people want to be friends with them. They're manipulative and will say anything to get what they want."

Brian looked down at his feet and shook his head. "A lot of the younger girls think Nataliya is the greatest thing because she still dresses and carries on as if the virus never happened. I guess she reminds them of how everything used to be. And a lot of the boys are afraid to cross her. But in truth, Aspen would be much better off without her or her friends. She doesn't lift a single finger around here either, and that irritates the shit out of me."

"She had other people cooking for her last night," Morgan remarked with a frown. "She was ordering them around like slaves."

"I know, it's pathetic. But like I said, some girls think she walks on water around here. They'd rather be her slave than actually do something useful. I'm just glad Susan isn't like that. She can't stand Nataliya, thank God."

"So you just have to put up with it?" asked Jim.

"Yeah, unfortunately, until more people see things my way. But I can't force others to think like I do. So in the meantime, Nataliya and three of her friends are on the council, and she's technically the leader, but it's really just a title to feed her ego. I'm sure you'll meet them all soon, but my advice is not to trust any of them."

"What about Mikhail? What's his story?" said Andy.

"No story," Brian said matter-of-factly. "He's just a pain in the ass kid, that's all. Spoiled and lazy, just like his sister."

"Do most people here own guns?" Ben asked, abruptly changing the subject.

Brian nodded.

"I think almost every home here has a gun of some kind. With all the wild animals in these mountains, people need to protect themselves—and we use them for hunting, of course."

"Was there ever a concern that people would use them against each other?"

"Sure, at first. But most people here knew one another growing up, and after the virus, nobody could stomach the idea of killing more people. It's actually safer knowing that everyone has a gun. You're less likely to get into a serious argument."

"Sort of how everyone did in the Old West, right?" Charlie added with a smile.

"Exactly, although we don't have shootouts in the middle of the street like they did."

"What about us? What can we do for work?" asked Andy.

"Well, it's sort of up to you really, although I can tell you that we really need more mechanics and people who are handy with equipment, and we need help on the farms. Raising crops and animals is a lot of work."

"We can help you with the mechanical stuff. Ben and I, that is," Jim offered. "We're pretty good with fixing cars. My father was a mechanic."

Ben sat quietly and allowed his cousin to speak for both of them. Andy thought he looked distracted, as though he were thinking about things that had nothing to do with the present conversation. She could only guess that it had something to do with their earlier discussion and all the things he wouldn't tell her.

"That's perfect," Brian replied brightly. "You can start tomorrow if you want."

"I can help with that sort of thing too," Charlie volunteered.

"Um, sure," Brian responded, though he sounded uncertain, as if Charlie might not be up to the task. It was understandable, seeing that Charlie didn't immediately strike anyone as being either particularly handy or strong, given his younger age and wiry frame. Morgan quickly stood up for him.

"Charlie's brilliant. Seriously—he's got an insanely high I.Q., and when we were in Bermuda, he could fix just about anything."

"Oh, okay," Brian replied sheepishly. "Sorry, I had no idea."

"How could you? You just met me," Charlie replied, cleverly

stating the obvious.

"Well, great. Come tomorrow with Jim and Ben in the morning, and we'll put you three to work. There's lots to do."

"I can help on the farms," Morgan suggested. "I can also teach the younger children reading and writing and math. I did that in Bermuda."

"Awesome, you can help my sister if you want. She works too much already, though she refuses to work any less. Or you can help my friend Scott on his farm. He's got livestock too and could use an extra hand. And I know Diana at the school needs some help a few days a week. There are too many kids and not enough teachers."

"Perfect," Morgan said, beaming. "I'll help your sister, if she wants help. And I'd love to help Diana. I look forward to meeting them both."

Jim, meanwhile, seemed glad that Morgan had offered to help Susan, and not to spend time helping Scott, another boy who was probably his age.

"Great. And what about you, Andy?"

Brian was looking directly at her.

"That's easy. You need a doctor? Nataliya said you don't have one here."

"Nataliya doesn't know a lot about who does what jobs around here, but she's right. We don't have a doctor, and we need one. You any good at it?"

"Well, I'm no surgeon, but my father was. I watched him work sometimes, and I've read more medical and anatomy books than you'd care to know. I helped some of the survivors in Bermuda: prescribed them the right medicine, stitched up cuts, that sort of thing. Nothing fancy, but I hope to perform a successful heart transplant someday. My dad used to perform them all the time, so I figure anything's possible."

Brian almost laughed, but then stifled it when he realized that Andy was serious. Ben, meanwhile, perked up after Andy's remark, his dull gaze becoming suddenly sharp as his blue eyes narrowed on her face.

"She's an ace," Charlie piped up. "She saved my big toe from being cut off by gangrene."

"Wow," Brian muttered, impressed. "Well, I'm convinced. You'll be on your own, though. There's a hospital in town that you can work out of, but I'm not sure what kind of equipment it's got. Not that I would be able to recognize what any of it does anyway."

"Cool, I'll head down there later and check it out."

"How do the tokens work?" Jim asked.

Brian went on to explain that no job was considered more important than another, so everyone got paid the same amount for every hour they worked. One token per hour of work, whether you fed horses or taught a five-year-old their ABCs. While it wasn't always fair, it kept people from arguing that their job was more important and they should be paid more.

"Who keeps track of how many hours someone works, or does everyone just trust each other not to lie?" asked Morgan.

"Well, that's the tricky part. For most jobs, it's obvious how many hours you put in because you're working with other people, so you hold each other to the truth. Solo jobs are harder to track, but people around here know each other pretty well and know which people are more willing to lie about their hours than others. Those that lie get called out on it enough, and eventually they stop doing it."

"What about Nataliya?" Andy asked. "If she doesn't lift a finger, as you say, how can she earn any tokens?"

"She claims that her work as council leader is enough," Brian said with disdain. "Believe me, I've tried arguing against it many times. I'm on the council and so are five of my friends, but we still work all day. I've just accepted that that's a battle I'm not gonna win anytime soon."

"What a bitch," Andy muttered aloud.

"You're not kidding," Brian agreed. "I admit, though, that when it comes to planning parties for the holidays during the year, Nataliya is actually pretty good at it. Of course, she just orders people around to do the hard work while she sits back and takes all the credit."

"Sounds like something from a high school movie," said Andy. "She's the mean girl that everyone wants to be friends with, and you have no idea why."

"That's exactly it," Brian said, smiling warmly. He seemed glad that she understood his frustrations.

The group continued talking a while longer as Brian filled them in on some of the more mundane but helpful details about the town. Andy enjoyed listening to Brian. He was open and honest, which stood in contrast to Ben. And he seemed to genuinely care about the town and the people living in it.

After giving everyone the details for where and when to begin their jobs the next day, Brian departed in the middle of the afternoon. Before leaving, he invited them all over for dinner that evening.

"You'll have to drive because we live about ten miles outside of town. But if you've got any gas in your car, come on by."

Everyone agreed. No free meal would ever be passed up.

Chapter IX

Autumn 2020

The summer passed quickly, and though everyone was working long hours at their new "jobs", they actually enjoyed being busy, the work giving them all a sense of purpose. The council voted unanimously that the five newcomers could stay after the first month. Despite Ben's initial unwillingness to commit to staying in Aspen, he never mentioned anything about leaving again.

When Andy told Jim about Morgan's pregnancy and how it happened, he took the news hard, his eyes even welling up with tears. From that time on, he and Morgan grew close. They spent much of their free time together, their temperaments a perfect match.

After a week of strained conversation, Ben and Andy slowly reconciled, and over the course of the following weeks, they would spend an hour or two many evenings talking about anything that came to mind. Ben once asked her what she missed most from her childhood, and she told him, "Television, so I wouldn't have to talk to you every night." It became a running joke between them.

Andy never asked Ben about his past again. Whatever may or may not have happened was gone, forever locked in a time and place that no longer existed. At random moments, however, Andy would sense a melancholic side to Ben that she attributed to some painful event within his carefully protected past. Though he laughed and joked along with everyone as his guarded demeanor gradually dissolved, there were times when his mind seemed to be miles and years away, and his expression somber.

Andy jumped right into her work at Aspen Valley Hospital located within a short bike ride from home and usually spent eight or nine hours there every day. The first weeks were dedicated to cleaning up the place. The hospital was still well-stocked with drugs of all kinds that had barely been touched—much to Andy's surprise—and when she asked Brian what happened when people got sick or injured, he said they had simply let nature take its course.

"But what if someone broke a bone or got seriously ill?"

"If it was a broken bone they usually took painkillers and let the bone heal on its own. But no one has yet to get really sick, and antibiotics always seemed to cure infections."

"So that's it? Just painkillers and antibiotics?"

"Yeah, but don't think that I'm not uneasy about my sister and I working on a farm and not having a real doctor around in case something bad happens. I worry about that a lot. We've been lucky, but luck has a habit of running out."

The first thing Andy tackled after cleaning the hospital and organizing all the supplies was learning how to operate some of the equipment: the x-ray machine, the ultrasound, and the MRI. Once she figured out how to use the ultrasound, which turned out to be fairly easy, she used it to check Morgan's fetus. On the first attempt, she couldn't see anything distinguishable, although Andy blamed that on her inexperience with the machine. The second time, she saw something that looked to be about the size of a walnut. The third time, it was the size of a lime. From all outward appearances, Morgan did not yet look pregnant by the end of August, but the weeks of rest and consistent meals had greatly improved her appearance. Gone were the dark circles under her eyes and the look of fatigue on her face.

Once it became known that there was a 'doctor' working at the hospital, people began seeking Andy's assistance for injuries and aliments that they had typically ignored in the past. Using the x-ray, she reset dislocated shoulders and other small bones that had suffered from improper alignment when fractured the first time. She continued to stitch deep cuts and prescribe drugs for common illnesses and infections, and she even diagnosed a sixteen-year-old boy with a herniated disc in his lower vertebrae using the MRI. In early September, a friend of Brian's was accidentally shot in the arm when a bullet ricocheted off a tree while hunting elk. The bullet lodged in his shoulder, but after giving the boy a few shots of whiskey to dull the pain, Andy successfully removed the bullet from the muscle tissue. Brian later joked that no one had ever gotten hurt in Aspen until she arrived.

Gradually, Andy's expertise grew, and it pleased her to know that she was learning how to do things that very few others could. With Charlie's help, she learned how to perform blood analysis to diagnose illnesses and deficiencies. After testing her own blood and finding that everything was normal, except for a slight deficiency in Vitamin D, Andy tested Morgan's blood, and everything appeared to be normal. Her next goal was to perform a blood transfusion on someone. Since the leading cause of death during childbirth was hemorrhage, she wanted to be prepared to administer a transfusion in the event that Morgan suffered from complications during her delivery.

At night, Andy often stayed up late, studying books and old medical articles on childbirth. She was determined to do everything in her power to ensure than Morgan and her child would have the safest delivery possible. For his part as both brother and future uncle, Charlie studied the steps of childbirth with Andy, and together they planned for every contingency in the event that something went wrong.

Morgan, meanwhile, strengthened not just physically but emotionally. She enjoyed helping Susan care for the animals on her farm and found the work therapeutic. Three days a week she taught reading and math to children at Aspen Elementary School, which was less than a mile from the hospital. She and Andy would often walk or ride bikes together from home and part ways just west of the main commercial area of town. Diana, the young woman who was the head teacher at the school, was a quiet but genial girl of seventeen, and Morgan got along with her beautifully from the beginning. With the addition of Morgan, there were eleven teachers who taught nearly three hundred children between the ages of five and twelve. After turning thirteen, all residents stopped going to school and began working, although Morgan offered to teach some of the younger teenagers more advanced reading and writing classes two evenings a week. Several students accepted her offer, and she quickly became one of the favorite teachers at the school, if not *the* favorite. Gradually, Morgan came to see herself as something other than a rape victim. The pain of that awful event would always be there, like a scar on her soul, but it no longer defined her or the life of the child growing inside of her. Her undeniable strength, often overshadowed by her fragile, delicate exterior, finally re-emerged.

To Andy's surprise, she and Ben slowly formed a close friendship, and though both wondered privately about the possibility of it becoming something more, neither acted on it. She was too timid—scared even—which made him uncertain, and so they remained as they were. Andy would then suffer moments of extreme self-doubt regarding her own attributes as a woman, and consequently Ben grew frustrated whenever she shyly withdrew from him after an innocent touch or prolonged gaze. It became an unending dance of tiptoeing around the boundaries but never daring to cross them.

Yet their friendship was solid, founded on mutual respect. They shared many interests, including a profound love of history. Both had read several books on various periods of human civilization, from ancient Greece to the end of the twentieth century. American history was Ben's favorite, while Andy preferred European, and the two would often debate late into the night on how the course of human history would have changed if one small and seemingly minor event had occurred differently, or had not occurred at all.

For his part, Ben appreciated the fact that Andy was the only girl he'd ever met who could not only use a gun with great skill and accuracy, but could also shoot an animal without flinching. When he mentioned this to her, she explained that it had been difficult to kill her first fish in Bermuda before adding, "I hope you don't think of me as cold-blooded just because I don't mind shooting a deer."

Ben laughed. "Of course not. No one wants to kill Bambi, but we don't want to starve either."

As for Charlie, he was like a kid in a candy store when it came to deciding what to do each day. He picked tasks as he liked, though everything he did was of value. Some days he would help Ben and Jim, proving to be a competent mechanic and repairer of various machines. Other days he would help those who were trying to fix the cellular service throughout town, but soon informed them that their efforts were in vain.

"You're trying to repair different networks that were built to provide coverage throughout the entire country. It's not possible to fix such a miniscule part of each network just to provide service to Aspen and only Aspen. Cellular networks weren't designed to work that way. We should just create our own network from scratch…if we have the right materials."

No one understood the technology as Charlie did, but everyone listened to him and tried their best to help him find the components necessary to build an entirely new cellular network. However, Charlie soon realized that the computer circuitry required for undertaking such a task could not be found in Aspen alone, and rather than travel aimlessly to other towns and scour for such hardware, he proposed that they instead set-up an encrypted, Internet-like service for the town using a local server. Though only a fraction of the size of the old Internet, people could still send messages to one another and even post their own websites. Within two months, the entire town was wired, and emails began flowing back and forth once again.

Other days, Charlie often helped Susan and Brian on their farm, and Susan quickly developed a crush on Charlie. Though initially wandering into unfamiliar territory, Charlie's hormones soon got the better of him. The pairing made sense to everyone. After all, Susan was a fun, vibrant girl of fourteen who worked hard and enjoyed being outdoors with her horses. Her main passion, however, was photography, and she was often seen with a camera hanging from her neck. "You never know when the perfect photo op will come along. If you miss it, it's gone forever," she would say. And though some people thought it was odd to be taking pictures the old-fashioned way with film, she insisted that film produced much better quality photos and were worth the hassle. When someone argued that you couldn't cut and edit film like you could with digital photos on the computer, Susan would make a face and say, "Why would you want to cut things out of a picture that were there to begin with? It's like turning your picture into a lie." Everyone liked Susan immediately; the girl had spunk and wasn't afraid to speak her mind.

Ben and Jim both fell right back into fixing cars and making them more fuel efficient by stripping them of excess body weight. Since electricity was available, they also began focusing their repair and maintenance efforts on the hybrid vehicles that existed in Aspen. When not working on vehicles, they assisted in fixing other mechanized equipment needing repair, from meat grinders at the grocery store to the centrifuges at the wastewater treatment plant. Ben admitted that he didn't care for working at the wastewater plant, but consented that if he wanted to keep taking showers, someone had to fix the machines when they broke down. At first it was trial and error fixing such unfamiliar equipment, but both Ben and Jim quickly demonstrated that they could figure out how to repair almost anything and soon became the leaders in their field. Those who had already been working as mechanics learned quite a bit from them.

In general, the residents of Aspen were pleased to have the five newcomers in their town. Susan and Brian were particularly pleased, and a special camaraderie quickly developed among the group. The two often came over for dinner and hung out afterward before heading to their own home north of town. The offer to spend the night in the enormous house was always extended, but they were never able to accept since their cows required milking early in the morning.

Being the only one without a blood-relative, Andy could have easily felt left out, but instead, she had gained an extended family of six that she came to care a great deal for. Here were seven very different people—with different interests, pasts, ages, and even nationalities—but they all treated one another with respect and compassion. Of even more importance was the fact that they all shared the belief that in the post-virus world, if you worked hard and didn't complain or give up, life could be worth living again; a life without the constant struggle to merely survive, but to actually thrive. This shared belief, though tested again and again, would bind them together for years to come.

Despite all the efforts to keep the town living comfortably as teenagers performed the work of adults, there was also time for fun. The habits of a generation born and raised during the age of online social networking, cell phones, and high-definition television were replaced by more old-fashioned entertainment. For the first time in years, Andy played games like "tag," and "hide-and-go-seek" with many of the younger children. Football, soccer, and baseball games became a regular occurrence after dinner during the longer summer and early autumn evenings. Storytelling around campfires would often follow, or they'd watch old movies shown on a big screen downtown in Wagner Park. All of it brought back a piece of childhood, something that had been missing during the years of pain, fear, and uncertainty. Andy knew that they were lucky to have found a life in Aspen, and she silently thanked Morgan for her insistence on leaving New Mexico. Sometimes she would think about Maria and her brother and sister, and how they would be much happier living in Aspen. She hoped to see them again one day, but doubted she would.

There was, however, one subtle rift in the group that Morgan noticed first. Though subtle, as both young men maintained considerable control over their emotions, Morgan recognized a tension that had developed between Ben and Brian, which, as she correctly guessed, involved Andy. Though both respected the other's capabilities and intelligence, and though they had become genuine friends as the weeks and months passed, an unspoken rivalry existed between them whenever Andy was around or when her name was mentioned.

If Andy commented that Brian had done something impressive, like the day he finally broke a particularly obstinate feral mustang, Ben would make a disparaging comment that he would pass off as a joke. Brian, in turn, would make fun of Ben's taste in music and movies, knowing full well that Andy often switched the CDs that Ben played and complained about his choice of DVD whenever it was movie night. Morgan sensed that Brian would be the more willing of the two to admit to having feelings for Andy; Ben would rather suffer a gunshot wound, he was so stubborn.

At one point Morgan confided her observation to Jim, after making him swear not to speak about it to anyone.

"Ben's in love with Andy. He just doesn't know it yet."

Jim responded by looking at Morgan like she was crazy, then lightheartedly poked at her slightly swollen belly.

"I think that tadpole swimming inside of you is making you see things that aren't there."

But Morgan stood by her suspicions and hoped that the triangle of emotions wouldn't disrupt the happy harmony the group shared.

* * *

The only constant source of aggravation that marred an otherwise tranquil life was the very existence of Nataliya and her friends. While Nataliya and her brother had been the children of a wealthy foreigner, most of her friends were the spoiled offspring of famous celebrities who had once owned homes in Aspen but spent most of the year elsewhere, and just by chance were in Aspen with their children when the virus struck. In fact, their jet-setting lifestyles likely increased the rapidity of the virus's spread by carrying the organism around the world.

These celebrity progenies believed that because their dead parents were once well-known, they themselves should continue to receive special treatment from everyone else. In a time when money and fame in the traditional sense no longer mattered, it was shocking to witness their atrocious behavior. More appalling, however, was how very few people dared to challenge them.

As Brian had mentioned, Nataliya barely lifted a finger when it came to doing any actual work for the benefit of the town in general, and her friends were no different. They lazed about, reveling in their idleness while others worked tirelessly around them, and Andy often wondered how they filled their days.

There were three girls who were especially close with Nataliya: Juniper, Sparrow, and Krista-Lynn. Juniper and Sparrow were sisters of nineteen and seventeen respectively, and the daughters of two world-famous actors who had not only appeared in numerous films throughout their careers, but had also conformed to the celebrity tradition of giving their offspring bizarre names. Both daughters were rather dimwitted, although they had mastered effective manipulation techniques by shamelessly using their feminine assets.

Krista-Lynn, the daughter of a movie director, had appeared as a child actress in some of her father's movies. Andy, Morgan, and Susan secretly watched a couple of these films one evening and unanimously decided that she was a terrible actress. In person, however, there was nothing fake about Krista-Lynn's heartlessness. Like her vapid friends, she was physically beautiful but downright mean to those she decided, for whatever shallow reason, to dislike. She was also a member of the council, and someone Brian despised more than Nataliya.

Andy's initial description of the girls was accurate: Nataliya and her friends *were* the popular but mean girls in high school. Unlike school, however, they had to be dealt with all the time, seven days a week. They ate the food others worked to produce and used the water and electricity in their homes despite their unwillingness to comprehend the work required to maintain such luxuries. And they treated people as servants while demanding things they had no right to demand.

Andy managed to avoid interaction with these girls, though Juniper did visit the hospital once and asked rather nonchalantly for a pregnancy test. Andy suggested first using an over-the-counter home pregnancy test but was rudely informed that the last one had been used more than a year earlier. As Andy was left to ponder this interesting statistic, she informed Juniper that she would have to draw blood to determine pregnancy.

"You mean, there's no other way to find out if I'm pregnant or not? Are you fucking kidding me?"

"Not unless you want to wait for the classic signs of morning sickness, then a few more months to have an ultrasound," Andy had snapped back.

Miffed, Juniper ultimately decided that she couldn't wait and grudgingly allowed Andy to draw her blood. Color drained from Juniper's face as the two women waited in awkward silence for the results. Once the test revealed that Juniper was not pregnant, and though she pretended not to care, color rushed back to her cheeks.

Others in Nataliya's inner circle included Aiden, seventeen-years-old and Sparrow's sometime-boyfriend. He was the son of an Olympic champion downhill skier who had gained wealth from product endorsements. Aiden was as promiscuous as his father had been, which created a fair amount of drama between Sparrow and her female friends, as she often accused several of them of sleeping with him. Aiden was also on the council. Though Brian didn't care for Aiden, he remarked that Aiden was rather harmless. Narcissistic, yes, but not a real threat.

Then there was Garrett and Heath, brothers aged eighteen and fifteen. Their mother had been a supermodel-turned-actress whose career reached its peak at the beginning of the twenty-first century. She married a successful Swiss financier, and after Garrett was born, they bought a home in Aspen to spend winters and part of the summer months. They were supposed to have been in the south of France when the virus struck, but a last-minute change in their father's business plans sealed their fate. For the sake of everyone else in Aspen, it would have been better if the brothers *had* ended up in France. Garrett and Heath were both menaces who loved to play cruel pranks on the other residents. The previous summer, they played a gag on Brian's friend Scott that took three days to clean up. After sneaking onto his farm and rounding up all of his cattle, the brothers released the animals in Wagner Park several miles away. By the time Scott discovered that his cows were missing the next morning, the animals were wandering all over the streets of downtown Aspen and leaving feces everywhere.

Unfortunately, both Scott and Garrett were members of the council, which made meetings both uncomfortable and unproductive. After Garrett's prank, the meetings often began or ended with the two of them arguing. Fortunately, Brian and his friends outnumbered Nataliya and her clique six-to-four, and even Aiden would side with the majority from time-to-time, though usually on matters that the minority cared little about.

And so an uneasy truce existed between the two groups. Though grossly unfair that one group did next to nothing to help the town while the other group worked tirelessly day after day, Brian remarked that he would rather keep the peace than topple the entire process with a violent but ultimately fruitless confrontation.

"Can't you just force them out of town at gunpoint?" Andy would often ask, partly joking but mostly serious.

"No, they have guns too. And they also have allies beyond their inner circle of friends. It's hard to tell which side actually outnumbers the other. It's not as if we've taken a poll that asks everyone, 'Do you like Nataliya and her friends? Yes or no? Do you want them to leave? Yes or no?.'"

"Did you and your friends ever think of leaving Aspen and going elsewhere?"

"Sure, but our farms are here. Plus, I would feel like I was giving into them if I left. They'd win out of forfeit."

"I understand. I wouldn't give in either."

For the most part, Andy and her friends ignored Nataliya's inner circle and their transgressions. As new residents of Aspen, it wasn't their place to make waves. If anyone was going to challenge Nataliya and her friends' behavior, it would have to be someone else, at least for the time being.

* * *

13 November 2020

The day tensions escalated was a snowy one in mid-November. As usual, Andy was working at the hospital. That morning, she gave Morgan another sonogram. Though Andy had studied many sonogram pictures in medical books, it was still difficult to determine with absolute certainty the sex of the fetus. Morgan didn't care either way, however, and was just glad that everything appeared to be all right.

Following an uneventful afternoon, Andy headed toward the main entrance of the hospital to end her day. As she passed one of the operating rooms, she heard a commotion from inside. When she entered the room, three boys were in the midst of a struggle in the far corner. One of the boys, Nathan, a rather frail kid of eleven that Morgan taught, was pinned against the wall by Mikhail and Heath, Garrett's younger brother. They were threatening Nathan with the defibrillator and were about to shock him when Andy quickly intervened.

"What the hell are you doing?! Let go of him!"

Mikhail and Garth immediately looked as if they'd been caught with their pants down around their ankles, though they still held a firm grip on Nathan.

"Did you hear me? Let go of him!"

"And if we don't, what are you going to do?" Mikhail sputtered as Heath sneered viciously at Andy.

Staying calm, she reached her hand inside the backpack she carried to the hospital every day and fished around until she found her loaded pistol. Using both hands to hold the weapon, she pointed the barrel back and forth between Heath and Mikhail.

"Let him go or you'll both get a bullet to the leg, and I won't pull them out."

After a tense silence, Heath and Mikhail realized Andy was serious and reluctantly released Nathan. Gesturing with her pistol, she ordered the two out of the OR. Fuming with anger, Heath and Mikhail skulked to the door.

"Fuck you, Andy," Heath hissed as he stepped outside.

"Yeah, you'll regret this, bitch!" Mikhail added with a flourish as he followed Heath.

Wordlessly, Andy followed them and watched them exit the hospital with her pistol grip remaining firm. She then returned to the OR and tucked the pistol back into her bag.

"Did they hurt you?" she asked Nathan as she moved toward him.

Nathan shook his head. He had tears in his eyes.

Andy reached out to him in a maternal fashion, placing her hands on his shoulders, and peered into his eyes focused firmly on the floor. Only after touching the boy's slumped shoulders did she become aware that her own hands were shaking.

"What happened, Nathan?"

But the boy was too upset to answer. A tear that had been hanging on precariously to his left eyelid finally gave up its fight and fell to the floor.

"Nathan, it's okay, you can tell me. I won't let them get away with it, I promise."

Wearily, the boy lifted his gaze to meet Andy's, and she took a step back to give him space. Huddled in the corner, Nathan appeared smaller than usual, and his tear-streamed face looked more tired than an eleven-year-old face should.

"They thought I saw something that I wasn't supposed to, but when I told them I didn't see anything, they didn't believe me."

"What did they think you saw?"

Nathan shrugged weakly. "I don't know. I mean I don't know exactly what I saw."

"But you did see something. What was it, Nathan?"

The boy bit his lower lip and his gaze returned to the floor.

"Nathan, please. I can't help if you don't tell me."

Andy's reasoning did the trick. Nathan wiped at his tears and looked up once again. "It was last night. I was over at a friend's house for dinner with a few others from school. It was Alison's house. Her older sister makes the best hamburgers."

This remark brought a brief smile to Nathan's face, and Andy smiled in return.

"Anyway, after dinner, I went to the store to see if Mark was still there and if he needed any help."

Mark was Nathan's older brother who ran the grocery store in town. Andy would often see him there cleaning up after hours, and Jim had once fixed a freezer there that stored butchered meat. Mark was a nice kid of about fifteen whom Charlie had befriended.

"I didn't see Mark inside the store when I got there, but I saw that the lights had been left on. I have a key to the store, so I went inside to turn them off, figuring Mark must have forgotten."

Nathan paused and wiped at his eyes again. Andy waited patiently.

"So I go to turn off the lights and I hear noises coming from the back of the store, like people talking or something. I go to the back of the store and see the back door open, and the freezer doors, you know the ones at the back of the store? Well, they were open too and all the meat was missing. I figured that the store was getting robbed, so I hid behind one of the shelves near the freezers. I should've just left the store, but I wanted to see who was robbing us."

Nathan took a deep breath and went on.

"I could see from where I was hiding that there were three people standing in front of a truck. The engine was running and the headlights were on, and I could see Heath and Garrett talking to the other person. I could hardly see his face until he moved. When he did, I didn't recognize him, which I thought was strange, because I know everyone in town. Then I decided to leave before they saw me, but when I started to move, I accidentally knocked over a jar of applesauce, you know those big ones that Amy makes every fall when apple season is over?"

Amy was a teacher at the school. Andy nodded and let Nathan continue without saying a word.

"Well, it crashed and broke on the floor. Heath and Garrett and the other person heard the noise, and they came running inside the store. I didn't see them come in because I was running to the front door, but I heard them. I turned off the light switch when I ran past it 'cuz I wanted to confuse them in the dark. When I got outside, I ran as fast as I could all the way home. I don't think they saw me, but they must've figured it was either me or Mark. We're the only ones with keys to the store."

When Nathan stopped speaking, Andy remained silent in case there was anything else he wanted to add. When he didn't, she said, "Did you tell Mark?"

"Yeah, when I got home. Mark went down to the store, but no one was there. The back door was closed and the jar of applesauce had been cleaned up. The freezer was still empty, but its doors were closed."

"And you have no idea who the third person was?"

Nathan shook his head firmly. "Never seen him before."

"And Heath and Garrett thought it was you in the store and not your brother?"

"I guess so. They probably waited until Mark locked up and left for the night before breaking in through the back door."

Andy nodded.

"What does Mikhail have to do with this? He wasn't there, right?"

"I don't know, but he and Heath are friends. There's something weird going on. No one has ever robbed the store before."

"Has anyone else ever been robbed before? Like in their house?"

Nathan shook his head slowly.

"No, I don't think so."

When Andy could think of nothing further to ask, she escorted Nathan out of the hospital. They both zipped up their coats and pulled wool hats snugly over their heads.

"Do you want me to walk you home?"

Nathan hesitated before nodding sheepishly.

"If you don't mind. I feel like Heath and Mikhail will be somewhere waiting for me."

"Okay," Andy replied tenderly as they set off along the snowy road. She felt sorry for the boy. He was a nice kid who didn't deserve to be bullied. It made her angry, and she would've punched Heath and Mikhail personally if she thought it would do any good.

The events that Nathan had described were more troubling. If Heath and Garrett were stealing from the store, what else were they doing? And if Mikhail knew about it, who else knew? Nataliya, probably, and likely her entire circle of friends. And who was this third person, the stranger? Was he from another town? Did Heath and Garrett give the stolen meat to this stranger, and if so, why?

There were too many unanswered questions. She would have to talk to the others at home as well as Brian and Susan. Hopefully together they could figure out the mystery.

* * *

After safely dropping Nathan off and explaining to his brother what had happened, Andy returned home. Mark was visibly shaken by news of the incident, and his expression was an intense mixture of worry and anger.

As she walked home, Andy couldn't shake the image of Nathan being pinned against the wall by Heath and Mikhail, each holding a charged defibrillator paddle mere inches from the boy's chest. Or Mikhail threatening her before leaving the OR. She wasn't physically intimidated by Mikhail, but his sister and her allies would make formidable enemies. The last thing Andy wanted was to disrupt the fragile balance of power that existed in Aspen, even as unfair and absurd as it was. It wasn't her place to challenge it, and getting kicked out of Aspen in the middle of winter with Morgan more than five months pregnant was not an option. Still, she refused to sit by while kids like Nathan were being bullied and tortured.

Distracted by her thoughts, including the need to take better security measures at the hospital, Andy nearly ran into Ben on the street outside their home.

"Jesus, Andy, didn't you hear me calling your name?"

But upon seeing her face, Ben immediately recognized that something was wrong.

"What is it?"

"I'll tell everyone inside," Andy replied after an exhausted sigh. "Right now, I just want to get warm."

"Okay, sure. I'll build a fire."

"Thanks, you're the best."

As they walked up the driveway, Ben put a reassuring arm around Andy's shoulder. Grateful for the gesture, she allowed herself to lean into him all the way to the front door.

Half an hour later, Andy recalled the entire story to everyone in front the fireplace. Both Brian and Susan were over for dinner, so everyone heard the story together.

Andy wearily recounted both what she had seen and what Nathan had told her. Morgan was visibly upset, for Nathan was one of her favorite students. When Andy finished, everyone looked to Brian, whose expression had grown increasingly tense as he listened. They all expected him to speak, or at least provide some sort of explanation for what Andy had witnessed. When he finally did, Brian asked the same question that Andy had asked of Nathan.

"And he had no idea who the third person was?"

"Nope. Nathan said he never saw him before."

Brian frowned.

"Mark and Nathan have lived in Aspen their whole lives. They know everyone here, so if this person lived here, Nathan would recognize him."

"Have there been any other robberies or anything similar lately?" Ben asked.

Brian thought about the question for a moment and started to shake his head when Susan stopped him.

"Hey, remember back in the spring when Gracie's sister lost her snowmobile?"

Brian scratched his head, slowly recollecting the memory.

"You mean Cathy? Yeah, I remember."

"Yeah, she kept saying that she didn't lose it but that someone took it right after the last snow storm of the season. Remember how no one believed her?"

"Yeah, she wanted me to bring it up at the next council meeting, but I didn't think it was anything serious, especially since it happened to Cathy. She's a nice girl but she's pretty spacey and is always losing things," Brian explained for the benefit of those who didn't know Cathy or the story.

"Maybe Cathy was telling the truth?" Morgan asked.

Brian shrugged. "I know *she* thinks she was telling the truth. Cathy may be a lot of things, but she's not a liar, and she was pretty insistent that the snowmobile was stolen. I've never seen her get so worked up over anything before."

"Are snowmobiles rare enough in Aspen that people would want to steal them?" Andy asked. "I don't see that many around."

"They used to be everywhere," Susan answered.

"Yeah, a lot of homes had them, and of course the ski patrol had a ton for the slopes," Brian added. "But most of them either broke down or disappeared the first winter after the virus. That year was pretty rough, and a lot of kids left to go to other towns and took snowmobiles with them. They don't have great gas mileage, though, so I don't understand why they would be of much value. Their only advantage is that they can go where cars can't."

"Maybe that's exactly what the person who took Cathy's

snowmobile was looking for," Jim offered as the others nodded.

"Are you going to say something to Nataliya about her brother?" Andy asked Brian pointedly.

Brian pursed his lips together.

"I'm sure she knows whatever Mikhail's up to, so she probably knows about what happened with Nathan. I'll say something to her tomorrow."

"What about Garrett and Heath?" Charlie piped up. He was angry on Mark's behalf. "They can't get away with this. Someone has got to say something to them."

Ben gladly volunteered.

"I'll say something to those assholes, but only if you say so, Brian. This is your town, man. We're just visitors."

The word 'visitors' sounded odd to Andy, for she didn't think of being a temporary resident anymore, not after nearly four months.

Brian obviously didn't think so either.

"No, you guys are more than visitors now. But let me talk to Garrett and Heath, though I'd be more than happy to have you back me up, Ben."

"I'll be there too," Jim offered. "It's totally unacceptable what they did, especially to a kid as young as Nathan."

"He's the sweetest boy," Morgan remarked with a sad frown, and Jim gave her hand a consoling squeeze. "I can't believe they would do that to him."

"I can believe it," Ben countered. "Look how they treat everyone in broad daylight. I'm surprised they didn't do more to Nathan than what Andy saw."

"They would've done more if I hadn't gotten there in time," said Andy. "Defibrillators can stop a heart as much as start one."

No one said anything for a moment, and Andy noticed that Brian had become particularly pensive.

"What is it, Brian?" she demanded, rousing him from his thoughts.

"Nothing," he began, shaking his head. "I was just thinking about some things I've noticed recently that seemed odd, but now I think they might actually be related to what happened today."

"Like what?"

"Well, for about two months at the end of last year we didn't have any gas in town. I mean *no one* was driving *anywhere*. Susan and I came into town only once a week, on horseback, to pick up supplies and check on how things were going."

"It sucked," Susan added bluntly. "I thought I was gonna kill Brian, we were so sick of being stuck in the house together."

"Yeah, it was pretty bad. It wasn't until the refinery outside of Denver started producing gas that we were finally able to start using our cars again. But about a month before that, I noticed Aiden driving around in his big SUV that has terrible gas mileage, and I asked him where he got the gas. He told me he had some stored in his garage at home, but at the council meeting a few days before he had complained how there was no gas left in town and that it was killing his social life not being able to get around to see all of his girlfriends. Of course, I had no sympathy for him since he could easily walk to where they all lived while Susan and I were stuck ten miles up the road and driving each other crazy. I don't know where he got the gas, but at the time I just figured he'd found some he'd forgotten he had stored somewhere in his garage. But I'll be damned if I didn't see him driving around in that SUV every single time we came back into town that last month before the refinery was running again."

"What about the liquor?" Susan remarked. "Remember at Juniper's birthday party last spring?"

"Oh, yeah, I forgot about that," Brian replied before explaining to the others. "Nataliya likes to throw these elaborate parties for her and her closest friends' birthdays, mainly so she can show off her house and her wardrobe. She also likes to have tons of liquor. Bourbon, scotch, vodka…you name it. Except at Juniper's birthday party in April, her supply ran out, and so had everyone else's by then."

"Nataliya was pissed," Susan said with a giggle.

Charlie turned to her and asked, "Why did you go to a party for someone you abhor?"

"Are you kidding? I didn't go, but Brian did," she replied. Susan was finally getting used to Charlie's extensive vocabulary.

"She invites everyone on the council. I only go because it would create more problems if I didn't," Brian quickly explained. "Anyway, after Juniper's party, all the liquor in Aspen was supposedly gone."

"But then June comes, right before you all got here," Susan continued, "and it's Sparrow's birthday. I actually went to that party, but only because my friend Karen really wanted to go."

Out of the corner of her eye, Andy thought she saw Ben flinch after Susan spoke, but she quickly ignored it and continued to listen.

"I kept trying to convince her not to, but she's always trying to make friends with the 'popular' people." Susan sarcastically made quotations with her fingers. "So I go to the stupid party with Karen, and Sparrow, Juniper, and all their close friends were drinking liquor and getting drunk. But this time they weren't sharing it like they'd always done in the past. Instead they were keeping it for themselves and hiding it from everyone else until they got too drunk to care."

"Where did it come from?" Charlie asked, frowning.

"Who knows?" Brian replied flatly. "The simple explanation is that one of Sparrow's friends had some liquor in their house that they'd forgotten about, just like Aiden could've forgotten about some containers of gas. But I doubt it. They must've gotten a fresh supply from *somewhere* between April and June."

"Is liquor something the town tries to resupply when it runs out?" Andy asked. "I gave your friend some whiskey when I pulled that bullet out of his shoulder, but it was a small bottle that I happened to find in some desk drawer at the hospital…probably belonged to some doctor or nurse who used to drink on the job or after a hard day."

Brian shook his head. "No, liquor is the least of our priorities. It's not something we ever worried about when we ran out. And I'll admit, when we had liquor in our house it was nice having a shot of whiskey on a cold night before going to bed. It was something my dad always did in the winter, and I guess I inherited his habit. But once the liquor ran out, that was that. No more whiskey before bed. Big deal. We've all sacrificed worse. I'm not worried if Nataliya and her friends have liquor. I'm worried about how they got it."

"You mean are they trading what they steal from the residents here to people from other towns in exchange for gas, liquor, and probably other stuff?"

It was Ben who posed this obvious question, and no one tried to contradict what had become so apparent.

"I'm just afraid of what else they're all up to," was Brian's eventual response. His eyes were closed, and he rubbed his temples while looking increasingly distraught.

"God, why can't they just disappear?!"

Chapter X

23 December 2020

In the six weeks since the incident at the hospital, little had changed in the daily routines of Andy and her friends. Work continued as usual, though everyone tended to stay indoors more during the cold, snowy days. Ben spent more time gathering and chopping firewood to keep everyone warm than doing any of his normal work. The electricity, though fairly dependable, was still temperamental, and a day without heat was not uncommon.

Brian spoke with Nataliya the day after Andy saved young Nathan from electric shock. Though she defended her despicable brother and unconvincingly denied involvement in robbing the store or any other nefarious behavior, Nataliya was no idiot. She knew that her comfortable living depended on the work of residents like Brian and his friends, so she promised to confront Garrett and Heath in private about what happened at the store. Knowing Nataliya's promise was worthless, however, Brian raised the incident at the council meeting two days later. A full-fledged war of words erupted.

"You have no proof!" Garrett barked at Brian. "Nathan will deny anything that Andy told you."

"That's because you've made him too scared to talk! And I'll believe Andy any day of the week over you, you lying piece of shit!"

The meeting spiraled out of control even further, with old feuds resurfacing until they climaxed into threats of violence. The only thing that prevented actual blows was Garrett recognizing that he was outnumbered, not just numerically but physically. Aiden was too much of a coward to defend his friend against six boys his own age and size, while both Nataliya and Juniper were as helpless as damsels in distress.

Before storming out of the meeting, however, Garrett came within inches of Brian's face and snarled at him: "Get ready to pay for this, motherfucker!"

No one saw much of Brian after that. Susan still came by the house often, but mainly to spend time with Charlie. She told him her brother was making himself scarce until everything blew over. When Charlie asked if anything like this had ever happened before, Susan shook her head firmly.

"No. Never."

Two days before Christmas, Brian finally came over to the house for dinner. It had been two weeks since anyone but Susan had seen him.

"Well, look who's at the door," Jim said as he moved aside to let Brian inside the house.

"Yeah, I know."

Everyone couldn't help but notice how tired Brian looked, as if he hadn't slept in weeks. Susan was standing beside him, and they both quickly entered the house to escape the cold.

"Sorry we're late," Brian commented as he took off his coat. "It took us a while to get all the cows and horses water. Our pipes froze, so I had to take care of that while Susan melted snow one bucket at a time."

"Did you fix the pipes?" Jim asked. "If not, I'll come over tomorrow and help you."

"Thanks, but I fixed them. I didn't want 'em to rupture, and it's looking to be a pretty cold night."

"It's too bad you two can't just move in here with us," Andy remarked from the kitchen where she was steaming frozen vegetables from the early fall harvest. "Or at least move the animals somewhere closer, like Scott's farm."

"He and I talked about that," Brian remarked. "Unfortunately, his farm isn't big enough for both his cattle and mine."

"Well, let us know if we can help," Andy added.

"Thanks, I will."

"How are Daisy and Suzie?" asked Morgan, who was also in the kitchen helping Andy. "I miss seeing them every day."

Daisy and Suzie were two of Brian and Susan's horses. It had been almost a month since she stopped working on the farm, as the weight of her belly made it too difficult to continue. Nearly seven months pregnant, Morgan's daily routine now consisted of a few hours of teaching in the morning, a long nap in the afternoon, and helping with chores in the house in the evening.

"They're good, but I think they miss you too," Susan replied as she kicked the snow off the bottom of her boots onto the mat at the front door. "Daisy's been in a mood lately."

"Who's been in a mood lately?"

Charlie emerged from the garage where he'd been working with Ben on his truck.

"Daisy," Susan repeated for Charlie, who came up to her and removed her coat before giving her a quick kiss on the forehead. "I think she misses your sister."

"Morgan? Why would anyone miss Morgan?" he teased, which earned him a scowl from his sister.

"Oh, piss off, Charlie."

While everyone continued talking, Ben came inside a moment later and headed to the sink to wash his hands. As he passed Andy at the stove, he gave her a friendly nudge with his elbow. "What's up?" he muttered as he scrubbed the grease off his fingers.

"Susan and Brian are here," she replied without turning away from the stove. "You hungry?"

"Always."

He dried his hands off on a towel and was just about to ask Andy if she needed any help with getting dinner ready when Brian approached.

"You need any help?" he asked, taking the words right out of Ben's mouth.

"Yeah, thanks. Can you defrost the steak in the microwave and then chop it up into pieces? I'm making fajitas."

"Wow, sounds great," Brian remarked while reaching for the frozen steak seating on a plate next to the microwave.

Suddenly feeling very much in the way, Ben backed out of the kitchen and wordlessly moved into the living room where Jim, Charlie, and Susan were sitting. He knew he was being irrational, but Brian's offer to help Andy irritated him. The mere fact that he was bothered by any of it was irritating.

The distance between the kitchen and the living room, though not enormous, was greater than the average American home, and it was necessary to elevate one's voice when speaking back and forth between the two rooms. However, moments later, Ben and the others in the living room clearly heard Brian's cry of pain as he cut his left index finger while chopping the steak.

"Jesus Christ!" he yelled as he instinctively raised his hand away from the cutting board.

Upon realizing what had happened, Andy quickly grabbed a towel, took Brian's hand, and applied strong pressure to his finger. Brian winced in pain, but remained calm. The others came into the kitchen, and a concerned Susan scurried over to her brother.

"What happened?" she cried, but one look at the blood on the knife answered her question.

"It was stupid, really," Brian replied with a strain in his voice as Andy continued to press firmly on his finger. "My grip just slipped."

"Will he need stitches?" Susan asked worriedly as she peered down at Brian's covered hand.

"I don't know yet," Andy remarked coolly. "I need to stop the bleeding first."

Sensing that the injury was serious enough to require a trip to the hospital, Ben went into the garage and fired up his truck. He moved it outside and left the engine running before returning inside.

"I'll drive you both to the hospital," he announced upon reentering the kitchen, his arms hugging his chest for warmth.

Andy removed the towel and inspected the depth of Brian's cut.

"Yeah, we need to go," she decided. "It's pretty deep."

* * *

It usually took Andy about fifteen minutes to walk from the house to the hospital. Using Ben's truck, they arrived in two minutes despite the snow.

"Do you want me to come inside?" Ben asked Andy as he dropped her and Brian off at the main entrance.

"No, we'll be fine," she replied. "It won't take long."

"You don't have to wait for us, Ben," Brian added. He had taken over for Andy and was keeping pressure on his finger with his good hand, still using the same blood-stained towel. "We can walk back. Go get some food and get warm, man."

"You sure?"

"Yeah, we'll be fine," Andy repeated as she moved away from the truck. "Seriously, it's too cold for you to wait here."

"All right," Ben mumbled, and reluctantly drove off.

But he wasn't "all right." In fact, he became acutely conscious of the fact that he was actually jealous of Brian for slicing his finger and would now be spending time alone with Andy at the hospital. This sudden awareness was startling and put him in a foul mood, and after returning home, his behavior did not go unnoticed.

"What's the matter?" Jim asked his cousin. "Is Brian all right?"

"Brian will be fine," Ben replied more sharply than intended.

Everyone was in the kitchen trying to salvage dinner, but with his appetite ruined, Ben excused himself and quickly ascended the stairs. He remained in his room for the rest of the evening.

Following his cousin's departure, Jim turned to Morgan and whispered so that Charlie and Susan couldn't hear. "Remember when you said Ben was in love with Andy but hadn't realized it yet?"

Morgan hesitated before raising an eyebrow at him. "Yeah?"

"Well, I think he's beginning to realize it."

* * *

"You're really good at this, you know?"

"What, stitching a finger?"

"Well, just in general. You're a good doctor."

Andy scoffed at the compliment. She had just completed the final stitch and was sterilizing the wound one more time.

"Thanks, but I'd hardly consider stitching up a finger qualifying me as a doctor."

"I wouldn't say that. Whenever I went to the doctor as a kid, all he would ever do is look into my ears and throat and bang my knees with that little hammer. Didn't seem too difficult."

Andy laughed heartily. "There are so many other things I haven't even begun to learn or that I'm too scared to try."

"Like what? Surgery?"

"Yeah. I mean, I've never cut open a person before, and I know that if I ever do, I'll probably end up killing them."

Brian cocked his head to one side and said, "Maybe, but if someone gets sick or injured enough where they need surgery, they'd probably die without it, right? All you'd be doing is giving them a chance to live, no matter how small. And if they die, it's not like anyone can sue you."

Andy laughed again and recalled how Ben had once told her the exact same thing.

"I know. And you're right about all that." Then, sighing, "It's the act of cutting someone open and trying to save them that scares me. Not to mention giving anesthesia first. That's an entirely separate specialty, you know. Anesthesiology."

"See, that's why you're a good doctor—or at least you will be one day. You understand what it takes to do something right."

Andy was done treating Brian, but they didn't leave the hospital right away, continuing to chat despite that it was almost as cold inside as outside. The heat was turned on only during the day and in certain rooms to conserve energy.

"You make it sound like I have a rare quality or something."

"You do, Andy."

Brian looked down at his bandaged finger, his expression solemn.

"What's wrong?" Andy asked.

Brian looked back up. "It just feels like everything my friends and I have worked so hard to build is about to fall apart and there's nothing I can do about it. It makes me so mad that people like Nataliya and Garrett get away with doing whatever they want, regardless of the consequences."

"I know. It's completely unfair."

"Life isn't fair, though."

Andy cracked a smile. "You sound like my dad."

"Yeah? Well, he was right."

"What I don't understand," Andy continued, "is why everyone puts up with their bullshit behavior. Doesn't everyone see that they do absolutely nothing to help out in this town?"

Brian said nothing. The question was merely rhetorical.

"I know what you said about it being like high school and they're the 'popular' kids, but this isn't high school Brian, it's survival. It's about being able to feed yourself, having clean water to drink, and staying warm in the winter. I would gladly make enemies with anyone if it meant that my friends and I could stay alive."

"I know that," Brian acknowledged. "I just wish more people felt the way you do, but no one wants to rock the boat. As long as everyone is getting what they need, people will continue looking the other way. Just human nature, I suppose," he added with a heavy shrug.

"Maybe, but I swear to you, if Nataliya or any of them do anything to hurt me or my friends, I'll fight back. I promise. Going after poor Nathan was bad enough. Going after those I care most about…well…" Andy raised an eyebrow. "Things would get ugly."

Her conviction caused a smile to emerge on Brian's face. After a pause, he started to speak, hesitated, but ultimately decided to continue.

"So, if one of them tried to hurt me, you'd go after them for me?"

He said it more as a joke, but partly to test her reaction.

"Of course," Andy replied matter-of-factly while completely failing to notice the subtleties of Brian's question.

He tried a different approach.

"Your friends are lucky to have you, and I'm glad you consider me one of them, especially since you already had such close friends when you got here."

Andy shrugged casually at the observation. "I don't think you can ever have too many friends. I've known Morgan and Charlie more than five years, but I only met Jim and Ben a few weeks before coming here. I consider them all my friends."

She looked down at her hands and brushed her palms on her jeans. "Plus," she went on, "I'm the only one without family, so I consider myself lucky to have the friends I do. Otherwise, I'd be alone. Morgan and Charlie will always have each other, so will Jim and Ben. And you and Susan. You're all so lucky to still have each other. I try not to be jealous, but in a way, I am."

When Andy finished, Brian continued his attempt to steer the conversation in such a way as to provoke the response he was seeking without being obvious.

"And Jim and Morgan are together, so I guess that brings everyone closer together." Then with a light chuckle, he added, "And now my baby sister and Charlie. I would've never guessed that, but she's almost fifteen, so…"

"See, all six of you are connected now, but I'm still just everyone's friend," Andy remarked with a hint of regret in her voice.

"What about you and Ben?" Brian asked, going for the direct approach after sensing an opening.

Andy blinked, clearly taken aback by the question. "Me and Ben?" Following an uncomfortable pause, she blurted out, "We're just friends. Why?"

Trying to appear indifferent, Brian casually shook his head. "Just curious. You two seem…I don't know…sometimes more than friends."

To this, Andy struggled with a response.

"Well, we've become good friends, but it's tricky to get beyond a certain point with Ben. It's like there's a part of him that he keeps hidden from everyone. I don't know why, but unless that changes, I don't think I'll ever be more than just his friend."

"But you've thought about it? Being more than just friends, I mean?"

Andy looked down at her boots and smiled awkwardly. "Sure, I guess." Then, feeling the need to explain further, she quickly added, "I think most girls do that with guys they know. We put each of them into one of two categories. There are the ones you know you will only ever be friends with because you only feel friendship for them, and then there are the ones that you always consider the possibility of something more happening. At least that's how it is for me. But I haven't known too many boys my age, so I could be wrong."

Andy drew her gaze up from the floor and looked directly at Brian, then shrugged as though to say she had no further explanation to give.

Brian was working up the courage to ask her which category she had put him in when a sudden crash erupted from outside the treatment room. Being closest to the door, Andy opened it and peered outside. Glancing left and right, she realized what had caused the noise. An IV stand that had been placed in the hallway to the right of the door had fallen over. Confused as to how it could've fallen over on its own, Andy's eyes darted in all directions, looking to see if someone was nearby and had knocked it over.

"What was it?" Brian called from behind.

"Just an IV stand that fell over. I meant to move that today."

"It just fell over by itself?"

"I know. I was thinking the same thing, but no one's out there."

Andy turned back toward Brian. "Weird," she said, and they both shrugged it off before heading back home.

* * *

All day long, Krista-Lynn, Nataliya's former child-actress friend, had a headache that wouldn't go away. Of course, she hadn't bothered to think that it might have something to do with the copious amount of alcohol she'd consumed the night before with her friends.

With her medicine cabinet bare and after spending the entire day waiting for the pain to subside, she grudgingly made the short trek in the snow to the hospital in search of aspirin, or hopefully something stronger like Vicodin. She cursed Garrett's name during the entire walk. He had taken her last two aspirin after a party a few weeks earlier, and now she was forced to go outside in the cold with a headache, and none of her friends cared enough to accompany her. It wasn't fair.

She knew that Andy, one of the new girls, locked some of the rooms in the hospital where the drugs were kept, something that had never been done before. But of course Brian and his friends, being the rule-abiding, control freaks that they were, gave Andy complete control over the hospital. Until today, however, Krista-Lynn hadn't cared. She possessed her own stash of drugs for every ailment imaginable, and thanks to her pill-popping mother's influence, her knowledge of pharmaceuticals was extensive. But sadly, her stash was running low to the point where even aspirin was gone. She would fix that today and grab any spare drugs she could find once her headache was taken care of.

It was dark inside the hospital, but Krista-Lynn had remembered her flashlight. After attempting to open three different treatment rooms, she discovered each was locked.

Fucking Andy. Why did she have to be so goddamned responsible?

Neither Krista-Lynn nor any of her friends liked Andy, but only because she seemed to have all of Ben's attention. Ben was simply gorgeous to look at, but he rarely said more than two words to any of them. Though always polite, he was distant, which only made him more mysterious and therefore more attractive. Nataliya had made the greatest effort to win his affection, but she had failed to spark any interest from him. Consequently, she vilified Andy further. They didn't like Morgan either, although they thought it was hilarious that she was pregnant. They all believed that Jim, who was also quite attractive, was the father.

As Krista-Lynn continued down the dark hallway, she noticed a light inside one of the rooms, and when she drew near, she saw that the door was open an inch. Voices could be heard from inside. There was a small glass window in the center of the upper half of the door, and after carefully peering through it without being seen, she recognized Andy and Brian inside. Though difficult to see, she could make out Andy doing something to Brian's finger with a funny looking pair of scissors that unbeknownst to her, was actually a needle holder.

She watched for a few minutes and eavesdropped on their initially boring conversation. Only when Andy had finished doing whatever it was to Brian's finger did things become more interesting.

"What's wrong?"

This was Andy speaking, followed by Brian:

"It just feels like everything my friends and I have worked so hard to build is about to fall apart and there's nothing I can do about it. It makes me so mad that people like Nataliya and Garrett get away with doing whatever they want, regardless of the consequences."

Then Andy again:

"I know. It's completely unfair."

Krista-Lynn listened for a few minutes longer. At first, she could barely contain her outrage at the way that they were speaking about her and her friends, and she almost opened the door completely to confront them when the conversation quickly changed. Her anger quickly turned to amusement as she listened to Brian's feeble attempts to flirt with Andy, and she nearly laughed out loud at Andy's own obliviousness to his interest.

It was around that moment when she accidentally backed into a tall, T-shaped metal pole with two loops on the top that had been leaning against the wall near the door. It fell over and made a loud clanging sound when it hit the ground. Knowing she'd get caught, she bolted away from the door and flew around the corner of a nearby hallway perpendicular to the first one. She then heard Andy open the door and say something indistinguishable to Brian. After another tense moment, she slowly looked around the corner and watched the two leave the hospital.

After finally finding some aspirin and a few other drugs, Krista-Lynn left the hospital and made a beeline for Nataliya's house. An hour later, Nataliya had managed to calm herself after listening to Krista-Lynn's account and was now contemplating revenge. As she stared through the large floor-to-ceiling window in her grand living room and watched her friend return to her home a block away, Nataliya muttered under her breath, *"Ya buduh ehteem naslazhdatsa."*

I'm going to enjoy this.

* * *

12 January 2021

New Year's Day came and went amid a blizzard that knocked out much of the power throughout Aspen. Brian and Susan were stranded in their home for more than a week, remarking afterward that it was the biggest storm they'd seen since their parents died. Before, people would have rejoiced at the record snowfall and the superb ski conditions it created, but now it was merely a nuisance.

The snow finally ceased during the second week of January, and one day, after the town worked tirelessly to turn the power back on, everyone decided to take advantage of the fresh powder and go sledding. Susan and Brian reemerged from their home and rode into town on a horse-drawn sleigh their family had owned for decades. Susan stayed inside with Morgan, while the rest of the household decided to join everyone outside. People scurried to the southern edge of town to Aspen Mountain, or "Ajax," as it was called. Though there were chairlifts for ascending the mountain, two years earlier the town council decided not to waste energy on them. Brian had also argued that the neglected lifts would require maintenance to ensure their safety, which at the time was hardly a priority. But Nataliya and her friends ignored common sense and wanted to operate the lifts so they could ski whenever they wanted. Ultimately, however, Brian and the rest of the council made the reasonable decision in yet another six-to-four vote.

After a few hours of sledding and scrambling up the foot of the mountain, Andy left the slopes early and returned to the house to check on Morgan and Susan before heading over to the hospital. She had a nagging feeling all afternoon that she'd accidentally left the door unlocked to the room where most of the drugs were kept. After some had gone missing a few weeks earlier, she had moved all the drugs to one room and installed a more secure lock on the door with Ben's help. But the lock was useless if she forgot to use it.

"I'm just gonna check on something at the hospital," Andy said to Morgan and Susan as they played cards by the fireplace.

"Okay, I'll start cooking dinner when you get back," Morgan replied without looking up from her hand of poker.

Daylight was fading as Andy began the now-familiar route to the hospital, and the sun began its descent behind the mountains by the time she arrived. Once inside, she quickly checked the door in question and discovered that she had indeed locked it the day before.

Feeling stupid, Andy unlocked the door and checked supplies inside, just in case. After verifying that nothing was missing, she relocked the door before heading back home.

She never made it there.

* * *

As twilight turned to dusk, Morgan began pacing back and forth in front of the fireplace. Something was wrong; Andy should have been back long before this.

By now, all the boys had returned to the house, and Brian and Susan were about to head home until it became clear that Morgan's worries could be serious.

Ben and Charlie went to check out the hospital, but they came back less than an hour later without Andy and without any answers.

"Where the hell could she be?" Morgan cried out.

Jim did his best to calm her down.

"She probably just wandered down to Main Street or got caught up talking to someone on her way back. Maybe someone got sick or injured and she went to help them."

This explanation seemed to soothe Morgan for a while, and Susan and Brian decided they needed to head back home before it got too late, though Brian was weary of leaving without knowing that Andy was safe.

"I'll come back in the morning," he said before heading outside.

"We both will," Susan added.

Morgan managed to fall asleep, as did Jim and Charlie. Ben, however, lay awake almost the entire night, save a few restless hours of sleep and dreams of Andy walking along the beach and swimming with dolphins somewhere far away.

At dawn, he rose out of bed and immediately went into Andy's room, hoping she had returned in the middle of the night. But her bed was empty, and a terrible, sinking feeling hit him in the gut.

Before the others awoke, Ben threw on his clothes and outerwear and headed back to the hospital on the off-chance that Andy was there. He trampled through the snow with haste while following a pair of tracks that were likely hers from the evening before. The sun was rising off to his right, and the rays of light hit his cheek with sobering harshness. With every step he took, he felt more and more certain that something terrible had happened. And after desperately searching every room and closet he could find at the hospital, he reluctantly accepted that Andy was not there and headed back home.

Roughly halfway back, Ben spotted a few things he missed seeing earlier as well as the night before with Charlie. On the side of the road, where the curb rose up many inches beneath the snow, was a dark piece of fabric that turned out to be a glove. It was a woman's glove, which Ben recognized as Andy's. A few feet away and nearly hidden after falling through the snow was a small, dark bottle with a white label. Ben reached down into the hole and retrieved the bottle: half-full with large print on the label that read, "Chloroform".

Ben shoved the glove and bottle into his coat pocket as a theory began to take shape in his mind. He looked carefully at the snow in and around the area where he'd found the glove and bottle and noticed a sudden cluster of footprints of various sizes that stopped abruptly in the middle of the road where a few sets of tire tracks crisscrossed in both directions. Ben counted three different boot prints, including those he guessed to be Andy's.

Minutes later and out of breath, Ben was home. He went directly to Jim's room, knocked first, and when there was no answer, he peeked inside and saw that the room was empty. He darted down the hall to Morgan's room and just as he was about to knock on the door, Jim opened it.

"Good, you're awake."

"Yeah, we both are," Jim replied, looking back at Morgan, who was lying on her side on the bed and facing Ben. Exerting great effort, she held her bulging belly with one hand while using her other to push herself into a sitting position. She looked exhausted, and Ben realized he wasn't the only one who hadn't slept.

"Did she come back last night?" Morgan asked, her voice heavy with worry yet containing the faintest hint of hope.

Ben gravely shook his head. "No, she didn't."

He then revealed what he found on the side of the road.

"I think Andy's been kidnapped."

Chapter XI

January 14, 2021

A monstrous headache greeted Andy when she woke. Her ears began to ring, and she immediately wished for her iPod to listen to her mother's cello music to make it stop. Then she opened her eyes.

It was dark, wherever she was. She was lying on what felt like a cold cement floor, and yet she was sweltering in her winter coat. Due to the pounding in her head, she carefully sat up and blindly took off the coat, placing it on the floor beside her. Still warm, she stripped off her thin sweater, underneath which was a T-shirt. Her jeans felt thick and heavy, but there was nothing she could do about that or her weighty winter boots. She groped around with her hands until her eyes adjusted to the darkness. The outline of what appeared to be a large door emerged to her left, a faint glow of light around its edges. Confused, scared, disoriented, and famished, she waited. Her last meal had been forty-eight hours earlier, though she did not yet know it had been that long.

Her mind gradually recalled what had happened. After leaving the hospital a pickup truck similar to the one Ben and Jim owned pulled over the side of the road beside her. Thinking it was one of them, she thought nothing of approaching the truck. But then the passenger door flew open and someone she didn't recognize jumped out. He lunged for her, and when she stepped back to evade his grasp, she fell backward into the snow. Following that, she remembered was the distinctive, sweet smell of chloroform…then nothing.

Back in the dark, an indeterminable amount of time later, a set of lights illuminated above Andy and revealed that she was sitting inside a cavernous warehouse, and that the large door was actually a garage door of sorts. The warehouse itself was empty, except for a large stack of cardboard boxes sitting in the center of the large space. The garage door suddenly began to open from the bottom, and bright light came pouring inside. Andy squinted until her eyes adjusted yet again, this time to sunlight. A wave of warm air hit her face as she stared straight ahead at a crisp blue sky, against which she made out a tall, skinny tree. She blinked once—then twice—with the realization that it wasn't a pine tree.

It was a palm tree.

* * *

From the beginning, Andy's friends knew that a panicked search for any sign of her whereabouts would be an entire waste of time, and with their suspicions sufficiently piqued after Ben's discovery on the road, they went straight to the top of the list of suspects, beginning with Nataliya.

"So you are accusing me of somehow *arranging* for Andy to be kidnapped? Is that what you are telling me?"

Brian, Ben, and Jim had practically stormed into Nataliya's home, all three of them armed and ready for a fight. They were standing in the vast living room, the same room where Ben and Jim met Nataliya on that first day in Aspen nearly six month earlier. Today's conversation, however, was far more unpleasant.

Nataliya lounged casually on her plush sofa in an attempt to appear unaffected by either their forced presence or their accusations, but her audience wasn't buying the act.

"You can cut the bullshit right now, Nataliya. Tell us where she is."

Out of respect for his position in the town, Ben was willing to let

Brian speak first, but only for so long. If answers weren't given quickly, he wouldn't hesitate to take over. Meanwhile, Jim knew he would have to be the voice of reason; both Ben and Brian were too emotional when it came to Andy. And he needed to be levelheaded for Morgan's sake as well. Fortunately, being levelheaded was something Jim was very good at.

"Get out of my house right now, or I'll call the guards and force you out."

"I've already called them."

The voice came from behind. It was Mikhail, descending the grand staircase in the foyer entrance. Ben, Brian, and Jim all turned around at the same moment just in time to catch the self-satisfied sneer on his face.

"They should be here any minute."

And *that* was Ben's limit. He lifted his rifle and aimed it directly at Nataliya.

"The safety's off, bitch. Now tell us where Andy is."

Mikhail scurried down the rest of the steps in a vain attempt to defend his sister, but Brian held him back at gunpoint with his own rifle.

Seeing the object of her desire aim the barrel of a gun at her face rattled Nataliya. Hearing him call her 'bitch' affected her even more, but she remained defiant.

"I'm not telling you anything. There is nothing to tell."

She pronounced the words slowly and deliberately.

Undeterred, Ben moved the barrel a few inches to the right and pulled the trigger. The deafening shot landed squarely in the headrest of the sofa mere inches from Nataliya's head. She let out a piercing scream and retreated to the furthest corner of the sofa.

"I've got twenty-nine more," said Ben in a strangely calm voice as he followed her movements. "And unless you tell me where Andy is, I swear the next one will draw blood."

Then, lowering his head, he lunged forward and shoved the end of the gun barrel into her chest.

"Are you fucking crazy?" Nataliya cried out, her eyes wide with a strange mixture of fear and anger as she pressed her back as hard as possible into the sofa.

Ben's eyes narrowed, and he moved the pressure of the barrel from her chest to underneath her chin, pining her in place.

"At this moment…yeah, I probably am a little crazy, and I don't want to have to put a hole in that pretty face of yours, but I will. *Now answer me!*"

But Nataliya could say nothing. Any anger she'd felt had disappeared, and now her face reflected only fear, and it dawned on Ben that perhaps she was telling the truth. As tears pooled in her eyes, she slowly shook her head as if pleading with him to believe her. But he wanted answers, and he knew that someone in that room had them. His hand began to tremble on the trigger, and suddenly, Mikhail burst out in a panic:

"She doesn't know where Andy is!"

All eyes turned to Mikhail as Brian edged closer to him, nudging him with his own rifle.

"But you know, don't you?"

Mikhail's characteristic foulness had entirely vanished, and all that remained was a scared boy whose shoulders began to quiver.

"Tell us, Mikhail," Jim demanded evenly. "Tell us, and no one will get hurt."

* * *

Andy pulled her gaze away from the palm tree when a large truck came roaring toward her through the garage door. The truck was different from the one she'd been forced into two days earlier, and when it came to a stop and the engine was turned off, three older boys—different from the ones who had grabbed her in the snow—emerged from three different doors and approached her. The tallest one, a dark-skinned young man with remarkably bright green eyes, like emeralds and similar to hers, was in front.

"You Andy? Andy Christensen?" he said to her in a deep, rich voice. His words were curt but not impolite. The sound of a complete stranger saying her name was startling.

After blinking a few times, she replied, "Yeah?" Her voice was hoarse.

"You're coming with us."

Dazed, Andy looked back and forth between the three men.

"Who are you?"

"It doesn't matter."

They were each openly carrying pistols on their belts, giving Andy little chance to argue. Rising tentatively, she picked up her coat from the ground, her legs nearly buckling in the process.

"Sit in the back seat," the tall one said as he climbed into the passenger's seat. Andy obeyed as her heart began to pound in her chest and ears. The other two young men climbed into the left side of the car, one in front and the other in back next to Andy. The driver was also black, but shorter than the other, and built like a bulldog. The third appeared to be Hispanic and had tattoos covering his arms. Andy kept her gaze focused outside her window, though she spoke to the tall one sitting in front of her as the truck backed out of the warehouse.

"Where am I?"

"Just outside of L.A."

"Los Angeles?" She couldn't contain the surprise in her voice.

"You know of any other L.A.?"

Andy didn't respond but instead thought of another question.

"What day is it?"

"Thursday," Emerald Eyes responded after looking at his beautiful Rolex watch.

"Thursday? You mean I was out for two days?"

Emerald Eyes turned around halfway to glance back at her.

"Look, I don't know how or when you got here. I just pick up the package when and where I'm told. That's all."

"Package?" Andy repeated with confusion. "Is that what I am? A package? What does that mean?"

Emerald Eyes turned back, this time looking directly at her. His irises were hypnotic.

"It's just what we call merchandise," he said slowly and more methodically now.

"I'm merchandise? What, someone paid money for me?"

Emerald Eyes laughed, and so did the driver and Tattoo Arms.

"Money? Fuck, no. There's no money anymore. What planet are you from?"

"Colorado," Andy said flatly, her voice hollow. Glancing down at her hands, she noticed a small circular bruise on the inside of her left forearm that appeared to be caused by a needle. Knowing that chloroform was only mildly effective despite what TV and the movies portrayed, Andy correctly guessed that she'd been injected with something to keep her unconscious for so long.

"Colorado? Damn!" Emerald Eyes said, interrupting her thoughts. He shook his head in disbelief. "I never delivered someone from so far away. Girl, you must be special."

"Special?" Andy repeated. She hugged her arms around her defensively.

Emerald Eyes seemed to read her mind. "No, not that kinda special. Shit, there's plenty of skin walking the street here willing to give it up for half a G of blow. We don't need to import sex from Colorado."

Ignoring this unfamiliar drug slang, Andy pressed her case further. "Then why am I here?"

Emerald Eyes shrugged. "You must be someone who knows how to do something important. Whatever it is, I dunno, but I hope for your sake that *you* do."

"Where are we going?"

"Why? Do you know L.A.?"

Andy shook her head. "Never been here before."

"Then what difference does it make where we're goin'?"

"Just humor me. I've had a bad day."

Emerald Eyes actually laughed.

"You like the ocean? 'Cuz that's where we're goin'…Santa

Monica, baby."

"Great," Andy muttered under her breath.

I'm Alice tumbling down the rabbit hole, she thought. *I'm Dorothy in Oz.*

Inside the truck was silent for a while, and Andy leaned her head against the window and stared outside. The bright sun reflected off the pavement in a haze. The number of surrounding houses and buildings gradually increased with each passing mile. A web of freeways, overpasses, and interchanges whizzed by. People were seen walking along the sidewalks and sometimes on the freeways. But all Andy could think of was how the hell she would get back to Aspen.

* * *

"Traded? She's been traded? What does that mean?! Traded for what?"

Jim demanded that Morgan sit down if she wanted to continue the tirade of questions she had every right to ask. He was home now with Ben and Brian. Morgan, Charlie, and Susan had been anxiously waiting in the living room for their return from Nataliya's.

"A kilo of cocaine," Ben replied bitterly. "Seems our good friends here enjoy more than just liquor at their parties."

"Cocaine!" Morgan cried. "My best friend was taken for some fucking white powder? Christ! Petrol, maybe, or food. I could wrap my head around that, but bloody drugs? Are you fucking kidding me?"

It was the first time anyone had ever heard Morgan curse, including Charlie. And no one had an answer for her. Charlie and Susan were too stunned to say anything, and the others were still reeling over the cold facts about Andy's disappearance that they had forced out of Mikhail.

"She was taken to Grand Junction, which is west of here," Ben continued wearily. "From there, she was sent somewhere else. She could be anywhere by now."

"Sent by whom?" Charlie asked.

"People who trade and bargain for things," supplied Jim. "This particular group operates out of Grand Junction, but they're just one link in a whole chain of people who do this. Apparently, Andy's skills as a doctor were considered valuable enough to be worth more than a kilo of cocaine. These groups always get more than they give. It's how they make a profit."

"So they don't just trade *stuff*, they trade people too? Is that what you're telling me?" Morgan demanded.

No one answered. It wasn't a question.

"Do we know where to find these people who took Andy?" asked Susan. "Did Mikhail tell you their names?"

"We know their names, but that's all. I'm going there tonight to find them," Ben declared.

Everyone looked at him, but he ignored them and instead turned only to Brian.

"I'll need some gas, as much as you can give me. Whatever doesn't fit in the tanks of my truck, I'll store in the back."

Brian stared back at Ben for a long moment but eventually nodded. It was decided.

"Mikhail said they chose Andy because she threatened him that day with Nathan at the hospital," Jim explained, as though this would make everything easier to understand. "He said they all wanted to get back at her after that. Nataliya did too, but she let her brother and Garrett handle it. All she told them was to somehow get rid of her."

Leaning back in the sofa, Morgan cupped her hands over her eyes and rolled the back of her head from side to side across the headrest.

"I can't stay here," she announced with unwavering resolve. "I can't live down the street from people who traded Andy's life for a kilo of drugs. Staying here would be betraying her."

"None of us should stay here," Ben added. "If we don't leave soon, someone could get hurt or even killed. We've made some serious enemies now, and that can't be reversed."

Jim looked up at his cousin, and Ben knew exactly what he was going to ask.

"You want me to come with you?"

But Ben shook his head firmly. "No, I'll go alone."

He sounded so determined that no one dared question him. Meanwhile, a mixture of relief and doubt appeared on Jim's face, and before he could change his mind, Ben offered him and Morgan a suggestion.

"You two should head back south to New Mexico. Go back to Santa Rosa and meet up with Maria. She should still be there."

Jim and Morgan looked at each other as he squeezed her hand.

"Yeah, okay," Morgan uttered faintly. She was doing everything in her power to keep from crying. "Maria will take care of us."

"Yeah, she will," Jim repeated before looking at Brian, then at Susan. "What about you two?"

Brian and his sister exchanged glances. It was one of those questions that they never thought they would ever have to answer, but the consequences of the day's events had changed everything. The fragile stability of their lives had been shattered.

"We'll stay here through the winter," Brian began as he improvised a plan. "When spring arrives, we'll move some of our livestock south and meet you. The rest we can give to Scott."

Brian silently verified with Susan whether she would go along with his plan, and she agreed with a single nod. However, she knew her brother wanted to go after Andy, and it made her sorry that his responsibilities to her and the farm were keeping him from doing just that. Had it been summer, Susan could manage the farm alone, but things were far different during winter.

Charlie was the last of the group to make a decision. Had Morgan not been pregnant, he may have answered differently. Tortured by choosing to stay behind with Susan or go with his sister, he ultimately put family first; he would head south with Morgan and Jim. With the exception of Ben, the situation had forced everyone to choose obligation over desire.

* * *

Los Angeles was enormous. Andy never knew just how big until it flew by at eighty miles per hour. It was an endless expanse of the machinations of Man now crumbling after years of neglect.

Her heart was still pounding, but it had slowed to a more steady rhythm. Some of her fear had dissipated into anger, and she wanted to let out a scream of rage. But being outnumbered three-to-one, and three-to-zero in terms of weapons, she remained silent and instead waited for an opportunity to escape.

She thought about her friends and visualized each one of them in the present moment. Morgan was probably out of her mind with worry, while Jim would be trying to calm and reassure her. She pictured Charlie discussing with the older boys a way to find her. Would they even know where to begin? Susan would be trying to help in any way she could, while Brian likely blamed himself in some way for her disappearance. And Ben? It was hard to imagine what Ben would do.

The truck slowed down as it pulled off the Santa Monica Freeway and headed north onto the Pacific Coast Highway. Andy could see the waves crashing against the sand as the water sparkled like diamonds beneath the waning sun. She immediately thought of Bermuda and her life there, which now seemed like an eternity ago.

"We're here," Emerald Eyes announced as the driver pulled the truck off the highway and headed east into a neighborhood just off the beach. Less than a minute later, they entered a long, gated driveway that ended at the front of an expansive home likely inhabited by a rich movie star at one time.

Andy's "escorts" got out of the truck first. Emerald Eyes opened the door for her.

"Follow me," he said, and she obeyed. She scanned the area, looking for anything that might provide a way out. The front door to the home was open, but Emerald Eyes gave it a quick warning knock before entering. Andy followed him, while the driver and Tattoo Arms came in behind her.

They entered a vast living room that spilled into an impressive kitchen, and Andy wondered if the water and power were working in the house. Her question was answered soon enough, for planted on three different sofas in the living room sat half a dozen teenage boys with their eyes transfixed by the images of a video game flashing in front of them on a huge flat-screen TV. Two of the six were actually playing the game while the other four merely watched. When the door closed behind Tattoo Arms, one of the players paused the game and turned around. The others followed suit.

"Everything cool?" the player asked Emerald Eyes.

"Yeah, no problems. She's right here."

The player stood up from the couch and approached them. He gave Emerald Eyes a friendly fist punch as he passed by and stopped a few feet in front of Andy. The young man was as tall as Emerald Eyes with broader shoulders, but lacked the spectacular eyes of his comrade. Andy also noted that he didn't seem to be carrying a weapon. If he was, it was well concealed.

"I'm Michael," he said, and to Andy's surprise, he extended his hand. She shook it tentatively.

"Andy."

"Good. Let's go to the den and chat."

Michael led Andy alone down a long hallway until he reached a door at the end. He opened it and they stepped inside. He gestured for her to sit in a chair in front of a mahogany desk while he took the seat behind it. The desk was covered in various papers and photos, which reminded Andy of what a private investigator's desk might have looked like. A laptop computer sat to Michael's right, but it was closed and didn't appear to be powered on.

"So, you're probably wondering why you're here?" Michael began.

"Uh, just a bit," Andy replied with overt sarcasm. "It's not every day that I get kidnapped and shipped, what, more than a thousand miles away from my home without explanation."

"A thousand miles?" Michael replied, his eyes widening.

"Uh, yeah, if not more. Now I'm even more confused because *you* seem to be confused. Can you please tell me what's going on?"

Michael put up his hands as if to surrender. "Okay, chill. Lemme ask you first…where you from?"

"Before the virus or after?"

"After."

"Colorado. Aspen, to be exact."

Michael let out a whistle.

"Wow, you weren't kiddin'. That's far. Always wanted to go to Colorado. Used to watch the Olympics, you know, before everything. Wanted to be one of those downhill skiers since I was this tall."

Michael indicated a height of about three feet with his hand.

"Fantastic," Andy replied impatiently. "Now why am I here?"

"I need a doctor for my girlfriend. But you think there's a doctor anywhere 'round here? Hell, no."

"So that's why I'm here?"

"I told my boys back there that I needed a doctor. They do what they do and meet with our boys in Vegas. From there, I ain't gotta fuckin' clue how they found you. It's a nice, long chain. Untraceable…that's how we like it."

"Who is 'we' exactly?"

"'We?' You jokin'?"

Andy shook her head wearily.

"I'm not from around here, remember?"

"You heard of the 'Bloods?'"

Andy thought a moment. A sudden recollection of hearing certain rap songs with lyrics referring to L.A. street gangs jogged her memory.

"Yeah, vaguely."

"Well, that's us…what's left of us. Me and some of the older boys were already members before that fuckin' virus killed everyone on top. But we carried it on. And now we're the biggest and strongest in L.A."

Michael beamed with pride. Andy was entirely underwhelmed.

"Uh, good for you…and who's your rival?"

Michael looked at Andy as though she had asked him to explain quantum physics.

"Shit, girl…you been living in a cave or somethin'? Those

motherfuckin' Crips are still rattlin' cages every day 'round here."

Andy nodded as if she gave a damn before getting back to the point of her being there.

"So, you want me to treat your girlfriend, is that it?"

"You a doctor? A good one?"

"Better than you'll find anywhere these days. Is she sick?"

"She's pregnant. I need someone to deliver the baby. But I wanna know first if it's a boy or girl."

"Does it make a difference?"

"Hell, yeah it makes a difference! If it's a girl, I'll need to get to work on makin' a boy with someone else. Gotta keep the ranks up, ya' know?"

"Yeah," Andy mouthed absently. She just wanted the whole bizarre experience to be over before dealing with the headache of getting back to Aspen. Luckily, no one seemed to be interested in hurting her.

"How far along is she?"

"What?"

"How many months pregnant is your girlfriend?"

Michael let out another whistle.

"Shit, hell if I know. But her belly is ginormous! I can't even touch her, she's a freakin' whale."

Michael made a face of disgust, which did nothing to entice Andy to help him. Jim would have never said that about Morgan.

"All right, take me to her, and I'll get her a sonogram."

"Is that the thing that tells you if it's a boy or girl?"

"Yeah, we'll need to go to a hospital for the sonogram…a hospital where the power is working. And I can't promise I'll be able to determine the sex of the baby. It depends on position of the fetus inside the uterus, and it's harder to tell the closer the mother is to her due date."

Michael gave Andy that same look of sheer puzzlement again, but this time because he clearly had no idea what she was talking about.

"I'm just warning you," Andy quickly explained, "that I might not be able to tell the sex with one-hundred percent certainty. It's not an exact science."

Michael shrugged.

"Whatever, my boys will take you and my girl to the hospital today. You tell 'em when you find out what the baby is."

"Fine," Andy muttered, realizing that while Michael still neither understood nor cared about the technical difficulties of a sonogram, going to the hospital might be her chance to escape.

"After the baby is born, then what?"

"That's it. Go back to…Colorado, right?"

"Yeah."

"Well, you can go back. I'll even throw in a car with a full tank to get you started."

"Perfect."

Andy wanted to ask for a bike along with a car in case she got stranded on the highway going back, but seeing that she was in the presence of members of one of the formerly biggest and most violent gangs in the country, she decided not to press her luck. There were, however, a few things she couldn't do without.

"Before I do anything, I need to eat and go to the bathroom. I haven't done either for two days. And I need some water."

Michael's demeanor shifted. "Think you're a fuckin' princess?"

"No, I think I'm human. If you want me to help you, I need food and water to function. It's pretty fuckin' simple."

Hard-pressed to argue something so obvious, Michael relented, but he wasn't happy about it. "Okay, but don't expect nothin' special. We ain't exactly cooks 'round 'ere."

The discussion was over. Andy followed Michael down the hallway and back into the living room where the video game had recommenced. The three young men from the warehouse were still there and had joined the rest of the group on the sofa as everyone stared numbly at the TV. On the screen, an alien-looking creature was biting the head off a human, presumably one of the players, and several groans and cursing filled the room.

"Yo, Derek!" Michael boomed over the noise.

Emerald Eyes, aka Derek, turned around and shot up from his seat before moving toward Michael.

"Get this bitch some food and water and show her the bathroom. Then go to Sherri's place and take 'em to the hospital on Wilshire. If she gives you any problems," Michael nodded toward Andy, "you know what to do."

Andy frowned. "I won't give you any problems. Just let me do my job and we'll both get what we want."

"Good. Now get outta here. I got shit to do."

Andy and her escorts left and got back in the truck, occupying the same seats as before.

"Sherri's got food at her place," Derek explained to Andy as the engine started. "And water. You can use her bathroom too."

"Sherri is Derek's girlfriend?"

"Yeah."

The driver darted carelessly out of the driveway and nearly hit the side of the gate.

"Shit, man! Learn to drive," Derek snapped at him.

"Fuck you," the driver barked.

Andy grabbed the handle above the window and held fast. After a couple more jarring turns, the driver made a right onto Wilshire Boulevard. None of the stoplights along the road were functioning, and he made a quick left-to-right swivel of his head to check for other cars before cruising through each light. The road was empty but several people were walking along the sidewalk. After seeing a pale girl with a sickly skeletal frame carrying what appeared to be an infant in her arms, Andy immediately thought of Morgan and a dull ache hit her stomach. She became so engrossed with thoughts about her best friend and the baby that would soon arrive that she didn't see the red SUV come out of nowhere and pull up beside the truck. Nor did she see its passenger's side window roll down.

"What the hell—?" Derek yelled, but the sound of gunfire cut him off. Several shots rang out, and Andy instinctively threw her head into her lap, covering her head and ears with her arms. She let out a scream that went unheard, and she could feel the truck swerve uncontrollably for what felt like an eternity as the gun shots continued. The truck suddenly hit the curb and came to an abrupt stop. The gunfire had stopped as well, and for about ten seconds, Andy kept her head down amidst the startling silence that followed. Finally, she lifted her head, bracing herself for the carnage she knew she was about to find.

There was no sign of the red SUV anywhere. It had done its job and had fled the scene. Within the truck, the driver was dead, a gunshot to the left temple and another to his left shoulder. Tattoo Arms had, unbeknownst to Andy, jumped out of the car during the assault and was now a crumpled body in the middle of the street at least fifty yards behind the truck. Derek had suffered a gunshot wound to the chest, which would have been treatable, but a second bullet had ripped through his jugular vein, which was now spurting blood. He was still breathing, but the life was draining out of him quickly. Andy grabbed the sweater that she had removed in the warehouse and leaned over the front seat. As she pressed the sweater into his neck in a vain attempt to stop the bleeding, their eyes met, and she could see that he knew his end was near.

"I'm sorry," she whispered.

Derek said nothing. He couldn't speak. Instead, he blinked once, then twice as he sucked in the last few breaths of air that he would ever take. Then silence came as death arrived, and with her fingers, Andy gently closed his beautiful green eyes one last time. A second later, amazed that she was still alive, she silently thanked God for saving her.

With blood on her hands and her sweater soaked, she numbly reached for the door handle. Before she opened it, however, the sound of a car engine emerged from the distance, growing louder as it approached. Andy whirled around until she caught sight of the same red SUV. It was headed directly toward the truck.

"Shit!"

Certain they were coming back to see if everyone was dead, Andy's mind panicked. Should she leave the truck and try running away, or hide herself in the backseat? She desperately searched inside and out for something to conceal her. Her winter coat was big, but it wouldn't cover her. Feeling her chances of escape slipping away, Andy sneaked out of the truck and crawled underneath it, hoping to hell that whoever was coming would miss her.

The SUV slowed down when it approached Tattoo Arm's body in the middle of the road. Seeing that he was dead, the driver pressed on toward the truck. By then, Andy was lying beneath the truck. With her belly to the ground, she strained to look behind her and caught a glimpse of the SUV's tires coming to a halt directly behind the truck. Seconds later, she saw two pairs of feet hit the ground and walk toward her. She heard the doors of the truck open, followed by voices. After hearing the doors slam shut, she thought she might be safe when suddenly a head poked underneath the truck. The person looked directly at her.

"Who the fuck are you?"

Scared to death, Andy sucked in a quick breath. Her voice was gone.

From the other side of the truck, an unseen pair of hands grabbed her right arm and shoulder and dragged her out from underneath. Andy let out a scream of terror.

"I'm no one...please! They kidnapped me...!"

Tossed to the ground next to the curb, she looked up, but the person who had grabbed her stood directly between her and the sun, and she couldn't see his face. The second person, the one who had spoken to her, drew up beside his comrade. They stared at her for a moment before speaking to each other in Spanish. Seconds later, one of them aimed a rifle of some sort directly at her head.

Instinctively, Andy held up her arms to cover her head and face, morbidly expecting the sound of a gunshot at any second. But instead, two sets of arms grabbed her and dragged her across the ground and into the backseat of the SUV. It all happened so fast, she didn't have time to scream.

Her journey down the rabbit hole continued.

* * *

Life is what happens to you while you're busy making other plans…

Ben's mother said this often, repeating the famous quote from a John Lennon song. Despite being the stereotypical homemaker, Mrs. Kelly had been a smart woman, much smarter than her son had given her credit for. Ben had taken his mother for granted while all of his respect went to his father. Mr. Kelly worked for the Department of Defense and travelled the world to support his family, and in the eyes of his son, he was a hero. Cooking, laundry, and running errands, the things his mother labored over day after day, simply could not compete.

Life is what happens to you while you're busy making other plans…

Now, he could hear his mother's voice repeating the words. Karen, his sister, had always appreciated their mother more. But now it was Ben who was finally listening to his mother from beyond the grave.

The summer of the outbreak was supposed to be their family vacation to New Mexico. Jim and his family were going along as well, and at age thirteen and fourteen, the two cousins were so excited about whitewater rafting on the Rio Grande that they could talk of little else that spring. Years later, they remembered their lost vacation and chose to head in that direction after their escape.

'The plan' consisted only of going to New Mexico, alone. Meeting Andy and her friends had never been part of 'the plan.' But instead of living a quiet life of watching the sun rise and set along the Rio Grande, Ben found himself in the dead of winter driving west on icy Interstate 70, hoping with the smallest of hopes to reach Grand Junction before nightfall.

He didn't want to care so much about another person again in his life, not after what happened the year before. It wasn't part of 'the plan.' But then Life made other plans, which included meeting a girl named Andy, a girl unlike any he had ever met in his life, and that was the end of the discussion. He never intended to feel for anyone they way he did for her, but there it was. Stubborn, compassionate, beautiful, and the most intriguing person he had ever met, she had slowly, yet unknowingly, bewitched him from the very first day they'd met. The first month of their acquaintance, he had resisted acknowledging her effect on him, but with each passing day his resistance gradually wore down. And now the thought of her being held captive by ruthless strangers who wanted nothing more than to bargain with her life for material exchange was beyond bearing.

And so he drove alone as the windshield wipers shoved the wind-driven snow away, his best friend and cousin staying behind because he himself had fallen for a girl equally as worthy as Andy in his eyes. Ben couldn't fault Jim for wanting to stay behind with Morgan. Together, they had passed through the threshold into adulthood where meeting the right girl was everything. Morgan was dear to his cousin and more fragile than Andy, not only in terms of her physical state but emotionally too, and with her best friend inexplicably gone, she needed Jim to get her through the last few weeks of her pregnancy.

Brian, meanwhile, had made the responsible choice. He followed his obligations as brother and friend to stay behind in Aspen until it was the right time for him and Susan to leave and follow Jim, Charlie, and Morgan south to New Mexico. Ben had nothing but the utmost respect for Brian, but it was difficult to accept him as a friend knowing how much Brian wanted Andy for himself. The mere fact that the two were rivals was truly regrettable. Far inferior young men had never affected Ben the way Brian had. He was decent and hardworking and deserved to be happy. But why in the world did he have to pick the same girl?

And so Ben battled through the weather alone, listening to the CD that Andy had made for him months earlier: a mixture of classical music and classic rock from the 1970s and '80s that his father listened to as a child and young adult. Aerosmith, Pink Floyd, and Metallica mingled seamlessly with Bach, Vivaldi, and Beethoven as the mile markers on the Interstate passed by. The music evoked memories of both the recent and distant past and gave Ben a feeling of overwhelming sadness, yet he couldn't turn it off.

The road conditions were unforgiving. Ice coated the Interstate like a skating rink, and without local government to salt the roads, efficiently or otherwise, Ben knew the conditions wouldn't improve unless the weather gave him a break. The speedometer read 40 mph on a highway meant for much higher speeds, which did nothing to improve his mood. The journey was fatiguing, and he nearly fell asleep behind the wheel as Grand Junction approached. The snow eventually stopped, but nightfall had come. Dark and cold, Ben had no idea where to begin. Mikhail had confessed a couple of names but nothing else. And without a soul in sight to ask, there was nothing to do but wait until morning and hope to find a place to sleep. Even if he wanted to start knocking on people's doors in the middle of the night, his body was too exhausted to try.

Chapter XII

15 January 2021

Morgan managed to get a few hours of sleep the night before, but it had been a restless sleep. The baby had been kicking all night, reminding her that she would soon have another person to worry about. As dawn approached through her bedroom window, the harsh reality of the entire situation had become shockingly real. Today she was leaving Aspen, a place that she had grown to love despite the friction among its leaders.

As she rose out of bed and glanced down at her belly, Morgan told herself that women had raised children in worse conditions and in times when modern conveniences like disposable diapers or baby monitors had not yet been invented. If women living in caves could manage, she could too. She would have to.

But now Andy was gone.

Morgan didn't want to think about it, but the reality was that her best friend could be lying dead somewhere, killed by her captors or a victim of hypothermia in the cruel winter cold. With her whereabouts unknown, as well as the people who took her, the possibilities of what happened to Andy or what she could be experiencing were she still alive were endless. It was maddening to think of.

Morgan reassured herself that if anyone could find Andy, it was

Ben. He seemed to be blessed with the ability to survive anything. Whatever had occurred in his past, events that Jim still refused to reveal, surviving it surely required certain faculties, both mental and physical, that went beyond anything the average person possessed.

The group quickly scattered. Brian had returned to his home the night before, but Susan had stayed over to spend more time with Charlie. An hour after sunrise and with a heavy heart, she said her goodbyes.

"I'll see you in the spring," she whispered into Charlie's ear before giving him the most intense kiss either of them had ever experienced. Morgan was almost embarrassed to witness her younger brother kissing a girl that way, but she also understood what it was like to feel as he did. She had told him the night before that he could stay in Aspen with Susan, but Charlie refused to budge on his decision, and secretly, she was glad.

After giving both Morgan and Jim a hug, Susan mounted her horse she had kept in the garage overnight, and rode back to her home.

Shortly thereafter and without saying goodbye to anyone else, Morgan, Charlie, and Jim left Aspen for New Mexico.

* * *

Ben hated Grand Junction. He hated it because it was everything that Aspen wasn't, and yet he had to be there. And he hated spending the night in a cold and filthy motel that likely had been in that condition for decades prior. Were it not for the wonderful layers of goose down filling in his thick winter coat, he would have easily shivered all night and lose any chance of getting the sleep he needed.

But Ben would keep doing things he hated for as long as it took to find Andy.

At dawn, he immediately began his search for two people named Jake Andrews and Kyle Hartzell. In the lobby of the motel, under a pile of six-year-old newspapers and a thick layer of dust, he found a 2015 edition phonebook for Grand Junction and its surrounding areas, as well as a detailed road map of the city. He flipped through it, searching first under 'Andrews' and finding exactly what he feared: almost one hundred people listed with that last name. There was no way of knowing which home was Jake's, since his name would not be in the phonebook; only his parents' names would be listed. Ben tried 'Hartzell' next and had more luck. There were only three people with that last name living in Grand Junction that year, and if luck played any part, Kyle might still be living at home. There was, of course, the possibility that both Kyle and Jake weren't from Grand Junction but had migrated to the city after the outbreak, but Ben could only hope that wasn't the case. If it was, he had other ways of finding them. Unfortunately, this would involve questioning others in the city, which could get back to both Jake and Kyle and drive them out of town.

Ben had brought food from Aspen, and after a quick bite in the truck, he used the map to maneuver his way to the neighborhood where the first 'Hartzell' in the phone book lived. The home at the first address was empty, as was the second. Discouraged, he went to the third house and knocked on the door. This time, someone answered.

* * *

The two boys who grabbed Andy took her directly from Santa Monica to Malibu along the coast. Unsure if her new captors spoke English, she racked her exhausted brain for some Spanish words she'd learned long ago in the seventh grade. She repeated "agua," "comida," and "baño" until they mercifully threw her a bottle of warm water and two oranges. She sucked down the water in seconds and ravaged the oranges. By the time she finished the second, they had reached Malibu, where she was dropped off at a large beachfront home. Apparently, people's taste for living in expensive homes remained constant, regardless if it was a winter chateau in Colorado or a prized beachfront property in Southern California.

Prior to leaving the house, Andy's captors received a small bag of something that she could not identify, and she realized she had been traded yet again. Inside the home were five people, but only one spoke to her. His name was Jeremy, and Andy vaguely recognized him from somewhere that she was unable to immediately place. After a few minutes, however, she realized why he looked familiar. He had appeared in a few TV movies as a child actor.

Great, more celebrities…

After her previous experiences with spoiled children who had evolved into grotesque teenagers, the last thing Andy wanted to contend with was another person with a similar history. But Jeremy barely spoke to her, and when he did, it was always direct and to the point. He wasn't particularly mean to her, but he wasn't pleasant either, and he forced her at gunpoint into one of the bedrooms and locked her inside for two days and nights. An explanation was never given despite her desperate queries.

Andy considered every escape imaginable but was thwarted at every attempt. There was the bedroom window, but the drop to the ground on the beach below was at least thirty feet. Then there was the bedroom door, which proved to be incredibly sturdy. When she tried kicking it, it refused to budge, and she received a short but fierce scolding from Jeremy in return. During the first hour inside the room, she searched high and low for objects that could aid an escape, but the room was virtually empty: a double bed with sheets, pillows, and blanket, two hand towels in the bathroom, a tiny bit of toilet paper on the spool, and an old toothbrush that she dared not use inside an otherwise empty medicine cabinet.

She slept a lot and ate a little. In the morning and evening, a plate of food was delivered by someone other than Jeremy. The amount of food was meager but the quality was good. She had fresh fish, eggs, and fruit that didn't upset her stomach. Someone obviously wanted to keep her alive and in decent physical condition.

She got angry at times and paced around the room, often talking aloud to herself and asking what she had done to deserve being in the situation she was in. Other moments were more pensive. Her friends remained at the forefront of her worries, but when she thought about her parents and her life years before the virus, she felt strangely better. Before falling asleep each night, music her mother once performed played over and over in her head.

Around four in the afternoon on the third day, there was a perfunctory knock on her door before it opened. Jeremy came inside and handed her a pistol, the same model Glock she'd left behind in Aspen.

"It's not loaded, but you'll need it for tonight."

"What for?"

"You'll find out soon."

He turned and left the room without another word.

* * *

The Hartzell residence in Grand Junction had mercifully remained habited by Mr. and Mrs. Hartzell's children, Kyle and Amy. Amy was young, only ten, and probably a nice girl on her own accord, but her brother Kyle was someone to be reckoned with. Though he was courteous and polite enough, from the very beginning he refused to discuss anything regarding his 'business,' as he called it.

"I buy and trade things and people. That's how I keep my sister and I fed," he explained straightforwardly. "If I start telling the friends of the people that I trade where they are, that wouldn't be good for business, would it?"

Kyle spoke in a manner that reminded Ben of how a stern police officer once spoke to his mother when she had been pulled over for speeding. Civil yet firm and authoritative. And Kyle seemed to have no scruples about what he had done to Andy, which led Ben to believe he had done it before.

When it became apparent that they had reached an impasse, Ben briefly considered using little Amy as leverage by grabbing her and holding her at gunpoint, but his conscience got the better of him. Doing such a thing would make him no different than Kyle or Nataliya or Garrett, and that was something he couldn't live with. So he did the only thing left to do—he bargained.

"I'll tell you a location where you can find a ton of gas if you tell me where you took Andy."

Gas was obviously the magic word.

"How much gas?" Kyle demanded.

They had been standing outside the front of his home up to this point. Ben asked if they could go inside to continue their discussion, which Kyle allowed. The house itself was modest, nothing compared to the mansion Ben had left behind in Aspen, but it was warm thanks to a roaring fire in the fireplace and a few propane space heaters. There were boxes and brown paper bags everywhere in the living room, all taped and sealed to keep the contents inside well-hidden. Things Kyle was probably trading and bargaining with, Ben assumed.

In the kitchen, Kyle spread out a Colorado state map on the counter.

"Show me where," he demanded curtly.

"If I show you, how will I know that you're telling me the truth about where Andy is?"

Kyle shrugged nonchalantly.

"You'll just have to trust me."

"I don't trust anyone I don't know…much less a human trafficker."

"I could say the same for you. You could be lying about the gas."

"True," Ben admitted. "But it's not close to here, and I won't be making my way there anytime soon, so I'm not losing anything by telling you. But you, you have something to lose by telling me where Andy is, so you're more likely to lie."

Again, they seemed to be at an impasse. But unbeknownst to Ben, Kyle was in great need of gasoline at the moment, and protecting the location of where he'd taken Andy was rapidly losing its importance.

"Salt Lake City," Kyle said, ultimately relenting.

"Where exactly?" Ben pressed.

Kyle flipped over the map, which displayed neighboring Utah. Within the small inset at the bottom was a detailed map of Salt Lake City. Kyle pointed to an intersection of two major roads south of the airport.

"I took her there, but she probably won't be there now. Merchandise moves fast."

Ben cringed at the word 'merchandise,' but he kept his cool. Moral altercations would accomplish nothing at this point, so he turned the map back over to the Colorado side and kept his end of the bargain. He pointed to Glenwood Springs, a small town forty miles northwest of Aspen where I-70 and State Highway 82 intersected.

"Here. There's a small regional airport just south of the town. It's called Glenwood Springs Municipal Airport. You'll find the gas there."

The conversation ended and Ben quickly left the house, taking the map without bothering to ask. He figured it was payment for the hassle and his time, which he knew was working against him. After starting the engine of his truck, which was sitting along the curb a few houses away on the quiet neighborhood road, he caught a glimpse in his rearview mirror of Amy running toward him. She had been in the living room during his entire conversation with her brother, listening to everything but saying nothing. But now she scurried down the sidewalk and approached the driver's side window with a piece of paper in one hand.

Ben quickly rolled down the window.

"What is it?"

"My brother lied," she said, catching her breath. "He didn't take her to Salt Lake City. He took her here."

She held out the piece of paper. Ben snatched it from her a little too forcefully and read it. There was an address scribbled in black ink.

"Las Vegas?" he muttered aloud.

"I'm sorry my brother lied to you. He lies to everyone."

Ben pulled his eyes off the paper and looked down at the girl who had just done him an enormous favor. She was a tiny girl for her age, though most children these days were malnourished. Her hair was parted into two long, stringy ponytails, and her round face was highlighted by bright green eyes that reminded Ben of Andy's. He looked at her with a mixture of gratitude and sadness. Sadness that her brother was the kind of person he was.

"Thank you for telling me the truth, Amy."

"Was she your girlfriend? The girl my brother took?"

The question caught Ben off-guard. He blinked at first, and then slowly shook his head.

"No, she's just a friend. A very good friend."

"I hope you find her."

"Me too."

Just as he was about to pull away, he looked back at Amy, hesitated, then put the truck back into park.

"You know, Amy, you don't have to stay here with your brother. I know a place where you can go and be with good people who will help you."

But Amy looked doubtful. She frowned and said, "I can't leave my brother, even if he is a liar and kidnaps people. He's still my brother, and he takes care of me."

Ben nodded. He understood. Still, he grabbed an old pen from inside the glove compartment and scribbled down something on the corner of the paper Amy had given him. He then ripped off the section with his writing and handed it to her.

"What's this?"

"It's the name of a town in New Mexico. If you change your mind, you can find my friends there. It's pretty far away, but I'm sure you can find a way there. Ask for someone named Jim or Maria. There's hardly anyone left in the town except my friends, so you should find them easily. Tell them how you helped me and they'll take care of you." Then in a stern voice, he added, "Just don't tell your brother, okay? Don't tell anyone."

Amy shook her head firmly, her eyes dancing with hope.

"I won't. I swear!"

"Good. Thanks again, Amy. You better get back inside before

your brother suspects anything. But remember to hide that piece of paper. Or just memorize it and throw it away."

"Okay, I will…bye!"

"Take care."

As Ben drove off, he watched in the rearview mirror as the girl ran back to her house and wondered if he would ever see her again. He also wondered if he had made a mistake by revealing his friends' location to a ten-year-old girl he hardly knew. But his instincts were telling him that he had done the right thing, and from experience, his instincts had never failed him. Only when he ignored them did he run into trouble.

Roughly five hundred miles of highway sat between Grand Junction and Las Vegas. Ben had more than enough gas to take him that far. He just hoped he was going in the right direction. Once the snowy roads of Colorado and eastern Utah passed, Ben kept the speedometer at 80 mph despite the fuel inefficiency of driving at such a speed through the Rockies. He made one stop in the majestic landscape of southwestern Utah to go to the bathroom, and by early afternoon on the fifteenth, he reached Las Vegas.

Ben had witnessed firsthand both the immediate and long-term effects of neglect on a large city's infrastructure. Crumbling roads, broken windows in dark homes and buildings, and downed telephone lines became the new landscape of post-virus America. The often unseen and underappreciated labor of millions of blue collar American workers had kept the nation running, and with their absence, a gradual decay ensued. In Las Vegas, with its distinctive skyline once ablaze with the glitter and glitz of every color imaginable, this deterioration was even starker.

Ben had only one stop to make. I-15 was still cluttered with abandoned cars that had become piles of rust and rubber. He skillfully swerved between them before exiting onto East Flamingo Road. Moments later, he pulled into the front entrance of the Bellagio, passing the famed nine-acre lake with its fountains that once mesmerized millions of tourists. Now, it was nothing more than a foul smelling pond, its stench wafting thickly through the air. Ben left his truck parked near the overly-grand hotel entrance and ran inside.

It was cool and dark. Ben scurried beyond quiet gaming tables and slot machines, their seizure-inducing lights long extinguished. Winding his way through the maze of the lobby floor, he found an "Employees Only" staircase that led to the top floor of the hotel. After climbing nearly forty floors, he found the correct penthouse suite. With his right hand, he grabbed hold of the loaded pistol tucked into the back of his jeans before knocking on the door. When it finally opened, he aimed the pistol directly in front of him.

* * *

16 January 2021

Apparently, Saturday night was still a busy night in L.A. In the backseat of a late model Mercedes, Andy stared numbly outside as the car headed east from Malibu on the Santa Monica Freeway. The sun was descending over the horizon behind her in the rear window. Two other people, two older boys, were in the front seat. She had seen both at the house in Malibu, though neither had spoken a word to her. She had no idea where they were going, and the continued uncertainty wore on her nerves. More than once along the drive she considered jumping out of the car. It wouldn't hurt too badly to jump out of a moving vehicle going 70 mph, would it? Even while wearing handcuffs?

The Mercedes exited the freeway and headed south on I-110 for a brief moment before approaching the University of Southern California. After the campus passed by on the right, the Mercedes took another turn south. People were crowded everywhere on both sides of the road, and they all appeared to be moving in the same direction: to the Coliseum.

Built in the early 1920s, the Los Angeles Memorial Coliseum had the distinction of being the only stadium in the world to host the Olympic Games twice, in 1932 and 1984, as well as both the Super Bowl and the World Series. Home of many L.A.-based teams over the years, including the Dodgers, Raiders, and Rams, the Coliseum was the one and only home of the USC Trojans since construction finished in 1923. With a capacity just over 93,000, it wasn't the largest stadium in the country by a long shot, but no one could argue the richness of its history. Declared a National Historic Landmark the day before the opening ceremonies of the 1984 Summer Olympics, it was originally built as a memorial for veterans of World War I. Tonight, however, it would not be showcasing any sport. Instead, it would live up to its moniker inspired by the original Coliseum in Rome, as it had done every Saturday night for the past year.

Sitting in the back seat with the empty Glock resting beside her, Andy watched helplessly as the Mercedes headed toward the stadium. It maneuvered its way around the front of the stadium, passing the two bronze nude statues of a headless male and female athlete at the main gate, then encircled the entire south side of the stadium before pulling into the a rear gate near the west side. Throngs of people coming from every direction were moving toward the front entrance as though they were bring drawn inside by some unseen force. Then suddenly, the Mercedes disappeared into a dark tunnel under the stadium. Moments later, the car stopped and the engine quieted, but the headlights remained on to provide light.

"Get out," the driver ordered.

Andy had no choice but to obey. The other young man in the passenger's seat stepped outside and gestured for her to follow. Had he and the driver not been armed, she might have made a run for it, but as she descended further into the underbelly of the stadium with her hands clasped in front of her and holding a useless gun, she could feel any chance of escape evaporating.

They reached the locker room formerly used by opposing teams playing the Trojans and went inside. With the exception of a single light bulb on the ceiling, the room was dark. There were seven other people inside; five handcuffed like Andy and sitting on benches near the lockers and two standing over them with rifles and keeping guard. These two nodded to the young man leading Andy inside, indicating that they all knew each other. Of everyone in the room, Andy was the only female.

"Sit down," one of the two armed young men ordered Andy, and again she grudgingly obeyed and took a seat at the end of a bench beside a frail boy who could not have been more than twelve.

"What time is it?" the other guard asked the one who had brought Andy inside.

"Almost seven-thirty."

"Let's go grab a drink. We've got time."

The three young men left the locker room and locked the door behind them, leaving Andy alone with the five other captives. She turned to the frail boy sitting next to her.

"What's going on? What are we doing here?"

The boy didn't answer right away. In fact, his eyes remained fixed on the floor, even when Andy spoke to him. His face was deathly pale and his forehead was sweating. Andy turned to the other four and saw the same catatonic expressions on their faces.

"Why am I here?" she asked the boy again, this time more softly.

"Shut up!" he suddenly snapped back violently.

Startled, Andy slowly inched away from him until she reached the end of the bench. Confused and scared, she looked back at the others and implored them with her eyes to explain. When no one answered or even glanced her way, she finally got up and moved to stand firmly in front of them.

"Somebody better tell me what's going on, now!"

"Or what, you'll kill us? We're all dead already, you included. So please leave us alone."

Andy stared dumbfounded at the boy who had just spoken. He was less frail than the first, but still miserable looking. She eyed him with disbelief and slowly dropped to her knees until her gaze was level with his.

"Please," she begged. "Until a few days ago, I'd never been to Los Angeles in my entire life. I don't know this city or anyone here. I was kidnapped from my home in Colorado and passed around between different gangs or groups or whatever until I ended up here, handcuffed and carrying this gun, and I have no idea why. Can you please, *please* tell me what's going on?"

The boy stared back at her, dark circles hanging beneath his lifeless eyes. He blinked once, then twice before finally answering.

"It's a game, and we're the losers."

"I don't understand…"

"It's called 'One Shot' because we each get a bullet. Just one."

And so the rules were painfully explained to Andy. One at a time, each of them would be taken up to the field where thousands of spectators would be waiting for them, and while still in handcuffs, they would be forced onto the field. At this point, one of the eight "referees" would load the Glock with a single bullet. The captive would then be ordered to stand on the ten-yard line on the east end of the field. At the thirty-yard line on the west end of the field stood the captive's opponent, but instead of a pistol with only one bullet, the opponent, wearing body armor, was given a fully-automatic M4 rifle and four magazines of thirty rounds each.

The goal of "One Shot" was brutally simple: to determine who could kill the other first within two minutes. Both the captive and the opponent were allowed to move around the field, but neither could cross the fifty-yard line at midfield. This rule was the captive's sole advantage, for the opponent, with far superior firepower, would want to get as close to the captive as possible. The captive, meanwhile, spent most of the two minutes dodging bullets and thinking little of the single bullet in his Glock. If the captive managed to survive these two minutes, he would have to undergo two more rounds. After surviving the third round, the captive was free, at least in theory.

As Andy listened to the rules being explained, it became horribly clear why everyone in the room appeared they way they did: they knew they were already dead.

"How long has this been going on?"

Her own voice had become weak and hollow.

"Every Saturday for more than a year."

"Has anyone ever survived the game?"

The boy who had just finished explaining the rules gave her a look that required no further answer. But he said it anyway.

"No. Never."

"Never?"

He said nothing more. There was nothing more to say.

"And people come to watch other people die?"

The boy responded with the faintest shrug. "It's entertainment."

"But I still don't understand. Who runs the game?"

But before Andy received an answer, the locker room door opened again and two guards returned. One pointed to the frail boy sitting on the bench that Andy had first attempted to speak to.

"You're up."

The boy could hardly stand, and his knees buckled with fear when he did. He couldn't have weighed more than a hundred pounds, and he stood little more than five feet tall.

The boy didn't look back as he left the room, and no one else seemed to react to the sound of the door locking shut after he left.

A minute later, the noise of the crowd began to swell from above. It was interrupted by scattered rounds of gunfire, and within another minute, the crowd erupted. Andy looked at the four other captives, but none reacted to the noise. Instead, one sat praying, his eyes squeezed tight and his lips barely moving. Another rocked back and forth ever so slightly with his knees hugged to his chest. The boy who had spoken to Andy was completely still now, like a statue. He seemed to be the one most at peace with his fate.

Soon after, the door opened again, and the two guards returned. They gestured to the boy who was praying.

"You're next."

And the cycle repeated itself. The next captive disappeared, followed shortly after by a wave of noise from the crowd, then gunshots, then a burst of cheers. It was after this second cycle when Andy finally grasped the hopelessness of the situation, and she joined the remaining three boys in silent agony. Everything that had led up to this point, from being kidnapped in Aspen four days earlier to narrowly missing stray bullets on Wilshire Boulevard to spending two days locked inside a bedroom overlooking the ocean in Malibu, none of this compared to the overwhelming despair that now consumed her entire body and mind. It transcended tears, for even tears could release sorrow and make way for hope. But all hope had gone, and this was it. This was the end. Despite the daily reminder of the mortality of the human race, Andy somehow believed that because she had escaped death more than once, she would live forever. But rather than a day many years from now during the quietness of old age, today would mark the end of her life, a random day in January five months before her twentieth birthday. The minutes that remained were just a formality in the shape of public humiliation. She would die amidst the cheers of thousands of strangers who knew nothing about her, not even her name.

The third captive was soon taken away, followed by the fourth. Only two people remained, Andy and the boy who had spoken to her. Soon the locker room would be empty.

As the noise from the crowd began to grow above them once again, Andy gritted her teeth and willed herself not to give up. Her eyes frantically searched the room for something that could help her flee. She stood up and looked inside each of the lockers but found them all empty.

"You won't find anything," the boy muttered in a flat, monotone voice.

But Andy ignored him. "When they come back, we should try to make a run for it."

But the boy shook his head. "They'll find us," he said with utter certainty.

"Don't you want to live?" Andy cried.

The boy's eyes met Andy's. His expression was resolute. "No, I'm ready to die. There's nothing worth living for anymore."

Andy blinked. "You don't mean that. There's always something worth living for."

"Like what?"

"Like family and friends."

"I don't have any. They're all dead or gone."

"You can make new friends."

"Not here. Unless you're a part of a gang, you're nothing."

"Then leave. Leave L.A."

But the boy shook his head firmly. "No, it's too late. It's time to go."

The door abruptly opened and the two guards entered to retrieve yet another victim. One looked at the boy and said, "I hope you last longer than the others. Folks aren't too happy with the performances tonight."

The boy said nothing as he slowly rose from the bench and walked toward the door with more dignity than the previous four captives combined. Before disappearing through the doorway, he looked back at Andy one last time.

"I'll see you soon."

And with that, the door slammed shut, leaving Andy alone with the haunting echo of those final words.

* * *

Ben pushed his way through the crowd to get as close to the field as possible. He'd already missed witnessing four innocent young boys get slaughtered to death, though he had heard the roars of delight from the crowd several blocks from the stadium. Now he feared that he was too late.

Every spectator entered the stadium through a single gate on the western side of the Coliseum, and everyone was checked for weapons by one of a dozen young men heavily armed themselves. Though the evening was unseasonably warm, even by L.A. standards, Ben wore a baggy sweatshirt over his T-shirt. He needed someplace to conceal his M4, which he had separated into two pieces. The lower receiver was jammed into his right sleeve and the upper receiver in his left. He had just one thirty-round magazine with him, which he had slipped into his sock underneath his jeans. When he passed through the gate, one of the entry guards asked him to lift up his sweatshirt, which he did without hesitation. Satisfied and anxious to let the remaining stragglers through, the guard quickly waved Ben off without a second look. Once beyond the entrance, Ben scrambled to a secluded corner beneath the stadium in the perimeter ring outside the numbered gates and quickly reassembled the M4. He removed his sweatshirt and inserted the magazine before concealing the weapon by wrapping the sweatshirt around it.

Inside, the crowd steered clear of the seats on the entire eastern side of the stadium. The reason became immediately clear to Ben when he saw the fifth captive take his position on the field as two minutes on the scoreboard began its countdown. The opponent simply rained bullets toward the east while the captive ran frantically back and forth. Though the opponent was aiming for the captive, most of the one-hundred and twenty bullets he fired lodged into the peristyle steps behind the eastern end zone and in front of the long-extinguished Olympic Torch. The single nine millimeter round in the captive's Glock posed little threat to the spectators, for not only did most of the captives fail to get the round off before they were gunned down, but unbeknownst to everyone except the unknown controllers of "One Shot," the single bullet was always a blank.

Standing now in the lower section on the southwest side of the stadium and thirteen rows up from the fifteen-yard line, Ben had a good vantage point of the field and the opponent. He arrived just in time to see the fifth captive become yet another victim of the gruesome sport as several bullets entered the boy's torso. Ben flinched. Violence of this sort was not new to him, but it was something he would never grow accustomed to.

"How many rounds have they had so far?" he asked a bystander as the body of the fifth captive was dragged off the field.

"Five," the bystander said as the noise of the crowd began to die down.

"All boys?" Ben asked as calmly as he could manage despite his racing heart. He was terrified to hear the answer.

"Yeah, but there's supposed to be a girl tonight, I heard," the bystander remarked nonchalantly.

"Really?" Ben replied casually though his internal reaction was mixed. He had prayed the information he had received earlier that day had been wrong, but at least now he knew he wasn't too late.

"I think she's the last one, so she'll probably be next," the bystander continued.

Just then, the crowd began to make noise as the next and final victim stepped onto the field. Though she was more than a hundred yards away, Ben could tell instantly by her stature and gait that it was Andy.

Chapter XIII

After passing through the end of the dark and dingy tunnel that both the USC Trojans and the visiting team once shared prior to emerging on the field, Andy stepped outside and was greeted by the jeering crowd. In the distance, the latest victim of "One Shot" was being dragged off the field by two of the referees. As she crossed the field from the west end to the east, she passed her opponent who was waiting for her to get into position. Tall and broad-shouldered, he looked every bit the ruthless killer he was. Too busy reloading his M4 with a fresh magazine, he didn't look at Andy as she walked by.

Her heart was pounding so fast that she could feel the blood pulse through her head, her neck, and even the arteries in her wrists. The noise of the crowd behind her and to her right and left was thunderous. Her eardrums were not accustomed to the strain, and a sudden memory of a discussion with Morgan months earlier in New Mexico resurfaced.

Where could everyone be?

Apparently, everyone was in Los Angeles, where people flocked to the Coliseum every Saturday night to witness a depraved spectacle of bloodshed. More than fifty thousand people were cheering at the anticipation of her death.

Daylight was long gone, but the lights of the stadium kept the field well-lit. As Andy approached midfield, she swore she heard someone calling out her name. Her eyes darted all around, but it was no use. There were too many people; her nerves had tricked her hearing. In her right hand, which was still handcuffed to her left, she held the Glock, though she would have been just as well off carrying a brick. A referee approached her and snatched the pistol out of her hands. He placed one round in the chamber—one *blank* round. Andy's eyes narrowed on him with a mixture of contempt and disbelief.

"You like watching people die? Haven't you seen enough death?"

The referee, however, dealt her a repugnant smirk as he handed her back her pistol and quickly returned to the sidelines.

Alone amongst thousands, Andy looked up at the scoreboard. It still read "00:58" from the end of the previous round. She moved slowly past midfield, her heart pumping nearly two hundred beats per minute.

So this is how I die.

Her palms were sweating profusely, and she switched the Glock from her right hand to her left in order to dry her hand on the jeans she'd been wearing for four days.

I will die in these clothes…these dirty jeans, this filthy shirt…my hands bound together like an animal…

As her palm pressed firmly against the right front pocket, she felt something small and hard inside by the outer seam. Carefully, as she continued her death march to the ten-yard line, she reached inside and retrieved a small object. When she looked down at her hand to see what it was, her heart skipped a beat. It was a single 9x19mm bullet, and Andy instantly recalled how she had shoved it into her pocket during her last hunting trip in Colorado when empting a box of ammo. All her magazines had been full and her pocket was the only place to put it at the time.

It was amazing how such a tiny object could create such an intense spark of hope, and an unexpected idea formed in her mind. She seized the bullet, careful not to be seen by one of the referees, and stuck it inside her mouth underneath her tongue. Then she marched, more quickly now, to her position on the ten-yard line.

Before turning to face her opponent and the surrounding crowd, she closed her eyes, took a deep breath through her nose, and let it out. Then, she opened her eyes and saw the scoreboard. A split-second later, the clock changed to reflect "02:00".

She turned around.

* * *

When Andy crossed the fifty yard line as she headed toward the east end of the field, the noise of the crowd swelled. Ben vainly called out Andy's name three times before giving up. To make matters worse, his view of the field became blocked as people's heads and arms started flailing about. In a move he would later regret, he shoved his way forward and managed to reach the thirteenth row before stepping out into the aisle to gain a better line of sight to the opponent. But the step downward from off the bleachers erased any chance of that. Frantic, he pushed through other spectators in the hopes that he could make his way to the first row and onto the field, but the first four rows closest to the field around the entire western half of the stadium were packed so tightly with spectators that it was impossible to get any closer.

With time running out, Ben made a split-second decision to scramble back up the aisle staircase and scurry across one of the higher rows that was less crowded. He shot a quick look at the press box above him and saw that there were people inside. Likely the anonymous people who organized the entire game. Whoever they were, Ben prayed that their reaction time to what he was about to do would be slow.

Crossing over from Section 9 to Section 8, he glanced down at the field and saw Andy approaching the ten-yard line. There wasn't much time. He weaved his way through the crowd to Section 7, cursing at people who refused to move. Then he cursed at himself for not adequately gauging the situation soon enough.

The scoreboard flickered "02:00" on the clock.

He pushed and shoved and yelled his way to the outer edge of the crowd in Section 7 at midfield, the furthest east any of the spectators dared watch without being in the opponent's range of fire. As he turned ninety degrees to face north and bounded down the aisle of stairs that divided Section 7 in half, he heard the first round of gunfire, followed by many more in rapid succession. Then, just seconds later, there was nothing but a riotous roar from the crowd. Panicking, he looked up and saw Andy lying on the ground. She wasn't moving.

Collapsing to the ground as his concealed M4 fell beside him, Ben shoulders began to shake.

* * *

When the first shot went off, Andy bolted to the right and immediately aimed at the opponent while sprinting sideways and released her single blank round. She continued to sprint north to the sidelines. A rapid succession of shots followed. A single bullet grazed her back and left a bloody, scorched line three inches in length across her scapula, but adrenaline prevented her from feeling any pain. After another burst of shots, she fell to the ground, rolled over once in the overgrown grass, and came to a stop on her right side.

And then she waited.

As the crowd roared, she maneuvered the bullet inside her mouth and spat it out toward her hands lying near her face, the Glock still in her right. After retrieving the bullet with her left hand, she discreetly pulled back on the slide release on her pistol, carefully inserted the bullet into the chamber, and then slowly let the slide release move forward.

Out of the corner of her eye, she sensed someone approaching. The pain in her shoulder finally hit her, but she managed to remain still. She forced her eyes to stare straight ahead in a dead-man's gaze.

Judging by the size of the person approaching, she guessed that it had to be the opponent, the large, husky young man. He was about five yards from her now.

Not yet…

Three yards…

Wait…wait…now!

Like a jack-in-the-box, she sprung upright and faced her opponent squarely and so quickly that any reaction was impossible. Her arms were already outstretched with the front sight of the pistol aimed directly at his forehead. Without hesitation, she pulled the trigger.

The sound of the bullet shattered the drone of the crowd.

The opponent flew violently backward and fell to the ground with an audible thud. The shot had been dead-on, her bullet landing right between the eyes.

David had killed Goliath.

A strange silence fell over the stadium. Even Andy sat frozen for a long moment, her arms still holding the pistol in the same position she'd fired it. Finally, a voice inside her head urged her to move.

Acting entirely on instinct, she scrambled to her feet, awkwardly tucked the pistol into the side of her jeans, and grabbed the M4 lying next to the opponent, averting her eyes from his bloodied face. With her hands still constrained by the handcuffs, she struggled to maintain control of the heavier weapon but could still fire it if she had to.

Suddenly, more gunfire originated off to her left, disrupting her tunnel vision. Her head spun wildly around until she saw someone running toward her.

"Andy!"

The sound of her name was jarring until she realized it was Ben heading toward her after he mortally wounded two referees. As he approached, he immediately grabbed her left arm and pulled her toward the end zone behind her, but the sight of him shocked her.

"Ben! What…?" she stammered.

But there was no time. He yanked at her arm again more forcefully and begged her to move to the east end of the stadium, to the peristyle steps leading to the center arch that held the Olympic Torch and away from everyone else.

"Run, Andy! Run!"

Regaining her senses, Andy turned her back to the crowd and her legs began to move. She followed closely behind Ben as he ran through the end zone and under the goal post.

They didn't look back. The remaining referees ran after them as the unruly crowd began spilling over the sides of the barrier and onto the field. They scrambled up the steps as two of the referees began firing after them with their own weapons, each widely missing his mark. At the top of the steps, Ben continued to sprint beyond the outer gate with Andy only mere strides behind. He looked back once to make sure she was keeping up with him.

They sprinted nearly a mile as Ben guided Andy north toward the USC campus. When they reached Ben's truck parked along a quieter street in the campus area, they quickly climbed in and Ben started the engine. Minutes later, they were heading north on I-110 before exiting onto the San Bernardino Freeway.

Finally safe, the city passed by them in the dark. Neither spoke for many miles until Ben turned north onto I-15 and left the City of Angels behind.

"Are you hurt?" were his first words to her.

"No…no, I'm fine."

Her voice was flat and barely above a whisper. She was staring down at her hands as an uncontrollable barrage of thoughts and visions began to fill her head, and when she closed her eyes, she saw herself pulling the trigger as the opponent flew backward. Then she heard the boy's voice saying to her, *I'll see you soon.* Meanwhile, deep within another corner of her mind, she wondered how the hell she was going to remove her handcuffs.

"I thought you got shot."

At the sound of Ben's voice, Andy opened her eyes and stared straight ahead as the truck's high beams illuminated the darkness of the highway just before it could envelop them.

"No, I faked it."

But as she said this, Ben turned to her and saw in the dim light a blood stain on her back near her shoulder.

"Are you sure?"

He glanced once at the road before taking a closer look. A nearly four-inch square section of her T-shirt was soaked with blood. He reached for it with his right hand, but Andy jerked away the moment he touched her.

"I'm sorry, I'm sorry," he repeated, pulling his hand away.

Shaking now, Andy slowly looked behind her left shoulder. She couldn't see anything, so she reached behind with both hands and winced as her finger hit the wound.

"Let me stop so I can get a better look," said Ben as he began to slow down.

"No, keep going. It's nothing."

But Ben was already applying the brakes. He didn't bother pulling over onto the shoulder. No one else was on the road.

"I said it's nothing," Andy insisted.

"You don't know that, you can't see it."

Andy let out a sigh of annoyance but kept quiet as Ben put the truck into park and turned on the overhead light. Then he carefully pulled downward at the collar of her T-shirt, but that only caused further pain.

"Here, lift up your shirt in the back."

Andy gave him a look.

"Jesus, Andy, now's not the time for modesty. I just want to make sure there's not a bullet lodged in your shoulder."

Agitated, Andy went a step further and pulled her T-shirt completely over her head so that she was wearing only her bra. Out of both annoyance and awkwardness, she avoided looking at Ben and turned her back to him and faced the side window, which gave him a better view of the wound.

The sight of Andy without her shirt gave Ben a moment's pause, but he quickly recovered and leaned in closer toward her. With one hand, he brushed her long hair away from the wound and gently felt around her shoulder with the other. He felt Andy tense beneath his hands from the pain, but she remained still and didn't make a sound.

"It's just a graze. A deep graze, but that's all. It'll definitely leave a scar."

The relief in Ben's voice was unmistakable, but he still insisted on treating the wound right then. Andy made no move to object, and in fact, she began to relax a bit as Ben used the contents of the first aid kit he kept behind his seat to clean out the gash and cover it with gauze.

"That'll do for now. We'll change it when we get to Santa Rosa."

"Santa Rosa?" Andy repeated as she put her shirt back on. "What are you talking about?"

Ben got the truck moving again before answering.

"We left Aspen after you got taken. No one could stay once we found out that Mikhail and Garrett had traded you for drugs."

Andy blinked.

"Drugs? They traded me for drugs?"

Still burning over what Mikhail, Garrett, and the others had done to her, Ben replied with a firm nod. Then, he turned away toward his left and muttered, "Everyone wants drugs."

"So Morgan and Charlie are in New Mexico?"

"By now, yeah. Jim, too. They were going to meet up with Maria."

Andy nodded, satisfied that Maria had been considered as part of this sudden change. However, it bothered her that the decision to leave Aspen had been made without her, though she knew this was a completely irrational reaction. Her friends had done what they thought was best during what were probably terrifying hours and days after her kidnapping. Still, she couldn't help but be a little irritated by it, and with both her mind and body reacting to the severe stress of the events at the Coliseum, she suddenly felt like either crawling out of her own skin or letting out a deafening scream.

"What about Brian and Susan?"

"They're staying in Aspen through the winter. They'll join us in the spring."

"What about their farm? They'll just leave it behind?"

Ben nodded. "Uh-huh. They'll try driving as much of their cattle as possible, but the rest they'll leave behind."

Andy frowned.

"Poor Brian. That farm means so much to him."

And with that remark, Ben lost it.

He slammed on the brakes until the truck came to an abrupt stop once again on the dark, lonely stretch of I-15. Andy let out a yelp as her body flew forward, straining the seat belt across her chest.

"Poor Brian? Poor *Brian*? Are you fuckin' kidding me?"

"What the hell…?" Andy snapped back as she steadied herself.

Ben turned off the engine before squaring his body to hers. He grabbed the shoulder of her seat, leaned forward, and stared directly into her eyes.

"Andy, I just spent the last two days and nights running after you. Do you have any idea how difficult it was to find you? Do you know what kind of people I had to beg information from?"

Despite restraining his frustration and jealousy, he spoke in earnest. This concession, however, was lost on Andy. His outburst only enraged her.

"So what? You want a gold star or something?! I just spent the last *four* days being tossed around between gangs and other strangers with guns, all using me so that I could end up shot to death like a wild animal in front of thousands of crazy people!"

Her voice had become hysterical, but she didn't stop. "And now you expect me to *thank* you? For what? For saving me? Well, fuck you, Ben! *I* saved me…*I* did! *I* shot that guy right between the eyes! *I* killed him!"

As she spat out these last words, she pointed to her chest with both of her constrained hands for emphasis. Then she threw herself back against her seat and looked down at her hands. Her eyes welled up, and she turned away from Ben completely and curled into a ball.

"Just drive, Ben," she mumbled dully as she shut her eyes, spilling tears down her cheeks. "Just drive."

But Ben made no move to obey. Instead, he remained quite still, gazing at her for a long moment as his heart broke over and over. He was angry with himself for thinking only of his own troubles and not realizing the ordeal she had been through. But he was also resentful that she didn't seem to care that he'd found her, or that he was even there at all. He had imagined that she would throw her arms around him and kiss him endlessly after reuniting with him. The worst part, however, was that he knew she didn't deserve any of his resentment. It was only the situation that deserved his contempt.

"When I saw you fall to the ground on the field, I thought that was it. I thought you were dead, and it nearly killed me."

There, I've said it, he thought before restarting the engine.

But Andy hadn't heard him, for she had already fallen asleep. When she didn't answer or make any sound of acknowledgment, Ben looked over and saw the rise and fall of her ribcage as she slept and realized that his words had been spoken in vain, and he doubted that he would ever have the courage to say them again.

He released a sigh and leaned against the window, holding his head with his left hand as the miles passed by.

* * *

When Andy awoke, she noticed the truck wasn't moving. As she blinked her eyes open, she glanced at the clock on the dashboard. It read 4:07, which was based upon the time in Colorado. Thanks to Ben's meticulous care of his truck, she knew it was accurate.

She rolled over and realized that Ben had pulled over the side of the road to take a nap. In the moonlight, she saw that he had reclined his seat as far as it would go and was lying on his back with his arms crossed over his chest. His face was turned slightly toward her.

Her slumber had restored her rationale, and a sudden wave of guilt struck her as she lamented her earlier words to him. Ben was the last person who deserved her anger. What he must have gone through to find her, traveling across hundreds of miles in only two days, she would never know and could only imagine. The feat itself was impressive, and he had done it alone. She should have thanked and hugged him a thousand times for dragging her off the field and getting her out of the city alive. Yet she had scorned him and cursed at him for not reaching her sooner. Yet again, Andy found she was acting in ways toward Ben that belied her true feelings.

Quietly and tenderly, she reached toward him until the rattle of her handcuffs forced her to withdraw. She turned away and opened the door to step outside. Her legs ached and her hunger and thirst were overwhelming. She stretched her legs and glanced back and forth along the dark, abandoned highway before shutting the door. The sound awakened Ben, and by the time she had walked around the front of the truck and opened the driver's door, he was already rubbing his eyes.

"I didn't mean to wake you. I'll drive if you wanna sleep."

Ben looked up at Andy and bobbed his head drowsily.

"All right," he mumbled. "Thanks."

He stepped outside and started to move by her when she grabbed his arm.

"Wait," she uttered before throwing her encumbered arms over his head. "Thank you," she whispered in his ear as she hugged him tightly. "Sorry for earlier."

Suddenly awakened by this unexpected contact, Ben wrapped his arms around her waist and pulled her close to him. He didn't want to let go.

"Thank you for finding me."

He gently pulled her head toward him and kissed her forehead, once then twice.

"I almost died."

"I know," he whispered back, and his whole body ached. He wanted to kiss her and hold her like that for as long as possible, but as suddenly as she had taken hold of him, she pulled away and slipped into the driver's seat.

"Let's get moving," she said crisply in an effort to push back more tears. "Is there any food and water?"

Composing himself after the abrupt break in physical contact, Ben walked to the other side of the truck. "Yeah, there's a bag behind the seat," he answered, climbing in. "You must be starving."

"More than I can ever remember."

They drove in silence as Ben fell back asleep. Andy, however, was wide awake. It was as though all her senses had been heightened. The wound in her shoulder throbbed. Strangely, it didn't bother her but merely reminded her that she was still alive.

The first mile marker she noticed read "157", and shortly after that, she saw signs for Grand Canyon National Park. She glanced at Ben, who was still asleep, before checking the gas gauge, which Jim had recalibrated to reflect the two additional tanks that had been added. The needle currently stood at just over half a tank, which really meant that more than a tank and a half of gas remained, not including the two five-gallon containers in the truck bed. Andy performed a quick mental calculation and determined that there was more than enough gas to get to Santa Rosa.

A quick side trip would be nothing but a frivolous waste of a rare commodity. But then the image of the boy leaving the locker room with his haunting last words to her reentered her mind.

Screw it.

When she reached the exit for State Route 64 heading north, Andy didn't hesitate.

* * *

17 January 2021

"Where are we?"

It was mere minutes after sunrise when Ben awoke. The truck was parked and he realized that Andy was not inside. Stepping outside, he saw that the truck was nowhere near the highway. Then he saw Andy standing in front of the Canyon, several meters away on the observation platform known as Mather Point. The light cast by the rising sun inflamed the layers of rock off to the west that descended more than a mile downward to the earth.

Andy heard the sound of tiny rocks shifting as Ben's footsteps approached.

"It's amazing, isn't it?" she whispered aloud.

Her eyes remained fixed on the majestic view as Ben drew beside her.

"The summer after my mother died, the same summer of the virus, we were supposed to come here for a vacation. It was a Christmas present for my mother from my father. She'd wanted to come here for years, but her concert schedule and my father's practice always seemed to prevent it. But she always talked about bringing me here."

Ben watched Andy intently as she spoke. The gentle morning wind played with her hair, the red-orange light reflecting off her glowing cheeks.

"My father never got to give my mother her present," she continued. "She died two weeks before Christmas. He traded in the three airline tickets to Flagstaff for two tickets to Bermuda, and that was that."

Andy looked down at her foot and kicked at a rock. She let out a tiny laugh and looked back up.

"It's funny…my mother travelled all over the world for her concerts, but the one place she really wanted to come was here, and now I finally understand why."

She looked over at Ben for the first time.

"Have you ever been here before?"

He shook his head.

"No. I've seen plenty of pictures…you know, in magazines and on the Internet."

"But it's not the same as actually seeing it, is it?"

"No. Not even close."

They remained silent, like statues staring at a view that once drew millions, and Andy wished that Susan was there with her camera so she wouldn't have to rely on her eyes and memory to capture the image.

"Wish I had a camera," Ben said suddenly, breaking the silence.

"I was just thinking the same thing."

"Yeah, too bad Susan isn't here."

Andy looked at Ben and opened her mouth to repeat her last words, but she merely smiled and said, "I know."

Ben turned away from the view and looked behind him. Andy had driven off the visitor's parking lot and onto the sidewalks that lead directly to Mather Point. The laws of the road, or National Parks for that matter, no longer applied.

Suddenly, an idea struck Ben.

"Are the keys in the truck?"

"Yeah, I left them in the ignition."

"Did you pass a visitor's center or something like that?"

"Yeah, it's right back there," Andy replied as she gestured toward the direction with her head.

"Good, I'll be right back," he said and headed toward the truck. When he returned about twenty or thirty minutes later, Andy was sitting on the large slab of stone that was elevated off the main ground at the observation point. Her gazed remained fixed on the view.

"I hit the jackpot," Ben remarked as Andy slid off the slab and onto the ground. She saw that he was carrying a plastic bag with its flimsy handles stretched to its limit.

"Yeah? What'd you find?"

"Trail mix and dried fruit in the gift shop at the visitor's center. There were bottles of water too, but all plastic, unfortunately."

Andy nodded. It was always the same problem with water. Over the years, the chemicals in the plastic broke down and contaminated the water, making it undrinkable. Glass-bottled water was like gold, but since its production had been far less than that of plastic, all were gone by now. Trail mix and dried fruit, however, never really went bad, regardless of what the expiration date on the package said. The taste would always be a little stale, but it kept a person alive; the post-virus version of MREs.

"And I found a disposable camera," Ben added as he revealed the bright yellow and black box from behind his back. "The film's probably expired, but it's worth a shot."

He dropped the bag of food to the ground and quickly scanned the instructions on the back of the camera. Then he clicked a few pictures of the scenery before handing the camera to Andy. She grabbed it and snapped a picture of Ben when he wasn't looking. Afterward, he gave her a smirk.

"Thanks a lot."

"My pleasure."

Andy proceeded to take a few more photos of the view before placing the camera on top of the stone slab. She then met Ben at the rail that ran around the perimeter of the observation point used to keep people from falling over the edge. The rail itself was no longer stable after the years of neglect, which Ben cautioned as soon as she approached.

"Just don't lean on it."

They stood there watching the sun rise and its light dancing off the vastness of the landscape.

"So how did you find me?" Andy asked suddenly.

"Well," Ben began, "We all figured that Nataliya and her friends were behind your disappearance, so Jim and I went with Brian to confront her about it. Long story short, Mikhail ended up telling us that you were taken to Grand Junction, and that you had been traded for drugs."

Andy's face filled with disgust as Ben continued.

"I didn't want Jim to come with me and leave Morgan behind. He wanted to come, but I knew he wanted to stay with her more. Charlie was torn, but he chose to go with them rather than stay behind with Susan."

"Of course he did," Andy remarked. "Charlie's too selfless to leave his sister."

"He is," Ben agreed. "Anyway, I left before they did and followed the trail of people that took you to L.A. From Grand Junction, I went to Las Vegas, where you'd been taken next, and then to L.A."

"I don't remember anything from the moment I was kidnapped leaving the hospital in Aspen to the moment I woke up in some warehouse outside L.A. For all I know, I could've been flown on a private jet from Colorado to California. I think I was drugged with chloroform at first and then drugged with other stuff along the way."

Andy glanced down at her left arm and saw that the bruise from the needle had completely faded.

"It was chloroform," Ben confirmed. "I found a bottle of it on the side of the road in the snow where you were taken."

Andy nodded and then recounted for Ben her own journey from the warehouse until being brought to the Coliseum. He listened intensely, stunned by what she had endured.

"How did you know I'd be at the Coliseum?" she asked once she'd finished.

Ben smiled sheepishly, and Andy was once again struck by how handsome he was.

"I didn't. It was total dumb luck. Your trail ran cold at the warehouse, but once I got to L.A. some random people told me about the game. They mentioned that a girl would be 'playing' that night, so I took a stab in the dark and went to the stadium. If it hadn't been for them, I would've missed you."

"But you didn't. You found me and got me out of there."

Ben nodded gravely but said nothing. He didn't want to think about what would've happened had he not made it in time. The fact that he had found her was a miracle, and the relief he felt was immeasurable.

"Maybe I got you out of there, but you shot the guy on the field. How did you do it? I thought they gave you just one bullet."

"There was a bullet in my pocket from one of our hunting trips. I just happened to find it when I got to the field."

Ben's eyes widened. More dumb luck.

"Why didn't you just shoot him with the first bullet?"

"Because I wanted him to think that I didn't have anything left to kill him." Then, after a pause, "I also suspected that the first bullet was a blank."

"A blank? You think so?"

"Yeah, why not? Whoever runs that game doesn't actually want anyone to win, so why risk using a real bullet when no one can tell the difference from a blank."

"You can tell from the recoil. Did it feel different?"

"Honestly, it's all a blur to me. My heart was racing so fast…I barely remember anything."

"Well, it was a hell of a shot you made. I couldn't believe it when I saw you sit up and fire it off."

"I was lucky it was a Glock." Andy looked down at her feet and kicked at another stone. "I'll still never get used to the idea that I've killed people."

"You'd be dead if you hadn't shot that guy."

"I know. I'm not sorry I did it, but it's still a weird thing to deal with…you know, knowing that I'm actually capable of doing it."

"You ever kill anyone before? Besides that one time in DC?"

"Nope, never. I don't think it's something I ever want to get used to."

"You shouldn't ever want to get used it, but you may have to."

Andy nodded vaguely but said nothing further. She didn't want to talk about death or killing anymore, nor did she want to even consider the fact that Ben's last remark might prove to be true someday.

"You know," she started, "if it hadn't actually happened to me, I would've never believed any of it."

"Believed any of what?"

"Everything that's happened these past few days. Being kidnapped. Getting shot at on the street, then being taken prisoner again. And then getting shot at by someone who didn't know anything about me while thousands of strangers cheered him on. And now I'm here, standing at the edge of the Grand Canyon, miles away from anyone."

She looked away and stared off into the view. "It's just so

unreal."

"I know," Ben said simply.

Andy turned to him with a frown.

"I don't know what to expect anymore. I mean, there was never any explanation for why I ended up at the stadium. It seemed like something that happened all the time…people getting kidnapped and forced into playing that demented game. And I just happened to be one of them. Just another person fulfilling someone's sick idea of entertainment."

"That's anarchy for you," Ben remarked solemnly. "Everyone out for themselves. No rules but the ones the stronger force upon the weak. And if they don't obey, things get nasty and someone ends up hurt or dead. It's been like that everywhere I've seen these past five years."

By now, Andy knew not to question Ben about his past, and she had long since stopped trying to make guesses about it.

"So nowhere is safe?" she asked, almost rhetorically.

"Nowhere I've been."

Andy looked back at the view.

"You don't think things will ever change, do you?"

Ben cast her a sideways glance.

"No, I don't. Nothing I've seen so far makes me believe anything will change anytime soon."

There was not a hint of doubt in his voice, but Andy still challenged him.

"I think deep down, most people want to be safe and have some kind of order in their lives. Look at all the people in Aspen who want it, and except for Nataliya and her friends screwing it up, it worked. It was a good system and we were a part of it. If it could happen there, it can happen again somewhere else."

But Ben was unconvinced. "Just because somewhere seems nice and organized doesn't mean it is. Aspen was the perfect example of that. In the end, Nataliya and her friends were running that place, regardless of how many others were really trying to make it work.

We're all fighting our own DNA, even those of us with the best intentions. We're programmed to look after ourselves and do whatever it takes to survive, no matter the cost."

"I disagree," Andy replied, crossing her arms across her chest. "If human beings weren't meant to live together peacefully, we would've been extinct long ago."

But Ben countered once more. "I'm not saying it's impossible for people to live peacefully ever again, but I don't think it'll happen in our lifetime. We're back in the Dark Ages. The first Dark Age lasted a thousand years."

To this, Andy pursed her lips together disapprovingly. "Well, if you keep thinking that way, you'll become a victim of you own expectations. Nothing that's worth having is supposed to be easy to get."

Then Andy faced Ben directly and took one step closer to him, halting his response.

"Ben, I know something awful happened to you, and I'm not asking you to tell me what it was, but you can't let it affect you for the rest of your life. Whatever it was, it's in the past. You can't change it or fix it."

With a sharp gesture of avoidance, Ben looked away and combed his fingers through his hair. When he turned back and opened his mouth to speak, a flash of light off to his right distracted them both.

"What was that?" Andy snapped, looking to her left. "Was that the camera?"

The camera, still sitting on the slab of rock, flashed again a second time.

"Whoa, that's weird," she said and walked over to retrieve it. "I wonder if that was just some glitch in the light or if it actually took a picture."

"We could give it to Susan to develop, but we'd have to wait until spring," Ben called after her. "I'm sure we could figure out how to do it without her."

"Yeah, maybe I'll try," Andy replied.

Ben motioned toward the truck.

"Let's get going," he said. "Everyone's worried about you."

"Yeah, okay," Andy remarked. She took one last look at the Canyon before turning away with a touch of sadness. Despite Ben's pessimism, the beauty of the place had reminded her that there were still things in life that were worth seeing and worth living for.

"Too bad we can't just stay here," she said wistfully as they drove off.

Ben said nothing. He glanced down at her hands and gave her wrist a gentle squeeze.

"We'll get those things off you as soon as we get back."

Andy frowned at the handcuffs stubbornly restricting her arms.

"They're really bugging the shit out of me. It would be nice to forget the last five days, but these things keep reminding of it."

* * *

They reached Santa Rosa by late afternoon as the sun was beginning to set and returned to the same homes that they had occupied during those few days the previous July. The reunion between Andy and her friends was filled with tears of joy and relief. Convinced she would never see her best friend again, Morgan was particularly emotional. She scolded Andy for making her worry so much before hugging her so tightly that Andy felt the baby kick more than once against her own stomach.

"She's happy you're back too," Morgan laughed through the tears. Since none of the sonograms Andy had performed suggested otherwise, Morgan was convinced she was having a girl.

"Then I'll be sure to thank her for the homecoming kicks when she gets out of there," Andy replied, sharing in the laughter and pressing her palm against Morgan's swollen belly.

Maria, Carmen, and Julio were there to greet Andy as well. Though it had been six months since they'd last seen one another, it felt as though hardly a day had passed.

"I'm glad you're back," Maria admitted. "But I'm sorry it didn't work out in Colorado. And I'm sorry for what happened to you. It's unbelievable."

And so, over a warm home-cooked dinner, courtesy of Maria, Andy and Ben each recounted their experiences of the past few days. The others listened intently, occasionally shaking their heads in dismay. Silent tears rolled down both Morgan and Maria's cheeks when Andy told her about the victims of "One Shot," while Jim and Charlie's faces crumpled into expressions of revulsion. Julio and Carmen listened with fear and confusion, neither being too young to understand the horrors of the world they now lived in.

The visit to the Grand Canyon, however, was never mentioned. For whatever reason, both Andy and Ben wanted to keep that experience to themselves. And before going to sleep that evening, Andy hid the portable camera under her bed for the time being.

Chapter XIV

02 March 2021

The comforts of life in Aspen were soon forgotten, albeit grudgingly. Gone were the large heated homes, the hot showers, and the grocery store with its fresh food. The people they had grown to care for during their six-month stay were missed as well, and Andy regretted that she never had the chance to say goodbye to them. But no one was more missed than Brian and Susan, and everyone anxiously awaited their arrival. Even Ben hoped that Brian and his sister would arrive safely despite the rivalry between the two young men. Naturally, Charlie was most anxious to see Susan again, though he rarely mentioned her name, perhaps to prepare himself in the event that she never came. After what had happened to Andy, anything seemed possible.

As January and February passed, the memories of Aspen slowly faded. One point of solace was that the New Mexico winter was considerably warmer than in the mountains of Colorado. Everyone busied themselves with work similar to what they had done in Aspen, though performing each task now seemed more arduous. Gone was the camaraderie they had shared with Aspen's many hardworking citizens. Without the desire to build and maintain a community, everything required to survive became tedious, and more exhausting.

Even Charlie, who had always liked learning new things and finding solutions to new problems, found himself resenting many of the activities he once enjoyed.

During the last week in February, Andy could feel Morgan becoming increasingly nervous as the birth of her child loomed. According to her own calculations, her due date was around the first of March. Morgan had accepted the idea of delivering an infant amongst the hardships of this new world, but as the event approached, she began to panic.

"How will I feed it? There's barely enough food for us."

Food was just one of her many worries. Jim did what he could to reassure her that everything would be all right, but it took Andy to remind her that she would never be alone when it came to caring for the child.

"All you need to know is that this baby will have not just a mother, but many uncles and aunts who will love and care for it as though it were their own flesh and blood."

In the early morning hours on the second of March, Morgan delivered a healthy baby girl after ten hours of grueling labor. The infant was named Kathryn Andrea Pemberton.

Maria assisted during the delivery, but the brunt of the work was performed by Andy, and of course, Morgan. Contractions began shortly after dinner the night before, and once her water broke, Morgan was moved to the unused bedroom in the same house Ben and Jim had occupied many months earlier. Despite all the hours he had spent with Andy regarding the birthing process, Charlie remained outside the bedroom at his sister's request, and he seemed relieved by this decision.

Everyone remained in the living room and waited for news from either Andy or Maria. Julio and Carmen entertained Charlie with multitudes of card and board games before falling asleep shortly before midnight. Charlie, Jim, and Ben, however, stayed awake until morning, pacing around the house and in the street. While Jim and Charlie were in a constant state of worry throughout, Ben remained calm. His faith in Andy's ability to safely and skillfully perform her duties seemed to comfort them both.

At 4:57 in the morning, after Morgan squeezed Andy's hand for one last push, little Katie, as she would be called, finally entered the world. Named after her grandmother and her mother's best friend, Katie was born healthy and strong, and the screams from her tiny lungs could be heard from across the street. When Andy cut the umbilical cord and tearfully handed Morgan her daughter, she looked at her child with the satisfied smile of a new mother and uttered, "She's perfect."

Then with a tired whisper, she thanked Andy before falling asleep as Katie squirmed helplessly in her arms.

When Charlie first held his niece, it suddenly dawned on him that it was also his birthday, his sixteenth.

"Bloody hell, Charlie…even *I* remembered that!" Morgan later teased as everyone was gathered around her bed and proceeded to sing "Happy Birthday" to both uncle and niece.

* * *

Spring 2021

Little Katie was the delight of everyone. Like her mother, she had delicate features, wide brown eyes, and the finest of brown hairs on her fragile head. Though no one ever said as much, it was a relief that she resembled Morgan so well and that there was no visible sign of the father and his degenerate genes.

As promised to her by Andy, Morgan received plenty of help with Katie during the first weeks of her life. Meanwhile, Jim's gentle temperament made him a natural father to the child, and he never once lamented that Katie was not biologically his own. If anything, the child seemed to bring him and Morgan closer than before. Their relationship was one of impressive commitment, and Ben often remarked to Andy that he had never seen his cousin so happy.

For her part, Andy was relieved beyond words that her friend had safely reached the end of the nine-month ordeal that had begun so violently the summer before. The birth had been hard on both of them, but Morgan had managed to pull through unscathed. Now it was time to enjoy seeing a new life grow and change right before their eyes.

By early May, the only thing that still concerned everyone was the continued absence of Brian and Susan. Neither had indicated exactly when in the spring they would leave Aspen and head south, which only made the waiting more trying. Everyone could sense Charlie's worry in particular. Many evenings during sunset, he would sit outside with the hope that Susan would suddenly appear with her brother.

* * *

28 May 2021

Minutes before midnight, there was a sharp knock at the front door. Andy was the first to hear it, so she quickly rose out of bed before a second knock could awaken Katie. As she made her way through the house, she heard the soft pitter-patter of rain hitting the roof. Before opening the door, she grabbed her Glock from a drawer in the kitchen and checked that it was loaded. As she leaned in toward the door to look through the peephole, there was another loud knock that made her jump back several feet.

"Jesus!" she hissed in the dark before leaning in once more to take a good look. In the moonlight, she could make out two figures wearing rain coats with hoods over their heads. As one of them turned sideways, she instantly recognized Susan's profile.

"Susan!" she gasped a bit too loudly and fumbled with the lock before finally getting the door open.

"Well, it's about time!" Brian exclaimed as he stepped inside. Andy quickly put her index finger to her lips to silence him. She was smiling, however, and when it registered who had greeted him, Brian's eyes grew wide.

"Oh my God…Andy? You're…you're here? How…?"

But Andy merely continued to smile and hushed him again. She then gestured for him to come inside as she placed her pistol on the kitchen table. Susan followed her brother and expressed the same degree of shock upon seeing Andy.

"We thought we'd never see you again!"

Andy let out a hushed chuckle and put her finger to her lips once again.

"I know, I know. You all thought I was dead…but right now we gotta be quiet."

"Oh, sorry!" Susan whispered. "Is everyone asleep?"

"Morgan and Jim are…and Katie, the baby," Andy whispered back.

"Oh! The baby!" Susan cupped her hands over her mouth. "Morgan had a girl? What's she like?"

"She's adorable. Now keep your coats on," Andy replied and nodded toward the front door. "Let's go across the street and we'll talk. I'm sure Charlie will want to see you anyway. He and Ben are staying over there."

Susan smiled in the darkness, flashing her teeth, and in seconds she was back outside. Brian, however, still couldn't believe he was actually standing beside Andy.

"What happened to you?" he wondered aloud in a heavy whisper.

"I'll tell you everything, but not now."

Andy gestured once more toward the door, but Brian shook his head.

"I'm exhausted. You go across the street with Susan. If you don't mind, I think I'll just fall asleep right here on this couch."

Without waiting for permission, Brian moved passed Andy into the living room. She followed as he removed his coat before plopping down on the couch.

"What about your livestock? Did you bring them?"

Brian looked at her, and in the moonlight, she could see how truly fatigued he was. Wearily, he shook his head.

"We had to leave everything behind."

"What? What do mean 'had to?'"

"I'll tell you everything, but not now," he mumbled, repeating Andy's earlier words. He kicked off his wet shoes, laid his head down on the couch, and quickly drifted off.

Andy found a spare blanket and discovered that Brian was already asleep by the time she brought it to him. She gently placed the blanket over him before putting on her coat. Susan was waiting for her outside.

"Your brother looks exhausted."

"He's just been fighting a cold."

"He's already asleep on the couch."

"I'm not surprised. He drove the whole way here, and it rained the entire time."

Andy pointed to the house directly across the street.

"It's that one."

The rain was steady but not too heavy, and the two girls made a dashed across the street. Andy knocked on the front door once then twice. Charlie opened the door with a wide grin on his face.

"Took you long enough!" was all he said before launching through the doorway to give Susan a long embrace.

Feeling suddenly in the way, Andy stepped inside to dry off, with Charlie and Susan following moments later. Then they heard a voice from within the house, followed by a bouncing beam of light.

"What's going on?"

Carrying a flashlight, Ben emerged from the end of the hallway that connected the bedrooms to the front of the house. When he saw Susan, no further explanation was needed.

* * *

The next morning began with a flurry of introductions and explanations. Maria and her siblings finally met the friends they had been hearing about for more than four months, and Katie was introduced to Brian and Susan.

"Oh my God, she's precious!" Susan squealed as Katie clenched onto her pinky with her tiny hand.

Morgan beamed and handed Katie over to Susan to hold.

Later, Andy and Ben recounted their saga in Los Angeles for Brian and Susan, who reacted with the same shock and disbelief as the others had upon their return in January.

"So people went to the Coliseum just to watch people getting murdered?" Brian asked.

Andy and Ben nodded solemnly together.

"They seemed to like it more than the opponent," Andy explained. "They were like a pack of wild animals."

"Sounds like gladiators, except with guns instead of swords," Brian commented.

"Funny…the Coliseum was named after the original in Rome," Ben remarked.

"Yeah, hilarious," Andy replied with sarcasm. "I still have nightmares about those poor boys in the locker room. I can still picture their faces and hear the words of the one who spoke to me before he left."

"What'd he say?" asked Brian.

"He said 'I'll see you soon'. That's it, but it will probably haunt me for the rest of my life."

The conversation then shifted focus to Brian and Susan's last months in Aspen.

"After you all left," Brian started, "things got worse. We stopped having council meetings, and every day people were reporting things of theirs getting stolen. Everyone kept coming by to ask us where you'd all gone. I swear, in all the years living on that farm, we never had so many people dropping by to visit. I think they wanted to know if you'd found somewhere better to live."

"What about the cattle? And the horses?" Morgan asked with concern. "I thought you were going to try to bring some of them here."

"We tried," said Susan, taking over for her brother. "We had everything all planned and ready to go. But the day we were going to leave, two days ago, Garrett and Heath showed up at the farm with guns. Somehow, they'd found out we were leaving, though neither of us told a single soul, not even our oldest friends."

"They threatened to shoot the animals if we tried to take them," Brian continued. "We tried to convince them that we weren't leaving, but it was a pretty tough sell. Our truck was sitting outside when they came by and was fully packed for the trip. We told them we would leave the cattle behind and go the next day, but then Mikhail and Aiden showed up and the four of them turned their guns on us and threatened to kill us if we didn't give them our cattle right then. So we had no choice but to let them take everything."

"Jesus, the whole bloody world's gone mad!" Morgan exclaimed.

"Everything fell apart these past few months," said Brian with unbridled regret. "What's worse is that they'll end up killing those animals because they have no clue how to take care of them.

"If things were becoming so terrible, why did you wait so long to come?" Charlie asked Susan directly with a hint of good-natured exasperation.

"Because winter lasted forever this year and the snow didn't melt off the roads until last week," she explained and reached over to give Charlie's shoulder a squeeze.

Returning a similar gesture, Charlie replied, "Well, at least you made it. That's all that matters."

Maria later invited everyone to her home for dinner, and as before, the meal was fresh and home-cooked. How she accomplished this still remained a mystery, but no one bothered to question it when their stomachs rumbled with hunger.

* * *

"It's still strange seeing my brother with a girlfriend."

Morgan said this to Jim later that evening after everyone had gone to sleep. Katie was already slumbering soundly in a crib they'd found in a neighboring house a few blocks away. The crib was kept in Morgan's bedroom, which Jim now shared with her most nights.

"Why? Because he's your brother or because he's never had a girlfriend before?"

Morgan shrugged. "Both. He's just always been so occupied with reading books and learning new things that I never imagined he could ever be distracted by anything else."

"Well, he *is* sixteen now," Jim replied pragmatically. "And it's funny what a beautiful girl can do to a guy."

As he said this, he gave Morgan an affectionate caress at her waist, and she giggled in response. He began to tickle her on the bed, and she quickly protested.

"Stop it!" she cried before quickly covering her mouth to muffle her laughter, and Jim started to laugh as well while continuing to attack her stomach.

"Stop! We'll wake her up!" Morgan pleaded through another fit of giggles until Jim finally relented and gave her room to sit up. Somewhat out of breath, she looked down at her stomach and patted it gently.

"I'm still not used to it being back to normal size. I'm just glad I don't look like a blimp anymore."

"What are you talking about?" Jim remarked with a groan of disapproval over Morgan's self-deprecating comment. "You've always been beautiful."

Morgan smiled warmly as Jim glanced over at Katie in the crib, her tiny chest rising and falling with each breath, and he smiled slightly.

"She looks so much like you, you know? She'll grow up to be beautiful, just like her mother."

"It doesn't bother you that she's not yours?"

Jim made a face. They had discussed this subject more than once before Katie was born, but Morgan still needed reassurance every so often, and Jim understood this.

"I've told you before that I don't care that I'm not her father, biologically. It's the person who's around when she's growing up who matters."

"But don't you ever feel…I don't know…constrained?"

"Constrained? No, I wouldn't be here if I didn't want to be. I love both of you. More than I ever thought possible."

But Morgan was still leery. "Do you ever miss your life from before? I mean, before we met and it was just you and Ben and you weren't tied down by anything? You were so free and could go wherever you wanted."

Jim let out a sigh and took hold of Morgan's hand. Then he looked at her with a serious expression, yet full love.

"Honey, for the first time since the virus, I'm actually glad I survived it. Until I met you last year, my life was…pretty miserable, actually."

Then he lifted up her hand to his mouth and kissed it. "You make me very happy. If I could, I'd marry you."

Morgan's eyes went wide. "What? You're joking."

"No, I'm serious. I'd marry you right now if there was anyone around to do it…a priest, a rabbi, a judge…whoever."

Morgan began to giggle again, and Jim quickly joined in.

"You're serious? You actually want to marry me?"

Jim raised a shoulder in a casual sort of way.

"Why not? I think it would be kinda cool to do something normal. You know, something that people used to do all the time…before the whole world became 'mad' as you say. Don't you think?"

Morgan looked away momentarily as a smile slowly spread across her face. By the time she looked back at Jim, she was grinning.

"I think it's brilliant. And you know who would find out how to do it?"

They both paused before saying, "Charlie" simultaneously.

After another burst of laughter that nearly stirred Katie from her sleep, Jim leaned forward and kissed Morgan again and again.

* * *

Summer 2021

The month of June brought with it increased temperatures typical to the region, but the intense heat that had driven the group away from New Mexico the previous summer was mercifully absent this year. Mornings in particular were cooler, and therefore made it much easier to sleep at night. Andy even found that she needed a sweatshirt in the evenings as the thermometer often dipped below sixty degrees.

In Charlie's quest to find a way to marry his sister to Jim, he discovered that performing a wedding was incredibly simple.

"Did you know that people could become ordained in a day or two on the Internet?" he asked Andy one day while hunting wild jackrabbits.

"I'm not surprised. I remember how anyone could do anything if they had a computer or a cell phone. Some days, I really miss the Internet."

The ceremony was another matter. Susan insisted on flowers and a proper dress for Morgan. She also planned to take multiple photographs to mark the occasion.

"Photographs are fine, but I don't need a dress or flowers," Morgan protested. "It's just us."

But Susan was determined, and within the old business district of Santa Rosa, she found a bridal shop that had plenty of dresses that had never been worn and dragged a reluctant Morgan to the shop one day in early June. Consequently, the two spent hours trying on various styles of gowns. Morgan eventually warmed up to the idea of wearing a dress upon seeing her reflection in the mirror, and Susan decided she was going to be a bridesmaid, which amused everyone. With contagious enthusiasm, Susan announced that everyone would play a role.

"Charlie will perform the ceremony. Andy, Maria, and I will be bridesmaids. Carmen and Julio can be the flower girl and ring bearer, and Brian and Ben can be groomsmen."

"But that leaves no one to be in the audience," Morgan pointed out later that evening as she, Susan, and Andy were making dinner.

"So? It's just us, like you said. We can be our own audience. We'll just be standing around you and Jim instead of sitting. It'll be better that way. You'll see."

"Susan, before you get ahead of yourself, you should know

something," Andy interjected while skinning a jackrabbit. "I don't do dresses."

"You don't 'do' dresses? Are you kidding?"

Susan was astonished. She opted for sundresses instead of shorts during warmer months. In many ways, she was more feminine than both Morgan and Andy combined.

"The last time I wore a dress was at my mother's funeral," Andy continued. "It was made of itchy wool, and I couldn't wait to take it off."

Andy then gave Susan a quick once-over in her sundress and said, "I really don't know how you can wear dresses all the time. They're so impractical."

"Oh, but they aren't. They're super-comfortable. You'd see that if you tried one on."

But Andy would not be easily swayed. Still, as difficult as she was about the idea, convincing all the boys to wear tuxedos was more difficult. But Susan was persistent, and when Morgan decided that she would indeed wear a white gown, everyone eventually relented. Of course, Andy was the last to consent, and she jokingly threatened to wear a sheet as a dress.

"What's good enough for the ancient Greeks is good enough for me. Or maybe I'll just cut out two eyeholes and be a ghost."

However, out of respect for her best friend, Andy mustered the courage to don a dress for the occasion that was, amusingly enough, Grecian in style. It was pale blue and made of soft linen, with spaghetti straps and an empire waist. Maria and Susan would wear the same dress, while Carmen wore a dress of identical fabric but one designed for a young girl.

"I look ridiculous," Andy said to Morgan and Maria changing into her dress on the day of the wedding.

"Stop it. You look beautiful," Morgan insisted, and Maria agreed.

"Well, whatever. It's your party, not mine."

Standing in front of a full-length mirror, Andy twirled around once in her dress.

"Okay, I'll admit that Susan was right. This thing is pretty comfortable. It's like wearing pajamas."

The ceremony was held at sunset in a quiet park just north of town. Morgan carried a bouquet of wild flowers and wore sandals with her dress. Andy stood to her left, followed by Maria and Susan, who took turns holding Katie. Due to the summer heat, the boys chose to wear slacks and light-colored dress shirts instead of more formal and confining tuxedos. Still, it was disarming to see them all scrubbed clean, standing straight, and out of their normal uniform of threadbare T-shirts and jeans. Ben stood beside Jim, with Brian to Ben's left, each stealing glances at Andy, while Julio and Carmen enjoyed their role of ring bearer and flower girl.

Charlie's voice was calm and clear as he spoke the words that would bind Morgan and Jim together forever. The two exchanged simple rings of silver to become man and wife and exchanged a kiss to end the ceremony. No paper or document would ever be signed or mailed to any local government to make the union legally binding, but there was no doubt by all present that the couple would forever honor their vows.

* * *

03 July 2021

A week after her twentieth birthday, Andy took a break one evening from reading a medical book that Charlie had rescued from Aspen and went across the street to talk to Ben. He was tinkering around with Maria's truck, which had been giving her problems for a few days. Besides Morgan, who was making dinner as she kept an eye on Katie, everyone else was either hunting or gathering water from the Pecos River that ran through town.

"How's it going?"

Ben looked up from under the hood and saw Andy standing beside him. His hands were covered in grease, and he was sweating. The truck's stereo was on, playing rock music. Andy recognized the song but the name of the band had slipped her mind.

"Her timing belt needed to be replaced, but I should be done soon."

"Is that difficult to do?"

Ben shook his head. "Not anymore. The first few times Jim and I tried it was hard, but now it's like changing a light bulb."

"I'll take your word for it. What band is this again?"

Ben took a swig of water from a thermos and wiped his mouth with the back of his hand. "Def Leppard. Gotta love the eighties. My dad listened to 'em all the time growing up."

Andy smiled.

"I think my dad did, too."

"So you know what today is?" Ben asked, changing the subject.

"Uh, Saturday?"

"Yeah, but it's also exactly one year ago today that we all first met."

Andy's eyes narrowed as she tried to recall the day. Remembering dates was not her strong suit, and she never wore a watch.

"I think you're right."

"Tomorrow's the Fourth of July."

"That's right," Andy suddenly recalled. "You wished me a Happy Fourth of July that morning in your truck."

Ben shook his head again, looking thoughtful this time. The sun was beginning to set, and they watched it descend behind the row of single-story homes on their street. Ben started to say something when he saw his own truck make a turn onto their street and head toward them.

"Good, they're back. I'm starving," he said as he wiped his hands off with an old rag and shut the hood of Maria's car.

Charlie, Brian, and Jim had gone off together hunting while Susan and Maria headed to the river, each taking separate vehicles. As the truck approached, two extra people could be seen riding in the back of the truck with Jim, while Charlie and Brian were up front.

"I thought this town was empty," Andy remarked as the vehicle drew near. "Who are these people?"

"No clue," Ben muttered distantly as his eyes followed hers.

The truck pulled up to the curb beside the house and Jim hopped out of the back before it completely stopped. Carrying a hunting rifle, he marched directly toward Ben.

"Don't worry, I checked 'em for weapons," he muttered under his breath to his cousin. Andy heard the words as her eyes darted from Jim to Ben to the two strangers in the truck.

"They're clean?" Ben mumbled back.

"They're clean."

The strangers were two older teenage boys, each carrying a large backpack as they stepped off the truck. Along with their scruffy appearance and three-day-old facial stubble, they wore expressions of fatigue and hunger. Being the Good Samaritans that Andy and her friends were, they immediately offered the two strangers water before any introductions were made.

"Thanks, you have no idea how grateful we are," one of them said to Andy after she returned from the house with two large glasses of filtered water. The strangers emptied the glasses within seconds and appeared as though they could drink half a dozen more.

Their names were Kevin and Matt, and their car had run out of gas fifteen miles east of Santa Rosa. They had been wandering west on I-40 when Jim, Charlie, and Brian came across them after their successful hunt.

The deer they had killed had already bled out, and while Brian and Charlie hauled it off the truck bed and laid the animal out on the front yard on top of thick plastic sheeting, Jim introduced Ben and Andy to Matt and Kevin.

"Wait, Ben? Ben and Jim?" Matt pointed back a forth between the two cousins.

"Yeah?" Ben replied wearily after a moment's hesitation.

"It can't be…your last names wouldn't be 'Kelly,' would they?"

Ben and Jim exchanged the quickest of looks before Jim took one step back and raised his rifle until the front of the barrel was pointed directly at Matt.

"Who are you?" he demanded in the steadiest of tones as Matt and Kevin's hands shot up in the air.

"Whoa, whoa! We're not looking for you two, believe me," Kevin pleaded.

"Yeah, the reward's not *that* good, trust us," Matt quickly added. "Besides, we're unarmed. If we were hunting you, we'd have guns."

But neither Ben nor Jim was satisfied. In the meantime, Andy had taken a step away from the group. She looked at Charlie and Brian, both of whom were as equally confused as she was.

"So if you're not after us, where are you going?" Ben challenged.

"To Phoenix," Kevin replied without skipping a beat as both he and Matt finally lowered their hands. "We both had family there before the outbreak and are hoping they're still there."

"Where were you before? New York? Philly?" Ben pressed.

"New York. Brooklyn," Matt answered.

"Why aren't you two armed?" Jim asked as he lowered the barrel of his rifle slightly. "Everyone carries something nowadays."

"We were, but our guns were stolen from us when we were sleeping one night in a campground in Missouri, along with all our ammo and food."

Suddenly, Morgan could be heard shouting, "Grub's up!" from across the street, alerting everyone that dinner was ready. Holding a squirming Katie, she emerged from the house and began to cross the street until she saw Jim holding a gun in front of two people she'd never seen before. She stopped dead in her tracks and twisted her torso to shield Katie.

"It's okay!" Jim called out to her, and Morgan continued to cross the street, though cautiously.

"Who's that?" Matt asked with curiosity. "And what's with the baby?"

"Just neighbors," Jim quickly responded in a tone that warned his friends not to contradict him.

"Why did you guys leave New York?" Ben asked, putting the questions back on the two strangers. "It's been shitty for years. Why leave now?"

Kevin looked away as he brushed his fingers through his hair in a similar gesture to the one Ben often performed.

"Yeah, well, it's gotten worse…much worse."

"You're probably not gonna believe this, but Sean's still got the virus, and he's still using it," Matt added as Morgan drew within earshot and stood beside Jim.

More confused than ever, Andy saw Ben and Jim give each other stunned looks.

Shutting his eyes and shaking his head as if he couldn't believe what he had just heard, Ben finally blurted out, "What are you talking about? How…?"

His voice trailed off.

"Sorry, man…what you and Jim did at the laboratory last year was legendary, but you didn't destroy it all," Matt replied rather apologetically.

"It's true," Kevin went on. "After what the famous Kelly cousins did, everyone thought there might finally be a chance to end Sean forever, but six months after you guys disappeared, people started dying again, but this time in larger numbers."

Kevin then made a sweeping motion with his arm.

"Whole towns and suburbs have been wiped out. Whoever Sean's found to replicate the virus is very good, and very quick."

"There must've been some sample he had stashed somewhere," Matt further explained.

Ben turned away. He couldn't take hearing anything more. Even Jim had to grit his teeth to stay composed, and he gestured absently toward the house across the street.

"C'mon inside. We'll get you both some food and we'll talk."

Seeing how disturbed their friends were, Charlie and Brian jumped in to escort Kevin and Matt into the house while the others stayed behind. Anxious and puzzled, Andy and Morgan looked at each other and then back at Ben and Jim with questioning gazes. Morgan's eyes narrowed hard on her new husband as Andy crossed her arms over her chest.

"Funny how you mentioned the one-year anniversary of our meeting earlier," she remarked coolly to Ben. "I remember you throwing similar accusations at us that day."

"I think it's finally time you told us the whole story," Morgan added firmly, speaking directly to Jim. "As your wife, I deserve to know."

Ben started to protest but Jim threw up a hand and cut him off.

"Fine. Just do me a favor first…take off your ring and don't mention anything about being my wife. In fact, pretend you don't care about me at all." He nodded to the house across the street and said, "I'm not about to trust those guys yet."

Both Jim and Morgan crossed the street with Katie and disappeared inside, leaving Ben and Andy alone on the driveway. She cast him a long and discerning gaze before wordlessly following the others inside.

Standing alone and feeling like he'd just been punched in the gut, Ben stared down at his dirty hands. He shut his eyes and pinched the bridge of his nose.

"Impossible," he breathed.

Chapter XV

His favorite character in all of literature was Iago, the "motiveless" villain from Shakespeare's *Othello*. He admired the character's great talent for manipulation, but he likened himself more as a modern Alexander the Great. Crowned King of Macedonia at age twenty, Alexander went on to conquer most of the known world before turning thirty. But it was easy to conquer when you began at the top.

Now twenty years old himself, Sean Taylor had started at the bottom with everyone else. Even his name was indisputably common.

What was extraordinary was how Sean had acted—so quickly and strategically during those first weeks and months after the outbreak. While most of the survivors remained huddled in their parentless homes, weeping wretchedly and wallowing in self-pity, Sean worked around the clock. He never shed a tear for his parents, and there was no older sibling to mourn in those lonely hours between dusk and dawn.

His father had been a Two-Star General in the Army and for a mere fifteen minutes had once stood in the very same room in which Sean now sat. General Taylor had uttered not a single word during that short meeting, and his presence had been overshadowed by higher ranking generals who ignored the unofficial policy of using "economy of speech" when addressing the President of the United States. It was as though he had never been there.

Sean knew nothing about this fleeting chapter of his father's history, but if he had, it would not have surprised him. The mere fact that General Taylor had managed to become a general at all was still a mystery to his son, for the man had been exceedingly dull, uncreative, and utterly oblivious to the motives and desires of others around him. It was this latter quality which had enabled Sean's mother to carry on an affair for years under her husband's nose without a hint of suspicion on his part. Thinking his father pathetic and his mother a whore made it easy for Sean to carry on when they died. If anything, the virus was the best thing that could have happened to him. Freed from the laws that civilized society once lived by—laws that were not his own—he could finally fulfill his potential.

For nearly an hour now, he had been lounging in the plush swivel chair with his feet propped up on the Resolute Desk in a display of gross disrespect and thinking it odd to be in a room without corners. He could feel the sunlight waning through the three windows behind him, the only indication that it was getting late. His musings that afternoon had erased any concept of time.

There was a certain decision bothering him.

Though less than a handful of people were arguably capable enough to watch over his interests in Washington DC, determining who would remain the most loyal from so far away was the real challenge. If only some of the Fixers could get their heads out of their asses and learn how to repair some airplanes, the decision wouldn't be necessary. Sean could control DC himself and not be forced to rely on another to bring order to the southernmost point of his realm.

DC was a mess. In terms of utilities, nothing within the city or suburbs worked, and the inhabitants who had been living out a sorry existence for six years were not accustomed to authority. Sean, however, lived to exercise his authority. He craved it the way Dregs craved drugs; it was the ultimate high.

Taking his feet off the desk, he spun around in the chair and stared upward, alternately fixing his gaze on and off the Seal of the President of the United States that had been artfully plastered on the ceiling decades earlier.

The task he needed to assign would be tough. None of the pleasures in New York or even Philadelphia existed in Washington at the moment. The pitiful girls and young women he'd seen earlier that day on the streets were so rough looking that they were nearly indistinguishable from the boys. How they had managed to live with themselves in such a sorry state all these years was incomprehensible to Sean.

Still, he was determined to reign in the former capitol city, and nothing would stop him or change his mind, not even the setback he'd suffered a year earlier. He had recovered from that unfortunate episode stronger than before, and taking over DC would grant him even more power. Beyond that, nothing would be impossible.

* * *

By the time Maria and Susan returned from the lake, Matt and Kevin had finished their donated meal and had fallen asleep on the living room floor in Ben, Brian, and Charlie's house across the street.

Everyone else was gathered inside the other house where Morgan had made dinner, although no one was interested in eating. Instead, they all sat in the living room with loaded weapons within arm's reach in the event that the two strangers sleeping across the street were not who they said they were. Once Morgan put Katie in her crib and a tired Carmen fell asleep in Andy's room, Andy began the inquisition.

"Sounds like you two were pretty famous back east."

She was sitting directly across from Ben, staring pointedly at him, which made it difficult for him to avoid her questions. But he was less than eager to begin any sort of explanation, so Jim spoke instead. He could feel Morgan's own impatience, and after a trying day dealing with Katie's bout of diarrhea, her temper was shorter than usual.

"What all do you know about the virus?"

It was apparent from the way Jim stated the question that some background information was necessary.

Andy shook her head absently.

"Nothing really. All we heard in Bermuda was something about a government project."

"Something supremely top secret, but that was it," Charlie added. "The news stopped being broadcast on the island once everyone started dying."

"What about you?" Jim said as he turned to Maria, Susan, and Brian.

"Pretty much the same thing," Maria answered.

"Us too," Brian said as Susan nodded in agreement.

"So the part about the virus being part of a top secret government project was correct," Jim confirmed. "What most people didn't know was that the virus was designed to be a humane biological weapon."

"How could a biological weapon be humane?" Morgan asked dubiously. "Was it supposed to kill people quicker or without pain or something?"

Jim shook his head.

"Not that kind of humane. From what Ben and I were told, the virus was designed to distinguish the difference between an adult male and everyone else based upon the level of testosterone and other hormones that naturally occur within the body. Those who came in contact with the virus and had high enough levels of testosterone would be killed; those who didn't should have been unharmed."

"Why would the government create a virus like that?" asked Susan.

But Maria had figured out the reason and answered before Jim could. "So they could go after men like my father without worrying about killing women and children in the process. My father always knew that the DEA and the Mexican government would never carry out a deadly raid on his home if they thought his family was inside. That's why he conducted all his business from our house."

Julio frowned as his sister spoke but said nothing. While Carmen remained unaware of her father's past, Julio was beginning to understand. His sister's contempt could not be contained forever.

"That's right," Jim continued. "Terrorists in the Middle East used the same tactics. The virus was supposed to be a way to get around that problem."

"So how did it end up killing everyone over a certain age, both men and women?" Andy asked. She looked directly again at Ben, but he maintained his silence.

"Because it wasn't finished being tested. The calculations were off. One day, a scientist accidentally left the testing facility with a microscopic sample of the virus on his clothes," Jim explained simply. "And the rest is history."

"Where was the virus developed?" Charlie asked.

"Fort Detrick. It's in Maryland, about fifty miles or so outside of DC."

"Fort Detrick?" Andy repeated with mild surprise. "I've read about that place in some of my medical books. I thought that lab was shut down decades ago."

"Apparently not," Jim replied with a slight shrug.

"How did you learn all this if it wasn't on the news?" Brian asked.

Jim quickly glanced over at Ben, signaling that the conversation was about to become more personal.

"We knew the son of the scientist who accidentally released the virus," Jim responded somberly.

"That's a strange coincidence," Andy remarked with a hint of sarcasm. "But who's this Sean person those guys were talking about?"

"And what's he doing with the virus?" Morgan demanded.

Jim held up his hands in a silent request for patience. "One thing at a time," he begged. "But this is really more Ben's story to tell, so I'll let him tell it."

Up to this point, Ben had been staring at the lit candles in front of him on the coffee table, his upper body leaning forward in his seat with his elbows on his knees and his hands clasped together, creating an altogether tense posture. Andy felt a sudden pang of guilt for pushing him so hard on the subject of his past, both that day and all the times before. There was obviously a great deal of pain associated with it, which she had always assumed but never really tried to understand. Only now was she beginning to.

Fixing his gaze on the candles, Ben swallowed hard before explaining everything. No one spoke once he began.

* * *

After soaking in the experience of hanging out in the Oval Office, Sean departed the White House by descending the steps on the south side of the building. He immediately grimaced upon seeing a rainbow of spray paint on the neoclassical white columns. Six years of unchallenged anarchy had taken its toll on the numerous monuments throughout the city, and the White House was no exception. The defacement didn't bother him as much as the boldness of the act.

But who could be trusted to turn this city around?

Jesse was a strong candidate. He was undeniably loyal to Sean and his interests, but more importantly he harbored no ambition of his own to challenge Sean's established position as undisputed leader of the Northeast. Jesse's negative quality, however, was his intelligence. It wasn't that he was stupid, but he lacked the ability to solve problems beyond the mundane. Worse, when things didn't turn out exactly as planned, he became severely flustered to the point of mental paralysis. In Jesse's favor, however, he was ruthless and didn't grow a conscience whenever Dregs begged for mercy.

Michael and Chad were also candidates. Michael was smarter than Jesse and just as ruthless, but Sean hesitated to select him because of the gnawing sense that he would someday double-cross him. Chad, meanwhile, was a wildcard. Intelligent and even more unfeeling than both Jesse and Michael combined, Chad had demonstrated great promise. The problem was that Chad had only come into Sean's acquaintance nine months ago. Though he had been very effective in helping him root out some highly damaging rebels amongst both Dregs and Fixers, nine months was insufficient to gain someone's trust and determine their true intentions.

As he walked across the South Lawn toward the car that was waiting to pick him up to take him back to New York, Sean thought about Ben Kelly. The memory of his former friend and present enemy was one of the few events in his past that could arouse fierce emotions.

Ben was an extremely intelligent, natural-born leader who had chosen to waste his talents tinkering with cars and other single-purpose machines rather than rise up above all the other Directors and become something far greater. His cousin and best friend, Jim, was a very talented mechanic as well, in some ways better than Ben, but he lacked the tactical and strategic intellect that Ben possessed, qualities essential for ruling a city as large as New York. But Jim had no interest in doing anything more than fixing machines, and his talent had served Sean well over the years. Ben, however, was different. Sean often saw in him the desire to govern those who couldn't govern themselves. Unfortunately, Ben also suffered from a nagging conscience that prohibited him from doing what was often necessary to keep the Dregs, and others ranked above them, in line. When he ultimately chose to betray Sean, Ben became Sean's worst, and most destructive, enemy. The previous summer's explosion at the laboratory had nearly toppled everything that Sean had worked so excruciatingly hard to build, and the sting to his ego would not soon be forgotten.

* * *

"His name is Sean Taylor. He's twenty years old, just a few days younger than me, and he controls almost everything in New York, Philadelphia, some parts of Boston, and everywhere in between. I'd say he's the leader, but that would actually imply that people were following him because they wanted to. Because they're...*inspired* to. But Sean doesn't inspire people. He forces them to do what he wants so that he can get what he wants, which is more power. He's a narcissist, he's manipulative, and he's dangerously intelligent. And he's sadistic…I mean no kidding, *evil.* I've never met anyone else like him in my entire life."

A sinking sensation brewed in Andy's stomach, her body already reacting to the ominous beginning of Ben's story.

"In the early days after the outbreak, while everyone else was scared shitless, Sean was plotting to take over the world, or at least New York City, his hometown. His father was a retired Two-Star General in the Army, so Sean knew to do things like stockpile weapons and food before anyone else could. And he had an uncanny way of getting people to do things for him. If you thought Nataliya and her friends in Aspen were bad, they were nothing compared to Sean. He made people believe that he cared about helping them and cared about getting the city working again. Today he barely lifts a finger, but back in the early days, he genuinely worked hard, which only convinced everyone that he was someone they could trust. Someone to save them. But it was all just an act. Just a part of his master plan.

"You all probably remember those early days…how being thirteen or fourteen was like being a king. Age was everything, and the older you were, the louder your voice and the more the younger survivors listened to you. Children are so impressionable. And if you were particularly persuasive like Sean, they did whatever you said and followed you wherever you went if they thought they would be safe and have food to eat. Sean took advantage of that and gained a large following of survivors in New York. Then he picked his favorites and they became part of his inner circle, and were later called 'Directors'. Sean came up with the name, like everything else. Directors were people who controlled specific resources, like food production or water treatment or getting power back to the city. Last year there were nine Directors in New York that Sean had appointed over the years, and each one is pretty powerful and influential on his own.

"But Sean also knew he needed some of the smartest survivors on his side to get things working again, so he went through hundreds and hundreds of school records at the best schools in New York, not just the city but the entire state. Then he tracked down the really smart kids, the ones who had skipped several grades because they were so intelligent and even some who were in college, and convinced them to work for him. Kids like you, Charlie."

Charlie cracked a slight, almost rueful smile as Ben continued, determined to finish now that he'd begun.

"The power grid was Sean's highest priority, and the kids he found to make that happen were amazing. They managed to fix a large part of the infrastructure within a year; pretty fucking incredible for a city that size. I mean, coal and natural gas production had to begin again in areas far outside the city limits…can you imagine?"

And Morgan and Maria shook their heads in silent agreement.

"But when Sean succeeded, he went from being just a persuasive voice to someone who actually made things work again. His power and influence grew. Everyone wanted to work for him, and he had his pick of smart, talented survivors to make him even more powerful.

"Over time, Sean developed a kind of class system for everyone living in the city. The first class, and the smallest, are the Directors. Including Sean, there are ten total, with Sean at the top. The next class is the army, or the 'Infantry,' as we all called it. After the power grid was restored, Sean spread the word that he was recruiting male survivors at least twelve years or older for the Infantry, and about ten thousand boys volunteered who fit the age requirement, all dying to work for Sean. From those, Sean selected three thousand, which became the Infantry. It has its own ranks like any army, and its leader is one of the nine Directors. Officially, the Infantry is like the police; they're meant to keep order among the survivors in the city. But power has made them brutal, and now they spend most of their time stealing anything of value from the rest of the population. In the early days, people wound up dead when they refused to give up their possessions, but now no one bothers to put up a fight 'cuz they know it means a bullet to the head."

Ben pointed to his temple to imitate a gun and cleared his throat while everyone anxiously awaited his next words.

"'Fixers' are the third class. All those smart kids that Sean recruited early on were the first Fixers. Then other survivors with useful skills were recruited; mechanics like me and Jim, cattle farmers like you two…"

Ben nodded toward Brian and Susan.

"…even kids whose parents had taught them to fly airplanes. Anyone with a rare but valuable skill was recruited to be a Fixer, and it was the job of the Infantry to find these people…and they searched far and wide for them."

"Why did he call them Fixers?" Andy asked when Ben took another breath.

"'Cuz Sean didn't want them to get an inflated sense of self-importance by calling them 'experts' or 'specialists' even though he never would have gotten to where he is today without them. I mean, how many kids do you know who can fly a plane? I didn't know anyone like that growing up, but Sean managed to find them. Now there are about two thousand of 'em…Fixers, that is."

Looking tired, Ben combed his fingers through his thick, dark hair.

"One thing Sean insisted upon when the Infantry found a possible Fixer was that the person had to be male."

Ben then looked up at Andy and saw the unmistakable expression of disgust appear on her face.

"No one in the Infantry and none of the Fixers has ever been a girl. Sean thinks girls are basically worthless except when he wants to get laid, so about three years after the virus, when the testosterone really started to kick in, Sean created the fourth class. He thought it would be amusing to find the prettiest girls in New York and keep them around to be sex slaves for him and his buddies…mostly the Directors. He called them 'Helens' because they were all beautiful like Helen of Troy. Sean is obsessed with Greek mythology.

"Most of these girls didn't want to have anything to do with Sean at first, but once he offered them certain benefits, they began to enjoy their new lifestyle. They lived in the nicest apartments in Manhattan, wore the best clothes, and always had enough food to eat. And since happy, healthy prostitutes were more fun to have around than sad, sickly ones, Sean didn't mind giving them these things as long as they did what he wanted. And the Helens made his Directors happy, and with a steady supply of drugs, alcohol, and parties, Sean created the ultimate playground to keep them and the Fixers loyal and…malleable. And eventually the Helens didn't seem to care that they were being used for sex as long as they kept getting things they wanted. They became addicted to the attention they received. Being treated like a celebrity does that, I guess."

Ben took a sip of water before continuing.

"The last class of people is everyone else in the city…the 'Dregs.' Even though they're by far the largest group, they're utterly powerless, which is exactly what Sean wants. The society he had created was based entirely on a system of reward and punishment. If you do something to piss off the Directors, the Infantry, or even some of the Fixers, the water and power in your house gets shut off and your food rations are cut. Or even worse, you're sent to one of the prisons Sean had reopened and are left to rot. But if you do something to help Sean, like ratting out a neighbor for claiming to have more people living in their house then they actually do in order to get bigger food rations, then you get rewarded. The whole system brings out the worst in everyone, which was Sean's plan all along. No one knows who they can trust, and as long as everyone remains suspicious of one another, there's no chance of people banding together to organize a revolt."

With his forehead glistening with sweat, Ben took another sip of water. He looked exhausted, as if he'd suddenly aged ten years in the last few hours. He took one more sip before saying, "All the faith people once had to restore some kind of civilized life is long gone. Now everyone just walks around the city like zombies, too scared to wake up."

Ben put down the glass of water and abruptly stood up.

"I'm gonna go for a walk. Jim, you can tell them the rest."

Then he gestured toward the window to the house across the street.

"We'll talk to those guys tomorrow."

Without another word, Ben picked up his rifle and left the house, bewildering everyone by this sudden halt to the story. When Andy started to rise from her chair to go after him, Jim motioned for her to leave him alone.

"You have to understand," Jim began slowly, "Ben knew Sean very well. He was a Director…and one of the few people Sean really trusted. He blames himself every day because he turned a blind eye to Sean's behavior for so long. But he had good reason."

Jim then hesitated because he knew the effect his next words would have.

"You see, Ben had a younger sister. Her name was Karen. And Sean killed her."

* * *

The roads on the Capitol Beltway and I-95 heading north were riddled with potholes. It was to be expected, but with every jarring hit to the car's suspension, Sean's patience dwindled.

The driver, a Dreg with high-level connections, had forgotten to bring extra containers of gas for the journey back to New York. The fuel gauge on the BMW indicated that less than a quarter of a tank remained, and they were currently between Washington and Baltimore with two hundred miles to go.

Sitting alone in the backseat, Sean leaned forward until his face was within inches of the driver's right ear.

"I'll give you ten minutes to find more gas after we run out. If you don't find any by then, I'll leave you on the side of the road with a bullet in your stomach."

Sean leaned back in his seat and rolled down the window. The summertime humidity in the mid-Atlantic was oppressive, but any use of air conditioning would only burn more precious fuel.

Sean hated being hot.

The driver said nothing, though fear in the form of beads of sweat rolled down his forehead and into his eyes, causing him to swerve the car slightly and strike yet another pothole.

"Hit another one, and you'll get a hole through your brain," Sean barked as the Infantry officer sitting in the passenger's seat beside the driver grasped onto the handle of the loaded pistol holstered at his hip.

The driver quickly steadied himself. However, his fate was sealed an hour later when the gas tank ran dry and the BMW came to a halt on the Interstate between Wilmington and Philadelphia.

"Jesus Christ, how stupid are you?!" Sean mocked the driver. "You didn't even try getting off at an exit and take a chance at a gas station. Now get the fuck out of my car!"

Stepping outside, the driver began to beg for mercy and apologized incoherently before urinating in his pants, but Sean gave the driver no notice as he went around the back of the car and opened the truck. After retrieving a long-range push-to-talk radio, he transmitted a few instructions to someone at the other end. Then, after grabbing a small bag containing food and water from the back seat, he signaled to the officer, who then removed his gun from his holster.

In one smooth motion and with chilling indifference, the officer fired once at the blubbering driver. As promised, the bullet struck directly in the abdomen, guaranteeing a slow and painful death.

The driver slumped to the ground, writhing in pain as Sean stepped coolly passed him. He and the officer continued walking along the highway for a few miles until the car he had requested over the radio to Philadelphia arrived.

The inconvenience of the entire situation left Sean in a foul mood for hours. Only Lily, the most beautiful and most desired of all the Helens, could cheer him upon returning to New York.

* * *

Despite the multiple expressions of shock upon learning of Ben's sister, Jim continued the story where Ben had left off.

"Karen survived the outbreak like the rest of us. She and Ben were very close…all three of us were, which was lucky for me since I was an only child. Ben's always been more like a brother than a cousin, and Karen was no different.

"Unfortunately, she was also a diabetic who needed daily shots of insulin. With the supply shrinking, this became a big problem for her…for all of us. We stocked up as much as we could, but there was only so much we could find. I mean, it wasn't as if Karen was the only survivor with diabetes."

Andy frowned. The lack of medical supplies was something she understood firsthand.

"We left Virginia and the whole DC area a few months after the outbreak. As some of you saw last year, DC became a wasteland, so we decided to take a chance and head north. We stayed in Philadelphia for about six months, but Karen's insulin supply was quickly running out. By then, Sean was close to turning power back on in New York, which we often heard rumors about, so we decided to check it out.

"Not long after we got there and found a somewhat livable apartment in Queens, Ben was approached by someone about his skills as a mechanic. He and I had repaired a few of the abandoned cars in our new neighborhood, and before we knew it, we were both given positions as Fixers. We repaired cars and other machines—no different than what we did in Aspen—but being a Fixer meant that you got better housing, more food, and most importantly, medicine. And because her brother and cousin were both Fixers, Karen never ran out of insulin.

"By the time we met finally met Sean, we'd already been living in New York for more than a year. I was fifteen and Ben was sixteen, but I remember the day because it was Karen's fifteenth birthday; she and I were only a few months apart. We had moved to Manhattan and were living right off Fifth Avenue in this huge apartment that was probably worth millions back in the day. Anyway, we had some friends over and there was even a cake for Karen. And suddenly, Sean showed up with some of his friends."

A look a concentration appeared on Jim's face as he recalled the details of that day.

"He seemed normal enough; no obvious sign that he was the monster that he is today, but you could tell right away that he was intelligent. At that time, his power and influence in the city was growing quickly, but he was still vulnerable. We didn't know why he came to the party, but months later we found out that Sean had wanted to meet Karen. She was a very pretty girl, and Sean had heard about her from his friends. Ben and I were protective of her because of her diabetes, but also because boys were constantly chasing her, even before the outbreak.

"Karen was always shy around strangers, and when she met Sean, she didn't say much to him. This didn't seem to bother him, though, and he began talking to Ben quite a bit instead. He seemed to be impressed with Ben, and Sean isn't someone who is easily impressed. A few days later, he asked Ben to become the Director of Transportation for the city. At first Ben was worried about accepting the position because rumors about what Sean was really like were already spreading. But he eventually accepted the position because he didn't want to offend Sean and risk losing Karen's supply of insulin.

"So Ben became a Director, but unlike the other Directors who abused their positions, he actually cared about his job. About two hundred people were assigned to his department, and he was in charge of them. A few of them, including me, were Fixers, but the majority were just average people…Dregs, as Sean would later call them, but they worked hard and learned quickly. Hell, we were all learning. Ben and I are good with cars, but we didn't know anything about fixing an entire subway system, which was part of Ben's responsibility. But we did it. It took us months to work out all the kinks, but we finally got it working, which made Sean very happy. After that, he began to confide in Ben more, sharing his plans of expanding his command south to Philadelphia and even DC. Ben had always been uneasy about Sean and his motives, and it was around this time after finishing the subway that Sean's true nature appeared. It all started when he began selecting girls to become Helens.

"Some of the other Directors told Sean to choose Karen, but he refused. Ben and I wanted to believe that he refused out of respect for Ben, but we realized too late it was because Sean wanted Karen all to himself. She had just turned sixteen, and it seemed like the number of boys chasing after her had quadrupled from the previous year. Some of them were decent enough and sincere with their intentions, but Karen wasn't interested in any of them except this kid named Timmy.

"Timmy lived in the same neighborhood in Queens when we first came to New York, and he and Karen clicked from day one. They spent a lot of time together, even after we moved to Manhattan. Timmy would ride his bike over the 59th Street Bridge from Queens every day to visit us, and after a while, he stayed with us in our apartment. He didn't have any surviving family, so we looked out for him. Ben and I showed him how to fix cars, and he actually became pretty good at it."

The memory formed a faint smile on Jim's face that quickly dissolved into sadness.

"Over time, Sean became more and more obsessed with Karen. It wasn't that he was in love with her. He wanted to *own* her, to *possess* her, and the fact that she had so many admirers only made him want her more. Ben and I were afraid that he would hurt her, but we couldn't confront him about it either. Karen needed her insulin, and the supply was becoming dangerously low. It was only because of Ben's position as a Director that she managed to get her shots every day. So we were trapped. Sean's network had grown so large that making an enemy of him meant making enemies with hundreds. So we kept quiet, made sure Karen was rarely alone, and came up with a plan; Ben and I would leave the city and search for enough insulin to last Karen for a long time.

"Since we knew we were going to be gone awhile, we had to justify our absence to Sean, so we told him we were going to check out the subway in Boston. He liked the idea because he was struggling to gain control there and knew that fixing the subway would give him a huge advantage. So we went to Boston and actually worked on the subway to avoid suspicion. We even got it partially working again, but most days, one of us would disappear for hours at a time and search hospitals, doctor's offices, and pharmaceutical companies within a hundred miles of Boston. We went to Providence, Concord, Manchester, and about a dozen other towns in New England. It took almost two months, but we finally gathered enough insulin to last Karen five years, which we hoped would buy her enough time until some genius with a microscope came along and figured out how to make it again."

"But doesn't insulin have an expiration date?" Andy asked suddenly.

"Yeah, it does, but Karen had been using expired insulin for years without any issues. The vials just become less effective as it gets older, but that just meant that Karen had to monitor her insulin levels more carefully as time went on."

Satisfied, Andy nodded and let Jim continue.

"So after finding all the insulin we could, Ben and I headed back to New York. All we had to do was pack our things and leave in the middle of the night. We didn't plan on coming back. We were going to head west somewhere and start over."

Jim let out a labored sigh that seemed to resonate throughout the room. He then rubbed his eyes before resuming.

"But when we got back from Boston, we couldn't find Karen anywhere. It was like she had vanished. We asked everyone we knew, but nobody knew anything. We went to Queens to see if she was staying there with Timmy. Before going to Boston, we had told him to stay with her as much as possible and keep himself armed at all times. But later we learned from other kids in the neighborhood that Timmy had been shot and killed by the Infantry."

A collective gasp erupted among the group, but Jim pushed on. "Sean had taken advantage of our absence and had the Infantry follow Karen day and night. When she and Timmy went to Queens one day, they followed them there and kidnapped Karen after killing Timmy in his own home, less than a week after Ben and I had gone to Boston. She became a captive in Sean's private apartment in Manhattan, where he drugged her daily with heroin until her body became addicted to it. By the time Ben and I reached Sean's apartment to confront him about Timmy and Karen's whereabouts, it was too late. The combination of the heroin and her diabetes had been too much for her body to take. She had died just hours before Ben and I showed up."

Another gasp escaped from both Morgan and Susan at the same moment, to which Jim responded with a firm nod as though reconfirming the horrible truth. Meanwhile, a single tear escaped Andy's eye, which she quickly wiped away.

"I was devastated, but Ben went into a rage when he saw her lifeless body. I swear he would've killed Sean with his bare hands had another Director not shown up to defend that sick bastard. We were lucky to escape. I held Sean and the Director at gunpoint while Ben carried Karen's body outside. We immediately fled New York and left everything behind except some clothes and our truck.

"That evening, we drove all the way to Washington DC and buried Karen in Arlington Cemetery. Ben wanted her put to rest somewhere important. He said that she was a casualty of war just like the thousands of soldiers around her. 'A war against evil' he said, and I'll never forget the tone of his voice when he said those words.

"For a few weeks after Karen's death, we hunkered down in the same neighborhood in Virginia where we grew up. Ben became depressed and started drinking whatever liquor he could find to kill the pain. He couldn't stop blaming himself for his sister's death. I tried to tell him it wasn't his fault, but he wouldn't listen, and for a while I thought he'd never recover. It's strange, but finding out that Sean was using the virus finally snapped Ben out of his depression.

"One day, I managed to keep Ben sober long enough to go hunting for rabbits and deer in the woods near our neighborhood. We weren't very successful, but on the walk home, we ran into three guys passing through the area. We often saw people wandering around most days, so we didn't think anything of it, but these guys were different. They looked healthier and were well-fed, and they were driving a car. Outside of New York and Philadelphia, most people got around by walking, biking, or riding horses that hadn't been killed for food. Nobody drove cars because there wasn't any gas being produced like Sean was producing it in New York, so Ben and I assumed they had come from up north. We approached them carefully in case Sean had sent anyone to come after us. But once we realized they weren't looking for us, we started talking to them about general stuff, like where they were from and where they were going. When they told us about Sean and New York and how things were so much better there than anywhere else, and Ben and I soon realized that we were talking to Fixers, and that they were in the area because Sean had sent them to look through the Pentagon and a few other buildings that were once vital to national security.

"We invited them to our house for dinner and offered them liquor to see if we could get them talking. Eventually, one of them started spilling secrets about Fort Detrick and the virus. He told us how his father had been one of the scientists who'd developed the virus, and he began describing the history of the virus's development and how it hadn't been ready to use when it was accidentally released six years ago. He told us that samples of the virus still existed at the Fort and that it was still lethal to many survivors who were now beyond a certain age…including most of us in this room."

A shudder shot down Andy's spine as she immediately thought of her father in his final days. Morgan, meanwhile, curled up into a ball on the couch and hugged her knees tightly to her chest. "Sean sent Fixers to the Fort to study the virus, and once they learned how to handle it without exposing themselves, he started using it to intimidate people into doing things for him. By the time we heard about it, he'd already killed dozens of people he decided were less than obedient. And because the virus and what it did six years ago is such a horrible memory for every survivor, Sean had found the perfect tool. People fear it more than guns. You can survive a bullet, but no one survives from exposure to the virus."

Jim stopped to take a sip from Ben's abandoned glass. As he leaned forward, Morgan placed a comforting hand on his back.

"It was Ben's idea to blow up the lab at Fort Detrick. At first, he saw it as a way to get his revenge for Karen's death, but later he realized that we *had* to destroy the virus forever. If we didn't destroy it, then not only would Sean continue to kill more innocent people, but if things got out of control, it could end up spreading like it did the first time and kill millions all over again. So, we went to West Virginia to some of the mining towns and found some peoples who knew about explosives used for coal mining. We learned how to use them and took some back to Virginia. We staked out the lab in Maryland to determine how many people worked there and when the place was empty. We wanted to destroy the place without killing anyone. So one night last summer, after months of planning, we placed about a dozen large barrels of gasoline throughout the building to magnify the power of the explosion before triggering the detonators.

"The explosion was enormous—a gigantic fireball that could be seen and heard from miles away. Afterwards, we headed south, and that's when we met you three on the highway. Ben and I were suspicious of you that day because we knew that Sean would assume we were behind the explosion and hunt us down. We suspected anyone we ran into and still do whenever a stranger appears."

Jim finally stopped. The story had ended, although in many ways, it had just begun.

No one spoke. The horrible truth about Sean and the virus was overwhelming. It took the piercing sound of a gunshot from outside to awaken everyone from their thoughts, and within seconds, everyone had scrambled out of the house.

Across the street and under the dim moonlight, Ben could be seen standing in the driveway with the outline of his rifle visible and held in the ready position. To his right and in the line of fire were the two strangers, Matt and Kevin, both of whom were holding their hands up in surrender.

Jim and Brian arrived first, and Ben said to them in a steady voice that matched the solid grip on his weapon, "They lied. They're working for Sean. I heard them talking."

Neither Matt nor Kevin tried to deny the accusation. In fact, the duo was strangely silent and their looks of defiance were unmistakable, even in near-darkness.

"Let's give them a ride to the desert," Jim declared after a tense moment. "We'll drop 'em somewhere west of here…far off the Interstate. They can walk back to New York for all I care."

"That's better than they deserve," Ben snapped bitterly.

"Yeah, it is, but we're not like them, Ben. We're not like Sean."

Restraining himself, Ben lowered his rifle before releasing a long and heavy sigh.

"No, we're not."

* * *

Assuming correctly that Ben and Jim would appreciate the additional security of outnumbering their 'prisoners,' Brian accompanied the two cousins on the long journey in the dark. While they were gone, the rest of the group dispersed and went to bed. The events of the evening weighed heavily of everyone's mind. Morning would soon arrive and bring with it new realities of a world where a person like Sean existed, and the threat of the virus had returned.

Just before falling asleep, Andy picked up an old dictionary she'd found in the house and flipped to the "D" section. Using her flashlight, she skimmed over the appropriate page and found the word "dreg." There were a few definitions, but only one caught her eye:

"The vilest and most worthless part of anything; as, the dregs of society."

Chapter XVI

04 July 2021

Andy arose the next morning just as the sun emerged above the visible horizon. Her sleep had been restless, with bizarre dreams weaving in and out of her subconscious; images of people she didn't know chasing her through dense forests that transformed into the busy streets of a large metropolitan city. In the dreams, she always managed to escape her pursuers just in time.

She tiptoed through the house as everyone slept and stepped outside. It relieved her to see Ben's truck parked across the street. As she crossed the vacant road, Andy saw the outline of someone sitting on the front steps of the house across the street. Startled, she took a few stumbling steps backward as the figure stood up.

"Andy, it's me."

It was Ben's voice, and when her eyes finally adjusted to the light, she saw that it was indeed him. Embarrassed, she approached the steps and took a seat beside him as he sat back down.

"Sorry, I didn't mean to scare you."

"When did you guys get back?"

"A few hours ago. We didn't go as far as we wanted. We were running out of gas."

"How far did you get?"

"About fifty miles. We left 'em on the side of a deserted road about ten miles west of Route 84. They'll have to walk for miles before they get to another town."

"Did they say anything to you, like how many others are after you?"

Ben shook his head. "They didn't speak the entire time. Brian and I sat in the back with them and Jim drove."

"Do you think they'll try to come back here? Should we leave?"

Ben bobbed his head once. "Yeah, we'll have to. I don't think those two will come back here, but if they somehow make it back to New York, they'll tell Sean where we are."

Andy nodded. This news didn't particularly upset her, for she held no great attachment to Santa Rosa. However, she hoped that Maria could be convinced to finally leave as well. In the months since their return to New Mexico, Maria and her siblings had grown close to everyone, as Brian and Susan had in Aspen. Leaving them behind once again seemed unthinkable.

"When should we leave?" was Andy's eventual response as she glanced back at her house.

"As soon as possible," Ben replied somewhat absently. "Though I don't know how we're gonna be able to go anywhere at all. We're almost out of gas, and I don't know what the alternative is."

"We'll figure it out. We always do."

There was so much Andy wanted to say to him but she had no idea where to begin. The past that he had concealed for so long turned out to be far more tragic than she'd ever imagined.

"Did you sleep at all?" was all she said while noting that Ben was wearing the same clothes as the evening before.

"A couple of hours."

Andy nodded lightly. How could she even begin to speak of a beloved sister murdered by a sociopath? Or was it a psychopath? Was there really a difference?

She chose a more neutral subject.

"It's impressive what you did…destroying the lab. That took

guts. And probably a ton of patience."

Ben merely shrugged off the compliment and looked down at his hands. "We just did what needed to be done."

He dropped his head down and combed both hands through his hair in a gesture of immense frustration. "It wasn't enough, though. He still has the virus."

"How was it transmitted when he wanted to infect someone? With a syringe?"

Ben nodded. "Yeah, and if he wanted to infect more than one person, he would inject one and lock the others in a sealed room with the injected person. Since the virus is airborne, everyone in the room would get infected. Sometimes the others would strangle the person who had been injected before they could be infected themselves, but that never worked."

"Why?"

"Well, according to the son of the scientist Jim and I met, the virus was designed to be what they called a 'rapid killing agent,' which means from the moment one person is infected, either by injection or through the air, that person can then infect another person within a minute or two."

Andy thought about this for a moment before speaking.

"So, if I was injected right now with the virus, and then a minute later, you came and sat next to me like you are now, I would infect you immediately?"

"That's right. It was designed that way so that our military could target an isolated group of people, say, in a house or remote building somewhere and all the men would be infected very quickly. They were also supposed to die within minutes so that they wouldn't move around and infect innocent people. But we all know it doesn't work that way."

"So there were *two* errors with the virus when it was released?"

"How do you mean?"

"Well, the first mistake was that it infected both men *and* women, and the second was that it took more than a week to kill a person."

Ben's eyebrows lifted as he listened to her point. "Yeah, you're right. Everyone was dying and infecting others without even knowing it."

Andy exhaled sharply. "Jesus Christ…no wonder it killed billions in just a few weeks."

"Exactly. Whatever made the virus so contagious worked, but the things that were supposed to prevent it from killing the wrong people or spreading too quickly didn't."

"Jesus Christ," Andy muttered again. "And he still has the virus?"

Ben cracked his knuckles and readjusted his sitting position before answering.

"He must've stashed some vials somewhere away from the lab. And now he's probably got some Fixer in another lab working to replicate it."

"But those guys…Matt and Kevin…couldn't they have been lying to you about the whole thing? Maybe it was just a trick to draw you and Jim back to New York."

"Maybe," Ben conceded. "Anything's possible."

The daylight had intensified to the point where Andy could finally make out Ben's expressions. He looked exhausted.

Out of nowhere, an off-topic question entered Andy's head. "What does he look like?"

"Sean?"

"Yeah."

It was the first time either of them had uttered the name.

"I guess he's about my height and build. Kinda brownish-blond hair."

Ben stroked at the stubble underneath his chin in a reflective manner. "What I remember most about him are his eyes. They're icy blue in a kinda terrifying way. And when he looks at you, it's like he's looking beyond your skull and into your brain and reading your thoughts."

He turned toward Andy and faced the sunrise. His gaze was distant, as though he were looking at something miles away. "Karen used to say that whenever Sean looked at her, it was as if he was telepathically injecting fear into her body." Then, with a faint smile, he shook his head slowly and said, "She was very poetic."

Ben talking about his sister in such a way made Andy's heart swell, and without even thinking, she rested her right hand on top of his left and gave it a firm squeeze.

"I'm sorry about your sister. And I'm sorry that I gave you such a hard time for not telling me about her…and everything else."

Wordlessly, Ben's gaze shifted down to Andy's hand on top of his. Then he put his right hand over hers, raised her hand upward and kissed the top of her knuckles lightly. He released her hand and slowly rose to his feet. Looking down at her, he said, "I'm tired as hell….going back to bed."

Andy stood up and met Ben's eye level by climbing one step higher on the steps leading to the front door. Without thinking, she reached out and placed her hands on his shoulders and stood up on her toes to lean forward and kiss him on the forehead. When she pulled back, she met his weary gaze for an unusually long moment. Though heavy from fatigue, his eyes became rapidly alert. A split second before he could move toward her, however, Andy turned away and stepped down. The moment had passed.

"Get some rest," she called back to him as she made her way across the street. "Sounds like we've got some planning to do."

She disappeared inside as Ben stared after her.

* * *

"Wouldn't it be nice to stay somewhere longer than a few months?"

Morgan said this to Andy later that morning in the living room as she fed Katie. Her words conveyed a desire rather than a complaint.

"Would you want to stay here longer?"

"I dunno," Morgan replied before shaking her head. "No. I miss trees and green grass. I don't think I'm cut out to live in the desert."

"Me neither. But at least we're all together this time."

"Thank God for that. I'm glad I don't have to wonder anymore if

Jim will stay, or if I have to give birth without you because you've gone and gotten yourself kidnapped."

Andy laughed heartily. "I don't think you were ever in danger of Jim leaving you. He was smitten with you from the first day we all met. And as for getting kidnapped, there's little chance of that happening again. Wherever we go from here, I won't be so trusting of people."

Andy rose from the sofa and moved over to the window facing the street and the house across it. "Poor Ben," she sighed. "Never in a million years would I have guessed any part of what Jim told us yesterday."

"Me neither," Morgan agreed. "But it explains a lot."

Andy turned away from the window. "Like what?"

"Like why he's so distant sometimes, like he's afraid to get too close to someone because he might lose them just like he lost his sister. It also explains why he was so determined to be the one to go after you when you were kidnapped."

Looking puzzled, Andy made her way back to the couch.

"He told me why. Because Jim wanted to stay with you and Brian needed to stay with his sister. It only made sense that Ben was the one who went after me."

Morgan rolled her eyes and let out a moan as she shifted Katie's weight in her arms. "Is that what you think?"

"What else *should* I think?"

"Forget it, I shouldn't have said anything."

Katie started to coo adorably, and Morgan stood up and began circling around the room, gently bouncing her daughter up and down and mimicking her sounds.

"God, it's so much easier now that she can hold her head up on her own."

But Andy wasn't listening. She rose from the couch, approached Morgan, and offered Katie her pinky finger to grab onto. The infant happily gripped it with her whole hand and squealed, making the two young women laugh in return.

When her smile faded, Andy turned to Morgan with a serious face. "So Ben went after me because…?"

"Because he's in love with you," Morgan quickly finished as though she were finally ready to rid her mind of the secret.

But Andy shook her head in refusal, and laughed at her friend's ridiculous suggestion.

"No…no, he doesn't. Why would…?"

"Why would he love you? Bloody hell, Andy…you're beautiful, smart, compassionate…and you're strong. And Ben isn't intimidated by any of that."

But Andy still wasn't convinced. "Has he said anything? To you or to Jim?"

"He doesn't need to. We both see it. How he acts around you and looks at you. So does Maria. Hell, even Charlie sees it, and my brother isn't exactly perceptive when it comes to this sort of thing. I mean, Susan had to practically snog him before he got the hint."

Andy gently retrieved her pinky from Katie and took a step backwards. Stubbornly, she placed her hands on her hips.

"I think you're all just imagining it. Ben's the kind of guy to go after what he wants. And if he wanted me, he would've said something by now."

"No, you're wrong. He's exactly the type of guy who *wouldn't* admit his feelings if he had any doubts about how you feel. He wouldn't risk it."

"Well, *I'm* not gonna say anything."

"Why? You don't feel that way about him?"

Andy quickly turned away and headed back to the window.

"It doesn't matter how I feel because I disagree with you. Ben is just a friend…a very good friend, I admit, but still just a friend. And it won't ever be anything more."

With a heavy sigh, Morgan gave up the argument. "Oh, Andy…I wish you wouldn't resist these things. It's wonderful to be in love."

"I'm sure it is, and maybe one day I'll be lucky and find out what that's like. But now isn't the time…"

"What, you think you're too young to fall in love?"

"I didn't mean that…but I *am* only twenty. My parents didn't get married until they were in their early thirties."

"Andy, the calendar might tell you that you're only twenty, but we're both so much older than that. As far as I'm concerned, we became adults years ago."

* * *

The conversation with Morgan gnawed at Andy all day, but she refused to let it consume her when there were more important things to worry about. Things like Sean and his virus.

That afternoon, she stopped by to see Maria at her home. Julio and Carmen were off swimming in the lake with Susan and Charlie.

Maria was busy making dinner when Andy entered the house.

"You sleep at all last night?" Andy asked as she closed the front door behind her.

Maria looked up from her cutting board and frowned.

"Barely. I still can't believe everything Jim told us."

"I know," Andy muttered as she took a seat at the kitchen table.

"All of you are still coming over for dinner, right?" Maria asked as she finished dicing an avocado.

"Yeah, I think so. Ben and Brian are out hunting, but they should be back in time."

"What time did the boys get back last night?"

"I dunno exactly. Sometime in the early morning, maybe."

"I can't believe those two strangers were actually hunting for Ben and Jim. Makes me wonder how many more are out there looking for them."

"Me too. And now we have to leave again."

Maria nodded calmly. She understood the reality of the situation.

"And when will that be?"

"Not sure, but probably not for at least a few days. Our biggest problem is that we're almost out of gas."

"How much do you need?" Maria asked as she began cutting a second avocado in half and scooping out the soft insides of the fruit.

Meanwhile, Andy rapped her fingers on the counter as she performed the math.

"Well, as much as we can get, but fifty gallons, maybe? It depends if we take one car or two."

Maria nodded again.

"I'll see what I can do."

"Really? If you can pull that off, you're my hero."

During all the months spent in Santa Rosa, the mystery of how Maria managed to acquire such valuable commodities like food and gasoline had remained a secret, but neither Andy nor anyone else ever pressed her about the issue. After all the generosity she had repeatedly bestowed upon them, respecting her privacy was the least she deserved in return.

"Are you still sticking with your eighteen-month timeline?" Andy asked, avoiding details.

Maria was now smashing the avocado fruit into pulp.

"I don't know," she replied, frowning again. "Things aren't going too well back home, and I'm starting to lose hope."

"So why don't you come with us?"

"And go where? You don't even know where you're going."

"I know, but we could use you, Maria. You're extremely capable, and I know that no matter where we go, we're gonna need all the help we can get."

"You sound like you're going into battle or something."

Andy smiled slightly as she stared absently at the surface of the kitchen table.

"You know, I keep wondering what we're doing here every day. I mean, we get up every morning, we find food to eat, we take baths in the lakes, we cook the food we find if there's wood or gas to burn, and then we go to bed and do it all again the next morning. And that's it."

"Yeah…so? You want something more meaningful in your life?" Maria remarked with mild admonishment. "You're also forgetting that you're safe, with friends, and you're helping Morgan raise her child. Isn't that enough?"

"Honestly, no it's not. Not for me. We're living the way people did back in the Dark Ages."

"This *is* the Dark Ages, Andy. That virus pushed us centuries back in time."

"But we have all the knowledge of a real civilization…all the scientific and technical knowledge. And we have the example of generations of people before us and what they did to make the world what it became."

"But aren't you forgetting that it was scientific knowledge that created the virus in the first place?" Maria remarked as she began adding dried spices to the avocado pulp.

"I know, but it was a mistake. Humans make mistakes."

"It was a pretty big mistake."

"I know, I know," Andy muttered as she closed her eyes and rubbed her temples. "And I just keep telling myself that it's just a phase and that I'm just…I dunno…antsy…"

Her voice trailed off and she released her head and opened her eyes. Maria, meanwhile, put down her knife and turned to Andy, her eyes narrowing keenly.

"What are you really saying, exactly?"

Looking up from the table, Andy met Maria's eyes with equal intensity.

"I'm saying that I want to do something that will make a difference…not just for us, but for people everywhere. Something… something that inspires everyone to work together and get life back to the way it was."

"And what would that something be?"

The words came out almost immediately.

"I think we should start by destroying whatever remains of the virus."

Maria absorbed these words.

"Which would mean going to New York, right?"

"If that's where Sean is, then that's where the virus is."

"What if those two strangers were lying? They lied about who they were, so they could've been lying about everything else."

"I thought about that, but what if they were telling the truth? Should we just ignore the possibility? We all know how deadly the virus is, and if there's a shred of truth to their story, then all of us are in danger."

Maria, however, wasn't convinced. "It seems like a long way to go just to prove a story that was told by two liars. Plus, after everything that Ben and Jim told us, New York sounds like the last place I would want to be."

"True, but victories aren't won in paradise."

"Very poetic," Maria observed with a smirk.

"Funny, that's how Ben described his sister this morning."

This surprised Maria. "You talked to him about her?"

"Just for second. He actually brought her up."

Maria shook her head sadly as she began dicing tomatoes for the guacamole she was making. "All of us lost people we loved when the virus came, but to lose someone afterward like that is horrible."

"I know. It's unimaginable…how she died."

Neither spoke for a moment as Maria folded the diced tomato into the avocado mixture.

"I hate to say it," she began, "But I think you will have a hard time convincing anyone to go back to New York. Ben and Jim left for good reason, and after what happened yesterday, I don't think they'll ever consider going back into the lion's den."

"But it would also be the last place that anyone would look for them."

"Then you'll have to convince them that destroying what's left of the virus is worth the risk."

"And what would I have to do to convince you to come?"

Maria raised her eyebrows. "Truthfully, probably not much. As I said, I've started to lose hope, and the thought of all of you leaving me again isn't comforting either."

"I'm sorry, Maria," Andy replied with genuine sincerity. "I know you wanted to go back home. But I know everyone would be glad if the three of you came with us."

Maria smiled faintly. "We'll see. But just between you and me, I understand what you mean by wanting to make a difference. That's why I haven't left here yet. I'm still trying to help people back home."

"Maybe one day you can explain all of that to me."

"I will, I promise," Maria said without a hint of doubt. "But in the meantime, I have something for you."

Moving away from the counter, Maria opened a cabinet drawer on the other side of the kitchen and retrieved a bottle of wine. She handed it to Andy, who grabbed it tentatively.

"What's this for?"

"Nothing. Just something I thought you might enjoy," Maria replied with a knowing smile before adding, "When you talk to Ben about your crazy idea, you should share this with him. He might be more willing to listen."

"Are you trying to get us drunk or something?"

Maria laughed. "It'll take more than that to get you both drunk, though I'm sure Ben would *love* to get you drunk."

Andy rolled her eyes. "Not you too. First Morgan, and now this. You're all imagining something that's not there."

Trying hard not to smile, Maria held her hands up as though denying an ulterior motive. "All I'm saying is that *that* might help your conversation," she said as neutrally as possible and pointed to the bottle.

"I doubt it," Andy replied with a frown while staring at the wine in her hand. "But what the hell, I'll give it shot."

* * *

"You're insane. I'm not going back to New York."

Ben and Andy were sitting alone on the curb in front of Maria's house while everyone else was inside chatting after dinner. Her first attempt was unsuccessful, despite going so far as to beg him to listen to his conscience.

"My conscience is clear. Jim and I did our best to destroy the virus. If Sean still has it, which we don't even know for sure, then there's really nothing we can do. Someone else can step up to the plate and try to stop him, but I'm done with it all."

"You don't really mean that, do you?" Andy implored. "Ben, I saw you last night. I've never seen you so upset than when you were told that the virus still existed."

"But that was before I overheard those two assholes talking about how they were going to persuade Jim and I to go back to New York and then hand us over to Sean. After that, everything they told us yesterday became a lie as far as I'm concerned."

Ben then narrowed his gaze on Andy's face. "Why are you so eager to go to New York?"

She quickly turned away. "I don't know…I can't explain it…"

Her voice trailed off, and she thought about the bottle of wine Maria had given her. It was hiding under her bed back at the house. For some reason, she didn't want Morgan or anyone else to see it.

"C'mon," she said as she abruptly rose off the curb. "Let's go for a walk."

Ben hesitated before slowly rising to his feet. "Okay…where're we going?"

"Doesn't matter, but first I need to get something at the house, okay?"

Ben shrugged. "Sure, whatever."

Fifteen minutes later, Andy emerged from her house with the bottle of wine in her hand and a rusty corkscrew in her back pocket. Even in the waning daylight, Ben could clearly see what she was carrying.

"I never would have taken you for a drinker," he teased.

"I figured I'd find out what the big deal is."

"You've never drank before?"

Andy smiled sheepishly. "Not really. Just at a couple of weddings when I was a kid. Some champagne, a little bit of wine…that sort of thing."

Ben asked to see the bottle by extending a hand. Andy passed it to him, and he took a glance at the label. "Cabernet Sauvignon," he read with proper pronunciation. "California…2014."

He handed the bottle back to Andy as they began to walk down the street.

"I'm sure it'll be good."

"What about you?" she began. "Did you ever drink…oh, shit!"

Andy stopped dead in her tracks and smacked her forehead with her palm.

"What?" Ben asked with concern.

Frozen with shame and embarrassment, Andy shook her head and muttered, "I totally forgot…"

"Forgot what?"

"Uh, yesterday, Jim told us that after…after Karen died, you…"

She couldn't finish, but Ben understood.

"Jesus, Ben…I'm sorry. I wasn't thinking…"

He put up a hand to stop her. "It's okay. There's no need to apologize. It was a long time ago."

"I'll go put it back," she said quickly, referring to the wine.

"No, don't," Ben insisted. "It's fine."

"But I wanted to share it with you."

"Then let's share it. I'm not in danger of becoming an alcoholic, if that's what you're worried about. Even if I was, there's not a lot of liquor out there to be found anymore."

"I wasn't worried about that, but…are you sure?"

"Yes, I'm sure. I admit that I was in trouble after Karen died, but I got through it…actually, Jim got me through it. But it's been almost two years."

Still uncertain, Andy shrugged tentatively. "All right."

They continued walking until they reached a small park near their neighborhood. There was a playground in the center, and they sat down next to each other on the swings. Andy opened the wine and threw the cork aside.

"Sorry, I didn't bring glasses," she said.

"No worries, I don't mind swapping spit with you."

"Very funny."

Andy took a healthy swig from the bottle and handed it to Ben.

"You were right," she said after swallowing. "It's not bad."

Ben tried for himself and took a long sip from the bottle. After finishing, he wiped his mouth with the back of his hand and nodded in agreement. "Pretty good."

They drank half the bottle before any significant conversation passed between them. After her fourth "sip," Andy could already feel the wine's effects. Her thin frame, meager diet, and inexperience with alcohol did little to protect her against its consequences. She did, however, find it easier to talk, though not physically, as her tongue grew heavy. Any hesitation to voice her thoughts, however, was fading.

When handing over the bottle to Ben, she dabbed her lips with her fingertips and said, "Did you ever think that you're meant to go back to New York and fight against Sean? Like it's your destiny or something?"

Ben looked at Andy as though she had lost her mind. "Man, you *are* a cheap date! I'll have to remember that."

"No, I'm serious. Don't you ever wonder what it is that we're all doing here? Why we survived the virus when others just a few months older didn't?"

With a somewhat strained laugh, Ben took another large gulp from the bottle and shook his head. "No, that's just how things turned out. I never read anything more into it."

"But what about Sean? How does someone like that get to be so powerful so quickly? And how does he manage to stay in power? Doesn't anyone try to challenge him?"

Ben actually thought about this, particularly since it was something he had often wondered himself.

"You know European history," he began, passing the bottle back to her. "So take Henry VIII, for example. A major asshole, right? Just a big baby who used his power to get whatever he wanted."

"Right," said Andy after another swallow. "Major asshole."

"Exactly. But he wasn't just a spoiled brat. He was ruthless, too."

"No shit…beheading two of his wives…going to war against France whenever he felt like it…spawned Bloody Mary…"

Andy could feel herself rambling, but Ben didn't care. It even amused him.

"See? He was a pain in the ass even after he was dead," he said.

Andy frowned as she turned to him.

"What's your point?"

"My point is that even though he did all these things that definitely pissed off the English people, he still managed to hold onto the throne for…how long?"

Andy looked up at the darkening sky as she reached deep into her memory. "Almost thirty-seven years…no, thirty-eight."

"So for almost four decades, this guy managed to stay King of England despite all his bad behavior. People were afraid to stand up to him, no matter how much they disagreed with him because if they did, they'd lose their head or get burned at the stake, right?"

"Right."

"Okay, now take Sean. He's probably more intelligent and maybe less, uh, emotional than Henry VIII, and despite how truly evil he is, he's smart enough to know that if you provide food and water to people and dispose of millions of rotting corpses, they're more likely to ignore your sins. So he does that. And he also knows how to manipulate those closest to him. He makes you want to please him, which is when you know that you're completely under his control."

"Sounds like you're speaking from experience."

Though Andy couldn't see it clearly, a look of shame crossed Ben's face.

"I hate to admit it, but yeah, at times I just wanted to do my job well just so he'd be happy with me. It's a weird thing to realize while you're doing it, but you just can't help yourself."

"So when did you finally snap out of it?"

"Around the time he started recruiting the Helens. Up until then, I ignored a lot of little things that I wouldn't today. But he was so good at justifying his behavior."

"Like how?"

"Like whenever he would punish someone by not giving them food for a week because they challenged his authority, he would say that he only wanted people to understand that getting life back to normal meant taking orders without question. That people need someone to tell them what to do or else there would be anarchy."

Ben shook his head slowly. "I bought his bullshit for a while until one day I looked at Karen and realized she could've just as easily been used for sex like the others…that Sean was using his power just to get whatever *he* wanted and to hell with everyone else."

"Did the other Directors agree?"

"Yeah, a few of them did, but they were all too scared to do anything about it. Not that I was any better. Three years went by before I woke up and saw Sean for who he really is."

"But you were young. Just a kid, and I'm sure he was pretty damned persuasive."

Andy could feel her words beginning to slur, but Ben didn't seem to notice. The wine was beginning to affect him too, though not to the same extent.

"Yeah, he *was* persuasive. Everyone was so vulnerable that when he came along and made things even a little better, they believed he was their savior."

"What about Jim? Did he see through Sean before you?"

"He didn't deal with Sean as much, but he never liked the guy from day one."

They were quiet for a bit as the bottle of wine quickly emptied. Ben offered Andy the last sip, which she gladly accepted. Her body felt warm all over and her vision became a bit unsteady, made worse by the increasing darkness. When she leaned over to stand the empty bottle on the ground, she nearly fell out of her swing and started to giggle.

"Jesus, Andy, you're drunk," Ben declared and began to laugh as well. He enjoyed seeing her relax a bit.

"I am *not*," she replied a bit too loudly as she steadied herself in the seat. "Maybe a little tipsy, that's all."

"Whatever you say."

"Oh, shut up."

Neither spoke for a lengthy moment as the wine's effects continued to settle, and after the giggling and laughter waned, Ben began to swing a little, gliding forward and back. Andy remained still and watched the red-orange glow of the remaining daylight fade away off to her right. She kicked absently at the rocks at her feet and knocked over the empty bottle.

"What are his weaknesses?" she asked, ignoring the bottle.

Ben put his feet on the ground to stop swinging. "What?"

"I said, what are his weaknesses? Sean's? Not his flaws…his vulnerabilities."

She slurred the word.

"Where are you going with this?"

"Just humor me. How could he be beaten?"

Staring down at the ground in front of him, Ben became pensive and inhaled a deep breath.

"Well, he's overly confident…thinks he's invincible. He's extremely careful about whom he trusts, but once he includes someone in his inner circle, he tends to trust them without question." Then after a pause, "Of course, after what I did, he's probably a lot more careful now."

"I'm sure," Andy muttered. "What else?"

"He underestimates women," Ben said without hesitation. "He thinks you're all less intelligent than he is, and since he surrounds himself with girls who don't question him or defend themselves, he has little reason to think otherwise."

"How very King Henry of him," Andy mused.

"Yeah."

Ben glanced sideways at Andy, and though the encroaching darkness dulled the view of her face, he knew every angle and curve well enough to imagine her expression.

"He wouldn't know how to handle someone like you, that's for sure."

Andy released a derisive laugh, and as its sound faded, an idea slowly formed in her mind.

"Maybe that's it. Maybe that's the key," she said, unable to conceal the growing excitement in her voice. "You throw him a curve ball. Something totally unexpected, something he would never suspect."

"What are you talking about?"

Andy rubbed her fingers through her hair in the same manner Ben often did.

"I'm not sure of what I'm talking about right now. I blame the wine."

"It's not just the wine. You're actually serious about going to New York, aren't you?"

"Now you're putting words into my mouth."

"C'mon, Andy, I know you too well. You get an idea into your head, and you turn into a bulldog."

"I do *not*," she replied defiantly.

"See, you just proved my point. You're the most stubborn person I know. So headstrong."

Ben leaned over to the side in his seat and shoved her shoulder good-naturedly.

"Oh, like you're any better," she retorted as she attempted to perform a similar shove. Due to her diminished reflexes, she missed her mark and hit Ben on the side of his ribcage instead.

"Whoa, where're you aiming at?" Ben teased as he deftly grabbed her hand, proving that despite the wine, his reflexes were in much better shape than hers. He didn't let go of her hand right away.

"See, I told you it was the wine," Andy managed to say between her giggles. "Now give me back my hand."

"No, not until you tell me why you want to go to New York."

After gently turning her hand into a fist, Ben pulled it toward his body until the back of her hand hit his chest.

"Now tell me," he repeated, his voice lowering to a more serious, and somewhat desperate, tone.

Despite her diminished physical sensations, Andy could feel Ben's heartbeat beneath her hand, and it gave her a start.

"No, I'm not falling for your…your boyish charms," she declared with drunken wistfulness as she freed her hand from Ben's rather tender grasp. "My mother warned me about people like you."

"What are you talking about?" Ben replied with utter confusion.

But Andy didn't have a clue. Frustrated by both her lack of mental clarity and the sudden stirrings of emotions, she stood up and turned toward the direction of the house.

"Wait, where are you going?" Ben called out to her in dark.

"To bed," she blurted out immediately as she stepped forward, and then stopped and muttered, "No, not bed…I don't know."

Andy put her hands up to her forehead as a dizzy spell struck her, and feeling a sense of vertigo, she took a stumbling step backward to steady herself. Ben quickly stood up in reaction and placed his hands on her shoulders to give her balance.

"Whoa, slow down…slow down."

"I'm fine. Just a bit dizzy, that's all."

"It's just the wine. Let's head back home."

"Okay," Andy surrendered without further argument and began to walk cautiously forward.

They made it halfway home when she abruptly stopped.

"What is it?" Ben asked her.

Andy's eyes first fell to the ground before she lifted her gaze to the vanishing horizon. Though her head was heavy, she had a sudden urge to speak plainly and without reserve. Thankfully, this was made all the easier by the wine.

"It's not that I *want* to go to New York, but I just have this nagging feeling that I'm supposed to be doing something else with my life. I just feel like I'm watching life pass before me here."

She made a sweeping, and slightly clumsy, gesture at the surroundings with her arm. She did, however, speak with relative clarity.

"I'm just…restless! I can't stop thinking that I should be somewhere else, and that I'm meant for much more than this. It's like…it's like I'm not fulfilling my potential or something…God, that sounds so ridiculous, doesn't it?"

"No, not at—"

"—and arrogant too," Andy went on. "Like I'm somehow a better person than all of you because I feel these things. But I don't mean it like that, I swear I don't…"

"I know you don't," Ben insisted, cutting her off as he edged even nearer to her. "No one would ever accuse you of arrogance. If anything, you're too humble sometimes. You're an extraordinary person, Andy, more than you realize, but since you've spent most of the past six years so isolated, you haven't seen just how capable you are compared to other survivors. But *I* know what you're capable of, and if there was anyone who stood a chance at defeating Sean, it's you."

Ben spoke with such ardor, there was little doubt in Andy's mind that he meant every word and every meaning those words conveyed. Normally, he might have regretted his last remark, but the wine had affected his own inhibitions as well.

Though they were less than a few feet apart, Andy allowed herself to look directly at Ben and even dared to move a half step closer toward him.

"Then come with me," she urged him, nearly whispering. "Come with me to New York."

She uttered the name of the very last place in the world Ben wanted to return to. The pain of those days persisted like a scar on his heart. But when she asked him like that, whispering in earnest, it became impossible for him to refuse. And yet, he managed to gather his senses enough to deflect the question.

"You and I alone can't defeat Sean. It would take hundreds…no, probably thousands to finish him. How do you expect to pull that off? You've seen how things are…in DC, in Aspen, in L.A.…all over the country. If there's not anarchy, then there's…there's calculated deception. How are you going to get that many people to trust you and follow you when no one trusts anyone anymore?"

"I don't know all that yet, but we have to start somewhere," Andy replied in a strangely calm and logical voice. "What I do know is that there are ten of us here who are hardworking and capable…and compassionate. If anyone can do this, and I mean *really* do this, then it's us."

Revealing her characteristic stubbornness, she held Ben's gaze as if daring him to contradict her. Instead, he relented by letting out a long and weary sigh.

"Good luck convincing everyone else."

"You don't think I can?"

"It won't be easy, but I'd never think that you couldn't do something, Andy."

"I know. You just said I was extraordinary. Now watch me prove it."

Chapter XVII

05 July 2021

The faintest of headaches that greeted Ben when he awoke served as a reminder of his previous recklessness with alcohol following his sister's death. Her memory still haunted him daily; sometimes for mere seconds, other times for hours, but always daily. Every so often, her blue eyes—opaque like his—would dance in the hazy light of his dreams in the moments just before waking. Last night, however, had been dreamless.

Ben wandered to the kitchen and drank two full glasses of rainwater caught after a monstrous thunderstorm a few days earlier. Sitting at the table, his stomach growled with hunger, but Ben ignored it the way he suppressed most of his cravings these days. The early morning light streamed through the tattered venetian blinds and hit his left cheek. Squinting, he stood up and moved toward the front door. The muscles in his lower back ached for no apparent reason, and he stretched his torso from side to side, then front to back before opening the door.

The air was cool and refreshing to the skin. Taking a deep breath through his nose before exhaling at length, Ben opened his eyes and took a seat on the front steps as he had done the morning before. His gaze quickly fixed upon the house across the street where Andy slept, the painfully short distance between the two homes that taunted him more each day.

Logically, Ben understood that Andy wanted to help Morgan with Katie. But at times he detected certain words and displays of body language on her part that suggested that his feelings were not one-sided, like yesterday when she kissed his forehead and the lingering moment after, or her nonsensical ramblings while sitting on the swing the night before. But why then did she continue to resist, if that was indeed the case? Was it Brian? Did he feature more into the picture than Ben realized? And did he similarly torment himself over Andy?

Having long since grown weary of these endless speculations and the hours spent agonizing over them, Ben had become skilled in exercising the willpower of his mind to push aside futile, anxious thoughts. If he didn't, he felt fucking pathetic.

And, there were more pressing matters to deal with.

Yesterday had been wasted when preparations to leave Santa Rosa should have already been underway, and he chided himself for this carelessness. The two spies they had dumped in the desert were unlikely to be any further threat, but the fact that they had found him and his cousin in the first place was beyond disturbing. It reminded Ben once again how strong Sean's influence still was and that it could reach nearly two thousand miles away. Now the only question was where to go.

Last night, Andy was intent on going to New York, although Ben knew that words, when mixed with alcohol, were often prone to gross exaggeration, particularly for someone unaccustomed to drinking. And yet, *he* had not been exaggerating when he told her that if anyone could find a way to bring Sean to his knees, it was her.

There were innumerable qualities Andy possessed that stirred up images of great leaders and warriors among the pages of history Ben had often read about. It didn't matter that most of those people had been men and that she was a woman. Archaic beliefs disparaging a woman's mental and physical abilities could no longer afford to be even mildly entertained when Sean had resurrected those ideas with a vengeance. It wasn't just her strength and courage, or her intelligence, but something intangible that he'd recognized within her from the day they met. Maybe it was her sense of timing or her composure, both of which had saved her life in the Coliseum. Whatever it was, it lived inside of her and was a force to be reckoned with.

But should trying to defeat Sean even be attempted? And where would they even start? Perhaps Andy was right and that destroying whatever was left of the virus was the logical first step toward his downfall. He and Jim had done it before, and this time they would have several trusted friends to help them. And, Ben grudgingly admitted, attempting the task was not only the right thing to do, but could ultimately save their lives were the virus to be unleashed again into the world. Sean was no idiot, but he was still human and prone to fatal mistakes like anyone.

Engrossed in this myriad of intertwined thoughts, Ben's attention was roused when Andy appeared across the street, repeating their encounter from the morning before. Already dressed and ready for the day, she made a straight line toward Ben with an air of determination. By contrast, he was disheveled from sleep and wearing a worn T-shirt and boxers.

"We've got a lot to do today," she called out to him while crossing the street.

It seemed that pleasantries were going to be spared.

"We wasted yesterday when we should've been planning to leave."

"I know," Ben called back. "We gotta get gas first."

Andy nodded as she approached. "Maria said she was going to look into getting some for us."

"How?"

"Don't ask me. You know how secretive she is."

"Well, I'm the last person to judge anyone for keeping secrets."

"True," Andy remarked, letting the comment go as she took a seat beside Ben on the steps. "I'm sure she's trying to protect someone, and after everything we've all been through, who can blame her?"

"No kidding," Ben muttered before shifting gears. "So…any headache this morning?"

"Nope. I drank a large glass of water before going to bed. Of course, then I had to get up in the middle of the night to go to the bathroom. But Katie woke up around then anyway, so I fed her."

"I don't know how Morgan does it," Ben remarked with a shake of his head. "Taking care of a baby during these times, I mean."

"It's easy when you love the child as much as she does. And she has help from all of us, including you."

"It's not the same as actually being a parent though," Ben countered. "I'm not sure I'd ever be up for it."

"I could be a mother," Andy declared matter-of-factly. "Not now, but someday."

A sudden image entered Ben's mind, an image of Andy holding a child and twirling around playfully as the child squealed with delight in its mother's arms. It made him smile.

"Is everyone awake?" he asked, returning to business.

"Susan is still sleeping, I think, but Jim and Morgan are up with Katie. Are Brian and Charlie awake yet?"

Ben shook his head. "Not yet. Lately I seem to be the one who keeps getting up early."

"Yeah, me too."

Andy rose to her feet.

"Come over when you all are awake," she said before heading back across the street.

Ben gave her a teasing salute. "Yes ma'am."

* * *

"Are you up for it?"

"Sure, but why me? Why not Jesse or Michael or one of the others?"

"Because I have a feeling about you," Sean said simply, providing no further explanation.

He was sitting in the office inside his immense apartment on Fifth Avenue. In the room with him was Chad Heinrich, the person Sean had ultimately decided to appoint as his right-hand man in Washington DC. With the exception of some rather interesting facts about the young man's pre-outbreak past, Sean still didn't know much about Chad, but after several days of careful consideration, he decided to trust his gut and give the guy a shot.

"It won't be easy," Sean continued. "I spent three days there last week, and it didn't look like anything I remember from when I was a kid. Nothing works, and everyone lives like rats. In fact, that's probably what they eat."

"Rats?"

"Yeah."

The two young men laughed.

"I've never been to DC," Chad admitted before quickly adding, "But I don't think it would matter if I had. What's to know about a city except what you can find on a map?"

"Exactly, and speaking of which, I've got most of what you need to get started in here."

Chad followed Sean into the large dining room where organized piles of topographic and topological maps, satellite imagery photos, and blueprints of important buildings throughout DC sat on a table.

"Looks like you've done most of the work for me."

Sean scoffed at the remark. "I didn't, but I've been sending a handful of guys in the Infantry down to DC for a few months now to scout the city and collect all this stuff. Unfortunately, they're completely incompetent when it comes to getting information about anything other than maps. There's nothing here to help you get the power back on, but I've assigned two of my best Fixers to work on that for as long as you need them. Without those two, it would've taken me at least twice as long to get the power back in this city."

Chad placed his hands on his hips and said, "What's their story, these Fixers?"

"Both of them were already in college studying engineering

before the virus, one at MIT and the other at Stanford. They're both from New York and just happened to be home from school when the outbreak began. I found them early on. Fuckin' geniuses, but only when it comes to these technical things. They're both pretty helpless otherwise."

"How old are they?"

"Both seventeen, I think. They won't give you any problems. They know who's boss."

Chad raised an eyebrow. "They better. I can't stand how arrogant some of these Fixers have become."

"No shit," Sean replied after a frustrated sigh. "I've been dealing with them for six years now, and it doesn't get any easier. The only thing that keeps them in line is reminding them how dependent on us they are. Just keep telling them that having a high I.Q. doesn't magically create food and water…or drugs, for that matter."

"Either of these two into drugs?" Chad inquired.

Sean frowned and shook his head.

"No, they're your typical nerds…virginal prudes. They'd probably take a pass on cough medicine, and I doubt either of them have ever talked to girl about anything that didn't involve an equation."

"Really? What about the Helens?"

"They've never requested them. Like I said, virginal prudes."

"They're not homos, are they?" Chad asked with a look of concern, which made Sean laugh.

"No, just completely terrified of what they would do with a girl if they ever saw one naked."

"Good to know."

Sean walked back into his office as Chad followed.

"I want you to leave tomorrow for DC," Sean commanded as he gazed out the window in his office. Though it was almost midday, an overcast sky created a gloomy atmosphere in the apartment.

"You'll have two cars with drivers, four Infantry men, and all the supplies you'll need to lay the ground work. Then come back in two weeks and give me an update."

Sean turned away from the window and grabbed a folder from his desk, handing it to Chad.

"I've written a list of things I want you to focus on. The priority will be power, of course. The Fixers should be able to handle most of that, but I want you to focus on how we'll deal with the locals. Determine if any gangs have formed and find out how they operate and how effective they are. Then see what it will take to either crush them or gain their trust. Worry about the neighborhoods near the Capitol first, then work your way out. I want that area under control before anywhere else."

Chad nodded, accepting his orders without objection. He would look at the contents of the folder later. "Got it. Anything else?"

Sean bit his lower lip as he contemplated any instruction he may have overlooked.

"Yeah, take some coke with you and see if you can use it to bribe some people there to paint over the graffiti on the White House. I want it gone the next time I'm down there."

* * *

10 July 2021

"Maria, we need drugs. As much as you can get your hands on."

Maria only blinked once after glancing up from her plate of food.

"Which ones, specifically?"

She knew what Ben was asking, but she wanted him to say it to be clear.

"Heroin, marijuana, and cocaine, if you can get it."

Ben rattled off the items as though he were delivering a grocery list. A week earlier, this conversation would have sounded bizarre, but much had happened in the past few days.

Maria had travelled to Albuquerque and back during that time to meet up with friends from Juarez. She went alone, leaving Julio and Carmen behind with the others, and when she returned, she made a bittersweet decision about her and her siblings' future: they were going to leave Santa Rosa.

Similar to the way Jim and Ben had revealed the details of their past, Maria finally disclosed her own secrets. In an attempt to undo some of the sins of her father, she had been secretly working to free survivors who were now forced into slave labor to continue the production of heroin and marijuana throughout northern and western Mexico. The children of her father's enemies, those from the rival drug cartel, began kidnapping survivors in Juarez and other neighboring cities and had been forcing them to cultivate and harvest cannabis and opium poppy plants. The luckier ones avoided this backbreaking work and instead were used to transport cocaine still being produced in Colombia to Mexico. As gasoline became a vanishing commodity, the cocaine was brought north on sailboats from Colombia along the Pacific side of Central America to the Gulf of California. All three types of drugs were then sent throughout the United States.

"The outbreak hardly affected the drug trade between my country and yours," Maria had explained. "After the first six months, everything was business as usual, and moving drugs across the border was no longer a problem."

As Andy and her friends were already painfully aware, drugs had become the new form of currency in the post-virus world. With the use of cocaine, heroin, marijuana, and all their dangerous combinations, survivors could temporarily escape their miserable existence. Maria understood this grim reality and that drug production was not going to stop, so she and a small network of trusted friends still living in Juarez decided to exploit the drug transport system as a way to rescue the slave laborers from their plight. However, because she and her brother and sister had been living in forced exile in Santa Rosa since the attempts made on their lives years earlier, Maria had only been able to minimally assist her friends in Juarez. Still, in her own way, she had successfully helped smuggle nearly two dozen children across the border during the past year alone, freeing them from their captors and a life that sounded every bit as terrifying as the ordeal endured by survivors in New

York.

"Like the old days, the cartel now in control keeps track of every gram of every drug moved across the border. But when it comes to keeping track of their slave labor, they're sloppy. If a slave goes missing for whatever reason, the cartel can easily grab another as a replacement."

Still, the mission Maria had been engaged in was not without risk. Her friends had carefully maneuvered their way into the roles of the drivers and sailors of the trucks and ships that transported the drugs north to America. They would falsify the numbers detailing the amount of drugs they were carrying and keep the difference for themselves, which they would then use to trade for other necessities, like food, water, and gas. And within the cargo of each truck or ship, they would hide a slave or two, whatever they thought they could get away with under the watchful eyes of the cartel, and deliver them to Santa Rosa. Once there, Maria would secretly house and feed them until they regained their strength before sending them on their way, sometimes alone and sometimes with another shipment of drugs being driven by her friends from across the border.

"That's what you saw me doing that morning last year when that truck was driving away from my house," Maria recalled for Andy. "Those were my friends driving the truck, and we had just put two young girls inside the trailer. It took nearly a week for the lashes on both their backs to stop bleeding. Those girls had to sleep on their stomachs until their wounds finally healed."

Nearly half of the drug shipments that came from Mexico passed through Santa Rosa on I-40, and many of these shipments were bound for New York. Maria further revealed that she had heard rumors about what was going on in New York, but hadn't pieced together the entire puzzle until Ben and Jim had disclosed their story.

"Unfortunately, the cartel in Juarez has only gotten stronger in the last year. Their numbers have increased and lately they've been keeping better track of their laborers, which has made our work much more difficult."

But what ultimately made Maria decide that it was time to move on was learning during her time in Albuquerque that the cartel had stopped keeping handwritten records detailing each shipment and had started using computerized records. This now made it impossible to for Maria and her friends to continue falsifying the shipment records.

"In a way, it's probably for the best. We were fighting a losing battle, and the fact that we were still helping the cartel transport the drugs was only keeping them in control. And besides, every time we saved one poor slave, another innocent person was kidnapped to replace them."

Maria went on to say that although the ends justified the means, knowing that the food she and her siblings were eating had been bought and paid for with the drugs she and her friends stole from the cartel had taken its toll on her conscience. Her decision to leave Santa Rosa had been made. She wanted nothing to do with drugs ever again.

Sitting now at her kitchen table, she considered Ben's request carefully.

"Before I agree," she said to him, "I have to know exactly what you need the drugs for. If you really need them to help take down this Sean person, then I'll make this the last time I ever deal with the stuff."

"It's only to bribe people in Sean's network. People that might know where he's keeping the virus. And to buy some supplies that we'll need once we get to New York."

"And that's it?"

"That's it."

Maria became silent. Everyone watched as she stood and placed her empty plate in the sink. Later, Morgan and Andy would offer to wash all the dishes, as usual, and Susan would convince Charlie to help her fetch the water for the task. The older boys would clear off the table while Carmen and Julio would dry each dish meticulously before placing them back in the cupboards.

Standing with her back to everyone, Maria realized she wouldn't miss this house as much as she would miss the people who had magically entered her life and now sat at her kitchen table. At first, Santa Rosa had been a welcome refuge from the dangers of Juarez, but as those first chaotic months evolved into lonely years, a quiet melancholy had filled her life. Her only break from the endless mothering of her younger siblings involved taking care of the poor children she helped rescue from the snares of the cartel. The infrequent visits by her childhood friends and partners were brief and purposeful, not pleasurable and diverting. And they could continue on with their lives in Juarez, but she could never return.

Maria turned around and returned to her seat at the head of the kitchen table. Nine sets of eyes stared back.

"All right," she relented. "If you're all going to leave, then you might as well take advantage of my connections. I'll get you more than just drugs. I'll get you all to New York by the end of next week."

"Are you coming with us?" Andy asked anxiously.

"Do you want me to?"

The response was unanimous.

* * *

Though some were more reluctant than others, everyone had agreed to go to New York. Though Ben continued to struggle with the idea of returning to the place that held such painful memories, he accepted the fact that he and Jim couldn't hide forever. What finally sealed the decision was a conversation he with his cousin the same night Maria announced she and her siblings were leaving New Mexico.

"You and I can keep trying to convince ourselves that Sean will simply disappear and never send people to find us again," Jim said to him after dinner, "or we can figure out a way to finally destroy him, even if it takes years. But we'd be fooling ourselves if we thought that we could talk and argue ourselves into believing that he's a problem that will just go away."

Then, rather poignantly, he added, "People can become so lost in their own arguments to the point where they find themselves defending Hitler or calling Mother Theresa the Devil, so let's stop kidding ourselves. This is our fight, so let's finally finish it. For Karen, if not for us."

Jim rarely mentioned Karen by name, but he knew when he could use her memory to make a point.

Meanwhile, Morgan was surprisingly easy to convince, and Andy suspected that she had not only grown tired of the desolate isolation of Santa Rosa, but she wanted to personally see that the virus was destroyed, not just for her sake but for the sake of her daughter. Because her sole concern was Katie's safety, Morgan's only objection was living too close to the city. Jim quickly assuaged his wife's fears by making the executive decision that they would stay somewhere well outside New York's city limits and only go downtown when absolutely necessary. Too many people would recognize both he and Ben if they lived in Manhattan or any of the other four boroughs. Instead, they would live like vampires and sleep away from the city by day and sneak downtown at night.

Charlie was excited to go to New York, and despite the obvious risks, he viewed the move as a chance to learn new things. The library in Santa Rosa offered little in the way of books to challenge his thirsty mind, and from his desire for a more superior source of knowledge emerged the idea to live in Princeton.

"It's only fifty miles from New York, and since it's a university town, it'll probably be empty," Charlie explained with sound logic. "Oxford was a quiet town…just students, professors, and their families. And since all the students and professors are dead, it'll just be us."

Like Charlie, Susan was excited by the adventure and having a new place to take photographs. During her brief time in Santa Rosa, she had gone through countless rolls of film found at the local camera store and was ready for new scenery.

"I'm tired of desert landscapes. I want to take pictures of trees, especially in the fall."

"You do realize that we're about to go somewhere truly dangerous, right?" Charlie asked in jest during one of their last evenings in Santa Rosa. "It's not a holiday we're taking."

Making a face, she replied, "I know that, silly, and I don't want to die anymore than you do, but while I'm there, I might as well take some pictures."

"Then you can take a picture of me sitting on the steps at Princeton's library when the leaves change. I make a very handsome subject, don't you think?"

After delivering a smack to his shoulder, Susan gave Charlie a kiss on his cheek.

"Yes, you're my handsome genius."

Brian, however, remained strangely quiet about going to New York. He didn't seem to have an opinion one way or another on the matter, which struck Andy, in particular, as odd. In fact, Brian had been rather quiet in general since coming to Santa Rosa with his sister, and Andy wondered if he regretted leaving Aspen.

The night before Maria had arranged for her friends to come pick them up, everyone was busy packing their things. Finished with his own packing, Brian came by the house to talk to Andy. She was in her bedroom organizing her medical books when he knocked on her door.

"Come in!"

Brian entered and closed the door behind him.

"Hey, what's up?" asked Andy. She was sitting on the floor with small piles of books surrounding her.

"I, uh, I was wondering if you could look after Susan for me when you all go to New York tomorrow."

Andy immediately stopped what she was doing and looked up at Brian with confusion.

"What are you talking about? You're not coming with us?"

Brian opened his mouth to speak, but no words came out. He then closed his mouth and shook his head instead.

"No, I'm not. At least not right now."

Further puzzled, Andy pushed herself off the floor to her feet.

"I don't understand…"

"I need to go back to Aspen for a bit. There are some things I need to take care of first."

"Umm, okay," Andy muttered, still absorbing the news. She scratched her head.

"Does Susan know you're not coming?"

"Yeah, I already told her."

"And she's okay with it?"

"She's fine. I know Charlie will take care of her, but I'd feel better if you looked out for her, too."

"Well, of course I will, but I have to admit that I still don't understand why you need to go back to Aspen, especially after what happened to me there."

"It won't be forever, I promise. But I left some really good friends behind."

"Okay, I understand that, but aren't we your friends too?"

With Andy arguing like that and pleading with her eyes to reconsider, Brian found it difficult not to rethink his decision.

"Of course you are, all of you."

"Is it because you're worried about going to New York?"

"No, I'm not worried, and that's actually why I need to go back to Aspen."

"I still don't understand."

Brian took a deep breath.

"I know. I'm not explaining myself well. See, I really believe in what you're all about to do because in a small way, I was trying to do the same thing in Aspen. My friends and I were trying to get our lives back to normal, and we were mostly successful. Actually, we were *very* successful. We just didn't know how to handle people like Nataliya and her shitty brother and friends. And now I feel like I've abandoned my friends, so I'm going back to convince them to come with me and meet up with you all in Princeton."

Andy blinked. "Oh…"

"I don't know exactly what you'll all be up against in New York, but you'll probably need more people to help. And I know that I'll be more useful if I have my *old* friends around to help my *new* friends."

Taking a step toward her, Brian gently tapped Andy on the side of her arm.

"I miss my friends, Andy, and if I'm gonna do this thing with you all…take on this Sean character and destroy the virus, then I need to give them a chance to start their lives over again too. Or at least offer them the choice to leave Aspen." His eyes narrowed. "Does that make sense?"

Andy's mouth curled upward into a smile, and she nodded. "Makes perfect sense, but what you should've said is that you *are* coming to New York, but you need to make a detour first."

Brian let out a laugh. "I guess that would have been a better way of saying it."

"No kidding," Andy replied. "So when will you leave?"

"Tomorrow, when you all leave. And fortunately, Maria said she'd get me enough gas to get back to Aspen and then all the way to New York. I don't know how she negotiated that, but I'm not gonna argue."

"So you've already told Maria that you're not coming with us?"

"Right. And Ben and Jim. I figured that since New York is really their territory and their past, I wanted to run my plan by them first. You know, see if they didn't mind me bringing my friends along to the party."

"So Maria knows. And if Susan knows, then Charlie knows. And if Jim knows, then Morgan knows."

Brian looked guilty. "Um, yeah."

"So basically, everyone already knows you aren't coming with us? I'm the last person you've told?"

"Well, I knew you'd try to talk me out of it if I told you before the others, so by telling everyone else first, I knew I'd have to stick to my decision. It'll be hard enough leaving you guys without you trying to stop me."

"I wouldn't have tried to stop you if you had explained all of this to me sooner."

But Brian raised an eyebrow skeptically. "You can't blame me for thinking it, Andy. You're the most stubborn person I know."

And with that, Andy's hand flew up in the air.

"Why does everyone keep telling me that?!"

* * *

13 July 2021

Around eight o'clock in the morning, a large tanker truck pulled up to an intersection half a block away from the two houses. Behind it was parked a truck with a small trailer attached. It looked like the same truck Andy had seen at Maria's house the year before.

Charlie and Susan were first to spot the trucks. Maria was outside with Julio and Carmen and busily talking to three teenage boys in rapid Spanish. She stopped when she saw Charlie and Susan draw near.

"Don't tell me that that's what I think it is?" Charlie said as he pointed at the tanker with astonishment.

Maria laughed and said, "And it's completely full, too."

"God, how many gallons is that?" asked Susan, equally in awe.

"Gallons? I don't know, but in liters, I think around thirty thousand."

"Jesus!" Charlie exclaimed. "That's, what…almost eight thousand gallons?"

"Maria, you're amazing!" Susan cried. "How in the world did your friends get so much gas?"

"They stole it from the cartel in the middle of the night. It came all the way from Venezuela."

"They stole it?" Susan and Charlie repeated at the same time.

"Won't they get caught?" Charlie added. "Or killed??"

"No. My friends aren't going back to Juarez. They're going to Miami after they drop us off in New York. They've got friends and relatives there."

She glanced back at her three friends who were gathered at the front of the tanker and talking to Julio and Carmen.

"We all decided together that it was time to leave. The danger just isn't worth it anymore."

Maria then introduced Charlie and Susan to her friends, Andreas, Manuel, and Edgar. Friendly and polite, all three spoke English nearly as well as she did.

"The rest of my friends are meeting up with these guys in Miami. They've all tried talking me into coming with them, but I told them I wanted to help you all first. Then maybe we'll see about Miami."

"You're choosing *us* over your friends?" Susan remarked with amusement. "I hate to tell you, but we aren't worth it. Sure you don't wanna change your mind?"

"Susan, stop it. We want her to come with us," Charlie urged. "Don't give her any doubts."

"Don't worry, Charlie," Maria countered. "I'm not changing my mind. You're stuck with me, but Julio is going with them to Miami."

"You're leaving your brother behind?" Charlie asked, surprised.

"Hey, Brian and I are separating for a while," Susan reminded him.

Charlie shrugged. "I guess," was all he said, though he still looked uncertain. "I think it would be hard being separated from Morgan, but I guess if I felt like I had to, I would."

"It's only temporary," Maria assured. "And my friends are like my family, and I know they'll take care of Julio like he's their own brother. I'll miss him, but he understands. Right now I'm more worried about that virus still being out there."

"Why isn't Carmen going to Miami?" said Susan.

"She wants to stay with me. Plus, Julio has good friends going to Miami that he misses, and he's at that age where it's getting hard for me to tell him what to do."

Susan crossed her arms over her chest and gave Charlie a mocking smile. "See? Julio's not afraid to be separated from *his* sister, you big baby."

"I never said I was afraid to be separated from Morgan," Charlie retorted defensively. "I just said that I wouldn't want to unless I had to."

But Susan laughed, knowing she'd gotten the better of him. Charlie waved her off, though he started to laugh as well. Maria, meanwhile, just grinned slyly.

"You guys are cute. Soon you'll be married like Jim and Morgan."

"Hell no!" Susan squealed. "I'm only fifteen!"

"What, you don't wanna marry me?" Charlie said with feigned surprise as he grabbed Susan from behind around her waist and lifted her off her feet. She continued to squeal with delight as Charlie twirled her around once before putting her back on her ground. Maria looked on with amusement.

"Don't fight it, Susan. I think you're stuck with him."

Andy, Ben, and Brian approached just then. They were followed shortly behind by Jim and Morgan, who was carrying Katie.

"Whoa, is that thing full?" was the first thing Brian said, referring to the tanker.

"Just about," confirmed Maria as she beamed. "We'll give you whatever you need to get to Aspen *and* New York.

"Nice work, Maria," Ben announced as he came up next to her. "Are you sure your friends can't come with us back east? It looks like they've got some valuable skills."

"I've already tried, believe me. But their minds are made up."

"What's in the other truck?" Andy asked. Maria frowned and gestured for her and Ben to follow as she walked toward the smaller trailer while Brian stayed behind with the others.

Maria opened the back of the trailer with Ben's help, and Andy saw something she'd never seen before in her life: kilograms upon kilograms of illicit drugs. More precisely, three hundred kilos of high-grade cocaine, heroin, and marijuana, all wrapped and vacuum sealed.

Frozen with his arm still in the air from lifting the trailer door, Ben was stunned.

"Holy shit," he muttered.

"Holy shit," Andy echoed. "That's…that's a *lot*."

"Well, you said to get as much as I could get my hands on, and I don't like to disappoint people," Maria said as she climbed into the trailer and made a sweeping gesture to its contents with her arms. "This should be enough to get some people talking, I would think."

Ben said nothing, however. Still in disbelief, he stepped up to join Maria inside before gingerly placing his hand on top of the stack of wrapped heroin. He seemed almost afraid to touch it.

"It's sad that this is what it takes to do something good," Maria remarked as she turned and hopped out of the trailer. "It's time to find another way."

She walked past Andy and headed back to the rest of the group, leaving them alone. Ben looked down at Andy, then back at his hand still touching the stack of heroin.

"This is the shit that killed my sister."

His voice wavered slightly, but he quickly recovered and rejoined Andy on the ground.

"You sure you wanna do it this way?" she asked cautiously.

"No, I'm not sure, but I don't know of another way right now."

"Okay, then we won't worry about it until we need to."

Andy stepped up and closed the trailer door, then turned back to Ben.

"Let's just get to New York first."

With renewed vigor, he nodded. "Right."

Soon after, Brian put his things in Jim and Ben's truck, which they were lending to him for his trip.

"This way you won't have to fill up so often," Jim had told him the night before.

"Just make sure you bring it back in one piece," Ben joked after handing over the keys.

"I will, I promise."

After Maria's friends filled all three tanks of the truck, Charlie, Jim, and Ben helped Brian fill up thirty five-gallon gas containers and placed them in the truck bed. Even with the added weight and the mountainous terrain, it would be enough for Brian and a few friends to make the journey east.

Before leaving, Brian pulled Susan aside to say goodbye. He gave his sister a long hug and said, "Take pictures for me, okay?"

Pulling away from the embrace, she forced herself to smile. "I will. Don't stay there long, and watch out for yourself."

"Yes ma'am," Brian replied in jest in an effort to maintain his composure. "You be careful."

"I'll listen to Andy, I promise."

Brian feigned a quizzical look. "What are you talking about?"

Smiling more easily this time, Susan said, "I know you told her to look out for me."

"Yeah, well, I'm your older brother, and that's what older brothers do. We try to protect our younger sisters, even when we're not around."

"I know."

Susan gave her brother one more hug. "I love you."

"I love you, too."

Brian then said goodbye to everyone else before getting inside the truck. Andy was the last to speak to him.

"I'll take good care of her," she said, referring to Susan. "We all will. Don't worry."

"Thank you. I'll worry a lot less knowing that."

Andy then gave Brian a hug, which wasn't unexpected since both Morgan and Maria had also given him a farewell hug. But this hug Brian didn't want to pull away from, and when he finally forced himself to break contact, he sneaked a quick kiss to Andy's forehead before slipping into driver's seat.

"Be careful," he muttered to her as he started the engine.

As everyone waved goodbye while Brian drove off, Andy stood still and touched the spot on her forehead where he had kissed her. She didn't see Morgan come up beside her until Katie made a few noises in her arms.

"I know that Ben likes Brian well enough, but I'm sure he's glad he won't have any competition for a while."

And without another word, Morgan slid away with her remark still hanging in the air.

There wasn't time for Andy to think about what Morgan had said. Within an hour of Brian's departure, everyone else had piled into four different vehicles—the tanker, the trailer with the drugs, and two other pickup trucks. Soon, the desert disappeared behind them as they traveled in a caravan.

A new chapter had begun.

Chapter XVIII

16 July 2021

Chad found Sean's assessment of DC to be dead-on. Calling it a "mess" had been a generous understatement. Doing what he'd been instructed, Chad surveyed the neighborhoods by starting at the Capitol building and spiraling outward in a clockwise direction. Though obvious that some neighborhoods had been wealthier and more prominent than others, by now all of them were in varying degrees of dereliction. The hot, humid summers followed by unpredictably cold and wet mid-Atlantic winters had taxed the city's entire infrastructure. Roads were torn up and buildings were falling apart. In New York, the buildings were far taller and more numerous, but due to the continual toil of the Fixers, the ones Sean was most concerned with preserving had remained stable.

It was hard to know exactly how many survivors lived within the city limits. They seemed to hibernate during the daytime and comb the streets at night, either looking for food or trouble. Chad chose to sleep in his car every night to witness the nightcrawlers firsthand. Sleep was not something he required much of, much to the frustration of the four Infantry officers assigned to him. Though Chad had handpicked them based upon their skills, unquestioning obedience, and obvious fear of him, they didn't care for sleeping outside in the middle of a hot summer. But they kept their mouths shut and did their job as they slept in a different neighborhood of the city each night: Penn Quarter, just north of the Mall, then Capitol Hill and the Navy Yards in the southeast quadrant, followed by Georgetown to the west, then Columbia Heights and Catholic University to the north and northeast. Tonight they would head even farther north toward Takoma.

The two Fixers opted to spend their nights at the Four Seasons Hotel near Georgetown instead of on the streets, and Chad relented only to save his ears from their incessant whining. Every day he spent in their presence was more trying than the one before. Were it not for their undeniable talents, he would've drowned them in the Potomac.

Yet as wretched and unruly as Washington DC was, Chad saw only opportunity. He would use Sean's influence and resources to resurrect the Capitol, then make his move and claim the city as his own. The two-hundred mile distance to New York would become his greatest asset and would provide him the space to recruit his own army. Until then, however, he would continue playing the role of dutiful servant. *Patience* was his new mantra.

Sitting now on the roof of his car parked somewhere deep within Rock Creek Park along the side of the winding road, Chad opened the folder Sean had given to him a week earlier. Two of the Infantry officers were presently urinating behind a couple of trees just a few yards away, while the other two were off with the Fixers at one of the power stations near the Potomac on the west side of the city.

Chad took a quick glance at the list inside the folder. He had covered nearly everything Sean wanted him to investigate. The only thing left to be done was to examine the Metro, which would be taken care of within the next few days. That would leave him another few days to do his own reconnaissance around the city before heading back north.

Sunlight peaked through the canopy of summer trees above him, making the Park far less gloomy had it been a cloudy day. Off to his right, he heard a rustle of motion in the overgrown bushes. A rabbit emerged and came to a stop in front of the base of a tree less than ten feet away from Chad. Its left side was facing him, and he slowly retrieved a throwing knife from his back pocket. After completing a split-second analysis of the distance and angle to the animal, he gripped the blade of the knife with his callused hand. Then, after slowly raising his arm for the throw, he released the tension and sent the knife flying. With an audible thwack, the blade impaled the rabbit, and it writhed about helplessly for several seconds until all movement ceased.

Chad smiled with satisfaction at his accuracy. When the other two boys returned from relieving themselves and saw the rabbit lying dead on the ground, one of them asked, wide-eyed, "Is that your dinner?"

Chad cast the boy a cold stare.

"No, that was just for fun."

* * *

19 July 2021

"Man, I'm beat."

Andy rubbed her eyes one at a time, for she was driving. The clock on the dashboard read 11:57.

"It's midnight already? God, where did the time go today?"

"Want me to drive?" Morgan asked even though Katie had just fallen asleep in her arms.

"No, let's not wake her just because I'm a little tired," Andy replied after yawning.

"How much farther is it?"

"Not far. We should be crossing the Delaware River in a few minutes."

Morgan nodded, although she had no idea where the Delaware River was in relation to Princeton. She'd been too busy dealing with Katie the entire trip to have a chance to look at a map.

Andy realized this and added, "About thirty minutes at most, assuming that the roads are clear."

Between driving in a slow-moving caravan, tackling the spotty road conditions stretching between New Mexico and eastern Pennsylvania, and stopping multiple times to check the safety of bridges to ensure they could support the immense weight of the tanker, the journey had been exhaustingly long. What normally would have been a three-day trip had taken them six. Princeton could not be reached fast enough, and once they arrived, they would then have to find a decent place to live. More than once during the trip did Andy question her own decision to leave New Mexico.

Andy now glanced back at Jim in the rearview mirror. He was lying down in the backseat, fast asleep.

"I'm glad someone's getting some rest," she said quietly to Morgan.

Morgan craned her neck to look at her husband. She smiled down at him but said nothing, and returned her focus on Katie and the road ahead.

They were the last vehicle in the caravan. In front of them was the other pickup truck, which Ben was driving along with Charlie and Susan. Susan had taken dozens of pictures throughout the trip as a way to keep her mind off the fact that her brother was absent for the first time in her life. Maria, Julio, and Carmen had remained with their Juarez friends in the tanker and trailer.

Andy mused how the drive west the year before had seemed far less arduous, and she could only attribute this sentiment to the excitement of heading somewhere as new and mysterious as the two young men they had met along the way. But now they were soldiers going to war, and all the inevitable difficulties they would face seemed more real as the battlefield approached.

After crossing the Delaware River, they passed through Trenton and continued on with surprising ease along U.S. Route 1 until Princeton appeared in the distance. After getting off the highway just south of the university, the four vehicles pulled over to the side of the road. Everyone stepped outside and regrouped near the front of the tanker, except Jim and Morgan, who remained behind with Katie in the truck.

"Now what?" Susan asked once they were all gathered.

With a flashlight in hand, Ben placed a standard AAA map of New Jersey on the ground and positioned the light on the center. Everyone huddled together to get a better look.

"We gotta hide the tanker somewhere," he began, taking charge. "It's too big to take into the neighborhoods without risking others seeing it. The less people who know we're here, the better."

Andy pointed to something on the map.

"What about one of these parks? Or this golf course?"

Ben stroked his chin with his free hand. Of everyone, he seemed to be the most alert.

"Yeah, that could work. It's not exactly hidden, but it's better than putting it in some parking lot. We'll find a warehouse or somewhere else later, but for tonight, let's just get it off the road."

He looked at Maria and each of her friends.

"You guys okay with that? I mean, it's your gas."

"No, it's *our* gas," Maria corrected. "They'll just take whatever they need to get to Miami."

"Really?" said Andy.

Andreas and Manuel nodded as Edgar said, "Our friends are bringing two more tankers to Miami."

"You stole three tankers of gas from the cartel?" Charlie remarked, this news rousing him from the same mental fatigue everyone was feeling. "You blokes have got some serious bollocks!"

Maria's friends laughed, and though they weren't familiar with British expressions, they understood the context. It was funnier still to hear the proper-speaking Charlie say something vulgar, but then, exhaustion could do that.

"Okay, then we'll put the tanker here."

Ben pointed to a spot on the map that no one could read clearly, so he read the location aloud.

"The Princeton Country Club. It's just down the road from

here."

Ben picked up the map and turned to Edgar, who was the last one to drive the tanker.

"You can follow me."

Edgar nodded, and he and Ben returned to their vehicles while everyone else stayed behind and waited for them to return.

"So this is Princeton," Maria remarked to Andy as the others chatted amongst themselves in the dark. "Have you ever been here before?"

"A few times," Andy replied. "My parents took me to the theater on campus to see *A Christmas Carol* when I was about eight or nine. And my mother performed there once when I was a little older. It's a nice town, or at least it was. Quiet and peaceful."

"Hopefully it's still like that."

"Yes...hopefully."

Looking upward at the waxing moon, Andy took a deep breath. The air itself was humid, but not overbearing, and the temperature was very pleasant. The sound of insects performing their summer mating calls filled the air.

Charlie went to check on his sister and niece just as Ben and Edgar returned in one of the pickup trucks.

"Everything all right?" Andy asked Ben as he approached.

"Yeah, we decided to just park the thing in the middle of one of the holes...the big grassy area. I don't know what it's called."

"The fairway?" Charlie offered.

"Yeah, the fairway. Anyway, the course looked pretty overgrown, so hopefully no one will come by and stumble upon it for at least a few days. We can start emptying the gas tomorrow once we find some containers to put it in."

"That's gonna be a lot of containers," said Susan wryly.

"No shit," Ben replied as he rubbed his eyes with one hand. Fatigue had finally caught up with him..

"Let's find somewhere to crash for the night," Jim announced, seeing Morgan struggle to stay awake with Katie in her arms.

The group dispersed into the three remaining vehicles, and within a mile, they discovered a residential neighborhood that appeared suitable. After finding three homes that were both easy to enter and absent of any six-year-old corpses waiting to be stumbled upon, sleep came quickly and easily to everyone.

* * *

The next morning, Andreas, Edgar, and Manuel immediately set out to refuel one of the pickup trucks with gasoline from the tanker. A Home Depot sitting within half a mile from the golf course provided plenty of jerry cans to transport the rest of what they would need for their journey to Miami.

That same afternoon, Maria said a tearful goodbye to both her friends and Julio. After their departure, she spent the rest of the day comforting Carmen, who was particularly upset to see her brother leave. Later, Maria remarked to Andy and Morgan, "I hope I did the right thing by letting him go."

"It's impossible to know what the right decision is anymore, but you're doing what you think is best," Morgan consoled.

"And you wanted to protect him from any possibility of being exposed to the virus," Andy added gently.

Biting her lip, Maria still wasn't certain, but there was little anyone could say to ease her mind. Everyone was silently questioning whether coming back east was a foolish pursuit. But the visceral memories of the horrors of the outbreak served as a constant reminder that a repetition of such devastation had to be prevented at any cost.

That night, after a long day of settling in, Ben announced that he was heading into the city. He didn't expect anyone to go with him, as everyone was still worn out, but after gaining a second wind, Andy felt the desire to see the city she'd been visualizing for days. Ben was happy for the company.

"Take your pistol and wear something to conceal it," he instructed her. "We'll likely be on foot once we reach Manhattan."

Despite the summer heat, Andy brought a lightweight sweatshirt with her, which she tied around her waist to conceal her Glock. They also brought some bottles of water, dried fruit and beef jerky made back in Santa Rosa, two bikes, and two sleeping bags, just in case. Ben also took a kilo of cocaine with him, which he divided into ten smaller bags of a hundred grams each. He weighed each carefully with a food scale he had picked up at a Walmart in Oklahoma for this very purpose. The rest of the drugs had been transported into the garage of one of their new homes.

"Sure you're up for this already? You're not tired?" Morgan asked Andy after putting Katie to bed.

"No, I'm actually pretty wired right now."

"Just be careful."

"I'm always careful."

"I'm not worried about you. It's other people that worry me."

"Me too."

Ben drove, since he knew the way. Little was said during the drive. Many hours of comfortable silence had long since passed between them within the confines of a car. As Andy gazed outside, the darkness gradually lessened as street lamps and the lights within homes became visible from the highway. It seemed strangely contradictory that the person responsible for restoring this light could be so dark and twisted.

"Where are we going exactly?" Andy asked as they passed Newark Airport before merging onto I-78 from I-95.

"Jersey City. We'll have to park there since we can't drive through the Holland Tunnel."

"Why not?"

Andy had studied enough maps of New Jersey and New York during the drive from Santa Rosa to easily recall the locations that Ben was referring to.

"'Cuz only the Directors and certain people in the Infantry are allowed to drive cars in Manhattan. Not even Fixers can drive in the city. Jim spent every day working on cars, but he wasn't allowed to drive them on the island except to make sure they worked. The only way he and Karen could get around the city without walking or biking or taking the subway was if I drove them."

"You're kidding."

"No, I'm serious. It's meant to control the population, like a lot of other things—but it didn't start out that way."

They crossed Newark Bay and into the peninsula of Bayonne just south of Jersey City.

"How did it start?"

"It started because of the Holland Tunnel."

"Sorry?"

"Yeah. See, when the tunnel was built about a hundred years ago, a ventilation system was installed to remove the carbon monoxide emissions created by all the cars passing through. Without it, drivers would asphyxiate before they could get through the tunnel, especially if they were stuck in traffic getting in and out of Manhattan. When the virus was released, people literally died while passing through the tunnel, and by the time it was all over, the tunnel was clogged with thousands of stranded vehicles and dead people. You can imagine the stench in the summer heat, so the tunnel was cleared as quickly as possible. But without power, the ventilation system wasn't on, and it ending up taking weeks to clear both directions of the tunnel. So until power returned to the city, no one dared to drive through the tunnel even after it was cleared, and by the time Sean got the power back up and running again, everyone was used to crossing the tunnel on foot or on bikes. But with gasoline running out and with the subway working again, he decided to outlaw driving in Manhattan entirely. Except for himself and certain people, of course."

The truck continued on I-78, which veered north toward Jersey City.

"So we'll have to bike through the Holland Tunnel?"

"Yep."

"And you just thought to mention this to me now?"

"Well, I was afraid that if I told you we would have to bike across the Hudson to get to the city, you wouldn't come," said Ben with an unapologetic smile, to which Andy merely smirked and shook her head.

"So once we get into Manhattan, where are we going?"

"To see an old friend. Hopefully he's still living in the same place."

"You trust him?"

Ben hesitated. "I trust him more than most people."

"You don't sound very convincing."

"Well, he hates Sean almost as much as I do, so I'm willing to take the risk."

They pulled off I-78 before reaching the Holland Tunnel and searched for a place to park. They were in Downtown Jersey City now, just west of Manhattan across the river. Lights were on throughout the neighborhood and people were scattered everywhere, some huddled in clusters on street corners and others wandering about without purpose.

Ben parked on a quieter street in the area. After turning off the ignition, he reached behind his seat and grabbed the backpack containing the water, food, a flashlight and small tools, the ten bags of cocaine, and most importantly, his loaded pistol and a baseball cap. He put the cap on and pulled the brim down low over his eyes. In the dark, he was practically unrecognizable. His pistol remained in the backpack for the time being.

Though she did not have the same concerns as Ben had about being recognized, Andy wore a baseball cap as well after Ben assured her that wearing one wouldn't appear suspicious. Better to obscure her appearance now and avoid being identified later. As for her Glock, she holstered it at her right hip with a belt. The air had cooled to an unseasonable temperature, so she put her sweatshirt on, which easily concealed the weapon.

After retrieving their bikes from the back of the truck, Ben threw the backpack over his shoulders and mounted his bike. Andy followed him as he began to pedal in the direction of the tunnel. After a half-mile backtrack, they veered onto I-78 just before the vacant toll plaza and entered the tunnel shortly thereafter.

Miraculously, the lights inside the two-lane tunnel were working, although only every third or fourth light was actually illuminated. It made for a long, dim ride through the one-and-a-half miles of tunnel that stretched under the Hudson. The air became increasingly stale as they reached the halfway point, and Andy could only imagine the smell created by hundreds of decaying bodies trapped inside. A few people passed by in the opposite direction, some on foot and some on bikes. Ben stuck to the outside of the right lane and kept his gaze downward to avoid even a microsecond of eye contact. Andy stayed behind him and slightly to his left until they emerged on the other side ten minutes later.

The road curved to the right, and Ben pulled off the pavement before entering the traffic circle at St. John's Park.

"What day is it?" he called out to Andy as she pulled up beside him.

"Uh, Tuesday, I think."

"You aren't sure?"

Andy sighed.

"No, I'm not sure. The World Date and Time app on my iPhone stopped working six years ago. Sorry."

"Very funny."

"Why does it matter what day of the week it is?"

"'Cuz on Mondays, Wednesdays, and Fridays, there are random checkpoints throughout Manhattan to check everyone's ID going through."

"IDs? We don't have any ID."

"I know. That's what we're taking care of tonight. But we need to get to Chinatown."

"Is that far?"

"No, but there's usually a minefield of checkpoints between here and there. So to be safe we'll head south and circle along the edge of the island. You up for that?"

"How far are we talking?"

"A few miles."

"Piece of cake. I'll follow you."

"You're awesome, Andy."

"I know. Just don't forget it."

They rode south along the Hudson side of Manhattan, skirting beside the water on West Street until it ended at Battery Park. The Statue of Liberty was visible in the distance. Shrouded in the darkness, the Lady's silhouette could be seen in the moonlight passing through the clouds high above. Whatever array of lights once illuminating this icon of liberty had not been attended to. It obviously wasn't a priority.

They pedaled on, farther east, stair-stepping through the crowded Financial District that was now bustling with a very different kind of commerce than stocks and bonds: drugs and prostitution. As Ben made a sudden right turn onto Wall Street, Andy nearly fell off her bike while distracted by the half-naked girls wandering about and looking to trade their skin for either food or drugs. She caught her balance in time to avoid a large pothole and see Ben make another quick turn onto South Street at the eastern edge of Manhattan. After travelling north a few blocks, they turned west and headed back inland. Upon reaching Chinatown, the swell of people roaming the pavement forced them to dismount. Ben ducked into an alley to hide their bikes.

"You really know your way around this town," Andy remarked as she wrapped a chain around her front wheel and the frame.

"Yeah, I surprised myself," Ben replied as he strapped his bike to hers with a second chain.

Andy followed Ben back onto the street. The crowds of people were loud and a dizzying mélange of music blared from the storefront windows of defunct ethnic food markets and noodle houses. The majority of people wandering about were of Asian descent. Minus the heavy smell of food in the air, Chinatown was everything that Andy imagined it would be.

As they maneuvered through the crowd, Ben drew close to Andy.

"Don't tell anyone your name. You'll understand why soon," he said loud enough for her to hear above all the noise.

Andy nodded once.

"Just pick another name for now," Ben went on. "It doesn't matter what, but nothing that sounds like Andy or Andrea. And a last name too, all right?"

"Got it."

Half a block later, they made their way to the nondescript front door of a narrow residential building. The door was sandwiched between what used to be two restaurants on the bottom floor within the same building. Ben opened the door without any resistance. After passing through a tiny entryway, they climbed four flights of stairs before heading down the narrowest of hallways. The air was nearly as stifling as inside the Holland Tunnel. They passed three apartments on each side, and Ben paused at the fourth door on the left. He stepped off to the side to avoid standing directly in front of the door and gestured for Andy to move off to the other side, which she did. When he removed his backpack and retrieved his pistol, Andy placed her right hand on the grip of her own gun and prepared to retrieve it if necessary.

After a quick glance at Andy, Ben knocked on the door. Half a minute passed without any sign of life on the other side, so Ben knocked again, louder. This time the sound of footsteps approaching was heard. Following the rattle of at least three different locks being undone, the door partially opened, concealing Ben on the other side.

"Who the fuck are you?"

Andy blinked back at the person standing in front of her.

"Excuse me?" she blurted out defensively.

He was about Ben's age and height but had a slighter build. His head was shaved and his face was fairly ordinary, neither overwhelmingly attractive nor unattractive. The most remarkable thing about his appearance were three uniform scars running diagonally across the side of his neck as though someone had tried slitting his throat with a wide-tined fork.

"Excuse you? You're the one standing outside my door."

His voice was gruff and the accent was unmistakably Boston.

"Still haven't learned any manners, have you, Danny?"

After speaking, Ben stepped into view and gave the stranger a friendly smirk. Danny blinked as recognition sank in.

"Holy shit…Ben Kelly! What the fuck are you doing here?"

"Shit, keep your voice down!" Ben hissed back. "You know how thin these walls are?"

Danny recoiled after realizing his error.

"Man, sorry, but you scared the shit out of me." He opened the door wider. "Quick, come in."

Andy followed Danny inside as Ben shut and locked the door behind them. After passing through a short and narrow hallway, they entered the space that comprised the majority of the tiny apartment. Not surprisingly, everything from the paint on the walls to the carpet beneath their feet was in desperate need of a renovation that would never come. Sitting on the couch in the living room were two young men deeply engrossed in a video game, giving Andy a sudden flashback of her meeting with the gang leader in Los Angeles.

"Where's Jim?" Danny asked as he wandered into the living room as Ben and Andy followed.

"He's around," replied Ben with intentional vagueness, and Danny didn't press further.

"Dez…Liam…turn that shit off. You'll never guess who's here," Danny called out to the other two young men over the flash and bang of imaginary guns firing.

The two men ignored Danny until one of them finally defeated the other. He pumped his fist in the air violently and repeatedly as the other flung his hand controls halfway across the room in frustration.

"You guys piss me off," Danny declared as he bent down to pick the hand control off the floor before turning off the television. "It's a fuckin' miracle that I haven't reported you two in to the Infantry yet for driving me insane!"

"Dude, I just beat Li in *Halo* for the first time ever! You know how long I've been trying to beat him?"

"Dez, I don't give a shit. We got visitors."

Danny's friends turned around and realized that two other people were in their apartment.

"Ben?"

"Shit, no way!"

The one named Dez scurried around the couch to get a closer look. The other, Liam, blinked in disbelief but moved in closer as well.

"Oh my God, it is you!" Dez cried. "What the hell are you doing here?"

Smiling, Ben stepped forward and gave Dez a firm one-armed hug.

"Good to see you, Dez," he said before stepping back next to Andy. He then gave Liam a friendly nod of recognition. "What's up, Li? You keeping these guys out of trouble?"

The young man cracked a smile. "Barely," he said as he moved toward Ben with his hand extended. Ben shook it warmly.

Meanwhile, Dez was inching toward Andy, looking eager to make the acquaintance.

"And who is this fine-looking creature? Where have you been hiding?" he smiled brazenly, looking directly at her.

Remembering what Ben said about her name, Andy extended her hand to Dez and said as coolly as possible, "I'm Katrina. I take it you're Dez?"

Puffing his chest out, Dez shook her hand and took yet another step closer. "That's right. It's short for Desmond, and I'll be hurt if you don't remember it." Then while still holding Andy's hand, Dez made a gesture at Ben, saying, "What's a beautiful girl like you doing with *this* guy?"

"All right, take it easy, Romeo," Ben intervened good-naturedly. "It's too soon to be giving me grief. I just got here."

Though Andy had to practically pull her hand free from Dez's grasp, she laughed at his bold yet harmless flirting. "I won't forget your name, Desmond," she replied, emphasizing his name pointedly. Then, turning to the other young man, she said, "You're Liam?"

Liam's face brightened. "Actually, it's just Li. Danny likes to call me Liam because he's Irish and thinks that everyone is Irish."

Andy laughed as she shook his hand because Li was clearly Asian.

"Nice to meet you Li. I'm Katrina."

"Everyone *is* Irish," Danny called out from the living room. "Even if it's just one percent."

Dez rolled eyes. "Don't even start with that shit, Danny."

"What? It's true," Danny countered. "Geneticists proved it. All of us are Irish."

"You ever consider that maybe the geneticists had it backward? That all Irish people are really part-Asian or part-African, even if it's just 'one percent?'" Dez made mocking quotation marks with his fingers.

Danny, it seemed, would not be deterred. "Face it, Dez, you're Irish."

"How can I be fuckin' Irish *and* black at the same time?"

"Why do you think they call it 'Black Irish?'"

Meanwhile, Ben and Li were chuckling amongst themselves. Apparently, this was an ongoing argument, and Andy merely watched with amusement as Danny and Dez battled on.

"So why do you call him 'Liam' if that's not his name?" Dez went on.

"Liam *is* his name. You're the one who calls him 'Li.'"

"But he calls *himself* 'Li.'"

"He's just shortening his name. Everyone does that," Danny replied as if the answer was clearly obvious.

"His parents didn't name him 'Liam.' How do you explain that?"

"His parents didn't know he was Irish. Geneticists only discovered this like a year before the outbreak."

"Okay, smart ass, what about my name? Why do you call me 'Desmond' and not something more Irish?"

"Because, jackass, 'Desmond' *is* Irish. Its Gaelic for 'Man from Munster,' and Munster is a province of Ireland."

"I think you're bullshitting me now."

"I'm not!" Danny cried adamantly. "We'll hook up to the *Wikipedia* server later if you don't believe me."

Dez threw his hands up in the air. "I give up."

The *Wikipedia* comment piqued Andy's interest immediately, but before she could say anything, Ben cut in.

"Danny, as much as I love hearing you argue with Dez about this obsession of yours, can we get down to business?"

"Yes…*thank* you, Ben," Dez said with exaggerated intonation. "Let's talk about why you and this beautiful girl are here." Dez gave Andy a wink, and she merely shook her head, smiling demurely.

"We need IDs," said Ben bluntly.

"That's it?" Danny replied as though he were expecting more.

"Yeah, that's it. We need nine of them. If you give me something to write with, I'll give you all the information you'll need before I leave…names, ages, and physical descriptions. Of course, my name will be different."

"All right, no problem," said Danny. "I'll need two days. Can you come back then?"

"Depends on when the Infantry does their checkpoints. Is it still Monday, Wednesday, and Friday?"

"Yeah, that hasn't changed," said Dez.

"And today's Tuesday?"

"Yep."

Ben glanced at Andy, who returned a satisfied smile.

"Then I'll be back in two days around the same time. That okay?"

"Awesome," Danny remarked as he grabbed a scrap of paper and a pen from somewhere in the kitchen and handed them to Ben. He took a seat at the small dining room table and began to scribble feverishly as Andy inched closer to him, attempting to read his writing over his shoulder.

A minute or so later, Ben put the pen down and looked back at

Andy.

"Here," he said, holding the pen up to her. "I forget how old Julia and Michelle are. Can you look this over to make sure I didn't make any other mistakes?"

Andy stared at him awkwardly for a second until realizing what he was really asking for.

"Sure," she said as casually as possible before trading places with Ben at the table.

On the paper, Ben had written nine fictitious names for their friends, along with their age and a brief physical description that consisted of sex, height, hair color, and eye color. The list was nearly complete except for 'Katrina's' last name. Ben had already written names for everyone else but apparently was giving Andy the choice to pick her own. As she scanned the list, she quickly added a last name after her fictional first name before handing the complete list back to Ben.

"Looks fine," she said. "Julia's eleven, not ten, so I changed that."

It seemed that Carmen was going to be Julia from now on, at least if she ever came into the city.

"Thanks," Ben remarked as he exchanged the paper yet again, this time giving it to Danny. "Here you go."

Danny looked over the list as everyone else waited.

"There are three males on this list, all age twenty and about the same height, brown hair and brown eyes. I assume you're one of them?"

"Yeah."

Danny squinted as he took a hard look at Ben's face.

"But your eyes aren't brown."

Ben raised an eyebrow. "Don't worry about that."

"But which one of these three names are you gonna be?"

"Don't worry about that either," was Ben's definitive response, ending any further discussion about his new alias or the list of names in general.

Danny shrugged. As long as he got paid, it made no difference to him.

Ben glanced at his watch before removing the ten bags of cocaine from his backpack. He placed them on the kitchen table in a neat row. Danny looked impressed, as did Li and Dez, who let out a low whistle.

"Shit, that's a lot of coke. Where did you get this stuff?"

"Don't worry about that," said Andy, echoing Ben's earlier words.

"They're each 100 grams. You'll get another kilo on Thursday when I pick up the IDs."

"Fair enough," Danny replied as he shook hands with Ben to seal the deal.

Ben threw his backpack over his shoulder, signaling that it was time to leave. First, however, he nodded toward the cocaine on the table. "Promise me you'll use that stuff to buy food and not to string out prostitutes."

Danny took immediate offense to the comment and crossed his arms over his chest.

"Fuck, Ben, who do you think I am? Sean or his cronies?"

Realizing he'd gone too far, Ben held up his hands remorsefully. "Sorry, man. I forget…I know you're not like him."

Satisfied by this apology, Danny relaxed his stance and mumbled, "It's okay."

Ben turned toward the door to leave, but Dez caught him first. "Whoa, hold up! You're not leaving here without telling us where you've been all this time, or why you're back."

"Not tonight," Ben replied before waving. "See you Thursday."

Ben exited the apartment with Andy following closely behind. They went back to the alley to retrieve their bikes. Before leaving the area, they paused a few minutes for some food and water.

"So who were those guys?"

"Just some hackers who helped me last year before Jim and I left New York, after Karen was killed. Sean keeps records about everyone and everything in this city on a server uptown. These guys have access to the server, so they can add or change pretty much anything on record, including names of people living in the city."

"So they're Fixers?"

"Just Danny. Li and Dez could both be Fixers if they wanted to, but they'd rather fly under the radar. They just work with Danny on the side for jobs like the one I just gave them. It's risky, especially for Danny. If Sean found out what he was doing, he'd kill him. So Danny's pretty picky about what jobs they take. They can't mess with the data too much, but this one is easy to hide. Adding a couple of names among the thousands of people registered is nothing."

Andy nodded and ate another dried apricot.

"So everyone registered has an ID? Like a driver's license?"

"Yeah, except it's a bracelet with a barcode on it. And if you want to live anywhere in or near the city and have access to food, water, and electricity, you have to register yourself and wear the bracelet."

"That doesn't seem so bad. The government used to have birth records on all of us, so how is this any different?"

"It's not, really, and I never had an issue with Sean making everyone register themselves. It's everything else that he does that I have a problem with. Once you're in the system, then you have to work. Food and clean water and power don't just magically appear—I get that. The problem is that Sean uses the Dregs like slave labor."

"Slave labor," Andy repeated. She frowned as she thought of Maria.

"They're treated liked dogs by the Directors and Infantry, and everyone over the age of seven has to work."

"So why do people stay here…people like Danny? He seems smart. Why don't they try to go out and survive on their own like we've done?"

"Some do. A few stay because they doubt anything outside New York would be any better, but most stay because they're scared and helpless. Most people aren't like us, you know that. And when you're so hungry that you feel like you're digesting your own stomach, you'll do whatever it takes if someone is giving you food, even if it's someone like Sean."

Rather appropriately, Ben took a bite of beef jerky and offered the remainder to Andy. Starved, she finished the rest of it. Together, they chewed away in silence. Ben edged closer to the end of the alley and glanced around. The streets were as bustling as earlier.

"You don't trust these guys?" Andy said suddenly after she finished eating.

"What do you mean?"

"Well, you told me not to tell them my real name, and then you didn't tell them which name on that list was going to be yours. I take that as you not trusting them."

"It's not that I don't trust them. It's just safer for everyone if they know as little as possible about who we are and what we're doing here. Sean tortures people for information if he thinks someone is betraying him or is plotting against him. He's got spies all over this city just waiting to find people like us. The fact that I'm already at the top of his list of enemies means that I have to be ten times more careful. And so do people who are close to me."

"People like me?" Andy said as Ben paused to take a sip of water.

"Exactly. Believe me, hon, you don't want Sean knowing your real name."

"All right, so besides getting through checkpoints, what else do we need IDs for if we don't need food or water or power?"

"To get into nightclubs."

"Nightclubs?"

"Uh-huh. Sean kept a few of them open, and now they're wild and crazier than ever. They're every teenage boy's wet dream."

"Sounds terrific," Andy mumbled sarcastically.

"Well, it's also our ticket to getting the information we need about the virus. The Directors and Infantry love the nightclubs, and if anyone knows whether Sean's hidden the virus somewhere, it's them."

Ben finished his water and put the empty bottle back in his bag.

Andy, meanwhile, was still thinking about the nightclubs as she unlocked their bikes.

"So did you randomly pick 'Katrina' or did you know someone with that name?" Ben asked as he unlocked his own bike.

"It was my mother's name. Katrina Wilson. That was her maiden name."

"Really? How did I not know that already?"

He sounded almost disappointed, as if this were something that he should have known about Andy by now.

"Well, I don't know *your* mother's name. What was it?"

"Ingrid. Ingrid Andersen."

"Andersen…sounds Danish, like my dad."

Ben nodded. "Her family was from Denmark. She was the first one born here in the States."

"And Irish on your father's side?"

"Yep. You can't get more Irish than 'Kelly.' I think that's the only reason Danny even bothers to help me."

Andy moved closer to Ben in order to put the bike locks back inside his bag. She looked up at him and smiled faintly.

"I like that name. Ingrid, I mean."

"Yeah, my mom was cool," he replied, returning the smile. "You would've liked her."

Even in the darkness of the alley, Andy could still make out his translucent blue eyes.

"How did you know everyone's eye color?" she said, suddenly frowning. "I've known Morgan and Charlie for six years, and I couldn't tell you what color their eyes are."

Ben shrugged.

"I knew we were going to need IDs so I made a mental note of everyone's eye color and approximate height over the past few days."

"But your ID will say that you have brown eyes, not blue."

"Well, that's what colored contacts are for. I can't be walking around here and going through checkpoints looking like Ben Kelly. Anytime some guy pops up on the barcode scanner who's about my age with my height, hair, and eye color, they always get a second look."

"You have colored contacts?"

"Yeah, some disposable ones I've got stashed away, just in case."

Andy shook her head and turned away.

"That's too bad," she said as she got on her bike. "Your eyes are gorgeous. Be a shame to cover them up."

The words were flirtatious but the delivery was not, making the remark entirely ambiguous, and frustrating.

Back on their bikes, Andy led the way through the southern end of Manhattan, retracing with perfect memory the same streets Ben had taken to get to Chinatown.

Chapter XIX

22 July 2021

"So Sean wants you to start adding somethin' to everyone's ID file."

Danny merely blinked back at Doug, Director of Census and Labor. In his experience, guys named "Doug" were always a pain in the ass, and this Doug was no exception. It wasn't that he was particularly mean or power hungry, but rather he was just too dumb to fully understand the duties of the position Sean had given him. If anything, he had the easiest job of any of the Directors, but he still managed to botch it all the time. It was widely rumored that Sean only gave Doug the position because he wanted to sleep with Doug's sister, Lily. So while Doug bumbled about like an incompetent slug, Sean assigned him an "assistant," someone with a few more brain cells who ended up doing most of Doug's work.

"What is it?" Danny asked him with thinly veiled impatience.

"He wants you to add fingerprints to everyone's file. Can you do that?"

Danny blinked again. He didn't like the sound of this.

"Uh, you mean like *scanning* fingerprints into their computer file?"

Doug shrugged in a way that people did when they didn't understand what they were talking about.

"Yeah, I guess so."

"Okay, I'm asking because the only other way to do it is have paper records, which can't be linked to electronic records."

While Danny couldn't believe he had to explain something so basic to Doug, he knew if he didn't, Doug's confusion would rapidly escalate.

"Okay, then do whatever it takes to link the files together," Doug replied while looking at Danny as though *he* were the idiot in the room.

"Fine," Danny sighed. "So what about all the people already in the system? Are they also supposed to get their fingerprints scanned and added to their file? Or is this just something for new people registering and everyone else is grandfathered?"

Doug frowned, and Danny immediately knew he had just used a term that the former did not comprehend.

"'Grandfathered?' What the fuck does that mean?"

Danny let out another sigh.

"Never mind. Just tell Sean that unless I hear otherwise, I'm only going to have new people scan their fingerprints, okay?"

Danny waited for Doug to confirm that he understood, but all he received was a blank stare.

"Okay?" he repeated more urgently.

"Yeah, I got it," Doug replied defensively.

Danny looked down at his keyboard and resisted the urge to pound on it. *Jesus Christ, it's like pulling teeth…*

He looked back at Doug.

"Tell Sean it'll take me about a week to get all the hardware and software set up to scan in fingerprints, all right? Tell him this won't happen overnight."

"Yeah, okay."

"Is that it?"

"Yeah, that's it."

Without another word, Danny went back to typing on his computer, a cue for Doug that they were done talking. Doug took the hint and left Danny's office.

"Fucking idiot," Danny mumbled when the door closed and he was finally alone again.

Following another hour of mindless work, he turned away from his computer and noticed the sun was beginning to set. Soon Ben would come back for his IDs. Fortunately, he had already finished creating them the day before, so any new rules about fingerprints would have no effect on them.

After hearing his stomach growl for the third time in less than as many minutes, Danny shut down his computer and pried himself out of his chair. With his backpack in hand, he locked the door to his office and went down the fifteen flights of stairs to the first floor of the Empire State Building, the same stairs he climbed everyday to get to his office. The elevators in the building were functional, but to save electricity, only individuals who needed to go above the twentieth floor were allowed to use the elevator. Naturally, only the Directors and other "special" people either worked or had access to these higher floors. These lucky people received special treatment in all things, and elevator usage was no different.

Danny passed by the guards at the front entrance of the building and departed without looking at any of them. Once outside, he walked two blocks to where his bike two was locked and made a beeline to the nearest food bank. He hoped the lines wouldn't be too long tonight. Ever since the Director of Food and Nutrition decided to limit the number of days per week that each bank was open from four to three, the lines of people waiting for food had grown to monstrous lengths by mid-afternoon. Danny already knew he was going to have to wait. It was just a question of how long.

* * *

By Thursday evening, the last thing Ben wanted to do was return to the city. Most of Wednesday had been spent finding a more suitable location to hide the tanker. Eight thousand gallons of gasoline was too much to consolidate into smaller containers, so the group ultimately decided to store the tanker inside the Home Depot.

This meant clearing a space large enough for it to fit inside, which required several hours of moving multiple shelves of home improvement materials out of the way. Making the task even more arduous was the heat wave that seemed to have crept into the region since their arrival. By mid-afternoon, everyone was sweating through their clothes.

"Someday, I'm going to invent something the size of a small rock that will power a vehicle for hundreds of kilometers," Charlie declared once the job was finally done. "Petrol is only twenty percent efficient. That's eighty percent waste!"

No one doubted that Charlie was smart enough to accomplish such a task.

There was a small lake near their new neighborhood that Charlie had tested the day before for potability, and once the tanker was safely stored within the Home Depot, everyone headed to the lake and jumped in fully clothed. Afterward, it was dinnertime.

The day before, Morgan and Susan had taken Katie along for a drive in search of wild fruits and vegetables growing on the many abandoned farms in the area. What they ended up finding was a veritable gold mine. Within a few miles of their neighborhood they discovered a farm inhabited by three siblings: two sisters age sixteen and twelve, and a brother, age nine. Along with fruits and vegetables, they had two dairy cows. The two eldest also hunted and used old-fashioned methods to preserve meat through winter.

After striking up a friendly conversation with the siblings, Morgan and Susan offered them gasoline in exchange for any food they could manage to part with. The siblings gladly accepted the proposition, for they had been without any fuel for their tractor for more than three years. And so, in exchange for a gallon of fresh milk, half a pound of butter, and a large basket full of various fruits and vegetables, Jim returned that evening with twenty gallons of gas. It was a fair exchange, but even better was finding people in the area who were willing to barter.

Following the dip in the lake and a particularly satisfying dinner, everyone was sleepy from their physically taxing day. Ben, however, was determined to get back to the city that evening despite his tired muscles. Andy would again return with him, along with Maria and Morgan. Jim initially objected to his wife going along, but she quickly silenced him over dinner.

"Just because I'm a mother doesn't mean that I don't get to go places anymore. I want to see the city, and I want see it tonight, so lucky you…you get to babysit."

"Blimey, first she sends you to deliver petrol, and now you're stuck looking after my niece? What do you Yanks call that again?" Charlie teasingly asked no one in particular.

"'Whipped,'" Ben replied as he pushed himself away from the table.

Jim cast his cousin a look. "Thanks, man. Appreciate it."

"Anytime."

As everyone laughed, Morgan leaned over and gave Jim a consolatory kiss on the cheek, which quickly soothed him.

"Well, Uncle Charlie," Jim began. "I might have to watch her, but *you* get to change her diapers all evening."

Charlie let out a groan and looked over at Katie, who was contentedly sitting between Morgan and Andy in her highchair. With her chubby legs kicking at the air, she was currently engrossed in pounding raspberries and blueberries into mush on the tray with her little palm. Ben was already standing up to waken his body, and he now moved behind the highchair and picked Katie up off her seat. Everyone watched as he smelled the back of her diaper and immediately winced. Placing her back in the highchair, he said, "Time for a change, Uncle Charlie."

"Hey, how did I get stuck with changing nappies all evening?" Charlie said, looking utterly victimized.

"That's what you get for giving shit to her stepfather," Jim remarked. Everyone laughed again, and even Charlie had to smile.

"Father, not stepfather," Morgan quietly corrected as the laughter faded, and she and Jim exchanged a brief but intimate smile that only

Andy saw. She glanced over at Ben, but he was already walking out of the room toward what she assumed was his bedroom. He was preparing for the evening's outing.

Susan, meanwhile, rose from her chair and picked Katie up after first wiping off her sticky hands. "I'll change her this time," she said to Charlie. "But you get the next one."

"Aw, thanks, love." Charlie beamed as he watched Susan leave the room with Katie in tow.

"My girlfriend is cracking," he proclaimed proudly, but only Morgan understood the expression.

"You'll say anything to get out of changing nappies."

"I would not. Susan *is* cracking, even if she didn't change nappies. But the fact that she does change nappies makes her even more cracking."

"'Cracking?' 'Nappies?'" Jim commented with a chuckle as he placed his hand over Morgan's. "Sometimes I feel like I need a dictionary just to understand you two."

"No kidding," Andy concurred.

But before Morgan and Charlie could defend their native vocabulary, Maria and Carmen entered the house. Having eaten earlier, they'd gone for a walk in the neighborhood while everyone else ate.

"Hey, Maria," Andy called out in her best British accent as they entered the kitchen. "Did I ever mention how cracking you are?"

"What am I?" Maria called back, frowning with confusion.

"Cracking," Andy repeated before a fit of laughter took over.

Even more confused, Maria shook her head and turned to her sister for a clue.

"I don't understand. What does that mean? Like I'm going crazy or something?"

By now, Andy and Jim were laughing too hard to speak while Morgan and Charlie both rolled their eyes, mutually this time.

* * *

With an inmate population of just over two thousand, Green

Haven Correctional Facility had been one of the larger prisons in New York State. Sitting some seventy-five miles north of Manhattan, the facility was once the prison of choice for long-term inmates due to its proximity to the city and its comfortable conditions. Today, however, it was anything but a 'haven.'

Sean had chosen Green Haven not because it was close to the city, but that it sat in a quiet, rural area of the state. There were other prisons closer to the city, including the infamous "Sing Sing," but Sean had other uses for them that were far less sensitive.

There were eight cellblocks in the prison, lettered A through H. The first four on the west side of the prison, A through D, were closed cells, while blocks E through H on the eastern side were comprised of open cells in an aviary-style set up. Each of the eight blocks had two hundred and fifty-two individual cells. Most of the closed cells in blocks A through C were vacant with the exception of a few that some of the Fixers would often crash in after a long day of handling the virus in the confines of a hazmat suit. All of the highly specialized laboratory equipment and the virus itself were kept within cellblock D. No longer recognizable as a place that once housed convicted murders and rapists, cellblock D had undergone extensive renovations to emulate the conditions and protocols once employed by the Center for Disease Control and other national laboratories for handling Biosafety Level 4 agents.

Under Sean's watchful supervision, the renovations had been completed in less than six months, though most of the workers were kept in the dark about what exactly they were constructing. Despite some guesswork in terms of replicating exact CDC safety procedures, the overall result was quite impressive. Hidden within the walls of a prison, the last known strains of the virus were securely contained in a place no one would think to look.

That Thursday, Sean made a trip to Green Haven. After telling Luke, his closest advisor, where he was going, he made the hour-and-a-half drive alone and without a driver, something he rarely did anymore. In truth, Sean had been thinking about going to the prison for a few weeks now. He knew he was being a little paranoid, but over a month had passed since his last visit. And there was another reason for the visit—a personal one.

In the year following Ben and Jim Kelly's disappearance, Sean had dispatched twenty young men from the Infantry to search for the two fugitives. Traveling in pairs, the men headed in different directions. Their mission was neither to capture nor kill the fugitives, but merely to find them and lure them back to New York by revealing that their attempt to destroy the virus had failed. Naturally, the men all presumed that the virus no longer existed and that they were merely feeding the fugitives a tempting lie. Only twelve people knew about Green Haven: Sean, Luke, three Fixers who performed all replication and containment of the virus, and seven of the highest ranking Infantry men who guarded the three Fixers.

After months of tireless searching, nine of the ten pairs had eventually returned without any luck. Only one pair had yet to return, and since there was no way of knowing if they had been successful or not, Sean erred on the side of caution and assigned an additional thirty men to augment the prison's security.

Reaching Green Haven by early evening, Sean walked by a dozen or so guards, each greeting him a little too eagerly, and headed directly to cellblock F. Stacked on more than one level, only a fraction of the two hundred and fifty-two cells were occupied. The one that Sean was interested in was on the bottom level, and as he made his way toward the end of the bottom row, he passed by two prisoners incarcerated for more than petty offenses. They both cried out to him, desperately asking for mercy, but he callously ignored them. The only prisoner he was concerned with was in the fourth cell from the end of the row. When he reached this particular cell, he stopped and peered inside.

"Wake up," he barked between the bars to the person crumpled on the tiny bed in the corner of the cell.

The sound of Sean's voice was startling, and the girl quickly stirred from her slumber. She rolled over, turning her back against the wall of her cell and pushed herself up to sitting position as her feet hit the floor. Wordlessly, she stood up and walked the few feet to the bars to face her captor. Having barely eaten for nearly a week, it was a struggle for her to stand, and the fatigue showed on her face. More pale than normal, there was the faintest hint of circles under her eyes. Despite her weakened condition, however, Lily Haines was still a sight to behold. At eighteen, she was a stunning beauty whose physicality had suffered no ill-effects from the difficulties of life. Though most young women her age were thin from their paltry diets and the demands of their labor, Lily was still more petite than most but had all the curves that could excite every male from pre-pubescent boys to fully grown men.

Yet Sean's first remark to her was, "You look like shit."

Lily said nothing in response. She merely hugged her arms tightly around her chest as though freezing. Her long, dark hair draped over her folded arms, and her hazel-brown eyes averted Sean's own piercing blue stare. She remained silent not out of fear but out of defiance, and Sean knew it. A few weeks earlier, she had propositioned herself to one of the other Directors, and as much as he'd wanted to take her up on her offer, his loyalty to Sean was stronger. He mentioned the incident to Sean, and the result was a week in the cell.

"Fun being in here, isn't it?" he went on, finally taking his eyes off Lily to look around at the vast and empty space that surrounded them. "All alone and without any Directors to fuck."

With this last word, Lily sharply turned away.

"I only did it because you've been ignoring me for weeks now," she cried out. "How else was I supposed to get your attention?"

She then turned back again and came within inches of the bars. Color had quickly returned to her cheeks in the form of anger as her almond-shaped eyes narrowed on Sean.

"I'm sick of you fucking the other girls and then getting jealous if I even talk to another guy. It's not fair!"

"Life's not fair. Get used to it," Sean responded coolly as he stood perfectly erect. "And for that outburst, I'm leaving you here another day. Someone will drive your sorry ass back to the city tomorrow…unless I change my mind before then."

Looking as though she was either about to cry or scream, Lily did neither and instead hardened her jaw by gritting her teeth. She had no other choice but to remain silent. Finally, she turned away once more and retreated back to the tiny bed.

Wearing a smug smile, Sean watched her lie back down on the bed before stepping away from the cell without another word.

There was one more thing to do before leaving the prison.

* * *

"I don't know how you do it, man," Dez said to Ben not a minute after he entered the tiny apartment in Chinatown with Andy, Morgan, and Maria. "Where do you find these gorgeous women, and can you tell me so that I can go there too?"

The three young women laughed lightly. Andy had warned them about Dez's flirtatiousness, but insisted it was innocent.

"It won't do you any good if I told you. All the pretty ones left with me," Ben quipped.

"Well, it sure seems that way," Dez went on as he ogled each of the girls shamelessly.

"Yo, Dez, leave 'em alone," Danny called out from the kitchen. "They didn't come here to be harassed."

"I'm not harassing you, am I?" Dez asked the girls while wearing a mischievous grin.

"Dez, get the fuck outta here," Danny ordered. "We got work to do."

With his hands held up in a mocking surrender, Dez inched toward the door.

"Fine, Mister Grouchy Pants. I was gonna go to the food bank anyway."

Turning back to the girls, Dez bowed dramatically before grabbing each girl's hand to kiss the top of it.

"Good night, ladies," he said with exaggerated gallantry before leaving the apartment.

Danny came into the living room where everyone else was seated.

"My apologies. There's just no explaining him," he began.

"Don't apologize. He's funny," said Morgan smiling. Thus far, the diversion into the city had been an exciting and welcome change from the daily toll of motherhood.

"I'm glad *you* think so," Danny replied. "He can be a pain in the ass most times."

"What did he mean about a 'food bank?'" Maria asked.

"It's exactly what it sounds like…just a place for people to buy food. I think there's, like, fifteen in Manhattan and 'bout another thirty in the other boroughs. Of course, the lines are a fuckin' nightmare. It's like this scary film I saw in school once about Russians standing in line for hours during the Cold War for a single loaf of bread. Today I waited two goddamned hours, and by the time I got to the front of the line, the only things left to buy were apples and eggs. I'm so fuckin' sick of eggs that I feel like I'm gonna sprout feathers or somethin.'"

Everyone else immediately felt guilty for the deliciously well-balanced dinner they had eaten earlier.

"What do you buy the food with?" Andy asked as she silently wished they had brought along some extra food for Danny and his friends.

"Credit. It's like money. Each person has to work to get credit, and every job has a certain value. Most Fixers, like me, get a thousand credits a month, which is a lot. I usually have extra credits at the end of each month. Other jobs, like working in the water treatment plants, get less…maybe three or four hundred credits a month."

"The dirtier the job, the worse the pay?" Morgan commented aloud. "Well that's nothing new."

"And lemme guess, Sean decided what each job was worth?" asked Andy, her voice tinged with disdain.

"He and the Directors," Danny replied, nodding toward Ben.

"Wait, *you* decided what each job was worth?" said Andy, turning toward him, but Ben quickly shook his head.

"Not exactly. I had this whole idea where each job would be paid based on whatever the national average was for the same type of work before the outbreak. I thought it was fair and made the most sense, but no one listened to me, and in the end, Sean decided on his own what everyone would be paid."

"So why does Sean even bother hearing these Directors' opinions if he doesn't listen to them?" asked Maria.

"He wants 'em to feel like they're important 'cuz he trusts those motherfuckers to manage everything that keeps people fed and the lights on. Like my ol' man used to say, 'happy employees are loyal employees,'" Danny enlightened with his colorful Southie accent. "No offense, Ben, but you know that's true."

Ben waved away the comment without issue.

"So, about this credit that everyone gets," Morgan continued. "People get credit every month?"

"Uh-huh, and the credit is electronically linked to your ID," Ben explained. "So when you go to the food banks or anywhere that requires credit like the nightclubs, you scan your ID and the 'cost' gets deducted from your credit. Of course, Sean can then monitor everywhere you've been and everything you've bought."

"Yeah, it's like fuckin' 'Big Brother,'" Danny added as he suddenly pushed himself out of his grungy armchair. "Speaking of IDs, I've got all of yours ready. Hang on a sec."

He disappeared into what was likely a bedroom and returned moments later with a handful of metal bands in one hand, a small electronic-looking box in the other, and a laptop tucked beneath his arm. He sat back down and placed the bands and small box on the rickety coffee table in front of him before firing up the laptop.

"So today I was told that Sean wants to add fingerprints to everyone's ID file."

Ben frowned at this bit of news.

"Why?"

"Dunno. That shithead Doug told me, so you can guess how that went."

"Oh, Jesus," Ben moaned. "I forgot how stupid that guy is."

"Well, he hasn't gotten any smarter since you've been gone. I think I'm just getting better at dealing with his total failure to communicate the simplest instructions."

"Who's Doug?" said Maria.

"He's the Director of Census and Labor, which just means he's supposed make sure everyone is registered with an ID and is assigned a job. But he's a big, fuckin' idiot who only got the job because Sean wanted to bang his sister." Danny then paused to rub his eyes with one hand. "Most people just ignore him, but he's a daily headache for me."

"Sorry," Maria mumbled sympathetically, which made Danny smile.

"So why the fingerprints?" Ben asked. "Has there been a rash of people forging or stealing other people's IDs or something?"

Danny shook his head.

"No more than usual. Maybe Sean wants to get rid of the ID bands completely so that people just use their fingerprints, which, I gotta admit, would make sense. There's more than a million people registered in the five boroughs, and with people losing their IDs all the time, it's a major ass-pain for people to prove who they are without 'em. Fingerprints would solve everything."

"So you need to scan our prints," Andy said while nodding at the small electronic box. "But won't that completely defeat the purpose of you having an alias?" she asked Ben.

"It shouldn't," he replied, sounding certain. "It's not as if Sean's got a copy of my prints. And anyway," he went on as he combed his hand through his hair. "Jim and I burned and deleted all our medical and school records in Virginia last year, which was the only thing that had my fingerprints on them. We even destroyed Karen's records too. If Sean ever searches for our old records, it's too late. It's like we never existed."

Andy raised her eyebrows as she listened to Ben. She had no idea the measures he and Jim had taken to erase their pasts. Neither had Morgan, who muttered, "Good Lord," under her breath.

"As long as they're not asking for a photo ID, I'm not worried," Ben concluded.

"That ain't gonna happen soon," Danny assured. "With the data rates we gotta work with right now, photo files are too big to transfer from the main server to all the food banks and checkpoints. It would take five fuckin' minutes just to verify one person's identity. No one's got that kinda patience."

Not a moment later, the lights throughout the entire apartment began to flicker—once, twice, and after the third time, they went out completely, and the apartment became pitch-black.

"Terrific," Danny muttered as the others reached into their pockets and backpacks to retrieve flashlights. Maria found hers first and illuminated the room. By the time the others turned theirs on, the lights flickered back on.

Andy turned off her flashlight. "Does that happen a lot?" she asked.

"All the time," Danny replied with a sigh as he plugged his laptop into the wall. "And always when I'm about to do something with my computer."

Everyone waited as Danny hooked up the fingerprint scanner to the computer. Once everything was ready, he looked up at everyone.

"So I told Doug that I'd only scan prints for new people who were registering for IDs, but knowing Sean, he'll demand that everyone else start scanning their fingerprints at checkpoints to get them on record, so better to get yours on record now by me than some punk-ass Infantry kid."

Agreeing, Ben nodded slowly, and Andy could tell that he was thinking hard on something.

"Do you need all ten prints for each person?" he finally said.

Danny shook his head. "No, I just need one fingerprint per file. But I can add up to five prints per person."

"Good," Ben remarked. "I want you to add one of my prints to three separate names. Can you do that?"

Danny blinked a few times before his face broke out into a smile, making him look almost handsome. "What are you up to, Ben?"

"Only good things, I promise."

Danny shrugged and glanced at his laptop screen. "All right…whatever you want, Ben. If anyone ever finds the glitch, which I doubt, I'll just say I accidentally copied the same print to three different names."

"Also, I'll need to add another print, maybe two, to each of the three names, but it will be someone else's prints."

Danny looked up and gave Ben the same smile before breaking out into a chuckle. He held up his hands. "Like I said, whatever you want."

Morgan, Andy, and Maria exchanged glances as each silently attempted to decipher Ben's odd request. When Andy figured it out, she wordlessly expressed to the other two that she would tell them later. Ben, Jim, and Brian, when he returned, would be sharing multiple aliases.

Ben scanned the print of his right index finger first, which Danny copied to the files of the three aliases that he would be using: John Simmons, Michael Wilkins, and Matthew Thompson, all age twenty with brown hair and eyes and a height of six-foot-one. There was no meaning behind the three names; Ben had simply found them in a phonebook a few days earlier. Danny handed him the ID bracelets for all three.

Morgan went next. She scanned two of her fingerprints, which Danny quickly added to the file of her new name, Sarah O'Brian, his face brightening as he commented about her Irish name. Andy followed Morgan and applied her right thumbprint to Katrina Wilson's file before being handed her ID. It was similar to a medical ID bracelet except that there was a small black-and-white QR code where the person's medical condition would normally be inscribed.

"And last but not least…" Danny said, looking at Maria, smiling awkwardly at her.

"Isabel. Torres." Neither Morgan nor Maria had introduced themselves to Danny prior to scanning their prints.

"Uh, right," Danny muttered as he fumbled through the remaining ID bracelets to find her name. "Here we go."

Maria sat beside Danny as the others had done to scan her prints, but Danny appeared to be slightly flustered by her presence and made more than a few keystroke errors when updating her file. As she stood to return to her seat on the adjacent sofa, his gaze lingered on her for more than a few seconds, but he quickly caught himself. Only Ben seemed to notice, and he suppressed a smile.

Danny then held up the remaining IDs.

"I've still got three more…Henry, Kathy, and Julia."

"Here, give 'em to me," Ben said, holding out his hand. "They can get their prints scanned at the checkpoints."

"All right," Danny replied, handing the IDs for Charlie, Susan, and Carmen to Ben.

"Jim will come by in two days to scan his thumbprint, and he'll bring these."

Ben held up the bracelets for the three male aliases: John, Michael, and Matthew.

"And you want me to add his thumbprint to all three?" Danny asked.

"That's right."

"No problem. Just tell him to come by before ten."

Narrowing his eyes on Danny, Ben gave him a knowing look. "What, you hitting the clubs or something?"

Danny looked sideways at Maria for a spilt-second as he placed his laptop on the coffee table before addressing Ben. "Shit, what else is there to do in this town for fun?" he remarked unapologetically as he leaned back in his chair and cupped his hands behind his shaved head. "I gotta blow off steam somehow. I can't keep watching Li and Dez play video games every day. I'll go fuckin' insane!"

The girls laughed lightly at this, but Ben began to frown. His thoughts were elsewhere.

"Does everyone still go to *Papillon*?" he finally asked, sitting up straight.

"Yeah, I hear it's packed almost every night," said Danny.

"What's *Papillon*?" Andy asked, repeating Ben's perfect French pronunciation.

"A nightclub in the Meatpacking District," Ben murmured, still looking pensive. "You know if Luke still goes?" he asked Danny.

"Probably. Sean's there at least three nights a week, so Luke's gotta be there too."

Ben nodded and looked over at Andy. He could tell that she wanted to know what he was thinking, and who Luke was, but now was not the time for explanations. Instead, he stood up and announced that it was time to go. No one objected to the command. This was Ben's show. As everyone else stood, he extended his hand to Danny, who shook it.

"Thanks, man."

"Hey, easy day, brother," said Danny with a laid-back manner that befitted him. "Part of me wants to know what you're up to, but the rest of me doesn't wanna know a fuckin' thing."

Ben understood. Sean's use of torture to literally bleed information out of people was well-known. Ignorance was always safer.

From within his backpack, Ben pulled out the second kilo of cocaine that he'd promised Danny. However, Danny waved it away.

"Nah, man. What you gave me last time was enough. Just tell Jim to bring me some food when he comes if you got any to spare. Something other than eggs or apples."

Surprised at this refusal, Ben shrugged before returning the drugs to his backpack.

After thanking Danny and saying goodbye, the girls stepped outside the apartment first, and with their departure, Danny seized the opportunity to ask Ben something in private.

"Hey, I know I give Dez a lot of shit for almost every word that comes outta his mouth, but I gotta admit that I agree with him on those three girls. They're fuckin' gorgeous, particularly that Isabel. Instead of a kilo of coke, I'll take one night with her."

"I'll be sure to pass that along," Ben replied with good-natured sarcasm.

"Seriously, what the fuck did you do? Go to L.A. and find all the leftover models and movie stars or something?"

Ben just laughed and shook his head. "I met them all just like I met you—speed dating."

As Ben chucked, Danny shooed away the gibe with a wave of his hand.

"Oh, fuck you, too…lucky bastard. Maybe if I looked like you, girls like that would fall right into my lap, too."

* * *

Sean looked at his watch with impatience. It read 9:17. He wanted to be back in the city by ten, but now there was no chance of that. More than five minutes had passed since one of the guards who kept watch over the secret activities in cellblock D went to find him a hazmat suit. Were it not for the dangers of entering the cellblock without a suit, he would've tracked the guard down and thrown him into "The Pit" without a suit for making him so late.

Five additional minutes were spent in the "waiting room," as it was called, before entering a series of three hermetically sealed rooms secured with combination cipher locks. The last of these three rooms was the "prep room" where the hazmat suits were double-checked to ensure everything was airtight. The two rooms between the waiting room and the prep room were called "safe rooms." They were completely empty and their sole purpose was to create a physical barrier between the virus and the outside world. Beyond the prep room was an unnamed room where the virus itself was stored in the same manner as back at Fort Detrick: inside a medical freezer kept at minus forty degrees Celsius, which was stored in a room lit by a single safelight, the same type of light used in photography darkrooms. Higher temperatures and visible light would risk degrading the life of the virus.

Beyond this room was the long and narrow "vacuum room," which contained multiple showers and intricate air filtration and vacuum systems used to destroy any traces of the virus after its exposure to the air. Another safe room followed the vacuum room, beyond which was "The Pit;" the room where prisoners condemned to virus exposure were kept. A large and empty room, roughly twenty-by-thirty feet in dimension, there was currently only one prisoner inside—and the second reason for Sean's visit.

After yet another five minutes, the guard finally appeared from behind the first safe room. He was wearing a cumbersome blue hazmat suit and carrying a second suit for Sean, who by now was livid.

"Jesus fucking Christ! How long does it take to find a suit? Aren't they supposed to be kept in this room and not beyond this door?"

From within the confines of the suit, the guard and the top third of his suit nodded up and down meekly, and a muffled "I'm sorry" could be heard from beneath his helmet.

Sean snatched the suit out of the guard's hands and hastily put it on.

"Let's go!" he barked, once all the seals and zippers of the suit were closed. The guard wordlessly obeyed, and after passing through the two safe rooms, they stopped at the prep room to check and recheck their suits. Satisfied that everything was in order, Sean gave the guard a nod to keep going. Once inside the next room, Sean turned on the safelight and carefully opened the medical freezer.

Inside were seven small glass vials sitting on a metal tray. Sean carefully picked one up with his gloved hand and examined it. The contents of the vial looked like water and appeared to be equally as harmless. It was hard to believe that what lived inside the tiny container had forever changed the course of humanity. In the six years since it had been unleashed on the world, the virus had never been called anything else. Perhaps it didn't need a name, like "hepatitis" or "smallpox" because no other virus had been even remotely as devastating. It had entirely redefined the meaning of the word.

In mid-2017, Sean sent a handful of survivors, still young enough to be immune, to Fort Detrick to verify the rumors of the virus's origins from within the infamous government laboratory. It turned out that the rumors were indeed true, and exactly sixty-eight vials of the original strain of the virus still existed, including the one that had been improperly handled with by a reckless scientist. Afterward, Sean maintained a constant presence of guards and Fixers at the Fort to protect and study the virus—and use it.

To date almost one hundred people—opponents of Sean's as well as the friends of his opponents—had been killed by exposure to the virus, and in doing so, a few things had been accomplished: the death of his most threatening enemies, the near-successful replication of the virus by the Fixers, and, most importantly, the near-development of a vaccine.

The explosion at Fort Detrick destroyed fifty-seven of the vials and all research documents regarding the virus, its replication, and the vaccine. Afterward, Sean nearly abandoned the whole notion of using the virus as a weapon and decided to destroy the remaining eleven vials. Without a vaccine, he knew he would only be prolonging the risk to his own life from exposure. But the nagging desire to control something so deadly overwhelmed him, and the eleven vials were transported north as plans to convert part of Green Haven into a lab began. Now, only seven vials remained. Four had been used to infect a dozen or so people, and the attempt to replicate the virus was nearly complete once again. His Fixers were brilliant, but never would he tell them that. Instead, he constantly berated them for not working fast enough.

Sean now placed the vial back in the freezer and closed the door before turning to the guard.

"When was the prisoner infected?"

"Uh, twelve days ago. I remember 'cuz it was my birthday."

The guard smiled weakly behind his helmet, knowing that it was a vain attempt to instill even a tiny shred of sympathy from Sean, but he remained stoic and impatiently waited for the guard to open the next door despite knowing all the door codes and having the power to change them at anytime.

Flustered, the guard hastened to open the door to the vacuum room. He entered the wrong code by accident twice, which made Sean even more irate.

"Stop fucking around, or you'll be joining the slumber party!"

On the third try, the guard finally opened the door. Both he and Sean stepped through the long room and quickly passed by all the safety equipment before approaching the door to the final safe room. Beyond that was their destination.

"The Pit" was nothing but an empty room, cold and sterile. The windows had been sealed off and covered to suppress the faintest beam of light from the outside world. The room itself was not kept dark, however. A single pair of florescent light bulbs in the center of the ceiling gave the room ample illumination, but its effect was nearly as life-draining as the infliction suffered by those unfortunate enough to inhabit the room.

His name was John, and he was no one of great importance or threat to Sean, but he happened to be a distant cousin of someone named Timothy Baker. Timothy had been the leader of an underground movement in the city whose sole goal had been to overthrow Sean and his closest friends from power. Nearly two years earlier, Timothy and the other leaders of the movement had been caught and later killed via injection of the virus. They died while detained at Fort Detrick, and with their demise, much of the advancing research conducted by the Fixers had been accomplished from studying their blood and tissue samples in the days both before and after succumbing to the virus.

John, however, was truly innocent of any crime against Sean. In fact, he had only met his cousin once, at a baptism for yet another distant cousin more than a decade earlier when John had been too young to even remember the meeting. But any surviving blood relatives of his enemies were too close for Sean, no matter how distant, and therefore, one way or another, John had to die. But first, he would be Sean's guinea pig.

The guard remained by the door while Sean approached the prisoner. The fact that only a few millimeters of protective material guarded him from infection did not stop Sean from coming within mere feet of John. For a long and intentionally tormenting minute, Sean simply stood over the wretched soul lying helpless on the floor in the center of the room.

Wearing only the thinnest of hospital gowns, John was experiencing nearly all of the major symptoms: large, puss-filled boils on his arms and legs, uncontrollable shivering despite suffering from a fever, and profuse sweating. Within hours, death would come, but not without severe pain. Soon, his lungs would fill with blood, ultimately asphyxiating him. In the end, the virus simply choked its victims to death.

In his agony, John barely registered Sean's presence, or that of the third person who had just entered the room. The intense shivering and pain from the boils that had rapidly covered his body numbed all senses to anything outside of his own skin. Only sixteen years old, he knew the end was near, and at the moment, it couldn't come fast enough.

Suddenly, a gloved hand grabbed his arm, and seconds later a needle was inserted into a vein in his forearm, and the contents of the syringe were injected into his body. The pain from the prick of the needle did not register, and John's arm was released without him realizing what had just happened.

"How long will it take to know if it works?" Sean asked the Fixer who was now standing beside him and holding the empty syringe.

"Hard to tell," the Fixer replied through his helmet. "But if he's still in the same shape by morning, we'll know it failed."

Sean said nothing. He stared down at John trembling with pain, and he wondered how excruciating the ordeal truly was.

"When you find out, send someone to let me know," Sean commanded the Fixer before turning to leave the room.

Chapter XX

01 August 2021

"This time turn your back to me."

Bent over at the waist with her hands on her knees, Andy looked up at Ben like she wanted give him a hard kick to the groin, but for real this time and not a simulated one. She was breathing heavily, as was Ben, though he managed to stand upright while catching his breath.

"C'mon, I'm not doing this to be a pain in the ass. I want to make sure you can defend yourself," Ben insisted between breaths and beckoned her with his hands. "Let's go."

After slowly standing up straight, Andy raised her hand.

"Gimme a minute."

"No. Now. If you can do it when you're tired, you'll be able to do it anytime."

Knowing he was right, she grit her teeth and took another deep breath, though it still didn't lessen the urge to hit him.

"All right," she said, and turned her back to him.

They were in the backyard of one of their houses in Princeton. The cool weather enjoyed during those first days of their arrival had transformed into the persistent yet typical mugginess of summer, and despite being nearly eight o'clock in the evening, both Andy and

Ben's faces were glistening with sweat.

Andy prepared herself with another deep breath as the faint sound of Ben's shoes walking on the grass drew closer. Suddenly, he grabbed her from behind, his arms bear-hugging her around her chest and arms. The sweet scent of his sweat just barely hit her nose as she reacted swiftly to the attack by stepping one foot out to the side and squatting down to lower her center of gravity. Still moving fluidly, she jutted her elbows out to the sides, which loosened Ben's grip enough for her to break free.

"Good," he said approvingly. "Let's do it again."

Andy didn't complain this time, and they repeated the drill three more times before Ben decided she was ready for the next scenario.

"Now this time, raise your arms up, and my arms will go underneath them."

"All right," said Andy, nodding.

As with the other scenarios, Ben would slowly walk Andy through the sequence of movements until she understood exactly what to do to defeat her attacker. Now, with her back to him once again, she raised her arms, which allowed Ben to hug his arms around her even tighter than before, and as he did so, he consciously kept his hands closed tightly into fists to avoid any accidental grazing of his fingers against her breasts. Still, he couldn't stop himself from taking in the fragrance of her hair.

"God, you smell…"

"What, I smell?"

Horrified, Andy broke away, startling Ben, and she quickly sniffed underneath her arms.

"No, you don't smell bad," he said, laughing. "I was gonna say that you smell good…really good."

"Oh…"

Andy self-consciously brushed loose strands of hair away from her face.

"It's this new shampoo that Maria and Carmen made. It's got lavender and some other sweet things in it…chamomile, I think," she added hastily. "I don't really know."

"Well, whatever it is, it smells amazing."

And without warning, Ben stepped forward and leaned in to smell the top of Andy's scalp again, which caught her off-guard. She instinctively backed away.

"Relax. I just wanted to smell you again."

Then realizing what he had said, Ben shut his eyes and shook his head with embarrassment.

"Sorry, that sounded weird."

"Oh, no…well, maybe a little."

Then they both laughed and eased the tension.

"Wanna try again?" Ben asked.

"All right, but after this one, I'm done for the day."

"Fair enough."

Andy turned around once more as Ben stepped forward to wrap his arms around her. This time, he avoided thinking about how good she smelled, among other things.

"Now do the same thing. Step out to the side and squat down."

Andy obeyed.

"Good. Now since I have a tighter grip on you, you'll have to use your arms and feet to disable me. So look back and use your elbows to strike me in the face."

"Great, my signature move…hitting you in the face."

Andy looked back at Ben and smiled.

"Funny," Ben retorted lightly before continuing with the lesson. "You can stomp on the feet to further injure the person, but I would go for the face first, either with your elbow or the back of your forearm to disorient them. Remember, almost anytime you strike someone anywhere on the front or sides of their head, their instinct will be to close their eyes. If you're lucky, they'll grab their head. Either way, that's your window of escape."

"All right, lemme try it."

Andy returned her gaze straight ahead as Ben released his arms and stepped back.

"Ready?"

"Ready."

After Andy lifted her arms, Ben stepped forward and grabbed her again. With impressive speed, Andy deftly simulated the techniques that Ben had instructed, and after repeating the scenario a few more times, she declared she'd had enough.

"All right, we'll do it again tomorrow," Ben remarked.

Andy merely nodded, undoing the rubber band that held her ponytail in place. She rubbed her scalp which released the aroma of the homemade shampoo. It *did* smell good.

"How big is he?" she asked suddenly.

"Who, Luke?"

"Yeah."

Ben shrugged. "I guess he's about my height and build."

Andy nodded again as she studied Ben. He was a good eight or nine inches taller than she and easily seventy to eighty pounds of muscle heavier.

"Is he as strong as you?" she asked, her eyes looking anxious.

Ben didn't answer right away. Instead, he tilted his head to the side and looked away. The gesture made Andy uneasy.

"I'm not gonna lie to you. Luke is pretty strong." Sensing Andy's apprehension, he quickly added, "Just remember that he'll likely be drunk or high or both. That will take away some of his advantage."

Andy looked down at her feet. "Right," she muttered uneasily.

"You'll be fine," Ben said to assuage her fears. "You'll be the last thing he expects."

Looking up, Andy set her gaze to the rear of the house. Through the window that looked into the living room, she could see Susan and Charlie playing a game of cards with Maria and Carmen. Probably poker or rummy. Meanwhile, Morgan was reading a book at the kitchen table while feeding Katie, who would soon be put to bed. Lit candles flickered throughout both rooms, as there was no electricity in the area. Princeton sat outside of the zone where power had been restored, and they were too far north from Philadelphia to receive it from that end. By now, however, life without electricity was no longer the hardship it once had been, and Andy liked to joke that they would have made the early American pioneers proud.

"How did you learn to do this self-defense stuff?"

"You'll laugh when I tell you."

"Why?"

Ben stepped over to a wooden bench that separated a small rock garden from the lawn that covered the majority of the backyard and sat down. Andy edged over to him but remained standing with her arms across her chest.

"From watching *YouTube* videos that Danny gave me before leaving last year."

"*YouTube*?"

"Yeah. Danny has access to every video file that people uploaded on *YouTube* up to the days just before the outbreak. He's also got access to all the files from *Wikipedia* too."

"Holy shit…" Andy uttered in a near whisper.

"Yeah, but get this," Ben went on, "less than a year following the outbreak, Sean sent people to the headquarters of both of those companies to bring back *all* of their servers to New York. He didn't want anyone else to get their hands on all that information."

"Holy shit…" Andy repeated.

"Yeah," Ben breathed hoarsely. "That's the kind of person we're dealing with. While we were all scared and starving, Sean was busy transporting thousands of terabytes of data across the country, literally. Do you know where *YouTube* and *Wikipedia* had their headquarters?"

"No idea."

"California and Florida. Both thousands of miles from here."

"Jesus Christ…"

"Yeah, Jesus Christ is right."

Andy rubbed her eyes as her anxiety returned. "And Danny has access to those files?"

"Yeah. Part of his job is to go through all the video files and delete all the crap that has no real value, at least to Sean. You know…videos that parents used to upload of their kids doing really funny or cute things…useless stuff like that. But of course Danny keeps copies of the really funny things for himself and then gives 'em to Li and Dez to sell."

"People buy old videos from *YouTube*?"

"Sure," Ben replied with a shrug. "It reminds them of the old days, I guess."

It never occurred to Andy that such things would be so important to survivors, but upon consideration it made sense.

She took a seat on the bench and hugged her knees to her chest. Her left shoulder touched Ben's right, and she made no move to distance herself.

"He's a devious little fucker, isn't he?"

Frowning, Ben turned his head to look at Andy. "Who? Danny?"

"No, Sean."

Ben let out a grunt and said, "That's just one of about a hundred adjectives that you could use to describe him."

Still curled up in a ball, Andy rested her head on Ben's shoulder, and without thinking, he wrapped his right arm around her and pulled her an inch closer. Closing her eyes, she let her weight settle onto him. She would do this sometimes, convincing herself that it was just a friendly hug.

"Ben?"

"Yeah?"

"Please don't tell me 'I told you so,' but I'm beginning to think that this might not be such a good idea."

"What, going to *Papillon*?"

"Yeah."

Ben swallowed hard as Andy waited for him to say something.

"Andy, you already know what I think of this whole plan, but I've been racking my brain for weeks now trying to think of some other way to do it. So has Jim, but the fact is that neither he nor I can be involved. If Sean gets even the slightest hint that we've returned, he'll either add so much security to wherever he's hiding the virus or he'll move it and we'll never find it again. And since Luke is probably the only person who knows if Sean still has the virus and where he's hiding it, the only options are to either kidnap him and force the truth out of him with torture, or…"

"Or do what we're doing instead."

"Yeah."

Ben gently stroked Andy's hair, which made her relax even more. "I just…I feel like I'm throwing you to the wolves. I feel like a coward."

Andy abruptly sat up straight and turned toward Ben with a sharp and focused gaze. "Hey, we've been through this already. I insisted on doing this. And you're no coward, Benjamin Kelly. You just have to accept that this is one thing that you can't do."

Her voice rose in both intensity and volume, and she still wasn't finished. "I completely admit that I'm scared, but if we're gonna succeed, we'll have to do some dangerous things. You know that better than anyone, Ben. You've already sacrificed enough. Let some other people handle the burden for a while."

The sincerity and determination in her voice was irresistible, and it forced a smile from Ben. It also made his heart beat a little faster.

God, I love you.

"I don't want you to worry about me," Andy continued on, completely unaware of Ben's thoughts. "Maria will be with me the whole time, and between the two of us, we can kick some serious ass, especially after all these self-defense lessons you've been giving us."

Andy then delivered a gentle punch into Ben's arm. "So stop worrying so much," she ordered with amusement. "You've prepared me well, Yoda."

"Yes ma'am," said Ben after clearing his throat.

"Ugh, you make me feel old when you say that."

Laughing at her own words, Andy released her knees from her chest and planted her feet firmly on the ground.

"I need to wash up," she announced.

"Yeah, me too."

Ben followed Andy inside. He went upstairs to clean up while Andy stayed downstairs to talk to Morgan in the kitchen.

"Whatcha reading?" she asked.

"Calculus," Morgan replied, looking up from her book. "Charlie found it at the library on campus. He said it would be a good one to start with."

"Calculus? I didn't know you liked math that much."

Morgan grimaced, implying that she didn't.

"It's not that I like it, but I often thought that I should learn some more advanced math so that I could teach it."

Andy's thoughts turned to her medical books laying in a box in her bedroom, and she felt a pang of regret for neglecting her own studies of late.

"Sounds like a good idea." Then glancing down at Morgan's wristwatch, she asked, "When did Jim leave?"

"About an hour ago, right after you and Ben went outside," Morgan replied without lifting her eyes from her book.

Nodding lightly, Andy offered her pinky finger to Katie, who was lying in a vibrating chair positioned on the kitchen table that was designed to help infants fall asleep. She latched onto Andy's finger with her entire hand but without her usual vice-like grip. Her eyelids were beginning to look heavy.

"She's about to conk out. Want me to put her to bed?"

Morgan released the pen she had been using to take notes and looked up at her daughter. She smiled and reached into the seat with both hands to retrieve Katie.

"Nah, I got her."

While Morgan put Katie to bed, Andy wandered into the living room where Susan had just won the last three hands of poker.

"Not again!" Charlie lamented as Susan raked in the pot of chips to her corner of the table while imitating an evil laugh.

"Ha! That's right, sucker!" she cackled at Charlie specifically. "You can't beat me!"

Both Maria and Carmen threw their losing hands of cards onto the table with mild frustration as Andy assessed the damage Susan had caused to everyone's stack of chips. Susan's stack was easily triple that of the others.

"Wait, didn't Susan win last night too?" Andy asked the group. The question was mainly a dig at Charlie, for everyone knew that he and Susan had had a longstanding poker rivalry since their days in Aspen.

"Why, Andy, I do believe that you are correct," replied Susan as her voice dripped with sarcasm.

Charlie made a face, and Andy decided to rescue him from further torment. There was real work to do.

"You got a sec, Charlie?"

"Yes, I have more than a second," he replied, relieved to have any excuse to leave the table. He followed Andy into the kitchen while Susan, still gloating over her victory, cleaned up the cards and put them back into a neat deck. The stacks of chips, however, would remain intact until the following evening when the game would resume. Maria and Carmen, meanwhile, went outside for a stroll, an activity they referred to as 'sisterly bonding.'

"What do you know about truth serum?" Andy asked as she and Charlie took a seat at the kitchen table.

"Truth serum?" Charlie repeated with surprise. "Not much, I'm afraid."

"Do you know if it's actually real or if it's just something that Hollywood made up?"

"Oh no, it's real. It's called *sodium amytal.* But other than that, I don't know how it works or how reliable it is. *Rohypnol* might be better, and it causes memory loss." After a pause, Charlie added, "Why do you ask?"

Andy sat back in her chair and let out a sigh.

"I'm trying to think of all possible ways to get the location of the virus out of Luke, assuming he even knows where it is."

"Sounds like you've got some doubts."

"Well...yeah. I can't help but feel like we're all taking a giant stab in the dark here."

"Who's taking a stab in the dark?"

Susan entered the kitchen just in time to hear Andy's last words.

"Oh...nothing," Andy quickly muttered to contain the conversation. The last thing she wanted was for everyone to think she doubted her own scheme. After all, she had insisted on being the one to go to *Papillon*, an idea that Ben still hated despite all his efforts to appear perfectly at ease with her plan, and despite all of their preparations.

A week earlier, a heated argument had taken place between Andy and Ben when she declared her intent to personally target Luke by posing as one of the Helens. When Ben adamantly objecting to such a scheme, she snapped, angered that he would try telling her what she could or could not do. At one point, she even dared to mention Karen, saying, "I'm not your sister. You can't protect me from everything, nor do you have the right!"

Ben nearly lost it after that, and the two didn't speak for three days afterward. Andy's stubbornness prevented her from relenting, and while Ben took offense to her mention of Karen, he couldn't tell her that the real reason he despised the idea was because he was terrified that she would get hurt, or worse, killed. Only after Maria volunteered to go with Andy did things finally calm down.

"Maybe Luke prefers brunettes over blonds," Maria initially joked, though no one could deny that she might be right.

Andy later apologized to Ben for bringing Karen into the argument, and Ben apologized for being overbearing, and the next day, he began showing both Andy and Maria simple but effective self-defense techniques in the event Luke or anyone else in the club tried to overpower them. Both young women turned out to be quick studies.

"Did I hear you say something about truth serum?" Susan now asked.

Andy closed her eyes, feeling foolish for even considering the notion.

"It was just something that popped into my head earlier today. I'm sure it won't even work."

"I'll look into it," Charlie assured her. "You never know, right?"

"I guess," Andy muttered before mustering a smile of gratitude. "Thanks, Charlie."

"No worries." Charlie then turned to Susan. "Wanna come with me to the library tomorrow?"

Susan's face quickly fell.

"Oh, I would, but I'm going with Morgan and Maria tomorrow to find clothes, remember?"

"Oh, right. I forgot," Charlie said, frowning. "Oh well, then. It'll be boring anyway."

"What are you talking about? I love going to the library with you," Susan said as she reached over and tussled Charlie's hair. "I always feel smarter when I leave," she added as Charlie reached up and grabbed her wrist to stop her before he succumbed to her irresistible charms. Susan broke into laughter and surrendered.

Though smiling at the pair, Andy couldn't help but feel a twinge of envy.

Later, after Jim returned from his visit with Danny in the city, everyone convened in the living room except for Carmen, who had gone to bed shortly before.

"How'd it go?" Ben asked first. Sitting closest to him, Andy thought she caught the faintest hint of aftershave.

"It went fine. Danny came through, as usual."

Jim then pulled out two ID bracelets from his backpack and handed one to Andy and the other to Maria.

"You're both registered as Helens now. Nothing else has changed except your classification."

"So I'm still 'Isabel Torres' and Andy's still 'Katrina Wilson?'" Maria asked.

"Uh-huh."

"What's today? Sunday?" asked Andy, to no one in particular.

"Yeah, and I think if we're gonna do this, it should be this week," Ben stated with an edge of apprehension in his voice. "The sooner, the better."

"I agree," Jim echoed. He looked back and forth between Andy and Maria. "Are you two ready?"

The two exchanged a quick glance before nodding in unison.

"Yeah, we're ready," Andy confirmed. Inside, however, her heart began to pound.

"We're gonna go find clothes tomorrow," Maria added, referring also to Morgan and Susan. "After that, we'll be ready."

"Good. Wednesday is the best night to go," Jim remarked. "Danny said that's the night Dregs are allowed into the club, which means that the guards will be distracted with the crowd."

"Which means less focus on everyone else, right?" Andy correctly assumed. "Including the Helens?"

"Right. You and Maria should have no problem getting in without a second look. Once inside, you're in the clear."

Though Jim made that task sound easy, he knew differently. While both he and Ben were forced to remain on the sidelines, Andy and Maria would be placing themselves in the crosshairs.

By midnight, everyone was either asleep or getting ready to go to bed. Jim and Morgan went to their room where Katie was slumbering peacefully. Down the hall, Maria retreated to her room adjacent to Carmen's, who was already asleep. Meanwhile, Susan and Charlie headed next door to the house they shared with Ben and Andy, who followed shortly after.

"Are you wearing aftershave?" Andy joked as they crossed between the two backyards.

"Maybe," Ben replied somewhat sheepishly. "Hey, I can't let you be the only one who smells good around here. I'm just trying to keep up with your standards."

Andy laughed lightly. "Well, maybe I'll wear perfume on Wednesday. Lots of it. I'll probably end up looking like a hooker. Why not smell like one too?"

* * *

"You were gone for more than three weeks. What happened?"

Sean was careful with his tone as he addressed Chad so that his words sounded authoritative but not accusatory. It was always important to let people think you trusted them while still knowing that you were the one in control. This subtle nuance did not go unnoticed by Chad, however. He was one of only a few who saw through Sean's mind games.

"The Fixers you sent with me took longer to investigate the Metro than expected," Chad replied calmly. "You were right about them…smart but totally helpless."

They were sitting in Sean's office in his Fifth Avenue apartment. Both had just returned to New York; Chad from DC and Sean from Philadelphia.

"They have their uses, clearly," Sean countered. "But you're right. They can be a big pain in the ass. What about the people? Did you run into any problems?"

"No," Chad replied after what he considered to be a convincing hesitation. "They live like bats. They only come out at night. It's fucking weird."

That part was true.

Unaware of any deception on Chad's part, Sean recalled his own trip to DC weeks earlier.

"Yeah, I remember it being very quiet in the day. Every once in a while you'd see a few people running around, but that's it."

As they talked a bit more about the people living in DC, Chad carefully chose what information to feed Sean and what to withhold. When Sean inquired about the power and how damaged the infrastructure was, Chad was able to answer entirely truthfully, but only because it served his purpose to do so.

"The infrastructure is shit," he declared. "A lot of DC has power lines above ground, not like here where everything is underground, and six years of storms without repairs has done some major damage. We're talking miles and miles of power lines that'll have to be fixed.

It'll take months and probably a few hundred people to fix it all."

Sean frowned at the news, though he wasn't surprised. "It was the same in Philly, but I got that fixed."

Turning to his computer, he opened a few files that detailed every young man enlisted in the Infantry along with their age, rank, current location, and current duty. Over two thousand were located among the city's five boroughs, while the remaining thousand were either in Philadelphia or shuffling back and forth.

"I can give you fifty guys in the Infantry, and maybe a hundred and fifty workers," Sean ultimately assessed after staring at the screen for several minutes.

"I'd be better off with three hundred," Chad countered.

But Sean would not relent. "For long distance jobs, I never want Dregs to outnumber the Infantry by more than three to one. Otherwise, I risk an uprising. That's how I cleaned up Philly, and DC will be no different."

Chad chewed at his lip, partially out of agitation but mostly to keep from saying anything he would later regret. Finally, he said, "I'll take what I can get."

"You'll manage," Sean said coolly as he turned away from his computer. "It'll take a few days to move some people around, but you should be back in DC within a week. Also, since it sounds like this will take a while, I'll be rotating out those in the Infantry every two weeks. If they're away from either Philly or here too long, they get cranky, and I'll have bigger problems to deal with than power."

Chad nodded, indicating that he understood. "They're your men. Rotate away."

The average age of the Infantry was now seventeen, and they were used to the lifestyle that Sean had provided for them, which included the dependable presence of young women, either the ordinary prostitutes who now numbered in the thousands throughout the city, or if they were lucky, the Helens. Personally, Chad lived like a monk and could easily deal without seeing a single female for months, if not longer, and unlike Sean, he had no interest in controlling women by relegating them into sexually submissive roles. In fact, dealing with women was usually a waste of his time.

After discussing a few other mundane matters, Chad left Sean's elaborate home and headed back to his own sparsely furnished apartment in Chelsea. He walked the mile home, preferring to use his feet rather than a bike. He lived alone, his older brother Thomas having succumbed to the virus six years earlier.

Immediately after entering his apartment, Chad removed his treasured throwing knife from his back pocket and placed it on the kitchen table before washing his face in the bathroom with cold water. After a quick dinner of apples, milk, hard-boiled eggs, and bacon, he sat in the living room and spent the next half hour sharpening his knife.

Originally from a small farming town in western Iowa, Chad had traveled east to New York three years earlier after hearing the rumors of the city's miraculous resurrection. Shortly after his arrival, he joined the Infantry and quickly rose up the ranks after catching the attention of Luke, the leader of the Infantry and the second most powerful person in New York. Luke assigned Chad the task of hunting those involved in a growing underground movement plotting to overthrow Sean and the rest of the Directors. Chad proved to be very effective at flushing out this enemy, and he didn't shy away from violence the way Sean or Luke did. They preferred to have others get their hands dirty on their behalf, and Chad had no problem getting his hands, or his knife, a little bloody.

The knife, which he preferred to use over a gun, had been a gift from his father on his tenth birthday. Two days later, his father was killed in a car accident on a lonely country road just after dusk. The death was a serious blow to young Chad. He had lost his idol, and his protector. His mother favored Thomas more and never gave Chad reason to believe otherwise. For three years, he endured her endless criticism of his failings and her lamentations over why he wasn't more like his older brother. It all became too much to bear, and so one night, he staged a robbery before stabbing his mother in the chest with his beloved knife while she slept, instantly killing her. One month later, Thomas died without ever suspecting his brother.

All of that was well behind Chad now, as well as his days in the Infantry. Sean was now using him to further his own ambitions, which suited Chad just fine, for he was using Sean as well. His endgame required only time and patience, and he had plenty of both.

* * *

02 August 2021

"Where did you get your dress?"

The girl, probably no older than fourteen and little more than skin and bone, looked at Maria like she had two heads. "Where do you think? From a store."

"Uh, okay. Which store?"

"I don't remember," the girl scoffed. "I've had it for years."

Maria glanced back at Morgan and Susan with a look that said *this is hopeless.*

"Well, can you tell us where we can get more clothes like it?"

The girl was biting hungrily on her ragged fingernails as she contemplated the question.

"What's in it for me?" she finally replied.

"What do you want?" Maria countered.

"Whataya got?"

Maria offered food, hoping the girl would take it, as she so obviously needed to eat. The girl mulled over the offer, but asked if there was anything else to bargain with, implying drugs. Maria tried to persuade her otherwise.

"No offense, but you look like you need some food."

"Fuck off! Don't tell me what I need!"

Maria shrugged and turned around. "Forget it. We'll ask someone else," she said and began to walk away.

"Wait!" the girl called out upon realizing that a potential meal was about to walk away. "Give me something to eat, and then I'll tell ya."

Maria turned around and gave the girl a long stare. She was a pitiful sight, like so many other young girls they'd seen wandering the crowded streets of Manhattan. With bloodshot eyes, stringy hair, and a red, runny nose from obvious cocaine abuse, she was the picture of misery. The embodiment of Sean's legacy.

"Please," she begged. The attitude was gone. Only desperation remained.

* * *

"You went all the way to the city just to find some clothes? I thought you guys were just going to look around here. Aren't there shopping malls in New Jersey?"

Andy closed her pharmacology book as Morgan entered her bedroom in the early evening with several garments draped over her arms.

"You and Maria have to fit in with whatever the other Helens wear, so we had to go to the city to see for ourselves what they wear. And besides, you didn't even want to come."

"That's because I hate wearing dresses, and looking for them is even worse."

Morgan ignored the remark as she placed the dresses on Andy's bed and held up each one. Andy eyed them all with revulsion. They reminded her of little more than lingerie.

"Seriously? Those aren't dresses!" Andy cried after Morgan held up a blue piece of fabric that was sheer everywhere except where her bra and underwear would be. "I'll look like a whore!"

"Well, you *are* pretending to be a prostitute, so you might as well fit the part."

"Where the hell did you find these?"

"You don't want to know."

Morgan then plucked a black dress out of the pile and analyzed it. "This one is not as…"

"Slutty?" Andy offered, though looking doubtful.

"Well, it's not," Morgan urged. "Try it on."

With a sigh, Andy stood up and slid her jeans off. She stepped into the dress and pulled it up to her waist before removing her T-shirt. The top portion of the dress was a corset design but without lacing. As she adjusted the thin straps, the wire boning hugged Andy's ribs and back, giving her more cleavage than she thought possible.

"Wow," Andy exclaimed. "Look at those!"

The dress was sexy indeed, and by contemporary standards, not "slutty." Hollywood starlets would have worn something similar on the red carpet, and Andy's figure did the dress justice.

"I've got shoes to go with it too," Morgan added before disappearing from the room momentarily. When she returned, she carried a pair of four-inch black heels. Andy eyed them suspiciously but tried them on nonetheless. She attempted a few steps but wobbled like a newborn fawn.

"You'll get used to them, but you should practice," Morgan instructed.

Andy nodded. She hated the shoes, but there was no escaping having to wear them. She would need to practice, not just walking in them, but running as well.

"You should show Ben," Morgan suggested as she fought to keep a straight face and contain the edge in her voice. "You know, to get a bloke's opinion."

"Uh, yeah…all right," Andy murmured absently. She was too occupied with the strain of the shoes on her toes to acknowledge her friend's instigating. "These are *not* comfortable."

"They're heels, Andy," Morgan called out as she left the room. "They're not supposed to be comfortable. Just practice!"

A minute later and sans shoes, Andy knocked on the door to Ben's room.

"Yeah?" he called from inside.

Andy opened the door slowly. "Will this work?" she asked meekly while remaining in the doorway. Her hand gripped the doorframe while the other rested flat against her stomach in a self-conscious manner.

Unprepared for the sight in front of him, a strange mixture of fear and desire came over Ben as his gaze froze on Andy in her dress. She was stunning, even more so than the day Morgan and Jim were wed. Unfortunately, she looked uncomfortable as well as terrified, like a deer waiting to become a wolf's prey.

As he opened his mouth to speak, his voice caught in his throat, and he cleared it quickly.

"Um, yeah. That'll work. Just don't look so scared."

Andy released her hands to her sides and adjusted her posture in an attempt to appear more confident.

"Better?"

Without responding, Ben sat up and got off his bed.

"Come here," he said to her.

Tentatively, Andy stepped inside the room a few feet.

"No, come *here*," Ben insisted, gesturing for her to stand right in front of him.

Looking confused, she slowly moved forward until they were a few feet apart.

"So pretend I'm Luke and you finally got me alone," Ben started off. "What are you gonna do first?"

"What do you mean?"

"How are you gonna get me to tell you where the virus is?"

"I'll pull a gun on him...you, I mean."

Ben inched closer. "What if I've got my hands all over you? How are you gonna get a hold of your gun *and* give yourself enough space to get a clear shot, or at least make me believe you've got a clear shot?"

"I don't know...I'll seduce you...him," Andy quickly corrected.

Ben raised his eyebrows. "Seduce him? How exactly?"

Andy's face grew red, and Ben couldn't tell if it was out of anger or embarrassment. Probably both.

"I'll...I'll kiss him," she finally said while trying to sound certain.

"You'll kiss him? You sure that'll work?"

Andy lifted her chin defiantly, her eyes flashing. "You don't think I can seduce someone?"

Ben shrugged. He knew he was baiting her. "How would I know? You've never tried to seduce me."

Andy froze. "No…of course not," she stammered. "What does that have to do with anything?"

"Nothing. I just wanna make sure that you've thought this whole thing through."

"Oh, really? And have you asked Maria if she knows how to seduce someone?"

Ben felt like he was about to walk into a trap, but rather than try to back-pedal, he went for honesty. "No."

Andy crossed her arms. "No? But you asked me."

"No, I didn't. *You* asked *me* if I thought you could."

"Now you're twisting my words," Andy said with a huff. "What you really mean is that you think Maria can seduce someone but I can't."

"I'm not worried about Maria. I'm worried about you."

"You don't care what happens to Maria?"

"Of course I do. Now *you're* twisting *my* words."

"Then what did you mean when you said that you're worried about me but not Maria?"

Ben let out a sigh, mostly to buy time. "Because I know the type of girls Luke goes after, and you fit the type perfectly."

It was a lie. Ben had seen Luke with a wide variety of girls. Blond. Brunette. Redhead. Skinny. Curvy. Athletic. He didn't discriminate. It was truly anyone's guess who he'd prefer: Andy or Maria. But lie or no lie, Andy's infuriation quickly turned to trepidation. Then, strangely enough, trepidation shifted to determination. She released her arms and let them hang at her sides as she had done before. This time, however, she wasn't trying to act confident. No, this was the real thing. This was the same Andy who had dared to punch Ben in the face the day they met, the same Andy who had dodged dozens of bullets from an assault rifle while managing to kill with just one. And this was the same Andy who would find the virus and destroy it.

But Ben didn't seem to notice this transformation. He was too preoccupied with back-pedaling.

"Andy, all I'm saying is…"

But she stopped him. Not with words, but with her mouth. In a single, fluid motion, she closed the gap between them, placed her hands on his shoulders, rose up on her toes, and tilted her head to kiss him.

It took a moment for Ben to realize what was happening, but once he did, it was impossible for him not to kiss her back. For her part, Andy did not hold back. After a few gentle caresses with her lips against his, she gradually opened her mouth. Ben reciprocated, though he somehow mustered the self-control to keep his hands from reaching out to grab her, but only by clenching them into fists. She, however, slid one hand up his neck until her fingertips dug into his hair, and what started as Andy simply proving a point turned into a mutual and rather lengthy embrace that only ended when she finally pulled away.

Stepping backward, Andy placed her fingers to her mouth. While averting her eyes, she gathered enough poise to ask him plainly, "How was that?"

Temporarily paralyzed and unable to think, let alone speak, Ben could only blink before combing a hand through his hair. "Uh, yeah…" he managed at last while trying to sound as nonchalant as possible. "Just do that."

"Okay," was all Andy could manage before backing out of the room, and for the rest of the evening, she kept touching her lips as though expecting the same feeling to return.

Chapter XXI

04 August 2021

The beat of the music was hypnotic, the melody sensual. It struck the bones and reverberated throughout the body, eliciting the desire to move without a care or worry.

It was the kind of music that made people rip each other's clothes off.

With their heads and shoulders flung back and their eyes closed, the bodies pressed tightly together swayed about in a blissful trance. A temporary spell was created by both the music and atmosphere, and from the chemicals flowing through their bloodstreams.

As she watched from the periphery of the main dance floor, Andy studied her fellow survivors en masse, contemporaries once cared for and protected by parents like hers and later thrown into a living nightmare before they were old enough to drive a car. Since learning of Sean Taylor's existence, she had been unable to entirely grasp how in six years' time, a single teenager could rise up to manipulate the lives of a million people as he had done. But watching them now, how they quelled their pain with dance, music, and drugs, the puzzle came together: Sean had created his own "brave new world," and the people of New York had let him.

Andy had read Huxley's visionary novel in Bermuda, but only

now did she recognize the parallels as the pages of the book came to life before her. The Directors were the Alpha males, the Helens the Alpha females. The Fixers and the Infantry were the Beta males, and the Dregs were everyone else: the lowly Gammas, Deltas, and Epsilons. But despite this caste system, Sean did not care what people did with their lives as long as they respected the society he had carefully designed. And since sex was abundant, and drugs, akin to *soma*, were readily available, the people had enough diversions to numb them from the realities of their existence—and everyone seemed resigned to it. It was simply easier to give up fighting and give in to hedonistic apathy, particularly when a place like *Papillon* existed.

"Excuse me."

A young woman brushed up against Andy's side as she dragged another girl onto the dance floor where they quickly meshed into the sea of people. Stirred from her thoughts, Andy regained her focus on the job at hand. As she scanned the area for Luke, she briefly locked eyes with Maria, who was several feet away in a seductive red dress and looking equally as stunning. Maria subtly shook her head, indicating that she had not yet found Luke. Though both Ben and Jim had described his appearance, Andy and Maria were told that the best way to identify him was based on location. He was second only to Sean in terms of power, and therefore would often sit in a secluded area of the club with a few guards nearby to protect him and the Helens who kept him company.

As her eyes and ears grew accustomed to the sights and sounds of the club, Andy strolled about the place with an air of belonging. The shoes that had troubled her only days earlier were now the pedestals from which she would mount her offense. Her dress hugged the natural curves of her torso remarkably, and her hair and makeup had been carefully arranged and applied hours earlier by Morgan and Susan in the safety of their home in Princeton. Assembled flawlessly for the role of a Helen, Andy now had to act as one: to laugh and flirt and preen for attention while revealing as much skin as possible. Such behavior was not natural to her, but for the sake of the unwitting survivors now surrounding her, she would forget who she was for the night.

* * *

From across the room, he saw her. Through the heady air, he saw her before she saw him. Keeping his eyes fixed upon her, he leaned over to one of his fellow Directors as he pointed in her direction.

"Who is that?"

His friend followed his finger. "Which one?"

"The blond in the black dress."

"No idea. I haven't seen her here before."

After callously shooing away the girl who had been sitting on his lap, Luke stood up to get a better look before quickly deciding that she was exactly what he wanted, at least for tonight.

"Bring her to me," he ordered one of the guards.

* * *

A few blocks away along Greenwich Street, Ben and Jim were waiting for their friends to return victorious from their mission. Susan and Charlie were waiting as well at the New Jersey end of the Holland Tunnel in two separate vehicles on the off chance one of them broke down. Morgan remained back in Princeton with Carmen and Katie, anxiously awaiting everyone's return.

Nearly an hour had passed since Andy and Maria had filed inside *Papillon*, and there was no way of knowing how long they would be gone. Under the shadows across the street from the club, Ben and Jim had watched the girls enter, Andy casting Ben an unsmiling glance before disappearing into the crowd. As he and Jim retreated to the alley they had designated as their rendezvous point, Ben silently prayed that everything would go smoothly. He prayed to God Himself, something he had not done since he was a child and was too young to understand who God was.

"She'll be all right," Jim reassured Ben.

"Who?" Ben muttered as he checked his watch.

Jim scoffed. "Are you kidding?"

"I'm worried about both of them."

In the darkness, Jim shook his head. "Whatever."

Ben ignored his cousin and rubbed his eyes instead. His colored contacts were bothering him, which only added to his stress.

"Danny was certain that Sean wouldn't be there tonight?"

"Yeah. He won't go on 'Dreg Night.'"

"Hmm, let's hope Sean hasn't lowered his standards," Ben mumbled.

* * *

"What's your name?"

Andy could smell the alcohol on Luke's breath, she was that close to him. He had pulled her aside from the rest of his group and immediately started to caress her shoulder and run his fingers through her hair.

"Katrina."

"And why have I never seen you here before, Katrina?"

Andy smiled coyly, thinking it the best reaction.

"Because I just came to New York a few weeks ago."

Luke smiled back, his eyes staring intently into hers. When she dropped her gaze for a moment, he lifted her chin up with his fingers.

"You have a beautiful face, Katrina. Don't hide it."

Andy said nothing as her eyes stared back into his once more. They were large and hazel, just as Ben had described. Despite wearing four-inch heels, Luke still stood nearly half a foot taller and was physically very fit. It was obvious he believed that no girl could resist him, and though Andy did find him attractive, she was in the habit of comparing every young man to Ben, and to her, there was no comparison.

"You thirsty?"

Andy wasn't thirsty, and she definitely did not want to be drinking alcohol, but she couldn't refuse the offer.

"Sure, but tell me who you are first," she replied, playing dumb.

"I'm Luke. I'm the Director of the Infantry."

Look impressed. Sound dumb. Be dumb. Be blond.

"Wow. That sounds really important."

Luke smiled. He was pleased with himself. "It is. What I do is very important."

"Really? Why are you here then, and not out there 'directing' your men?"

It was not a stupid question, but Andy's tone made her sound like she had left half her brain outside the club.

"Because everybody needs a break from time to time. Even me."

Then Luke slid his arm around Andy's back, sending a shiver up her spine, and guided her toward the bar. Along the way, she caught sight of Maria, but Maria did not see her as she walked by. Since they were pretending not to know each other, Andy could not call out to her.

"What's your poison?"

"Sorry?" Andy frowned.

"What do you want to drink?" Luke restated, clearly amused by the naïveté of his latest plaything.

"Um, whatever you're having," Andy quickly answered.

"Perfect. Whiskey and water it is."

Whiskey? Jesus…

Luke was served immediately. He passed Andy her drink and escorted her to the private area where his friends were sitting. Introductions were not made—Luke was not planning on staying on the main floor long. He had his own private room in the rear of the club, which he intended to use shortly.

Currently, Luke's group of friends consisted of three men and four women, each of whom was dressed similar to Andy. They were all very beautiful young women, and were Andy not preoccupied with the task at hand, she would have begun to feel self-conscious about her own appearance. Three of the girls were engrossed in heavy flirting with the three young men. Probably other Directors, Andy assumed. The fourth girl, and the most beautiful, sat alone and appeared rather bored.

Andy placed her drink on the edge of the coffee table that sat in the middle of the cluster of large sofas and chairs. Several other half-consumed drinks and small piles of white powder that could only be cocaine were scattered about the table.

"Come, sit over here," Luke instructed, indicating a spot beside him on one of the sofas.

But Andy decided to speed up the entire process by sitting on his lap instead.

"I hope you don't mind," she whispered in his ear after carefully positioning herself across his thighs. "But this seems more comfortable, don't you think?"

She pulled away just enough to stare back into his eyes while she lightly bit her bottom lip. Morgan had told her that guys liked this and to do it whenever possible. It seemed to work.

Visibly pleased by the progress he was making, a smile slowly spread across Luke's face.

"I agree," he whispered back before kissing her neck. Just as he was about to pull Andy's face toward his, the girl sitting alone reached over and gave Luke a slap to his arm with the back of her hand, causing him to abruptly turn her way.

"Who's that?" she demanded with a quick nod at Andy.

"Why the fuck do you care?" Luke snapped before turning his attention back to Andy.

The girl made a face.

"Excuse *me*," she said in an exaggerated tone before adding, "I just wanna know who I'm sharing my coke with."

"Hey, this is *my* coke!" Luke yelled.

But the girl flipped her hair angrily.

"Whatever," she sputtered. "It all comes from Sean anyway, so what difference does it make who he gives it to?"

Andy wanted to tell the girl that she wasn't interested in the cocaine but figured it was better not to say anything that may risk damaging her persona.

"Just ignore her," Luke muttered in her ear as he ran his hand up Andy's back before cupping his hand around the side of her right breast. "Lily's being a bitch because she's still getting over her little stint in prison."

"Prison?" Andy replied impulsively.

"Fuck you, Luke!" Lily shouted back before storming away from the group. Before disappearing into the crowd on the dance floor, she turned back and yelled to Andy, "Good luck with *that* one, honey. He can't stay hard longer than five seconds!"

Luke's face turned bright red.

"Fucking bitch!" he growled as he shoved Andy off his lap to go after Lily. He started charging toward the dance floor when his friend reached out and grabbed his arm to stop him.

"Dude, she's not worth it! Let it go."

His nostrils flaring in anger and hands gripped tightly into fists, Luke appeared incapable of calming down, but after several deep but labored breaths, he returned to his seat and beckoned for Andy to return. She forced herself to obey.

God, get me out of here…

"I'm *so* glad I'm not her," declared one of the other girls. "It's gotta suck being Sean's personal slave."

The others seemed to agree and continued to gossip about Lily and Sean. Looking sullen, however, Luke remained silent. His desire for Andy was gone, and she began to panic. Turning to the table, she grabbed her drink and took a sip before handing it to him. He stared at her and then at the drink before finally grasping it. He took a long, slow sip.

"Forget about what she said," Andy said in as seductive a voice as she could muster and leaned in closer while lightly grazing her fingertips down his chest until she could feel his stomach muscles tighten. "She's probably just jealous 'cuz she can't have you…and I can."

Sensing a reversal in his mood, Andy took the glass out of his hand, took another sip, and placed it back on the table. She leaned in even further until her lips brushed his ear and whispered, "Let's go somewhere private." Then, surprising even herself, she kissed his ear and then his neck.

Moments later, Luke was leading her toward his private room.

* * *

"Luke prefers blonds, at least he does tonight."

Maria reported the news after rounding the corner into the alley where Ben and Jim were waiting.

"What happened?" Ben demanded.

"Exactly what we wanted. She finally got him alone."

"Great, so you just left her there?"

"That was the plan, Ben" Jim gently reminded.

Pushing his hands through his hair, Ben let out a heavy sigh to quell his spiraling anxiety. "I know, I'm sorry. I just really hate this whole thing. I hate not being able to do anything."

"She looked like she had the situation under control," Maria firmly assured as she retrieved a pair of sneakers from her backpack. She slipped off her heels and stepped into the sneakers.

"I saw her carrying their drinks," she added as she began to tie her sneakers. "He should turn into putty soon."

* * *

Standing behind Luke as he unlocked the door to his private room, Andy adroitly retrieved a tiny plastic bag from underneath the lacey top of her sheer thigh-high stockings with one hand while carefully balancing her drink and Luke's in the other. Inside was a small, white pill. As Luke opened the door, she quickly shifted his drink back into her right hand and hid the bag between the bottom of his glass and her palm.

"Here we are," Luke announced proudly as he ushered Andy into the room. As he closed the door behind them, Andy quickly assessed the room. Likely an office back in the day, the space was modest, about the size of a bedroom in an average American home, which was what it had been converted to at present. There was a bed in one corner and a plush sofa in the other. A small table stood in the corner adjacent to the door, on which were several half-empty bottles of various liquors. Andy made her way over to the table and placed the two glasses down as Luke moved behind her and placed his hands on her waist. She could smell aftershave, which instantly reminded her of Ben.

"You still thirsty?" he said in a low voice into the back of her head before he kissed it.

Her heart pounding, Andy discreetly opened the tiny plastic bag and slipped the pill into Luke's drink. She let the bag drop to the floor. It floated downward and landed beside her foot, and she carefully kicked it under the table.

"Yeah," she breathed as Luke began to kiss her neck. "You have any Coke?"

"Uh-huh," Luke mumbled as he worked his way down her neck, and she wondered if she was going to have to use the self-defense moves Ben taught her. But suddenly, Luke realized something and stood up straight. "Fuck, I left my stash out there with those guys. They'll steal it if I don't go get it."

Luke stepped away from Andy headed for the door.

"I'll be right back," he muttered before leaving her alone in the room.

Releasing a heavy sigh, Andy realized that Luke thought she was asking for cocaine, not Coca-Cola. The Rohypnol that she had slipped into his drink would dissolve much quicker in a carbonated beverage, as she and Charlie had discovered the day before. They considered grounding the pill first and then placing the powder in the bag or another small object, but the powder clung to the sides of everything, making it nearly impossible to slip into a drink with speed. Grinding up two or three pills into a powder was another option until they realized that if too much Rohypnol fell into his drink, it would knock Luke out before she had a chance to interrogate him.

The only solution was to let the pill dissolve, and now that she had a few moments alone, Andy quickly searched the room for something to grind the Rohypnol. Unfortunately, nothing like a pen or a stick could be found. Panicking yet again, an idea struck just when she needed it.

Removing her shoes and quickly wiping off any dirt and dust from the base of the pencil-thin heel, Andy dipped it into the glass and pressed down several times on the pill to break it into tiny pieces.

"That'll have to do," she said to herself as she quickly wiped off the outside of the glass and the heel with the hem of her dress. She threw her shoes back on just as the door reopened.

"Here we go."

Luke smiled back at Andy and held up a small bag of white powder that he'd left on the table. Thinking fast, Andy covered her mouth with her fingertips and started to giggle.

"I'm such an idiot! When I said 'coke,' I meant soda. But at least your stash is safe."

Before Luke could say anything further, Andy grabbed the drinks and handed his to him.

"Cheers!" she squealed with delight and took a sip.

Luke frowned, apparently disappointed that "Katrina" wasn't interested in the cocaine.

"Uh…okay," he finally muttered and threw the drugs on the table. Andy eyed him impatiently as she took another tiny sip.

C'mon, drink…drink, goddamnit!

"This is good," she lied. "What kind of whiskey is it?"

"Jack Daniels," Luke replied before finally taking a large sip, which he quickly followed with another.

Andy smiled wryly back at him.

* * *

"Maria, you should get outta here. There's no point in you risking hanging around if things go bad."

Maria listened to Jim as she looked at her watch. Gone were her dress and high heels. She had deftly changed into jeans and a T-shirt while the two young men respectfully looked the other way.

"I left thirty minutes ago. Hopefully she's slipped him the roofie by now."

"And it takes, what, twenty minutes before the effects begin?"

Ben called out from a few yards away as he kept watch on the people rushing back and forth along Greenwich Street.

"At least twenty minutes, according to what Andy found when she researched the drug."

"That's too long," Ben mumbled out of earshot of the others.

"You sure you two don't need me to stay?" Maria asked Jim.

"No, seriously, we're fine," Jim insisted. "You've done more than your fair share already."

"All right, I'm off then."

"Be safe," Jim called out as Maria walked her bike toward the end of the alley. Ben stopped her as she passed him.

"Thanks, Maria," he said with sincere gratitude. "It took guts going in there."

Maria merely nodded, and after mounting her bike, she turned to him before departing.

"She'll be fine. Don't worry."

Ben managed a smile.

"See you soon, hopefully."

Maria pedaled onto Greenwich Street and turned south. The entrance to the Holland Tunnel was just over a mile away.

* * *

After intermittingly sipping his drink and forcibly kissing Andy, Luke finally finished off the last of his whiskey without any suspicion he'd been drugged. Andy, meanwhile, took any opportunity she could when he wasn't looking to spill her own drink on the dark-colored carpet. The last thing she needed was several ounces of Jack Daniels coursing through her veins.

After watching Luke fumble to place his empty glass on the table, she knew it was time to switch gears. She placed her nearly empty glass beside his and drew close to him. Acting purely on instinct, she placed the back of her hands against his bare and rather muscular arms and began to lightly feather his skin with her fingernails.

"So, you're the leader of the Infantry?" she murmured softly.

"That's right." His eyelids were growing heavy.

"So you must be good friends with Sean then, huh?"

"Uh-huh."

Luke impatiently grabbed Andy's shoulders to pull her in even closer, and his fingers ran over her scar, her souvenir from Los Angeles. He peered awkwardly over her shoulder to get a better look.

"Hey, what's that?" he said with labored speech.

Andy glanced behind her shoulder and smiled proudly.

"Oh, that? I dodged a bullet in Los Angeles."

Luke's eyes widened and he stumbled back half a step.

"You…you've been to L.A.?" he stammered in disbelief.

"Yep. It was pretty chaotic. Not like here. Of course, L.A. doesn't have a great leader like Sean."

"Yeah…Sean…he's the best!" Luke blurted in a manner that only an intoxicated person would.

"He is," Andy agreed. "But I'm sure it helps to have the virus on hand to keep people in line, huh?"

Luke frowned and his eyes narrowed as a window of mental lucidity emerged.

"What?! How…how the fuck…?"

* * *

Sitting in near darkness in his office, Danny ran his fingers over the width of the three parallel scars on his neck. He often did this subconsciously while staring at his computer screen for hours at a time.

A sharp knock on his door startled him, and he quickly removed his earbuds.

"You Danny?" the shadowy silhouette of a person standing at the doorway inquired.

"Uh, yeah?"

"You like working in the dark?"

"Uh, yeah…it's easier on the eyes," Danny replied nervously.

Suddenly, the light in the office illuminated, and Danny could see his visitor clearly. It was Sean Taylor.

"Oh, sorry, Sean, I didn't…"

"Never mind," Sean interrupted by holding up a hand. He entered the office and took a seat on the edge of Danny's desk.

"So, I've been told that you're updating the database to include fingerprints of everyone registered in New York."

"That's right," Danny replied carefully.

"And how's that coming along?"

"Uh, pretty well, I guess. More than half the population has added their prints to the database."

Sean listened intently as he stared back at Danny with his icy blue eyes, forcing the latter to avert his gaze.

"Excellent. Good work, Danny. It's people like you that keep this city running smoothly. I'll make sure to mention that to Doug the next time I see him."

Danny smiled uneasily.

"Uh, thanks."

Sean got off the desk and headed toward the door.

"You should go to *Papillon* tonight," he advised. "You know, relax a bit, maybe get yourself laid."

"Uh, okay, maybe."

"Yeah, I know…the Dregs are there tonight, but it's better than sitting here alone in the dark, right?"

Without another word, Sean departed down the hall, leaving Danny alone again. He looked up at the florescent lights and groaned before standing up to turn off the lights himself.

"Fuckin' psycho," he muttered before returning to his desk in the dark.

* * *

"It doesn't matter how I know. Just tell me where Sean is hiding it."

By now, Andy had backed a few feet away from Luke and was standing in front of the door. As he blinked back in disbelief at the sudden change of events, Andy reached underneath her dress in between her legs and retrieved the tiny Ruger LCP that she'd carefully holstered to her inner left thigh. A temporary gift from Ben, she pointed the barrel at Luke's chest. He instinctively took a step back and lifted his arms.

"Who…who are you?" he sputtered, this time managing to complete an entire question.

"Where's the virus?!" Andy demanded. "Tell me, or I'll shoot."

Luke gasped out a laugh.

"You won' shoot me. You're jus'a fuckin' wh-whore!"

"Hey asshole, I've shot people dead before, including the person who gave me this scar."

Andy nodded toward her shoulder but kept her aim steady.

Luke stumbled backward again. The Rohypnol was starting to take full effect.

"You…can' sh-shoo' me. They…they'll 'ear it."

"Nobody will hear anything with all that music. It's nice and loud out there. Now tell me where the virus is!"

"F-fuck you…bitch!"

And with that, Luke took one more step backward. His foot hit the base of the sofa, and he fell onto it.

"That's it!" Andy yelled and she let off a round. The bullet landed expertly in the sofa, an inch from Luke's groin. The sight of the bullet hole so close to his manhood nearly stunned him into sobriety.

"You almost shot me!" he said with remarkable clarity.

"That's right, and unless you tell me where the virus is, next time I'll make sure to hit your balls…or something worse, since I'm sure you don't care if you ever have children."

Andy stepped forward and aimed the barrel once again at Luke's groin. Looking dazed, his eyes slowly refocused on the gun.

"Did he send you?" he asked, suddenly sounding like a scared child.

Andy frowned.

"Who?"

"Ben. Kelly."

Luke uttered the name in two separate breaths, and Andy's stomach fell to her knees. Somehow, though, she managed not to react.

"Who's Ben? Who are you talking about? Tell me where the virus is!"

It was convincing enough, and when she pressed her lips together and looked as though she were about to let the gun off again, Luke finally cracked.

"It's the prison! Green Haven…Green Haven! Don't …please!"

Instinctively bringing his knees to his chest to shield himself while raising his hands in surrender, Luke began to cry. Only then did Andy lower her gun. She almost took pity on him.

"Green Haven Prison," she muttered under her breath so that she'd remember. Then, while keeping her aim on Luke, she stepped over to the table and poured another couple of ounces of Jack Daniels in his glass. She handed it to him and ordered him to drink. He obeyed and emptied the glass in seconds.

"Thank you very much for your cooperation, Luke," Andy said calmly as she gathered up his glass as well as hers. Then, she grabbed the keys to the office from within Luke's left jean pocket. He didn't bother to resist. The threat of bodily harm had passed, and the combination of whiskey and Rohypnol had sedated him to the point where sleep would soon take over.

Holstering the Ruger back onto her thigh, Andy hurriedly left the room and locked the door behind her while carrying the two glasses. She didn't want to leave behind anything with her fingerprints in Luke's "office" now that they were registered to her ID.

She left the keys dangling in the lock to make it appear as though Luke had inadvertently left them there, and she returned to the main floor of the club. Passing through crowds of people busy dancing, drinking, and getting high, she dispersed the glasses onto two different tables sitting far apart. Finally, she left the club looking as polished as when she'd entered it before disappearing into the night.

Andy kept her head down and stayed to the outer edge of the sidewalk. She didn't look at anyone as dozens of people passed her on the street, including Sean Taylor.

* * *

At first, Ben thought it was the contacts playing a trick on him, and he rubbed his eyes not just once but twice until realizing that he was indeed watching Sean Taylor approaching from the right on Greenwich Street. There was no mistaking that arrogant gait or that cold stare even from yards away, and as was his custom, he was walking with two guards behind him.

"Shit!"

Hastily ducking into the shadows, Ben retreated back where Jim was standing.

"I just saw Sean!" he whispered sharply.

"Are you serious??"

"I'm positive…shit!"

But before a real panic could settle, the sound of Andy's voice suddenly echoed off the walls of the alley.

"I got it!" she cried as she scurried toward the two young men. She moved impressively fast in her heels, and Ben released a huge sigh of relief upon seeing her.

"Thank God because Sean just passed you on the street."

"Are you kidding?"

"No, and it's lucky he didn't notice you dressed like, uh, like that."

"Well, I won't be for long. We better get moving."

Andy grabbed her backpack from the ground and quickly changed out of her dress and heels as Maria had done.

"So where is it? Where's the virus?" Jim asked with more impatience than usual.

"Green Haven Prison," Andy revealed proudly while kneeling down to tie her sneakers. "Any idea where that is?"

"Nope."

"None."

"Well, I know Luke wasn't making it up. He was very forthcoming…after I nearly shot him in the balls."

Unseen by Andy, Ben and Jim looked at each other, both clearly impressed and even a tad intimidated.

Ben turned away and looked straight up at the narrow sliver of sky between the walls. He could actually see a few stars.

It's really true. Sean still has the virus…

Meanwhile, Andy stood up and threw her bag over her shoulder.

"We'll figure it all out when we get back to Princeton. I assume Maria left already?"

"Yeah, about half an hour ago," Ben replied, returning to the present moment.

"She should be with Charlie and Susan," Jim added.

"Good. I didn't see her leave the club, so I wasn't sure."

Once they had gathered all their belongings, the three mounted their bikes and pedaled out of the alley.

* * *

Sean spotted Lily sulking in the corner of the club, but he ignored her for the time being and headed to where the Directors were sitting. He wasn't planning on staying long. Opening the club to everyone on Wednesdays was a concession he knew he had to give, but the sight of all the sloppy Dregs dancing and spending all their credit getting wasted wasn't something he enjoyed seeing.

"Where's Luke?" he shouted at one of the Directors over the noise of the pulsating music.

"Dunno. He left with some blond like an hour ago."

Sean frowned and walked away. He made his way to the back of the club where the offices used to be. The first room he came to was Luke's, and upon seeing the keys in the door, he frowned again before opening the door and switching on the lights.

Lying in a near-fetal position on the sofa was Luke, snoring loudly.

"Fucking perfect," Sean grumbled as he entered the room. Using the bottom of his foot, he tried shoving Luke to awaken him, but it was no use. His Director of the Infantry, the leader of thousands of young men, was comatose.

Disgusted, Sean left the room and slammed the door behind him.

He needed Luke to help him redirect some of the troops for Chad, but now he would have to wait until morning. Sean despised delays.

Storming back to the main floor, he found Lily and told her that it was time to go.

"Fuck off!" she slurred. "I wanna stay."

She was either drunk or high or both, and Sean had run out of patience. He grabbed her arm but she wrestled free and staggered off into the mob on the dance floor. Annoyed as he was, Sean did not go after her. The last person he wanted to have sex with was a moody, drunken whore, even one as beautiful as Lily.

She would come crawling back to him in the morning like she had done so many times before. She was entirely dependent on him, and they both knew it.

Sean found another Helen and departed the club with her in tow.

* * *

"The Rohypnol worked?"

Andy grinned back at Charlie as she climbed in the car.

"It worked. Well, that and a bullet."

"You shot him?!"

"Nearly. He needed a little…encouragement."

"Brilliant. So where is it?"

Andy repeated the location of the virus.

"Where's that?"

"No clue," she replied as Ben climbed in after her in the backseat. "But we'll figure it all out tomorrow."

Jim was the last one to put his bike in the back of the truck, and as soon as he climbed in the passenger's seat and shut the door, Charlie threw the vehicle into gear and sped off. Susan and Maria had already returned to Princeton.

During the drive back, Ben wondered how far Andy had to go with Luke before he gave up the location. Did she have to kiss him, and if so, did it bother her? In the end, he decided he didn't want to know. After all, the night had been a success…as long as Sean never found out.

* * *

05 August 2021

The hangover was unimaginably awful, far worse than any Luke had experienced, and there had been many. As he sat up, his temples pounded and uncontrollable nausea overwhelmed him. When he tried to stand up to make a run for the bathroom, his knees buckled underneath him. He slumped back down on the sofa and proceeded to vomit on the floor between his feet.

Doubled over in agony, Luke didn't notice the door opening.

"Man, what the fuck?"

Covering his nose, Sean stepped clear of Luke and the puddle of vomit and stood as far away as possible.

"What the hell did you take last night?"

Luke groaned and slowly sat up. He wiped his mouth with the back of his hand.

"You look worse than shit!" Sean spat out, even more disgusted than he'd been hours earlier. "Seriously, you're a fuckin' Director! If you can't handle your booze or coke or whatever else you've been chugging, then I'm done with you."

Half-listening, Luke struggled to voice a defense. "Man, I think someone slipped me something."

Pausing his tirade, Sean's eyes narrowed. "Who?"

"I dunno," Luke whimpered pathetically. "I don't remember anything." There were flashes and blurs of the evening, but nothing concrete. Hours had been wiped away and entirely erased, like a computer chip.

"Jesse said you were with a blond last night. You remember that?"

Luke shut his eyes and rubbed his head. "There were lots of blonds," he muttered dully.

Sean shook his head. His friend's behavior revolted him.

"This is the last time," he warned, his tone menacing. "You know too much, Luke. You can't be acting like everyone else, and you absolutely can*not* blackout. You understand?"

Luke didn't dare open his eyes. He merely nodded. This small action alone hurt his head.

"Learn to pace yourself," Sean ordered as he stepped to the door. "Now get cleaned up. We got work to do."

Chapter XXII

12 October 2021

A small forest butted up against the northwest corner of the prison, and the early fall foliage provided plenty of cover to conduct a safe stakeout. Everything was almost ready. The final step was preparing the escape route.

The previous two months had passed in a flurry of unending preparations. Learning where Sean was hiding the virus turned out to be the easy part. Infiltrating the prison would be much harder, but fortunately, this was the second time around for Ben and Jim.

"I count three guards in the towers again," Jim whispered to Ben while staring through his binoculars.

"The same guys?"

"Yeah, and they all seemed bored to death."

It was now their seventh day in a row of conducting surveillance of the prison compound, not including the five nights spent staring through the same pair of night vision binoculars they'd used the year before at Fort Detrick. But the surveillance of the building was just one part of the puzzle.

It had taken three days back in August just to figure out where exactly the prison was located once Andy learned the name. Without the Internet, nothing was easy anymore. Ben almost made a trip to see Danny and access his *Wikipedia* files when Charlie found a reference to the prison in a thirty-two-year-old newspaper article at the university library. Then the real work began.

"Bored is good," said Ben absently as he scanned the area with his naked eyes. Without his color contacts, he swore his vision was better, and after his last trip to the city, he was happy to know that he wouldn't have to wear them for a while, if ever.

"It's too bad they're all using night vision goggles. Otherwise we could go in at night."

"Yeah, well, nothing's perfect. If it was, one of us would know how to fly a plane," Ben remarked as he lowered the binoculars. There was a small airport just west of the small forest. Flying away would have been the perfect escape.

Grabbing their belongings, they left their observation point and began the grueling task of clearing an almost quarter-mile long path through the forest using machetes found at a specialty knife store south of Princeton. Sweat soaked despite the grey, fifty-degree weather, the two young men reached the western edge of the small forest an hour later, beyond which lay an overgrown field surrounding the airport. Tired and cold, they scurried into their truck parked on the runway and set off on the one hundred and twenty-mile trip back to Princeton.

"I wish Brian would come back," Ben remarked once they were safely away from the prison. "Then we could finally relocate up here and stop making this trip every day. It's too bad we can't just put a sign on our door telling him where we are."

"It's almost over," Jim countered as he applied more pressure to the gas pedal. "And I know you're not anxious for Brian to return."

"Yes, I am," Ben retorted in an effort to curtail yet another of his cousin's implications. "If he were here, Andy wouldn't insist on being involved when we finally do this. It's bad enough that Charlie's coming too. Susan's been giving both of us grief ever since."

"Give Susan a break. She's worried about her brother. He's been gone three months already."

"Yeah, I know…you're right," Ben answered wearily. He leaned his head sideways against the headrest and stared silently out his window until the vibration of the tires against the road closed his eyes for him.

Jim took his gaze off the road momentarily and looked over at his cousin.

Before Karen's death, Ben had been easygoing and fun. But now he was tense and withdrawn. Only around Andy did he seem to relax, although she had also become a source of frustration for him, and Jim could only hope that one of them would finally have the guts to make the first move.

Jim then wondered for the millionth time if it had been the same for his wife. There was no doubt that being brutally raped had changed her, but he had no way of knowing how much. Had she laughed more or cried less? She couldn't be a better mother, but would she have been less protective of Katie? The first time they made love, it was natural that she had been terrified, but how much less scared would she have been had she been a true virgin instead?

With these thoughts floating around in his mind, Jim returned his focus to the road that stretched before him.

"Well, like I said, it's almost over."

Still awake, Ben let out a grunt that reeked of skepticism before mumbling, "God, I fuckin' hope so."

* * *

14 October 2021

Luke had experienced drunken blackouts before. In fact, he experienced two in the last month, both of which he had managed to conceal from Sean because the latter had been in Philadelphia at the time. Yet that day in early August had been nagging him relentlessly for weeks now. He remembered the day exactly because it was the night before his birthday. And he remembered the blond…Kathy? Kendra? Something like that. He could not for the life of him remember her face. She had been beautiful, of that he was certain. He only messed with the pretty ones.

Ever since that morning when Sean found him in his pathetic state, he knew she had drugged him, and though details about the girl remained hazy, snippets of the words that had passed between them had gradually flickered in and out of some dark corner of his mind. But two days earlier, like a flashbulb going off in his brain, it all came flooding back.

The virus…the goddamned virus. She made me tell her…

It had always terrified Luke that the virus still existed. He had silently rejoiced when it was believed that Ben and Jim Kelly had destroyed it last year. They were his secret heroes. Sure, maybe they deserved some of the revenge that Sean had planned for them, but for all Luke cared they could disappear forever to an island paradise filled with beautiful, naked women.

Sitting now in his own apartment, Luke began to sweat, literally. He body began to shake with fear, like a violent shiver that he could not control. Two days of agonizing over these freshly recollected memories once blissfully erased from his mind had made him physically ill.

The only thing that terrified Luke more than the virus itself was if Sean ever found out he had revealed its location. The punishment would be severe, and painful. Being Sean's number one confidant did not guarantee immunity.

I gotta tell him…I gotta tell him…Fuck! He's gonna kill me…

Luke dragged himself off his couch and stumbled into the bathroom to throw water on his face. After shutting off the faucet, he stared at the tap at length.

He'll understand…I was drugged…it wasn't my fault…she nearly shot me…

It was early, only nine o'clock, but he was exhausted. There was no way he'd make it to *Papillon* or anywhere else tonight. He needed to silence the voices and the fears. He needed to forget what he thought he'd never remember from that night.

He needed to sleep. Tomorrow he would break the news to Sean.

Or maybe the next day. After all, nothing strange had happened at the prison in over two months. What difference would another day make?

* * *

17 October 2021, 2:20 pm

The weeks of planning were complete. Today would see the end of the road.

Maria and Carmen made a hearty meal for Andy and the boys before their departure. It was an unseasonably cold and grey afternoon, no more than a few degrees above freezing, and they would need their strength.

There was tension in the air, more so than the night Andy and Maria had gone to *Papillon*. This mission was incredibly dangerous, particularly for Ben and Jim, and Andy marveled at Morgan's strength and composure when she said her goodbyes to her husband.

After her own goodbyes and a gentle kiss on Katie's forehead, Andy climbed into the passenger's seat of the car and immediately cupped her hands to her mouth. Her fingers were like ice.

"Here, I'll get the engine running," was the first thing Ben said to her as he climbed into the driver's seat.

"Thanks," she muttered over a shiver.

It was only October but it felt like winter, and for six years, Andy hated winter. Without heat and only a meager amount of body fat to protect her, the months of short days and long nights had become an eternal effort to stay warm. Even in Bermuda, which was often mistaken for a tropical island, the winters had been windy and damp.

"Once this is over, how 'bout we go somewhere warm?"

Ben smiled at the idea.

"Where you thinkin?'"

"Dunno. Maybe Florida or the Caribbean?"

"You miss island living?"

"On days like today…"

Andy's voice faded. It didn't matter. The mindless chatter was meant to keep their minds off of the daunting task before them.

They were still sitting in the driveway as the engine of their beat-up sedan warmed up when Jim and Charlie emerged from the house. They would follow Ben to Green Haven in a second vehicle.

* * *

17 October 2021, 2:52 pm

Sean's jaw dropped.

"Are you shitting me? *Please* tell me you're joking!"

As if his body was no longer his to control, Luke's weight seemed to shift back and forth from one foot to the other on its own. Standing just a few feet from the window on the eighty-first floor of the Empire State Building only further toyed with his equilibrium. "Sean, I wish I were, but it all just hit me…just last night."

That part was a lie. Luke had recalled everything five days earlier.

"I'm positive that she drugged me," he pleaded. "C'mon, Sean. I've never felt so sick in my life. You saw me that morning…you saw how fucked up I was. Have you ever seen me anywhere close to that bad before?"

Sean raised a skeptical eyebrow but admitted that Luke had a point.

"No, I haven't. But right now I need to know more about this girl. Was she a Helen or just a random Dreg pretending to enjoy her Wednesday night out?"

Regaining his balance, Luke looked squarely out the window and shook his head slowly.

"I don't remember much about her. All I know is that she was blond and wearing a black dress and her name was something like 'Kathy' or 'Kaitlin' or something that began with a 'K.'"

"Or a 'C?'" Sean added with exasperation.

"Maybe…she didn't exactly spell her name for me, Sean."

"Great."

In a sudden motion, Sean pushed his chair away from his desk and shot to his feet.

"Let's go," he ordered and was out the door of his office before Luke could turn away from the incredible view.

In the elevator, the two descended more than sixty flights before getting off at the fifteenth floor. Sean advanced toward a specific office as a bewildered Luke followed. Without bothering to knock, Sean barged into the office and turned on the light, nearly scaring Danny to death in the process. He marched directly toward the startled young man's desk.

"Danny, right?"

"Uh, yeah…yeah," Danny replied as his heart rate struggled to return to normal.

With Luke standing beside him, Sean placed one hand on Danny's chair and leaned in toward the computer screen. "Danny, I want you to look up the ID records of every Helen that went to *Papillon* on August…"

Sean looked up at Luke.

"Fourth. August fourth," Luke supplied humbly.

Danny just blinked as the instructions sank in. "Uh, all right."

He had a bad feeling, but there was nothing he could do but obey.

A few minutes and many keystrokes later, he brought up a list of seventeen names before pushing his chair out of the way so that Sean could get a closer look.

"Good thing it was a Wednesday. Otherwise the list would be longer," Sean remarked with a smirk.

"Heh, yeah," Luke echoed in an effort to sound agreeable. "The Helens hate hanging around the Dregs almost as much as we do, huh?"

Sean didn't reply. He was too busy scanning through the list of names. All except two he recognized.

"You know who these two are?" he said to Luke as he pointed to the third name from the bottom and then the very last name. "Isabel Torres and Katrina Wilson?"

When Danny heard the two names, his stomach fell to his feet.

He remembered every letter of each name Ben had asked him to register back in July. Inching farther away from the screen, he pretended to be looking at some papers he was supposed to convert into softcopy.

Meanwhile, Sean and Luke continued talking as though Danny wasn't in the room.

"Katrina…that's the one, the blond," said Luke. "But I never met her before that night."

"Me neither."

Sean then turned to Danny and unleashed more orders. "I want you tell me the number of times these two names have been scanned going into *Papillon* in the past three months. Can you do that?"

Of course I can fuckin' do it…

"Sure," Danny mumbled as he rolled his chair back to his keyboard and typed away until he found the results. He wished he knew what exactly Sean was looking for, but even if he did, there was no way to manipulate the data with Sean standing directly behind him.

"Uh, looks like they were both only there that one night."

Sean frowned as he stared at the screen, thinking. "Tell me when these two names were registered."

"All right." As Danny performed a few quick commands, he silently thanked God that he had entered separate dates for all the names that Ben had requested. "Okay, Isabel was registered on May thirteenth and Katrina on June first."

"This year?"

"Yeah."

Sean looked away from the screen and turned to the window. As he mulled over what to do next, he noticed how unspectacular the view was on this floor. A minute later, he had a plan.

"Follow me," he barked at Luke without a further word to Danny.

Once the two had left his office, Danny got up to switch off the light. "You're welcome, asshole."

For a long while afterward, he stared outside his window and wondered what Sean was up to and whether or not he should do anything about it.

* * *

17 October 2021, 3:12 pm

"God, I miss my truck."

Ben was staring at the fuel gauge. They were still eighty miles from the prison, and though they had filled the tank and threw couple of full jerry cans in the trunk, he was still uneasy. Nine-hundred guaranteed miles of fuel was priceless.

"We'll be fine," Andy reassured. She could read his mind.

"Yeah…" Ben's voice trailed off.

"Hey, relax." Andy gave Ben's shoulder a shove and a lighthearted smirk to go with it. Except for the faintest of smiles, he barely reacted.

"I'll relax tomorrow. Shit, I'll open a hundred bottles of champagne if we can find any."

"Well, I'm sure between the two of us, we can find something to celebrate with."

This time, a genuine chuckle escaped Ben's mouth, and he took his eyes off the road to give Andy a proper smile.

"Oh, really? And what exactly did you have in mind, aside from champagne?"

She looked down at her hands, hands that were now warm, and averted a coy smile from his view. "Dunno…maybe dance."

"Dance?"

Andy lifted up her face. "Yeah, why not? People dance when they're happy, don't they?"

After a semi-shrug, Ben replied, "Yeah, sure."

"So we'll dance. You and me. But I get to pick the song."

Ben looked hard at Andy. Her voice sounded…different. Was it possible that she was actually flirting with him? "That's all? Just one song?"

Andy returned her gaze to her hands. She studied the crescents of her fingernails.

"Well, one song to start with. Then…"

Gripping tightly on the steering wheel, Ben's hands began to sweat. For the first time in weeks he wasn't thinking about the prison. Right now he just wanted to blow the whole place up to the sky and move on. He wanted the weight and the tunnel vision created by their goddamned selfless mission to vanish. He just wanted to live…and feel…like a twenty-year-old and not like some Navy Seal always preparing for another suicide mission.

"It's a deal. Just wear that dress."

Andy looked up. "What, the one I wore to *Papillon*?"

"Yeah. You looked…you look good in that."

"Oh…okay. I think I have it somewhere."

Both were straining to sound nonchalant.

"Great. But no Beatles, all right?"

"No?"

"No. Never been a fan."

Andy laughed lightly.

"Yeah, me neither. I never understood the hype. Of course, I wasn't a teenager in the sixties."

"No, we were both lucky enough to grow up after the fuckin' Apocalypse."

* * *

17 October 2021, 3:31 pm

Back on the eighty-first floor, Sean rattled off orders to Luke.

"I want you to send five…no, ten…of your best men up to Green Haven. I want them to ask the permanent guards if they've seen anything unusual since early August…and I mean *anything*. Even if it's a goddamned cow that got tipped over on some field a mile away, I wanna know about it. Then have two of them come back and report what they find by…" Sean looked at his watch, "seven o'clock. Got it?"

"Got it," Luke said confidently before heading toward the door.

"And, Luke," Sean called out before Luke disappeared. "I won't forget that you're the reason we're in this mess right now."

Like a scolded child, Luke swallowed hard and kept quiet. There was nothing to say. He merely nodded and silently left the room.

"Fucking idiot," Sean hissed as the door closed. He picked up the phone that sat on his desk and dialed a number. After three rings, someone answered.

"Yeah, it's me…I want all videos from the night of the fourth of August sent to my apartment within the hour."

Without waiting for acknowledgement from the other end, Sean hung up and left his office. Fifteen minutes later, he was back at his apartment. He had wandered back from his office alone, something he normally wouldn't do in broad daylight, but he needed to think without his personal bodyguards hovering around him. And it was during this walk when an idea suddenly struck him like a ton of bricks. It was something so obvious he couldn't believe he hadn't thought of it until now.

After locking his front door behind him, Sean went directly to his den. In the corner behind a desk stood an antique armoire, inside of which was a safe. He opened the doors of the armoire and hastily spun off the combination. The safe clicked open, and he grabbed a large stack of stuffed folders from inside and placed them on his desk.

There was a file for every Director and nearly every Helen and Fixer: school files, medical records, juvenile detention records, and even notes from old therapy sessions with over-priced psychiatrists. Most of the files were kept in a standard filing cabinet on the other side of the desk, but Sean stored the most important ones inside the bullet-proof safe.

Organized alphabetically by last name, Luke's file was on top, labeled "Luke Andrews" on the protruding tab. The contents of his file were underwhelming: a poor math student but decent in history and writing, several disciplinary infractions from grade school teachers but nothing out of the ordinary, and a mild case of childhood asthma that seemed to have vanished over the years. The rest of the details were mundane. Handsome, popular, but nonetheless impressionable. Rich parents and an older sister who died with them. Large house in Westchester. A typical profile of an upper-class, white male survivor.

Sean sorted through several others, including Lily's with scribbled notes dictated by her shrink detailing her history of sexual abuse by her stepfather, and Chad's folder with graphic crime scene photos of his mother's murder. Thousands of man-hours and road miles had been spent gathering the total sum of these personnel files.

At the bottom of the pile and out of alphabetical order was Ben Kelly's file. It was empty except for one small piece of paper. Sean had personally found it on the floor of what had been the guidance counselor's office at Ben's elementary school in Virginia. The rest of the file was gone, as was his cousin's, but the single paper had likely been missed when he and Jim attempted to erase all evidence of their past after fleeing New York the year before. It was cunning of Ben to destroy his files, but it was simply bad luck that such a critical piece of personal information had been left behind. But Ben's bad luck was Sean's good luck.

Sean held the paper up to the light and studied the ten individual fingerprints taken when Ben was ten-years old, as determined by the date stamped on the top corner. The private Catholic school that Ben and Jim had attended recorded their students' fingerprints with parental consent in the event that a student was kidnapped or went missing. Sean's school had the same child safety program, and he found it ironic that something meant to protect ten-year-old Ben might now help to catch him ten years later.

As for the mysterious blond who had drugged Luke, there was probably no correlation to Ben. However, following one's intuition was Sean's primary rule of survival.

A heavy knock on the front door interrupted Sean's thoughts.

"You're late," he barked at the poor kid delivering a single envelope. He slammed the door shut before the boy could squeak out an apology.

Sean marched directly to his massive living room. In three quick movements, he turned on the sixty-inch flat screen television, removed the first of three DVDs from the envelope, and inserted it into the DVD player beneath the screen.

Every single night at *Papillon* was captured on video camera, though only rarely did Sean bother to watch the DVDs. Still, he ordered the recordings to continue for situations like the one he was currently facing. Following more than half an hour of both real time and fast-forwarded footage from six different cameras positioned throughout the club, Sean found what he was looking for.

The camera angle was not optimal, but it was still clear enough to see what went on. Looking at the blond, it was easy to understand how Luke had fallen prey. She was wearing an enticing black dress that left just a little to the imagination and high heels that showcased her slender yet muscular legs. Her wavy hair extended to the middle of her back, and every minute or so it would glide back and forth over her shoulders as she moved. Where had she concealed the gun Luke spoke of? Likely in a holster strapped to the inside of her thigh.

Sean watched and re-watched the film several times. There was no doubt that he had never seen the girl before. He would have remembered. There was something different about her, and although he couldn't hear a word that either she or Luke said, he could just barely identify the subtleties of the act she had put on for Luke: a slightly forced smile here, a tentative caress there. But would he have noticed had he not been looking for some clue, or if it had been him instead of Luke? Probably not, he admitted, particularly with alcohol mixed in.

After the ninth or tenth time watching Luke's skirmish with Lily before the blond finally coerced him out of view, Sean rewound the video once more. The girl never looked directly at the camera, as there was no way that she would know where it was hidden. Still, her face was clearly visible from several angles throughout the ten or so minutes that she was on the screen. Sean pressed "pause" on the clearest shot and leaned in closer to the screen. His cold, blue eyes soaked in the image, and memorized every pixel.

"Pretty little thing, aren't you?"

* * *

17 October 2021, 4:32 pm

By the time they reached Stormville, the small town that surrounded the prison, it was pouring rain. Andy did not envy the job Ben and Jim were gearing up to do.

"Man, this sucks," said Ben, echoing her thoughts as he increased the speed of the windshield wipers.

"Just think of it as a strategic advantage. The guards will be cold, wet, and tired. They'll be slow to react."

"Easy for you to say. You and Charlie will be nice and warm inside the cars."

"Not the entire time."

"Oh, sorry…for like, five minutes you'll be outside." Ben was teasing her, but there was an edge to his voice. He was nervous, and so was she.

A few miles away from the prison, Ben steered the car into a vacant gas station and waited. Half a minute later, Jim and Charlie pulled up beside them in the other vehicle. Charlie rolled down the passenger's window.

"Smashing weather, 'eh?"

"Yeah, terrific," Ben called back. "Let's check the radios."

"Yeah, all right."

Andy fished in her backpack until she found the walkie-talkie that Charlie had encrypted weeks before and successfully performed a radio test with him on the other end.

"Good," Ben mumbled as he glanced at his watch.

It was time. The sky was dark but not too dark. Any later and they would risk trying to slip past the guards using night vision goggles.

Ben looked over at Andy. "You ready?"

She nodded once, and though her heart was starting to race, she pursed her lips together. "Ready."

Ben smiled thinly before turning to the others. "Jim, you ready?"

"Yeah, I'm coming."

Both Charlie and Jim stepped out of their car. Jim slipped into the backseat behind Ben while Charlie walked around his car and slid into the driver's seat. He then called out to Ben.

"I'll radio you just before I fire it off."

"Yeah, okay."

Charlie then gave a salute.

"Cheers…good luck."

Charlie drove off and headed in one direction while Ben went in the other, toward the airport. Once there, he parked inside one of the hangars.

The three got out of the car and donned black raincoats. Jim and Ben grabbed two large rucksacks from the trunk while Andy retrieved two loaded M4s. Once Ben and Jim slung the rucksacks over their shoulders, she handed each his weapon.

"Here we go," Jim said, trying to sound upbeat.

Together, they marched about half a mile from the hangar to the forest, crossing the runway along the way. As they descended underneath the canopy, Andy remarked favorably about the path Ben and Jim had cleared days earlier before asking, "Where's the rock?"

Ben pointed straight ahead. "Just up there."

Andy followed him as he stepped off the main path to a narrower path on the left, around the rock. She looked down at it and saw the "X" marked with red duct tape.

"Just don't miss it," she said.

"We won't," Jim replied.

They arrived at the opposite edge of the forest and knelt down behind some trees. All three withdrew their binoculars from their bags and scanned the area.

"Still three," Ben muttered, referring to the guards, each in his own tower along the perimeter wall. "Damn, I was hoping they all wouldn't be there."

"And I bet they're all miserable," Andy grumbled. "I dunno why they put up with it."

"Three words," he whispered. "Food, drugs, and sex."

Andy smirked. "I get the food, but drugs and sex? C'mon…how much of that do people really need?"

"Well, you're not an eighteen-year-old boy," Ben replied, referring mainly to sex.

"No, thank God," she commented as Jim chuckled lightly at the exchange, welcoming the break in the tension.

Andy put down her binoculars and picked up the radio. She ensured the volume was on the lowest setting. Meanwhile, Ben and Jim grabbed opposite ends of a large ladder they had hidden near the path during their last surveillance mission and awaited word from Charlie. Moments later, a crackle was heard coming from the other end.

"*I'm here*," Charlie's voice called out. "*You all ready?*"

Andy looked at both Jim and Ben for confirmation. When they both nodded, she pushed the transmit button.

"Ready," she whispered back.

Seconds later, a loud bang was heard off in the distance followed by the bright, red glow of a flare soaring vertically against dark, grey skies. Through her binoculars, Andy watched as two of the tower guards scurried down from their towers and disappeared from view behind the prison wall.

"Shit, there's still one left."

She radioed Charlie.

"Do it again."

"*Roger…*"

Thirty seconds later, another shot erupted in the distance, followed by another flare. The remaining guard looked around and hesitated, wondering what to do.

"*Once more?*" Charlie called back.

Ben nodded, and Andy called back. "Once more."

Charlie let off the third flare, and the remaining guard finally descended the tower.

"All gone," Andy announced to Charlie before turning to Ben and Jim. "Let's go."

They scrambled to the perimeter wall of the prison between the third and forth observation tower. Andy followed Ben and Jim as she carried their weapons. When they reached the wall, Ben raised the ladder and skillfully adjusted its height until it reached the top. Andy, meanwhile, pulled out a rope from within Jim's rucksack. It was thick, like climbing ropes in gym class with knots tied every two feet and a large metal hook on the end. She also grabbed a wire cutter, which she passed to Ben.

While Andy kept watch, Ben climbed the ladder to the top. Keeping his head low, he cut away at the spiraling loops of barbed wire and created a space large enough to pass unhindered. Once finished, he descended the ladder.

Simultaneously, Jim made two trips back to the edge of the forest to retrieve two hidden fifty-pound weights. Using smaller pieces of rope, he and Andy tied both weights to the first rung of the ladder to weigh it down. When they finished, Jim and Ben grabbed their rucksacks and weapons. Jim also grabbed the thicker rope and ascended the ladder. He hooked the rope to the top rung and dropped the rope over the other side of the wall. Then, he descended the rope and landed safely inside the prison compound.

Before following his cousin, Ben gave Andy one last look as she handed him the radio.

"I'll see you soon," he said.

"Don't do anything stupid," she told him, and he smiled back at her.

"I won't."

He climbed the ladder and disappeared over the wall.

Alone, Andy headed back to the airport beneath the fading daylight. She approached the rock with the red "X" and swerved around it to the right off the main path. Fifty or so meters later, she emerged from the forest and picked up speed. By the time she reached the hangar, she was out of breath. Charlie arrived moments later.

* * *

17 October 2021, 5:02 pm

"So you can scan them in and compare them to every print on file?"

Sean held out the paper containing the ten fingerprints to Danny. He had ripped off the top of the paper where Ben's name had been labeled, however. No need for Danny to know more than was necessary. The kid was already eyeing the paper suspiciously.

"Yeah, no problem."

Danny took the paper between Sean's fingers.

"Give me a few minutes," he added as he fired up the scanner.

"Be quick."

Danny ignored the remark. Outwardly, he appeared bored by the task, but inside his mind was racing. In the few hours since Sean and Luke had visited him, he had anticipated a return visit.

Sean stood by impatiently as Danny scanned the paper into softcopy. He then separated each individual print and stored them as "Unknown 1" through "Unknown 10" prior to instructing the software to compare each "Unknown" print to the more than one million prints on file, beginning with the left pinky first and ending with the right pinky. If the prints belonged to either Ben or Jim, as Danny feared, he wanted to stall as long as possible, and since neither had scanned a print from his left hand, Danny started with those. Each print took just over a minute to crosscheck with every other, giving him at least five more minutes to think.

"Anything yet?" Sean demanded.

"Not yet," Danny replied flatly. "It might take ten minutes. Each print takes about a minute."

In keeping with his role as a lowly, uninterested worker, Danny leaned back in his chair and began to squeeze a rubber stress ball with one hand. His demeanor angered Sean.

"Can't you make it work faster?"

Danny looked at Sean like he'd just said something terribly dumb, which logically, he had.

"It's a computer. It only listens to ones and zeros."

Slightly humbled by this remark, Sean backed off a bit. He wasn't used to people challenging him, but now wasn't the time for a reprimand.

The first three prints came up negative, so Danny entered the commands to crosscheck the left index finger followed by the left thumb. After both came up negative, he started on the right hand.

Jim had registered his right middle finger while Ben had registered his right index. If Danny's suspicions were correct, Ben's finger would pop up first.

"Six down, four to go," he muttered as he reached for the mouse.

Sean, meanwhile, was beginning to think he was chasing a ghost. He turned and faced the window. Daylight was fading, and he was wasting time feeding his paranoia.

And then a distinctive beep emitted from the computer speakers, followed by a second and then a third. Sean whirled around on his heels.

"What was that?"

With his back to Sean, Danny closed his eyes tightly. He was afraid to look.

Sean sprang toward the computer screen and read off the first name.

"John Simmons…"

And the second.

"Michael Wilkins…"

And finally the third.

"Matthew Thompson. Wait, three names for one set of prints…what the fuck…?"

As Sean stared at the screen, Danny finally opened his eyes. He scrambled for an explanation.

"It's probably just a glitch. I mean, I'm sure the guards at the checkpoints mess up…"

"Motherfucker."

Sean uttered the word plainly. He had figured it out.

Stepping away from the desk to allow Danny room to work, Sean spouted off additional commands.

"I wanna see every single checkpoint entry for those two girls…Katrina Wilson and Isabel Torres…along with these three names. I wanna see them all side by side."

Danny grudgingly obeyed and soon brought up five columns in a single Excel spreadsheet, one for each name. The lists were all short, no more than three time, date, and checkpoint location entries each, which would only make it easier for Sean to verify what Danny already knew.

"Move over," Sean ordered as he practically pushed Danny out of his chair.

As Sean sat down and rolled the chair as close to the desk as possible, Danny inched his way to the side of the desk. He desperately wanted to hit Sean upside the head to knock him unconscious and then chain him to the desk so that he could run off to warn his friends. Unfortunately, guards were waiting just outside in the hallway. Sean was always surrounded by guards.

Oblivious to Danny's futile scheming, Sean studied the screen. His eyes moved rapidly back and forth as they glazed over the spreadsheet.

Whoever Katrina was, she had passed through a checkpoint three times, each time within a minute of at least one of the other four names: John Simmons twice and Michael Wilkins, Matthew Thompson, and Isabel Torres on her third and last entry on the fourth of August. All entries had occurred at the same checkpoint, the one near the Holland Tunnel. Now there was no doubt.

"Son of a bitch!" Sean slammed his hands on the desk and sprang to his feet. He ran toward the door and disappeared in seconds.

Alone once again, Danny quickly shut down his computer and left his office minutes after Sean. Once outside, he rode back to Chinatown in the rain on his bike. By the time he reached his apartment, he was soaking wet. It didn't matter. He moved about the place like a tornado as he packed his backpack for the long, wet bike ride to New Jersey. Before leaving the apartment, he left a note for Dez and Li explaining that he would be gone for a least a day but didn't say where he was going.

During his last visit to the city just a few weeks earlier, Ben had entrusted Danny with the location of his hideout in Princeton. Now it was time for a visit.

Chapter XXIII

17 October 2021, 5:15 pm

"What's that?" Charlie asked Andy as they waited anxiously inside the hangar.

"Oh…just a photo that Susan printed for me a few weeks ago."

She handed it over to him. He studied it and frowned. "Where was this taken?"

"The Grand Canyon, on the way back from Los Angeles. Ben found one of those disposable cameras and we started taking pictures just for fun."

Andy paused, smiling faintly at the memory. "When we put the camera down on a nearby rock, the flash went off a few seconds later and that's the picture it took."

Charlie continued to study the photo. The quality of the color was noticeably distorted due to the age of the film, but the images were sharp. The stunning background of the canyon was clearly evident, but even more remarkable was the image of Andy and Ben standing squarely in the center of the photo, both looking at each other in a way that made one wonder what was going through their minds at the moment the flash went off. Though the handcuffs around Andy's wrists were visible, she appeared to be liberated from whatever it was that had shackled her. Ben's face, meanwhile, reflected a mixture of both relief and weariness.

Charlie handed it back to Andy with a smile. "It's amazing that the camera just went off on its own like that."

"Yeah…strange," was all Andy said, and she tucked the photo away in the back pocket of her jeans. She didn't know why she decided to carry it with her that day, but looking at it somehow gave her peace of mind during the agonizing wait.

* * *

17 October 2021, 5:27 pm

After an excruciatingly long ride up the elevator to the seventy-ninth floor, Sean barged through the door of Luke's office without knocking. Finding the office empty, he reached into his back pocket and grabbed his cell phone. He speed-dialed Luke's phone, but the call refused to go through. Even when hovering against the window, the cell service was non-existent.

"Goddamnit! What the hell am I paying them for?" he shouted, referring to the nearly one hundred Fixers he employed to maintain wireless service throughout Manhattan.

Before heading to the ground floor to improve the chances of his phone working, Sean first checked his office two floors above. There he found Luke sitting at his desk talking on the phone. Upon seeing Sean, Luke pulled the receiver away from his mouth.

"Sorry…my phone isn't working."

Luke returned to his call as Sean impatiently waited for him to finish. He abhorred people violating his private office.

"Well?" he said the instant Luke hung up.

"My men will be there in fifteen minutes."

Sean frowned. "Fifteen minutes? I told you two hours ago to send your men. It's only an hour's drive from here."

But Luke was quick to defend himself.

"It's longer than that, and you know it also takes at least an hour just to get out the door. They had to gear up and figure out where they're going first. They've never been to the prison before and most of our maps don't even have the prison labeled."

Goddamned paper maps.

If there was one technology Sean missed more than anything, it was GPS.

"You don't need to remind me of that. I'm fully aware of the limitations of *your* men."

The emphasis on "your" was clear. Any flaws or screwups from the Infantry were strictly Luke's responsibility.

"They'll be there and back before seven, which is what you asked, Sean. Sorry, but I can't give you anything more than that."

Sean didn't respond. Instead, he took a seat on the leather couch adjacent to his desk. Luke stood up to give back the chair, but Sean waved him back down.

"So guess who your Katrina has been coming in and out of the city with since August?"

"Who?"

"Ben."

Luke was stunned at first until another memory from that night came roaring back.

Did he send you?

Who?

Ben…

"You don't look surprised," Sean remarked.

Luke played it off with a shrug.

"Who else would be so interested in the virus?"

Sean resented Luke's apparent indifference. "Your lack of concern is disturbing considering you were the one who told her…the blond…about Green Haven. And now I find out that she's working with Ben."

"But nothing's happened at the prison since she found out."

"You mean since you told her."

Luke groaned and said, "Yes, since I fucked up and told her. But honestly, Sean, you've got the place covered."

Covered? Hardly. A dozen guards for a huge prison compound was grossly inadequate. But Sean couldn't spare anymore men, especially for a job that was so…boring. The ones he had assigned there hated it enough already, so much so that he'd had to double their salary from what the other guards earned.

"How'd you connect the girl to Ben anyway?" Luke went on.

"I had that kid Danny compare every one of her checkpoint entries with Ben's. All the timestamps matched."

"Ben's registered?"

"No, jackass, he's using an alias…three, actually."

"And how'd you figure that out?"

"I have his fingerprints so I scanned them into the system. He's recently registered his right index fingerprint to each of his aliases. How he managed to do that, I'd like to know. Might be time to interrogate some of our guys working the checkpoints."

Luke was still confused by the prints. "How'd you get his fingerprints?"

"From off a glass he drank from once," Sean lied. "A Fixer pulled them off for me."

Luke's eyes grew wide. "Seriously? Sounds like something out of the movies."

Sean sneered at the comparison. The secret files he kept in his apartment were indeed completely secret. Only those who had travelled all over the East Coast and farther to gather the files on Sean's orders were aware of their existence. And those few people were not the same people who knew about the dozen hidden cameras capturing video every night at *Papillon.* And still those people were not the same handful of people who knew about the virus at Green Haven. Only Sean knew everything. Compartmenting was the only valuable lesson he'd learned from his otherwise worthless father.

Sean shooed Luke out of his chair.

"I wanna know the minute you hear anything. Now get outta here."

* * *

17 October 2021, 5:37 pm

"Jesus Christ, this place is enormous," Ben remarked as he and Jim scurried from one building to the next.

Starting on the opposite side of the prison from where they had entered, they'd already scoured through the entire E through H cellblocks and found nothing but empty prison cells, a few of which appeared to have been recently occupied. The entire prison complex itself was a large series of buildings, outer walkways connecting these buildings, and expansive courtyards where inmates once exercised and took in fresh air. There was no way of knowing exactly where the virus was being stored.

Once back inside a building that appeared to contain the old dining hall, Jim laid out a copy of the schematic of the compound, courtesy of Susan and Maria after hours of combing through hundreds of public records at the county courthouse and administration buildings.

Jim pointed to the buildings labeled as cellblocks A through D. "Let's go here next."

"All right, but after we finish with this building," Ben replied.

So far, every building and cellblock they had wandered through had been cold and dark and contained stale air and an eerie sensation of abandonment. When they arrived at cellblock A, however, they no longer needed their flashlights. The vast space was illuminated.

They walked slower now, convinced that they were getting close. They turned the bend from cellblock A to B and heard a faint echo of voices that became louder with every step. Simultaneously, they flipped off the safety switches on their M4s.

"Who are you?"

The voice came from behind. Startled, both Ben and Jim whirled around on their heels. Their ears had been so focused on the voices coming from ahead that they had not heard the footsteps approaching from the other direction.

The person was a young male in his early teens, and his small body was encased in a hazmat suit. His head, however, was exposed. Eyes wide, he appeared equally as startled.

"Who are *you*?" Ben countered in a voice more threatening than intended, so he lowered the barrel of his gun.

"Sean sent us to check on things," Jim added quickly.

"He wanted to make sure everything was moving forward as planned," Ben continued, reciting lines from the script he and Jim had prepared for this type of situation.

The boy frowned. "Does this have anything to do with the noises outside?"

Ben did his best impression of looking confused.

"Noises?"

"Yeah. The guards here just got a call on their radio that there were some loud noises heard outside the perimeter. Most of them just left to go to check out what's going on."

Ben turned to Jim, who casually shrugged. "We didn't hear anything, but we just got here."

"How many guards are usually inside?" Ben asked.

"Seven, but only two are left. They're in the waiting room in case the noises have anything to do with us."

"All right," Ben replied. He had no idea what or where the "waiting room" was, but now his biggest concern were the two guards around the corner.

"So are you gonna be replacing two of the other guards?" the boy asked, his face looking almost hopeful.

"Uh, we're not sure yet," Jim answered slowly. "Why do you ask?"

"'Cuz no one is allowed through the front gate except me, the two other Fixers, and the seven guards. And Sean and Luke, of course. Not even the guards at the front gate are allowed through."

"Because of the virus?" Jim offered, continuing to play along.

"That and the vaccine."

Ben and Jim looked at other. *Vaccine?*

"Right, yes," Ben hastily answered. "That's actually why we're here. Sean wants an update on the progress."

The boy nodded.

"All right, I guess you should follow me. You'll both need a suit."

The boy led the way through cellblock C where some of the cells had personal belongings within them and rumpled sheets on the beds. The Fixers obviously spent most of their nights here. When they approached cellblock D, they came up to a door with a cipher lock. The boy discreetly entered the combination and opened the door.

"This is the waiting room," he informed them as he stepped through the door. At the mention of the "waiting room," however, Ben and Jim stood back and subconsciously gripped their weapons tighter. When they peered inside, however, the room was empty.

"Huh, I guess the guards are further in," said the boy with bewilderment. "You'll have to wait here. I'll go get your suits."

The boy then moved to yet another door on the opposite side of the room and entered the combination on the cipher lock. When he disappeared behind the second door, Ben and Jim turned to each other.

"Sean's developing a vaccine?" Jim said first.

"I guess so," replied Ben as he dropped his rucksack to the ground. "But it doesn't change anything. If he creates a vaccine, that'll just give him even more control over what he can do with the virus."

Jim didn't disagree, and they both checked their weapons to ensure they were properly loaded. The boy soon returned with two hazmat suits in his arms. They were big and bulky and nearly weighed him down.

"Here," he said breathlessly as he handed them over. He then showed them how to put the suits on properly before stepping back to the door.

"Leave your bags and weapons here," he said. "They'll be safe."

"It's all right, we'll carry them," Jim said casually.

But the boy hesitated. "Uh…you can't…"

"We're carrying them," Ben insisted sharply, and the boy's face grew scared. Defeated, he silently turned to the door and entered the combination.

They walked through two additional empty rooms with more locked doors before entering the prep room. There was still no sign of the two guards or anyone else.

"Here we check our suits one more time," the boy said timidly, still recovering from Ben's words.

The instructions regarding the suit were taken seriously, and after double-checking every seal, zipper, and flap, they finally entered the room that they'd come to destroy. The dim light, the super-cold medical freezer, and distinctive laboratory equipment were a figurative "X marks the spot." Strangely enough, however, the boy headed straight through this room to yet another locked door on the opposite end.

"Wait, where are you going?" Jim called to him through his helmet.

The boy turned back.

"To 'The Pit.' You said you needed to see our progress on the vaccine, right?"

"Uh, right. How much farther is it?"

"Just two more rooms."

Jim looked at Ben.

"You stay here and I'll check it out."

It was their opening, their chance. But the boy immediately protested the idea.

"I'm sorry but I can't leave anyone in here alone who doesn't know how to properly handle the virus."

They could see the boy was serious this time, and Jim made the decision for them both.

"All right, we'll both come."

Leaving their rucksacks in the room, they followed the boy through the impressive-looking vacuum room until they finally reached "The Pit."

When the boy opened the door, there was a distinctive sucking noise originating from the entire perimeter seal of the door. Though all the previous doors were airtight, this one seemed exceptionally adhesive.

There were five people in the room: the two guards and the other two Fixers, all wearing hazmat suits. The fifth was a young girl lying on the floor in obvious distress. Wearing nothing but a thin hospital gown, her bare legs and arms were likely freezing cold. Standing beside her was a shorter person in a suit holding what appeared to be a syringe.

Ben, who was in front of Jim, was loath to enter the room without knowing the identity of everyone, particularly the guards. But stopping now would only look suspicious, so they passed through the thick door as it closed behind them with another 'whooshing' sound.

"Who are *they*?" one of the other four people demanded of the boy. Even through the masking effect of the hazmat suit, his demeanor reflected that of an Infantry guard and not a Fixer, and Ben thought his voice sounded vaguely familiar.

"Sean sent them to check on our progress," the boy responded as Ben and Jim slowly entered the room. They kept their distance from everyone and stayed near the door.

"Why did you let them in here with weapons? You know they aren't allowed beyond the waiting room."

"They insisted on bringing them," the boy answered, sounding even more fearful than when Ben had snapped at him.

"So you just decided to let them in?" the guard roared back before pointing a gloved finger to Ben and Jim. "Get outta here and take your weapons with you!"

After exchanging one last pivotal look, the cousins knew they had been polite long enough. Raising their weapons in unison, they lunged forward into the room, Ben aiming at the outspoken guard while Jim fanned the others. Everyone except the girl stood frozen in place.

"All right, here's what's gonna happen," Ben's voice boomed

through his suit, and with his aim still on the guard, he turned to the Fixer holding the syringe. "You…you're gonna put down the needle and then all of you are gonna follow my friend here to the waiting room."

The guard took a hostile step forward, but Ben quickly subdued him with a threatening forward thrust of his M4. "There won't be any more argument about this," he snapped, persuading the guard to retreat backward.

Jim then took a step forward and nodded toward the unfortunate girl.

"Has she been infected yet?"

Through the confines of his helmet, the Fixer holding the syringe shook his head. "No," he said, and in reference to what he was holding, he explained, "This isn't the virus. It's the vaccine."

"Well, she's not getting that either," Ben ordered. "Now move! Everyone!"

With a wave of the gun, he motioned to the door as the three Fixers plodded awkwardly in their suits toward it. However, the two guards still refused to move.

"Who the hell are you?" the one with the familiar voice demanded, and Ben suddenly remembered who he was: the Infantry officer who was rumored to have murdered Timmy, his sister Karen's friend. A flush of anger rushed to Ben's cheeks.

"It's not important who we are," he answered with restraint. "Now move!"

The other guard finally backed away toward the door, but the first one remained defiant. He looked down at Ben's M4 and scoffed.

"You sure you know how to use that thing…wearing thick gloves and all? Kinda hard to pull the trigger, huh?"

Ben stared coldly back until a menacing grin spread across his face.

"You're right, it *is* kinda difficult, so maybe I'll just have to settle for this!"

And with a sudden flurry of motion, Ben flipped the gun around with the barrel pointed over his shoulder, and he slammed the stock into the guard's head. The flexible plastic of the helmet did little to cushion the blow, and the guard flew backward and fell to the ground. Dazed but not unconscious, he didn't get up.

Still as statues, everyone else could only watch.

Jim poked the other guard in the shoulder with his gun. "Get him outta here. Drag him if you have to."

Angry but obedient, the guard approached his fallen comrade and helped him to his feet. Though the downed guard's head bobbed about inside the suit, the whack to his head seemed to have induced some sort of memory recall, for when his eyes fixed upon Ben one more time, he mumbled, "You…you're Ben Kelly…"

The revelation didn't alarm Ben, nor did he care at this point.

"That's right, asshole. Be sure to give Sean my regards."

With Jim following closely from behind, the Fixers and guards left the room. The girl, meanwhile, had remained motionless on the floor during the entire episode. Ben walked over to her now and picked up the syringe. He lowered his weapon and extended his free hand toward girl.

"C'mon, sweetheart. Let's get out here."

Despite her frail appearance, the girl stood up with ease.

"Thank you," she uttered softly.

Her dark hair, blue eyes, and pale, tear-stained face reminded Ben of a younger version of Karen, and he smiled warmly at her. "C'mon, let's go."

She followed him to where Jim and the others were standing just beyond the door, which Jim was holding open with his foot.

"Take her with the rest of them," Ben instructed his cousin as they all entered the vacuum room.

When they reached the room where the virus was stored, Ben stayed behind while Jim directed everyone else to the waiting room. Before they left, however, Ben pulled aside their unwitting accomplice.

"What's the combination to all these doors? Is it the same?"

Eyes wide, the boy nodded. "It's three then five, then one and two together."

Ben repeated the combination for memory. "And they're all the same?"

The boy nodded again, and Ben gestured for Jim to keep moving with the others. Once alone with just the boy, he shut the door behind them and tested the combination to make sure the boy wasn't lying. The door opened, and Ben motioned for him to go through. The boy obeyed, but before leaving he spoke:

"I heard the guard say your name. I know who you are. You're here to destroy the virus."

Ben merely gazed back at the boy. "I am," he said.

"But why do you want to destroy everything when we're so close to creating a vaccine?"

Taking a step forward, Ben gently placed his gloved hand on the boy's shoulder. "Listen, kid…Sean Taylor is evil. He's using you and everyone else in here for his own twisted plan. He doesn't care about any of you, only what you can do for him."

Through his helmet, the boy blinked.

"Having the virus *and* the vaccine just makes him stronger," Ben continued. "But if the virus no longer exists, then there's no need for a vaccine and everyone will be safer."

Then, with a gesture toward the door, Ben made a final remark. "You should run," he began. "Run far away from here and use that super-genius brain of yours for something better than this. Now go."

Absorbing this earnest advice, the boy stared back at Ben for a few seconds longer. Then, without another word, he left the room.

Finally alone inside the room that contained the deadliest substance ever known to man, Ben moved with cautious speed. After a rapid scan of the room and everything inside, he placed his M4 on the floor and quickly retrieved several items from within his rucksack: half a gallon of gasoline, two bottles of nail polish remover, a bundle of balsa wood, a strip of wool fabric, a rubber band, a hammer, and a dependable cigarette lighter.

There were other things inside the rucksack, including C-4 and blasting caps, but these would not be needed. At Fort Detrick, they blew up an entire building because they couldn't gain close access to the virus. Today, however, Ben had the luck of being alone in the same room with the infernal matter. And he wouldn't have to use the C-4, which was always dangerous to use, particularly when demolishing a building.

Ben moved over to the medical freezer and carefully opened the door. Inside were two shelves, and on each shelf was a metal tray with several glass vials of what could only be the virus and the still-untested vaccine. He removed the trays with care and placed them on a nearby table before unplugging the freezer and moving it to the middle of the room. He then flipped the freezer over so that the door faced the ceiling. With the freezer door hanging open, he removed the shelves inside before placing the glass vials inside the freezer, one at a time.

There were three tables in the room, each with various stacks of paper and notebooks, along with a laptop. Not only would the virus need to be destroyed but all the carefully drafted notes and documentation the Fixers had compiled during their months of research. Everything would be vaporized.

Moving faster now, Ben gathered the notebooks and every single sheet of paper and placed them all inside the freezer. Lastly, he removed the hard-drive from the laptop and threw it on the floor before striking it multiple times with the hammer. He threw the warped drive into the freezer. After one final check of the room, he poured the gasoline and the two bottles of nail polish remover inside the freezer and on its contents.

Ben opened the door to the prep room and placed his rucksack and M4 inside, using the latter to keep the door propped open. Then with the bundle of balsa wood, he wrapped the wool fabric around one end and secured it in place with the rubber band. Lighting the end to create a torch, Ben backed toward the door before throwing the torch into the freezer.

A split-second later, a fire exploded from the freezer, its flames reaching the ceiling. Ben dashed though the door and slammed it shut. Peering through the small glass window, he watched as the fire raged. What he couldn't hear was the sound of the glass vials breaking as the last remnants of the virus became extinct.

Satisfied with his handiwork, Ben grabbed his rucksack and gun and rushed through the series of empty rooms until he reached the waiting room. Jim and the others were still there. No longer wearing a hazmat suit, Jim was now holding a radio that belonged to one the guards. A near-continuous stream of chatter could be heard from the speaker.

Ben hurriedly removed his helmet. "It's done."

"Good, 'cuz we gotta go," Jim urged. "There's a bunch of guards that just showed up at the security gate."

"Shit," Ben groaned as he yanked off the rest of his suit.

Without another word, the two fled the waiting room, leaving everyone else inside. They were no longer a concern. All that mattered now was getting back to the airport where Andy and Charlie were waiting.

They backtracked through the cellblocks. When they emerged outside, they discovered that the temperature had dropped substantially and that the earlier rain had returned in the form of sleet. It stung their cheeks and obscured their vision.

"This way!" Jim cried out once he'd found his bearings.

As nightfall approached, only the faintest amount of daylight permitted them to find their way back to the prison wall. With both rucksack and weapon dangling from his back, Jim climbed up the thick rope first using both his feet and hands as they grabbed for each knot. As he disappeared over the wall, Ben began his climb. Halfway up the wall, however, a moving flash of light caught the corner of his right eye.

"There they are!" he heard someone shout. When he turned to look, he saw three people with flashlights approaching fast. Then an even brighter light originating from the nearest observation tower was directed onto him.

"Hurry!" Jim called down to him from the top of the ladder.

With the pursuers not more than ten yards from the bottom of the rope, Ben scrambled to the top of the wall. Straddling it, he grabbed the hook at the end of the rope and dropped it over the inside of the wall just as the first pursuer grabbed at it. Then he flew down the ladder.

A chorus of cursing and shouts could be heard from the other side of the wall as the guard in the tower continued to direct his searchlight on the two fugitives. Waiting at the bottom of the ladder for his cousin, Jim had been listening to the chatter about their location over their stolen radio.

"Everyone knows we're outside the perimeter."

"Fine, let 'em chase us."

They ran toward the forest and found their path. Using a pencil-thin but powerful flashlight, Jim led the way. As the rock with the "X" approached, Ben heard voices and saw flashes of light coming from behind.

"Hurry," he shouted to Jim, who swerved around the right side of the rock. Ben followed with lightning-quick footing, and ten seconds later, a loud cry was heard. Ben's closest pursuer had just fallen through the hidden, six-foot-deep hole that he and Jim had meticulously dug a week earlier at the spot on the path where the "X"-labeled rock sat. If they were lucky, another one would fall in after.

As he cleared the forest and raced to the airport, Ben deftly retrieved his radio from within his rucksack, the one Andy had given him. "Get the cars started…we're being followed!" he shouted into the speaker between breaths.

"*Copy!*"

They ran through the field and across the runway, Jim leading by just a few feet. Ben chanced a look over his shoulder and saw the shadowy figures of people chasing them, the beams of their flashlights dancing in the dark. More than halfway to the hangar, he stopped and turned as Jim continued running. Ben brought his weapon to bear and squeezed off two rounds of suppressing fire, hoping to scare their pursuers off. Undeterred, however, they maintained pursuit like determined predators hunting their prey.

With two hundred meters to go, Ben closed the distance between himself and Jim, although his cousin was now roughly fifty meters ahead. As he approached the hangar, he saw Charlie pull his car outside. Jim reached the passenger's door and hopped inside. Seeing them hesitate, Ben yelled, "Go! Go!" and waved them off. He wanted to say, *We'll be right behind you,* but was too out of breath.

After a moment's hesitation, Charlie and Jim sped off toward the airport exit. Andy pulled up moments later in her car.

"Get in!" she cried as she leaned over and opened his door. Ben hurtled himself inside, and the moment he was seated, Andy pressed hard on the gas. The forward acceleration slammed the passenger's door shut.

"What happened?" she asked breathlessly as she rounded the corner and followed the hazy taillights of Charlie's car in the distance.

"We destroyed it but couldn't get out without being seen."

Ben looked back through the rear window but his pursuers were no longer in sight.

"But it's gone?"

"Yep, burned to Hell. Forever."

Andy gripped the wheel hard and roared the engine. The road had become slippery with sleet, and she nearly skidded off the road.

"Careful!" Ben reprimanded.

"I'm trying!"

After quickly regaining control, Andy watched as Charlie pulled a sharp left out of the airport. She prepared to follow him when a second car suddenly went flying by from the right just as she approached the turn. The car was obviously trailing Charlie and was immediately followed by a second vehicle. Upon seeing her headlights, however, the second once screeched to a stop, swerving in the process, and began to turn around.

It was going after them.

"Fuck!" Andy cried as she yanked the wheel to the left despite the threat and T-boned the rear of the vehicle before it could complete its turn. She kept driving as the other car spun around on the slick road.

"I'm going after the other one," she said while pushing hard on the accelerator. The car chasing Charlie was in sight.

"Get up close to it and I'll try hitting the tires," Ben instructed as he readied his M4.

Andy sped up while Ben rolled down his window, but when she came within a few car lengths of the pursuing vehicle, it suddenly turned ninety degrees to block the entire road and stopped.

"Goddamnit!"

"Go right!" yelled Ben as he pointed to a quickly approaching T-intersection.

Andy obeyed and turned north along a country road. The vehicle that had been chasing Charlie soon began chasing them and was quickly followed by another car, presumably the vehicle Andy had T-boned.

"Does Charlie have the other radio?" Ben asked suddenly, and desperately.

Andy glanced at the cup holders between their seats, in which sat her radio. "No, I have it."

"Shit…I have the other one."

"Great…"

Ben now attempted to stop the vehicles chasing them, but this time from behind. With gun in hand, he leaned out the window and aimed at their attacker.

"Slow down!"

Andy eased off the accelerator to close the gap. Ben focused on the front sight and fired several shots. The front vehicle swerved a bit but remained on course. Ben fired again, this time releasing every round of the magazine, but the vehicle still advanced. Andy, meanwhile, reached into his rucksack with one hand and fished for another magazine. After finding it, she held it out to him.

"Here!"

Ben released his empty magazine and grabbed her full one. He skillfully replaced it and took aim again.

"Slow down and move left!"

Andy obeyed, and this time when Ben fired, he hit vital components, including the front left tire. The car swerved out of control and was soon struck by the second vehicle behind it.

Ben dropped back into his seat. "Nice drivin'!"

"Nice shootin.'"

They continued heading down a road they didn't recognize.

"Where are we?"

"No idea," Andy answered.

Ben pulled out the map and turned on the overhead light. The sudden glare prevented Andy from seeing a deer crossing the road until it was almost too late. She swerved and missed the creature but soon went into a tailspin. Her attempt to recover was futile. The car careened off the side of the road into a shallow ditch.

"Shit!" Andy cried. She threw the car into reverse, but it wouldn't budge.

"Wait, I'll get out," said Ben.

He stepped outside and rounded the front of the vehicle. As Andy slowly applied the gas, Ben pushed as hard as he could, but after five attempts, the car was nowhere closer to breaking free of the muddy trenches that had formed around the tires. The rain had taken away any friction between them and the ground.

Accepting defeat, Ben returned to the passenger's side and began grabbing his things.

"We're just gonna leave it?" Andy asked incredulously.

"We got no choice. Whoever's chasing us will be here soon."

Cursing under her breath, Andy yanked off her seatbelt and grabbed her backpack and raincoat from the backseat. She threw on the coat and followed Ben to the other side of the road.

"Where are we going?"

"This is a residential area. We'll find somewhere to camp out for a while, but first we gotta get off the road."

Ben was right. On the road, they were vulnerable. They needed to put distance between themselves and their car. After a quick look at the map to determine where they were, the only plausible direction was to head east. Ben led Andy off the road and through a thick cluster of trees. When they emerged on the other end, they found themselves in a small neighborhood that contained several houses. But they didn't stop. Not yet, for they were still too close to the road. And so they continued to run in the cold and sleet, hoping that they could still disappear into the night.

Chapter XXIV

17 October 2021, 7:45 pm

With the exception of a scant handful of towers, the cellular network beyond the five boroughs had not been restored. To compensate, Sean had built a network of repeaters to extend the range of push-to-talk radios far outside of the city's limits. While nowhere near as capable or complex as a cellular network, these repeaters allowed the Infantry to communicate as far north as Poughkeepsie, as far west as the Pennsylvania-New Jersey border, and as far south as Philadelphia, where the cellular network picked up again. The prison sat at the northern edge of this communication zone.

After getting word about the gunshots and flares, Sean ordered Luke to go to the prison immediately. By the time he arrived, the trespassers had already escaped, and Luke then had the unfortunate job of breaking the news to Sean; not only had they escaped, but they had destroyed every last trace of the virus. The excruciating silence that followed on the other end of the radio lasted almost a minute as Luke visualized Sean hurling objects against his office wall in a rage.

"*So what are you doing to find them?*" were his first bitter words.

"We think there were three or four of them. My men tell me that one of them was a girl. They left the area in two separate vehicles."

"So what the hell happened to the two cars?"

"We chased both of them and they got separated. Unfortunately, one of them got away, but we found the other one deserted and stuck in a ditch on a nearby road."

"Deserted? So they got out on foot?"

"Looks like it. I've got everyone driving around looking for them. They can't be too far, especially in this weather."

"I hope you're right…for your sake. I'm coming up there now to sort out this mess. In the meantime, scan all the frequencies on this band and check for any signals that aren't ours. They're probably using radios to communicate. Out!"

Fearing for his rank and reputation, Luke soon ordered every single person at the prison, the three Fixers included, to scour a fifteen mile radius around the compound while he waited in trepidation for Sean's arrival.

* * *

17 October 2021, 7:59 pm

For nearly an hour, they stumbled in a northerly direction though the dark, passing trees, roads, more trees, and houses tucked away in quiet neighborhoods. But they continued on in the cold and rain, the desire to increase their distance from Green Haven propelling them ahead.

The sleet pelted Andy's cheeks, turning them red and raw. Both she and Ben were completely soaked through to their jeans, and their shoes weren't fairing much better. Their upper bodies were still dry, but they had grossly underestimated the temperatures. It felt more like January than October, and they hadn't anticipated being outside this long.

Andy began to shiver uncontrollably, the chill penetrating to her bones. As much as she wanted to keep going, she knew that hypothermia would consume her body if they didn't stop for shelter soon. Ben was visibly cold as well, and without a word, he took hold of Andy's icy hand and led her down yet another residential street. They had no idea where they were, and the map inside Ben's rucksack was not detailed enough to show anything more than major roads and highways.

The fallen autumn leaves coated much of the sidewalks, and Andy slipped on them more than once before regaining her footing. Ben continued to hold fast to her hand until they reached a two-story house at the end of a cul-de-sac. There were other houses on either side, but this one had a front porch with a stack of firewood sitting out of the rain. Hopefully, it was dry enough to ignite.

No lights were on, as expected, and the lock to the front door easily gave way with a strong push. Inside was pitch black and the air was stale, but it was dry and warmer than outside, which was all that mattered at the moment. Ben panned the entryway with his flashlight and led Andy down a hallway into the living room with a large fireplace. A pile of wood, considerably smaller than the one underneath the front porch, sat next to the fireplace. Ben touched the top piece of wood. Though covered in dust and cobwebs, it was blessedly dry.

Five minutes later, Ben was busy feeding a growing fire while Andy removed her wet jacket, shoes, and socks. Using the flashlight, she went upstairs and found a few blankets in a linen closet. Still shivering violently, she proceeded to remove her soaked jeans and sweater before wrapping herself in a blanket. With her wet clothes and extra blankets in one hand and the ends of the blanket firmly grasped in the other, Andy returned downstairs to the living room and placed her clothes in front of the fire to dry. Ben looked up from the fire to Andy. They hadn't said a word since entering the house.

"Here, sit down," he said to her as he stepped away from the growing fire that soon became a roaring inferno.

Andy obeyed, kneeling in front of the fireplace and drawing her knees into her chest beneath the blanket. Despite removing her wet clothes and the warmth of the fire, she continued to shiver violently.

"God! I c-ca-can-t-t-t…ge-ge-t-t…wah-warm," she stammered through chattering teeth.

Though chilled himself, Ben wasn't shivering nearly as bad. He quickly shed his own clothes down to his boxers. Andy was too preoccupied with trying to get warm to notice. After placing his wet clothing beside hers, Ben picked up one of the other blankets and sat down between her and a large ottoman. Only then did she finally become aware of what he was doing. Drawing up to her side, he straddled her and wrapped the blanket around them both.

"Body heat…such a cliché, I know," he muttered without further explanation as he pulled her head into his bare chest. Her head felt like ice against his skin.

"F-fun-ny…"

"What is?"

"Th-this. L-like a b-bad roh-mance nov-v-vel."

Ben let out a small laugh. "Andrea Christensen reading trashy romance novels? I'm shocked."

Andy released a laugh between her shivers. "R-ran outta real b-books in Ber-muda."

"Sounds like it…"

Leaning against the ottoman, Ben began to rub his hands through Andy's wet hair for warmth. Though her remarks regarding their compromising position may have been accurate, all he could think about was getting her warm, and all she could think about was getting warm.

"Not to sound like a complete asshole, but if you let go of your blanket so that more of our skin touches, you'll get warmer faster."

Andy didn't protest. She released her blanket and wrapped it around them both, creating an additional layer of insulation. She then pressed herself against every possible inch of his skin as he wrapped his arms around her. In time, the fire and the heat from Ben's body thawed the icy chill running through her until the shivering ceased. As she grew warmer, she didn't pull away but instead leaned in closer as her body began to relax. With her left ear pressed firmly against Ben's chest as she stared at the fire, she heard the steady beat of his heart.

Minutes later, Andy's eyelids began to flutter as the pulse of Ben's heart lulled her into a welcome sleep. His own slumber came shortly after.

* * *

17 October 2021, 8:45 pm

Sitting in the dark, Sean stared down at the pistol in his lap. Green Haven was just a few miles away.

For six years, he had managed to get where he was without killing a single person with his bare hands, but he couldn't decide whether that was something he should be proud of.

Many people had died under his orders, but he had never actually killed anyone. He'd never pulled the trigger or put a needle into someone's arm. Or plunged a knife into a person's chest as Chad had done to his mother. Though Sean still didn't trust Chad, he admired the boldness of the act. The police report from the small Iowa town made no conclusive accusation that young Chad had killed his mother, but a quick skim over the file said it all. Chad had snuffed the life out of someone he was supposed to love. And he had done it the hard way—by using a knife. Stabbing someone was an intimate act that required great physical strength. Sean couldn't help but feel a bit jealous.

He inserted a magazine into the gun and chambered a round.

Like Chad, Sean despised his mother. In fact, he had never really loved anyone. Ben's sister was the sole exception. Not since Karen had Sean felt such stirring of emotion for another, an emotion that he assumed was love. In a way, Sean had even loved her brother and once treasured their friendship above all others.

Lily was beautiful and fragile, like Karen had been, but she was just a poor, lost soul trying to make up for an abusive childhood. And she was suicidal, with multiple scars on her wrists to prove it. She didn't love Sean, nor did he love her, and they both knew it. They were simply using each other. He liked possessing her, and she allowed him to control her to maintain her status as both the envy and the lust of everyone. Lily wasn't anything like Karen. Karen had been a radiant creature. She could make anyone feel like they had just stepped into a cool stream on a hot, sticky day. Karen was irreplaceable.

Then there was Luke. He wasn't as smart or savvy as Ben had been, but he was predictable, and despite how furious Sean was with him at present, he would not be punished. Luke had made a grave mistake, but the Infantry was loyal to him, and he was loyal to Sean, and such loyalty was not easily duplicated.

No, if anyone was going to be punished, it would be Ben. But death was too good for him. Sean wanted Ben to suffer unimaginably. Even if it took him until the end of his life, he would find him and make him pay.

Sean exited the SUV the moment it pulled into the prison entrance. He spotted Luke and made a beeline toward him as he stuffed his gun into the back of his jeans underneath his rain coat.

"Well?"

Luke swallowed.

"We haven't found them yet?"

Controlling his anger, Sean crossed his arms over his chest. "Show me the map."

Luke nodded and led Sean to the rear of his SUV. The back door was open and sheltered them from the rain. Luke turned on his flashlight. Spread out in the back was a detailed map of the prison and the surrounding neighborhoods. The copyright date on the bottom-right corner revealed that the map had been printed in 2014, indicating that it was as up-to-date as possible.

"Where was the abandoned car found?" Sean demanded.

"Here." Luke pointed at a side road that ran perpendicular to the main road from the prison, Route 216, the same road that served as the entrance to the airport.

"And where were the two cars first spotted?"

"Here, at the airport. It's probably where they staged everything. I've got everyone searching five miles around the abandoned car, but so far, nothing."

Sean squinted at the map and shook his head. "They won't be down here," he said, pointing to areas south and west of the airport. "The second car was abandoned north of this road…216. They were heading north when their car was abandoned, right?"

"Right," Luke confirmed. "The car is facing north."

"Then they probably kept going north to put distance between themselves and the prison. They'll be up here somewhere."

Sean traced a circle with his finger around a large area north of the prison containing many residential neighborhoods.

"Move everyone searching south of this Route 216 up north to these neighborhoods. And tell everyone that the person who finds our fugitives will get an entire night with Lily."

* * *

18 October 2021, 12:07 am

Alone in the living room, Morgan kept the fire going. There was no point trying to sleep. Anything to stay occupied was better than lying in bed with eyes open staring at the ceiling. Not even the soft sounds of Katie's rhythmic breathing in the crib beside her could quiet her mind.

She hated this day. She hated it more than the day her parents died.

Morgan had never envied Andy for her daring ways. They were simply different: two perfect examples of distinct female archetypes. Yet during moments like these, when feeling useless became overwhelming, she regretted never playing the game and always watching from the sidelines. But mostly she was just tired of being perceived as the perpetual victim, someone too fragile to become too involved.

She had no idea what time it was but guessed that it was close to midnight. The other girls were all asleep. Susan normally slept in the house next door, but tonight they were all under the same roof. It was rainy and unseasonably cold outside. Upstairs, Maria shared a bed with her sister to keep warm while Susan huddled under a pile of blankets in a spare bedroom. The house was cozy but drafty, and the wind outside seeped through the cracks in the doors and windows.

Morgan placed another log on the fire. She was getting pretty good at building them and often teased Jim for his uncharacteristic lack of skill at building one himself. As this new log began to burn, there was a knock on the front door.

Morgan headed to the door and peered through the peephole. She could barely make out a shadowy figure standing in the darkness. She unlocked the door but kept the chain lock securely in place and reached for the flashlight on the small entry table.

As she opened the door a crack and turned on the flashlight, she was surprised by who she saw.

"Danny?"

"Yeah, hi…Sarah, right?"

Morgan nearly forgot her own alias.

"Uh, right."

Danny was soaking wet, and Morgan immediately took pity on him.

"Wait, I'll let you in."

Morgan closed the door, unlocked the chain, and ushered Danny inside.

"Take off your coat and sit by the fireplace."

"Thanks," Danny uttered through chattering teeth. "Sorry to bug you, but I found out something tonight that I know Ben and Jim will wanna hear."

"Oh, they're not here," Morgan replied as she shut the door and locked it again. "But maybe I can help. There are no secrets among us."

"All right," Danny replied as he followed Morgan into the living room. He stripped off his dripping raincoat and took a seat on the floor by the fire, then proceeded to hug his knees to his chest and rub his arms to get warm.

Morgan examined her guest. "You'll never get warm if you stay in those wet clothes."

"My shirt is dry. Just my jeans and shoes are wet. I rode my bike all the way from the city."

Sitting on the couch, Morgan looked at Danny as though he were insane. "All the way from the city? That's, what, fifty miles? In the rain?"

Danny only shivered in response.

"Good Lord, whatever you've come to tell us must be pretty bloody important."

"It is."

And Morgan could tell from Danny's expression that he meant it.

"You'll tell me, but first I'm going to find something dry for you to change into. And some socks too. Take off your shoes."

Morgan disappeared upstairs for a few minutes and returned with a pair of sweatpants and socks. She placed them on the coffee table near the fireplace.

"They're Jim's, so they should fit you. You can change in the bathroom over there."

Thanking Morgan, Danny stood and picked up the clothes. After disappearing for a minute or two, he returned to the living room and resumed his position on the floor next to the fire.

"How did you know where to find us?"

"Ben told me, on his last visit to the city a few weeks ago. He wanted me to update his and Jim's ID to indicate that they were members of the Infantry. Before he left, Ben asked me to listen for anything unusual…about any of you guys. And tonight, I did."

"What happened?" Morgan asked anxiously.

"It's Sean. He found out that Ben's been back to the city."

Morgan's eyes grew wide with fear. "What…how…?"

Danny then proceeded to explain the evening's events.

"I knew Sean was up to something when he found out your friends were at *Papillon* on the same night back in August, but I didn't know exactly what. When he came around a second time to scan Ben's prints, I didn't have time to stop him from figuring out that Ben had returned."

"I'm sure there was nothing you could do, Danny," Morgan consoled once she'd absorbed everything. "But how the hell did that bloody psychopath get a copy of Ben's fingerprints?"

Danny shrugged wearily.

"No idea. But he was fuckin' *pissed* when he found out Ben had sneaked back into the city."

To Danny's surprise, Morgan stifled a laugh.

"What's so funny?"

"Sorry, but in England, 'pissed' means drunk, not angry…still funny every time I hear it."

"England? I thought you were Irish…your last name being O'Brien and all."

Morgan didn't know exactly how much Jim and Ben trusted Danny, but the fact that they had entrusted him with their location seemed sufficient.

"Danny, I'll be honest with you. My name isn't Sarah. It's Morgan. We used aliases for our protection. Ben and Jim didn't want Sean or anyone else knowing the real names of their friends."

But Danny only nodded. The deception didn't seem to bother him one bit. If anything, he seemed to approve of it. "I don't blame you. Sean Taylor *is* a fuckin' psychopath."

Morgan frowned. "But then why do you stay in New York and work for him?"

Turning back to the fire, Danny pressed his lips together. It was a question he'd asked himself many times before.

"Because I'm a coward…because I'm…waiting…"

"Waiting for what?"

Danny stared, unblinking, at the fire.

"For something…or someone. Someone to come along who will change everything."

"Is that why you helped Ben and Jim? Because you think they could be the ones to change things?"

Danny tilted his head to the side. "Maybe…I dunno…"

He looked back at Morgan, who was merely listening without a hint of judgment.

"Anyway," he went on. "You don't seem too concerned that Sean found out about Ben."

Morgan smiled lightly. "Well, he and Jim only came back to New York for one reason, and after tonight, it won't matter anymore what Sean knows."

Danny, however, was doubtful. "Well, whatever Sean and Luke were worried about, it seemed pretty serious."

It was the first time Danny had said anything about Luke, and at the mention of his name, Morgan's stomach plunged.

"Luke was there when Sean asked you to look into the entry records for that night at the club?"

"Uh, yeah…everything started with them asking about Isabel and Katrina."

"It's Maria and Andy, actually..." Morgan murmured. She shut her eyes tightly and rubbed her temples.

Sean knows we're after the virus…

Danny, however, was confused.

"I don't understand. What's going on?"

Morgan started to explain when another knock on the front door echoed though the house, this time louder and more urgent. When she opened the door with the chain lock still attached, she saw Jim and Charlie standing in the rain on the other side.

"Thank God!" she cried out as she released the chain and opened the door.

Jim gave Morgan a tight embrace as Charlie entered the living room where he spotted Danny. The two had never met before.

"Who are you?"

Danny stood up. "I'm Danny."

"Oh, the hacker?"

Chuckling, Danny held out his hand to Charlie, who shook it.

"That's me."

Meanwhile, Morgan pulled away from Jim and guided him into the living room.

"What took you so long? Where're Andy and Ben?" she asked.

"What, they're not here?" Jim said with concern, causing Morgan's face to fall.

"They didn't come back with you?"

"We got separated leaving the airport," said Charlie. "Some guards from the prison chased after us, but Jim and I got away."

"But that's when we got separated," Jim added gravely. "We used most of what was left of our gas trying to reconnect with Ben and Andy, but we couldn't get too close to the prison or the airport and risk getting caught again."

"What about the radios?" Morgan asked in desperation, at which point Jim and Charlie exchanged weary glances.

"Ben and I were chased out of the prison, and in the confusion, Charlie and I drove off without a radio. They're both with Andy and Ben."

"So you had no way of communicating," Morgan uttered rhetorically, hardly believing the unfortunate turn of events.

"We had to come back because we were low on petrol," Charlie said, as if he needed to explain why he and Jim had returned without their friends.

"No, you did what you had to do, naturally," Morgan said as she placed a comforting hand on her brother's shoulder.

Jim finally took note of Danny. "What are you doing here?" he said a bit sharper than intended and quickly apologized.

"No worries, man. I came because I found out some things today that might explain whatever it was that happened to you all tonight."

Maria and Susan emerged from upstairs looking half-asleep. Upon seeing Charlie, Susan's face brightened and she ran into his arms. Meanwhile, Danny straightened himself up when Maria entered the room, but she was too preoccupied with rubbing sleep from her eyes to notice.

"Sorry, did we wake you?" Morgan asked.

"Don't worry about it," Maria replied as she plopped down on the couch nearest Danny. She greeted him with a friendly tap to the arm, which pleased him.

"So it's not Isabel, is it?"

Her mind still waking up, Maria looked confused until she finally realized what Danny really was asking. "Oh…no, it's Maria."

"Maria," Danny repeated with a smile. "I like that name better."

"Where're Andy and Ben?" Susan asked with a frown as she looked around the room, and Charlie quickly explained how they got separated.

"But they're okay, right?"

"I'm sure they're fine. They're probably either looking for us or are on their way back," Jim replied with genuine assurance.

"Those two can take care of themselves better than any of us," Charlie added before giving Susan a tender kiss on her forehead.

"So did you destroy it?" Maria asked both Charlie and Jim.

"Yep, it's gone," Jim declared. "As far as we can tell, the virus no longer exists."

Now it was Danny's turn to be confused.

"The virus? What are you talking about? I thought you two destroyed it all last year."

And so Danny was quickly filled in. Learning that Sean still had the virus came as a shock, but Danny was even more surprised to discover the dogged efforts taken to annihilate it forever. Afterward, he informed everyone about his two encounters with Sean and Luke earlier in the day.

"So Sean figured out that Ben and I returned?" Jim asked when Danny finished.

"No, just Ben. He had his fingerprints, not yours."

"And he just happened to figure everything out today, the same bloomin' day that we decide to finally break into the prison?" Charlie cried. "Is that just a coincidence or just the worst luck imaginable!?"

"It all happened pretty damn fast," was Danny's only explanation. "Maybe Luke suddenly remembered everything today and told Sean."

"I'm surprised Sean doesn't kill Luke for making such a mistake," Morgan declared and everyone agreed.

"He probably will now that we've destroyed the virus," Jim predicted. "He'll want revenge for this, I guarantee it."

And then, yet another knock at the door. Susan was the first to get up.

"That's gotta be them," she said, referring to Andy and Ben as she scrambled to the door.

"Why don't they just come in then?" Charlie wondered aloud. "It's unlocked."

But it wasn't Andy or Ben.

"Brian!" Susan cried as she dashed outside and into her brother's arms. "I can't believe it!"

"Hey, kiddo," Brian replied as he wrapped his arms around his sister, wetting her hair against his soaked raincoat. He sounded weary but elated. "Sorry it took me so long…we must've tried at least five hundred houses in this town in the last two days."

Standing behind Brian was Scott, his best friend from Aspen and the only person he managed to convince to come back east with him.

The two young men stepped inside and soon became acquainted and reacquainted with everyone. Once Andy and Ben returned, their victory would be complete.

* * *

18 October 2021, 1:35 am

Andy awoke sometime in the middle of the night. Her eyes opened as slowly as they had closed, and she became acutely aware of her body and its position against Ben's. In their mutual sleep, her cheek had landed firmly against the center of his chest, and her torso, wrapped snuggly under the thin blanket, was cradled within his. With her body temperature restored, the necessity of remaining pressed together had disappeared. But she made no effort to release herself from the grasp of the strong arms still draped around her.

The fire had dwindled in strength, but the area of the room near the fireplace was still warm. As Andy moved to relieve the crick in her neck, Ben stirred in his sleep but did not wake.

She checked the time on Ben's watch lying among their pile of clothes. They had been asleep for five hours, which gave her confidence that they were safe from discovery.

After placing a few more pieces of wood on the fire, she returned to her position beside him and gazed down at him as he slept. The rise and fall of his chest was hypnotic and prevented her from looking at anything but him.

From the day they first met, Andy could never deny that she found Ben to be very attractive; a young man blessed with the face and body of a movie star. But over the many months, she had grown accustomed to his appearance and had simply put that particular aspect of Ben in a figurative box and shoved it aside. After all, his looks had nothing to do with their relationship. They were close friends, confidants in many respects, and always would be.

And yet, as she stared down at him, at long last she allowed herself to admit that she wanted Ben as something more. She had denied her desires by hiding them deep within a secret compartment in her mind and heart. It had been her way of coping with her insecurities. But her efforts, as well as the mild envy she felt toward Morgan and Susan and their happy relationships, had worn her out.

Ben was absolutely everything she could ever want in a man, but what was she to him? She was a tomboy, wild and rough around the edges and not remotely sexy. Perhaps pretty, but she knew her place in the world of superficial appearance. Morgan was a graceful and elegant beauty. Susan, now nearly sixteen, grew more attractive every day, her smile and demeanor ever intoxicating to Charlie. Maria, meanwhile, was exotic…sultry.

But Andy? Strong. Intelligent. Daring. Yes, all of those applied. They were qualities she was proud to possess. But stunning? Sexy? Gorgeous? No, these did not apply, at least not in her mind.

But thinking rationally now, it wasn't entirely inconceivable to believe that Ben could possibly love her. Who else would have traveled alone hundreds of miles in the cold winter and hot desert to find her, and then enter a stadium filled with half-crazed, bloodthirsty spectators and dozens of armed men with only a single rifle for protection? Only someone who was more terrified of her death than his own.

As though under a spell, Andy's hand slowly reached out toward Ben, toward his abdomen. Whenever she had seen him without a shirt, his perfect set of muscles never failed to distract her. And now her hand was seemingly acting on its own as her fingertips delicately brushed his skin. They outlined each muscle and ran up and down the length of his stomach, slowly and lightly like feathers. Then, her hand became her own again, and she jerked it back, suddenly aware of what she was doing.

And then his hand grabbed her wrist.

Ben was awake.

Their eyes locked.

Without a word, he sat up and let go of her wrist, only to reach around her with both arms and pull her closer to him. Instinctively, Andy looked away.

She always looked away.

But Ben wasn't going to let it pass, and he quickly put both hands on her face by her ears, urging her not to turn away.

"Please…don't…"

With those two words, Andy realized that he had felt her fear, not just at that moment but all the other times as well—every aversion of her eyes from his, every inch of space that she had placed between them, every excuse that she had made to avoid her feelings. He recognized her hesitation once again, right there on a cold floor inside a strange, dark house. And he was refusing to let it happen any longer. He was tired of it, and so was she. And suddenly, she felt relief.

Before she could think or feel another thought, he pulled her closer toward him until their lips were a mere inch apart. Her breath caught in her throat in the same moment that he swallowed hard. Then he leaned in the rest of the way.

And when she kissed him back, it was not for practice or to

secretly play out a fantasy. This was actually happening. This was real.

Time seemed to both speed up and stand still as months of unspoken longing melted away. They kissed without restraint, the sensation of Ben's mouth and tongue against hers was electrifying, and when Andy began running her hands through Ben's hair, then over his shoulder and down his back, he knew he couldn't stop at this alone. He moved his hand down from her waist until his palm slid under her rear beneath the blanket. A soft sigh escaped her mouth.

With his other hand, Ben unclasped the hook of her bra. The straps slid over Andy's shoulders, and she flung the garment away without a thought as her mouth continued to kiss his. He then lifted her up and sat her down on top of his thighs, and she wrapped her legs around him. As he started to gently tug at the sides of her underwear, Andy suddenly pulled back. She looked anxious and uncertain.

"Ben, I've never…"

"I know."

And because he did know, he acted accordingly—carefully and gently. Instead of removing her underwear just then, he slowly ran a hand down the length of her stomach until his fingers slid underneath her underwear, and she drew in a sharp breath between her teeth as he began exploring between her legs. His fingers created such an alien sensation, one that she wanted to continue, and she began to move instinctively against his hand.

Feeling Andy relax, Ben withdrew his hand and pulled her underwear down around her thighs, at which point she removed them completely. Aching now, Ben leaned back against the ottoman and slid off his boxers. He gave her one last kiss before lifting her up once more. Then slowly, demonstrating both strength and restraint, Ben lowered her down as he entered her. She uttered a small cry, but the pain would soon pass.

"You okay?" he whispered.

Biting her lower lip, Andy nodded, and he brushed away the

single tear that had fallen down her cheek. He kissed her again before guiding her movements in rhythm with his. Any discomfort Andy had initially felt was soon replaced by the warmest and most enjoyable feeling she had ever experienced.

They made love twice more during those early morning hours, and by the third time, Andy no longer felt even the slightest hint of pain. In between, they slept close together by the warmth of fire, neither ever so happy as they were at that moment.

Chapter XXV

18 October 2021, 7:04 am

When Andy awoke, concern that they had stayed too long in the house immediately gripped her. She checked her watch and was stunned to find that it was after seven.

"Shit!" she hissed and quickly stood up. The acute soreness between her legs and the interior of her pelvic region was startling, but she ignored these unfamiliar aches and hastily got dressed. The room was cold once again, but her clothes and shoes were mercifully dry.

Once her shoes were laced, she knelt down beside Ben still fast asleep on the floor.

"Wake up," she murmured gently into his ear.

He stirred mildly, so she shook his shoulder to speed up the process.

"Sweetie, wake up."

Ben's eyes blinked open, and when he saw Andy, he smiled.

"Did you just call me 'sweetie?'"

"I did. Now get up. It's after seven, and the sun will be up soon."

Ben obeyed and sat up, but before reaching for his clothes, he grabbed Andy's waist and pulled her down to the ground. Squealing, she landed right beside him and laughed, which made him laugh in return until he leaned in and stopped her mouth with his. She kissed him back with equal eagerness as the tingling sensation returned in her stomach and between her thighs, but she forced herself to pull back.

"Stop it! We have to go!"

Reluctantly and with a groan, Ben released Andy and threw on his clothes.

"You're spoiling all the fun," he told her as he pulled his fleece sweatshirt over his head before reaching for his raincoat.

"I just want us to get away from here," Andy replied more sharply than intended, and she swiftly made amends by drawing near to Ben and kissing him tenderly once more. Wearing a knowing smile, she whispered, "We'll have more fun when we get home. You know, to celebrate."

Smiling in turn, Ben replied, "Promise?"

"I promise." And she kissed him again before adding as a final joke, "Was I better than champagne?"

"No comparison," was Ben's candid reply, and then his face grew serious. "I never thanked you for doing this," he added.

"Doing what?"

"All of this. For dragging my pathetic ass back east. For helping Jim and I finish what we started."

Andy grabbed at the neckline of Ben's sweater affectionately.

"I did it 'cuz I knew that deep down, you wanted to come back."

After one final kiss, they quickly gathered their things and headed for the door. But when Ben stepped outside, both he and his heart stopped cold.

Standing in the driveway surrounded by half a dozen guards was Sean. Upon seeing Ben, a repulsive, self-satisfied smile spread across his face.

"Well, well…isn't this cozy? We've been waiting forever for you two to wake up."

Acting on instinct, Ben placed himself in front of Andy and raised his weapon.

"I wouldn't do that if I were you," Sean yelled out in warning.

But Ben steadied his aim and shut his left eye as his right focused in on the front sight.

"Why not, asshole? Your head is right in my line of fire."

"Because your rifle has no firing pin."

Sean pulled out a thin metal object from within his jeans pocket. It was a few inches in length and resembled a long nail.

"You're bluffing," Ben hollered back, though his voice wavered.

Wearing a smug grin, Sean outstretched his arms as if daring Ben to fire.

"Go ahead…pull the trigger."

Without hesitation, Ben flexed his right index finger a second after Sean uttered his last word. Horribly, nothing happened, so he tried again and again until the hideous sound of Sean's laugh forced him to stop.

Both terrified and enraged, Andy fished inside her backpack for her pistol, but her hand found nothing.

"Looking for this?"

Sean suddenly revealed her Glock and held it up high as the guards began to laugh.

"You two really should've locked the doors last night. But I guess you were too busy fucking each other's brains out to think about it."

In a split-second motion, Ben whirled around and faced Andy.

"The back door. Go!"

Andy's feet propelled her back into the house. There was a door in the kitchen that led to a rear patio. She burst through this door and launched over the handrail that wrapped around the patio as Ben ran after her.

Beyond the small backyard of the house lay a cluster of trees that Andy ran toward, but just as she was about to disappear into them, two armed guards suddenly appeared from behind the trees and quickly subdued her. She stopped dead in her tracks as Ben nearly ran into her from behind. Within moments, they were surrounded.

Looking up at Ben, Andy saw only terror in his face. Even so, his eyes were scanning the area in a desperate search for even a remote way to escape. But the horrific reality was that any attempt to flee at this point would only result in one or both of them getting shot.

Walking intentionally slow, Sean came around the side of the house to the backyard. So confident was he in his captives' fate that he calmly pulled an apple out of his coat pocket and began biting away at it as though he were simply out for a stroll on a crisp, autumn day. He was enjoying every minute of this nightmare.

"You know, you two make a really cute couple," he said between bites and entered the circle created by his guards as they maintained their aim on both their targets. Taking another bite, Sean looked back and forth between Andy and Ben, his icy blue eyes dancing with delight. After swallowing, he said, "It's too bad that you won't be able to see what might've become of this beautiful relationship."

And with that, he flung the remainder of the apple to the ground. This action served as a queue for the guards, and two of them grabbed Andy and pulled her away. She struggled under their grasp, and Ben cried out her name in desperation as the remaining guards maintained their circle around him. One thrust the barrel of his gun into Ben's chest.

"Get off of me! Let…me…GO!" Andy screamed as they dragged her to the front of the house. She kicked her legs and squirmed violently, but the guards' grip was too strong. Sean followed them, marching behind her as he stared into her face and frowned with obsessive interest.

The guards let Andy go when they reached the front curb, flinging her crumpled body to the ground. When she tried to stand up, they rapidly restrained her. An SUV pulled up to the curb, and Luke stepped out of the passenger's seat. He looked down at Andy and sneered.

"Hello, Katrina. Nice to see you again."

"Actually, it's Andy," Sean corrected as he joined his comrade. "At least that's what our good friend Ben called her a moment ago."

Luke seemed to consider the name and nodded in approval.

"Andy, huh? Well, nice to see you again anyway, though you look like shit compared to the last time I saw you."

Seething, she stared up at Luke with overt hatred in her eyes but remained silent.

Sean gestured for Luke to follow him to the back of the house.

"Watch her," he ordered the guards before he and Luke walked away.

After rounding the house, Sean approached the circle of guards who were still restraining Ben. He waved them back to give him more room and turned to Luke. He leaned in close to his friend and said in a low voice, "Tell the two guards you trust the most to stay behind and send the rest to the front of the house."

Ben, meanwhile, was trying to figure out what was going on. His eyes flashed wildly between Sean, Luke, and each of the guards.

Luke took a quick look at the six guards surrounding Ben and pointed at two of them.

"You two…stay here. The rest of you go back to the front."

The guards obeyed, and as they broke off, Ben took advantage of the moment to break free and run. He managed to get beyond Luke and the guards. Only Sean reacted quickly and in a cruel twist of irony, he retrieved not his own pistol tucked into the back of his jeans but Andy's Glock from his coat pocket. With impressive skill, he aimed it at Ben and fired.

The sound of the gun shattered in the air, and the bullet lodged itself into the back of Ben's right shoulder as its momentum plunged him to the ground. The echo of the shot was still resonating off the house and trees when Andy released an ear-piercing scream from the front of the house.

In shock, Ben rolled over and opened his eyes. He saw Sean and Luke standing over him but their faces were out of focus. When at last the pain emerged, Ben grabbed his shoulder and groaned in agony. He couldn't hear what either Sean or Luke were saying, but soon after the throbbing began and the warm gush of blood flowed from his shoulder, he vaguely heard the thunderous crack of two more shots being fired. Neither of them were aimed anywhere near him.

More of Andy's screams could be heard in the distance; louder and more heart-wrenching than the first. Ben heard her cries, and they only added to his pain. The wound was unlike anything he'd ever felt, and his mind raced from thought to incongruous thought.

Should it burn this much? was the last before the butt of a rifle slammed into his forehead. His vision faded to black.

"You two," Sean said sharply to the two guards. "Ben Kelly is dead…got it? If I hear anything otherwise, *you're* both dead."

The guards nodded fearfully.

"Good. Now stand over there for a few minutes while Luke and I talk."

The guards did as they were told and stepped several yards away as Sean spoke to Luke.

"Take her back to the city. Put her in that closet across the hall from my office and make sure it's locked and guarded. I'll be there after I deal with him."

Sean stared down at Ben.

"What are you gonna do?" Luke asked.

Sean pursed his lips together, still staring at his unconscious enemy.

"I'm still working on that."

At that moment, Andy appeared around the corner of the house. Somehow, she had broken free from the guards who were now trailing after her. One of them raised his gun to shoot her.

"No!" Sean yelled out and waved his arms, stopping the guard just in time.

Andy collapsed to the ground when she saw Ben's lifeless body, and she began to sob uncontrollably as two guards dragged her away once more.

Smirking, Sean turned back to Luke. "At least now she'll believe that her beloved Ben is dead."

* * *

18 October 2021, 9:35 am

Staring out the living room window, Morgan held Katie in her arms as she fed her a bottle of formula. She normally would be breast-feeding her daughter, but this morning she wasn't in the mood. More accurately, she was exhausted. With the exception of Katie and Carmen, everyone had suffered a restless night, while Morgan hadn't slept at all.

Neither Andy nor Ben had returned, and by morning, it was evident that something had happened to them.

"I'll feed her," Jim said as he came up behind his wife. "You should try to get some sleep."

But Morgan continued to feed Katie.

"I'm tired but I can't sleep."

"We'll find them."

Morgan turned around and gave her husband a sharp look. "How do you know that?"

"Because I know Ben and you know Andy. They're fighters."

Morgan turned back to the window as Katie continued sucking away at the bottle.

"I won't just wait here for them."

"We won't. We'll go back to the prison today and see if we can find out what happened."

Morgan turned all the way around this time and looked hard into Jim's weary eyes. "When you say 'we'll go back,' you mean you and Charlie, right?"

Jim frowned. "Uh, yeah. And maybe Brian and Scott if they're up for it."

"Oh, and us girls get to stay back and do nothing, is that it?"

Jim sighed. "No, that's not what I meant…"

"Good," Morgan cut him off. "'Cuz here's what I'm thinking..."

She marched to the couch and sat down as Jim followed her with his eyes.

"You and Charlie will go back to the prison. So will Susan and

Maria. The four of you will do a search of the area and try to find out what happened."

"Uh, okay," Jim replied as he tried envisioning how her plan was any different from his.

"Danny will go back to the city, and as long as he thinks Sean doesn't suspect his role in any of this, he'll make new IDs for Brian and Scott. Then the three of them will listen for any rumors about Andy and Ben. They'll stay there in Manhattan for however long it takes."

"Uh, maybe you should run that idea by them, don't you think?"

"Oh, they'll agree," Morgan replied doubtlessly. "I know Brian would do anything to find Andy, and Scott will probably follow along with whatever Brian does. And if Maria asks Danny to return, he won't refuse unless he thinks his life will be in danger."

"Why would Danny listen to Maria?"

Morgan made a face. "You blokes sure are daft sometimes."

"Gee, thanks," Jim retorted. "Anyway, sounds like you've got it all planned."

"I do," Morgan replied, ignoring his sarcasm.

"And what are you going to do, my dear?"

Jim's patronizing term of endearment only annoyed Morgan. "I'll stay here with Katie and Carmen in case Andy and Ben come back."

Jim raised his eyebrows. "Oh, so you *are* gonna just stay here then?" he replied with amusement.

"Yes, but at least now it's my decision. My plan, my decision. Now, go wake everyone up. We've got work to do."

She was being brave, and Jim recognized her need to take charge. Rising to his feet, he approached her and leaned over to place a kiss on her forehead. "We'll find them, don't worry," he whispered.

Morgan's eyes welled up, and a large tear rolled down her cheek. It fell and hit Katie's bottle.

"What if he has them? What if he…"

She couldn't utter the word, so Jim sat down beside her and wrapped his arm around her.

"If Sean has them, he won't kill them. He'll play with them and torment them, but he won't kill them. That would be no fun for him."

Morgan looked into her husband's eyes and narrowed her own. "Then we'd better work fast."

* * *

18 October 2021, 12:12 pm

When Andy awoke from the torrent of despair that had knocked her out, her surroundings were pitch-black and the floor she lie upon was cold. Dazed and exhausted, a foggy recollection of the day in the dark warehouse outside of Los Angeles was the only thing to come to mind. Then suddenly, she remembered everything, and she began to weep.

And then, she cursed God.

She cursed Him for punishing her when all she had wanted was help others. She cursed Him for allowing her to be kidnapped and taken away from her friends in Aspen and for standing up to people like Nataliya. She cursed Him for her being a captive once again, all because she had tried to prevent a psychopath from having control over the virus.

But most of all, she cursed Him for forever taking away from her the only man she had ever loved. She choked when she said Ben's name aloud, and a great pain struck her like a knife stabbing her through the heart.

One night…that's all I got with him was one night. Why did I wait so long?

She didn't care where she was or how long she was going to be there. All she wanted was to die. Death was the only sure way to erase all the pain and the memories that would only haunt her forever.

And so she cried until mental anguish fatigued her to the point of unconsciousness, and she remained motionless on the cold, hard floor for several hours. Neither hunger nor the urge to urinate could wake her. The only mercy granted to her was a dreamless sleep, one without nightmares or images of Ben to cruelly disappoint her when she awoke.

* * *

18 October 2021, 5:12 pm

On the eightieth floor of the Empire State Building, Sean opened the door to a "room" guarded by two Infantry officers. Light from the hallway illuminated the dark space. It was a small closet, identical to the one he had placed the girl in. The space was empty, only measuring six-feet square that had once been used as a supply room to store cleaning materials. It was too small for his six-foot-two captive to lie down completely. Sean hadn't planned for that to be the case, but the discomfort the size would create pleased him all the same.

Conscious once again but now encumbered with a terrible headache to coincide with his gunshot wound, Ben was sitting with his back against the corner farthest from the door. Sean had earlier instructed a Fixer to check the wound and remove any fragments of the bullet. The wound had been a clean shot, however, tearing mostly through muscle and the very outer surface of the humerus bone, but the blood that had seeped from his shoulder through the bandages was visible even in the low light, and it was obvious that Ben was in excruciating pain. No sedative or painkiller had been given to him all day, and the unrelenting suffering was wearing him down.

Sean stepped inside and closed the door behind him. The darkness returned momentarily until he illuminated a hand-held electric lamp. Though the overhead light worked in the room, it was part of Sean's plan to keep Ben in near-permanent darkness.

Ben's eyes blinked at the sudden sensation of light as he recognized Sean's face.

"Where is she?" was the first thing he said in almost a growl through gritted teeth. Though the room was cold, his forehead glistened with sweat and his right leg shook from pain.

"Oh, she's a lot closer than you think." The self-satisfied smile on

Sean's face was sickening. "She's just upstairs. In fact…" Sean looked up and pointed his index finger to the ceiling. "Yeah…I think she's right above you. Just a few feet of rebar and concrete between you and her."

He looked back at Ben writhing in agony on the floor. "Unfortunately for you, she thinks you're dead. Shot through the head point-blank."

Ben's eyes grew wide. "No…she won't believe that!" he gasped, every word a struggle.

"Well, she seemed pretty convinced when I told her. She started yelling and then crying. And I'm sure you painted such a nice picture about me to her. You know, how evil I am and how many people I've killed…it would be harder to convince her that I *hadn't* killed you."

"You *are* evil, you miserable fuck!"

Ben spat out this last word with what remained of his strength. He let out a grunt in response to the pain and nearly passed out while Sean looked on with satisfaction.

"Why don't you just kill me then?"

"Because that would be too easy for you and less fun for me," Sean began. "See, you destroyed my plans with your little stunt at the prison yesterday, so now I'm going to destroy your life. I think it's a fair exchange."

Ben could only listen now. His will to argue was gone. All he wanted was to black out.

"But before anything else happens," Sean went on, "I'm gonna give you something for the pain 'cuz you really look like you need it."

He opened the door and the same Fixer who had cleaned Ben's shoulder entered. Without any instruction, the Fixer walked directly to Ben with a syringe in one hand and a flashlight in the other. Sean watched with delight as the Fixer leaned over and grabbed Ben's injured arm. Ben let out a howl, but the Fixer ignored him and injected the needle into the first vein he could find. After releasing the contents of the syringe, he departed the room, leaving Sean and

Ben alone once again.

"Did you know that heroin is synthesized from morphine?" Sean remarked flatly. "I understand that the two have similar psychological effects on users. Lots of soldiers became addicted to morphine after they came home from wars during the last century."

He spoke like a professor giving a lecture.

"But several of the Helens tell me heroin is the best high they've ever had. Of course, I can't afford to risk using it personally. Addiction doesn't really suit someone in my position, so you'll have to confirm that for me."

But Ben had barely heard anything. The drug was already numbing the pain in his shoulder, and his mind began to feel a strange sense of calm.

"It's the most difficult drug for me to get my hands on," Sean rambled on. "You should consider yourself lucky that I'm about to invest my limited supply on you."

He then took a few steps toward his captive. "But this time, I'll be more careful. You won't overdose like…Kar—like your sister."

Even in his deteriorated state, Ben heard Sean's voice waver, and his anger briefly returned. "You killed her…" he murmured.

"It was an accident. I never meant for…"

Sean stopped and cleared his throat. "I loved her."

"You never loved anybody."

Feeling a surge of rage, Sean took another step forward and delivered a sharp kick to Ben's stomach. Ben let out a sharp cough and rolled over to his side with his back facing Sean.

Sean knelt down and leaned over until his face was within inches of Ben's ear.

"I loved Karen. Just like you love Andy. So I'm gonna take her away from you. Slowly, one day at a time. One injection at a time. Soon, you'll love the drug more than you love her. And then one day, you'll forget about her completely. You won't even remember her name."

If vengeance ever had a sound, it was Sean's voice in that

moment. He stood up and left the room, his anger over losing the virus beginning to assuage.

* * *

18 October 2021, 7:32 pm

After enjoying his dinner, Sean decided it was time to pay Andy a visit. He had lied to Ben when he'd said that he had already spoken to her, when in fact the two had yet to exchange a single word. He had only checked on her once while she slept in her own tiny room hours earlier, and for some reason, he did not want to wake her.

The guards opened the door to the closet, and Sean stepped inside. Unlike with Ben, he turned on the light. Andy was still asleep, but the flicker from the bulb disturbed her senses enough to wake her. She rubbed her swollen eyes and looked about until she spotted Sean. Then her face fell and she looked away.

"Oh c'mon…is that any way to treat your host? And here I was so anxious to meet the person who started all this mess."

But Andy didn't move. Sean closed the door and stepped around Andy to face her. He sat down on the floor to meet her eyes. Andy recoiled and turned away.

"So that's how it's gonna be then, huh? I won't hurt you. I just wanna know who you are and how you got mixed up with someone like Ben Kelly."

At the mention of Ben's name, Andy's shoulders trembled. Sean crawled around her crumpled body and faced her once again. This time, she didn't move away. She was too overwhelmed by memories and regrets.

"Jesus Christ, he really did a number on you, didn't he?"

Sean leaned back against the wall and crossed his arms over his chest.

"I have to admit, I don't get the attraction. I mean, I guess he's good-looking…or *was*, I should say, but I never really saw him with a lot of girls before he took off last year."

He scratched his head as though he were trying to recall

something. Andy kept her head down, her hair covering her face.

"There was one girl…I think her name was Jenny…I saw her with him quite a bit, but she was just a Dreg, nothing compared to one of my Helens. She was pretty, but too reserved. I never understood why Ben wasted his time with her, and I doubt the two of them ever had as much fun as you two did last night."

Sean waited for a reaction but he would not be satisfied. He reached out and curled a thick strand of Andy's hair around his finger and brushed it aside to see her face. She jerked away.

"Calm down, princess…I'm just trying to see what Ben found so alluring. And Luke, too. I gotta say, that little act you performed back at the club was quite entertaining. I might've fallen for it too. You definitely looked the part."

Sean leaned forward and tried to force eye contact, but to no avail.

"C'mon, Andy! Say something…I'm asking you nicely."

"There's nothing to say," Andy mumbled hoarsely.

"Oh, she speaks!"

"Just leave me alone."

But Sean was blithe in his response. "Perhaps you're not aware that torture is not off the table when it comes to getting what I want."

Andy finally looked up at Sean with hollow eyes.

"You said you wouldn't hurt me, but go ahead…torture me all you want. There's nothing more you can do to me. But I'll take my life and what I've done with it to the grave."

Then she turned away and lie back down on the floor. The cold surface had become oddly comforting against her hot, tear-flushed cheeks.

"That's fine. You can remain silent for as long as you want. But until you tell me something about yourself, you'll stay in this room in the dark without food, water, or a bathroom."

At the mention of the bathroom, Andy became painfully aware of the pressure on her bladder. She had managed to ignore the sensation for hours, but now that it had been brought to her attention, she could no longer deny the urge. Lying on her side, she crossed her top leg over her bottom one in an effort to stifle the discomfort. The gesture made Sean laugh.

"See, you won't last another hour, so why don't you stop being so stubborn and answer my question."

Accepting defeat, Andy pushed with her arms to sit upright. She brushed her hair away from her face and stared defiantly at Sean, her eyes coming back to life.

"If I answer a question, you have to answer one of mine."

Sean pondered the proposition for a moment before casually shrugging. "Sure, why not. I'll start. When and where did you meet Ben?"

"That's two questions, not one."

"I'm changing the rules."

Andy frowned but didn't argue. "Over a year ago on a highway in southern Virginia. Now my question: who the hell do you think you are trying to control the virus? Who made you God over all of us?"

Sean held up his hands and snickered. "Whoa, slow down. That wasn't a question…that was an accusation."

But Andy remained stone-faced. "Answer it however you want, but that's my question."

Sean leaned back against the wall and kept an intent gaze on his beautiful captive. Looking back at him, Andy suddenly recalled Ben's initial description of Sean.

What I remember most about him are his eyes. They're icy blue in a kinda terrifying way…

The description was dead-on. His eyes were a beautiful, crystalline blue, but there was not even the slightest degree of warmth in them. Instead, they seemed to penetrate whatever they looked at.

With Sean's stare unwavering, Andy ultimately flinched and looked away. He didn't seem to notice, for her question had fully occupied him. He took a deep breath and released it before finally speaking. "I don't think I'm God, if that's what you're implying. I'm simply trying to save people from themselves."

Andy let out an audible gasp. "How? By killing everyone who gets in your way?"

"No, that's not it at all. I don't care what anyone does with their lives. They can eat and drink what they want and fuck whomever they want and stay out late and go to the clubs as much as they want and do whatever drugs they want. People in this city have the freedom to do all the things that they couldn't do six years ago."

"You actually believe that?! You distribute drugs in this city like it's candy…young girls of twelve and thirteen are out there prostituting themselves and are choosing cocaine over food…!"

"Twelve and thirteen is not young anymore, not when you and I are two of the oldest people on the planet. And why not let people do what they want? The world is a mess. At least I'm giving everyone some order and opportunity."

Sean was leaning in even closer as his voice raised in volume. He didn't know why but he wanted Andy to understand. "You're not from around here, are you?"

She didn't respond, and Sean didn't wait for an answer.

"Then you can't imagine what this city was like right after the outbreak. Things were brutal and chaotic and people were killing each other in the streets over a single can of food. I brought back stability for a million people! Who else can say the same? People want a leader to take charge, someone to fight the chaos and to do the worrying for them. There's only a tiny fraction of people who are smart enough and determined enough to do what I have done in the past six years. Most people are simply content to follow and watch the world go by. They're like grazing cattle waiting to be herded. Why can't you understand that?"

Andy didn't want to listen anymore. Listening to Sean was like listening to the ramblings of a vainglorious madman who believed without a doubt that his actions were entirely justified.

She raised her eyes once more to meet his. She spoke slowly and deliberately.

"You believe that people are easy to manipulate. You think everyone can be controlled, that they can be bought with drugs and sex and status, but people aren't like that. People want to be loved and to have the freedom to do what they want with their lives…they don't want what *you* think they want. They've been driven to act recklessly because you offer them no alternative. You encourage their self-destructive behavior to keep them from ever waking up and realizing just how *evil* you are."

With that, Andy's faced crumpled and she turned away as the tears began to flow once again. She slumped back down to the floor and pressed her ear to the cold tiles, completely unaware that Ben was lying just a few yards below her.

"You killed someone I love today," she murmured softly into the air just loud enough for Sean to hear. "You shot him in cold-blood because he was trying to destroy something that should've never existed. You think Ben did it to get revenge on you for killing his sister? No. He did it because he knew that someone like you should never have control over something so deadly."

And with that, Andy closed her eyes. Even if Sean asked her one more question, she would remain silent. Any further argument with this narcissist and self-proclaimed savior of civilization was futile, as were any additional threats of torture. Sean had killed her lover and friend, and sitting a moment longer in the same room with him was more unbearable than any physical torture.

"Go," she whispered. "Just leave me alone. Or just kill me and get it over with."

Sean wasn't used to being told what to do, but he'd never dealt with anyone like Andy before. He recognized that, and it both intrigued and scared him.

Accepting defeat over this round of interrogation, he stood up and left the closet after turning out the light. There would be other chances to prove himself.

Chapter XXVI

26 November 2021

On the thirty-ninth day of her captivity, Andy had her first real visitor. She was no longer in the Empire State Building, for Sean thought it was too risky to keep her someplace so exposed to the populace. So in early November, he had her moved to the infamous Sing Sing Correctional Facility located thirty miles north of the city along the Hudson. It was the only facility that Sean actually used as a prison.

Infuriated by her unwavering silence after two weeks in the closet and mere yards from his office, Sean grudgingly transferred her to a lonely cell in an isolated part of the prison. Sean came to visit her once a week to try to force her to speak, but each time she remained mute with an occasional glare as her only form of communication. Each time Sean threatened torture but never followed through.

On a cold day in late November, after finishing a particularly revolting meal of cold soup that tasted more like bleach than chicken broth, two guards approached Andy in her cell and informed her that there was someone coming to see her. For a wonderful but brief moment, Andy thought it might be Morgan or Charlie, but the lunacy of that idea quickly lulled her back into her near-permanent state of hopelessness.

She heard footsteps approaching, and a moment later came the now horribly familiar clanging sound against the bars of her cell. It was one of the guards taunting her with a baton, the same ones former prison guards had once used years earlier.

"Remember…two minutes," he said to the person behind him before retreating.

Andy looked and saw a fairly small person moving toward the bars wearing a baseball cap and a large winter coat. When the dim light hit the person's face, Andy recognized it immediately.

It was Susan.

Andy's eyes grew wide and she started to say something, but Susan stopped her by putting her index finger to her lips. She covertly reached inside her coat and pulled out what appeared to be a large padded envelope and tossed it between the bars. It flew past Andy and landed squarely in the center of her tiny bed.

"Open it after I leave," Susan instructed in a whisper. "There's a letter inside. Read it and memorize it. Then get rid of it. There's duct tape inside. Use it to hide everything else underneath your bed."

"How did you get in here?"

"Drugs. Works every time. Danny's been a huge help, too."

Andy cast her eyes down at her feet. "Ben's dead."

"We know."

"Sean shot him."

"I know. I'm so sorry."

Andy couldn't hold back the tears, but as soon as they fell she brushed them away and composed herself with admirable speed.

"How's Morgan and Charlie? And Katie?"

"Good, but they miss you. We all do. Brian came back with Scott. You remember him?"

Andy smiled weakly and responded with the slightest of nods.

"I want to get out of here."

Her voice shook as tears appeared once again. Susan reached through the bars and squeezed Andy's arm.

"You will. Read the letter. I gotta go."

Without another word, Susan left. She didn't look back as her footsteps faded away.

Andy waited nearly an hour before she opened the package. It had been meticulously packed, each object carefully arranged to fit snugly within the envelope. She removed the contents and placed them on the bed: a wristwatch, a key, a small flashlight, a collapsible baton, a small spool of duct tape, the four separate components of a Glock pistol, a loaded 9-mm magazine, a pair of thick rubber gloves, a construction worker's mask, and a small bottle filled with a clear liquid. The last item Andy pulled out was a small envelope with a letter and a hand-drawn map enclosed. She opened the letter and recognized Morgan's handwriting immediately:

Andy,

Today is the 26th of November. In twelve days, on the 8th of December, there will be a power outage in the entire prison at exactly six o'clock in the evening, or 18:00. The 8th is the day of the next guard turnover. The old guards will be replaced by brand new ones who have never worked at your prison before, making it easier for you to escape…

Andy reread the word a few times…*escape…escape…*

Her heart beat faster as she continued reading.

The watch has been synchronized with ours and shows the proper date and military time. We know you hate wearing watches, but try to get used to wearing it now. The small bottle contains an acid mixture that Charlie concocted. Starting today, spray the lock to your cell every day, twice a day. Wear the gloves and the mask while doing this, as the acid is highly corrosive. Make sure it doesn't contact your skin, and try to spray the lock when you think you won't be visited by guards or anyone else for at least an hour afterward, as the smell can be overpowering. By the time you're ready to escape, the acid should corrode the lock enough to kick the door loose. Worst case, use the gun to finish the job and to protect yourself against the guards. Same with the collapsible baton.

The key is for the car that we have staged for you about a mile away from the prison. On the map we've included, you'll find where we've parked it. It's a red SUV without plates and has a full tank of gas. Jim checked everything to make sure it's running smoothly. There will be warm clothes and food inside the trunk. Inside the glove compartment is a map and directions to get to where we are now living. We are no longer in Princeton.

On the other side of this map is a sketch of Sing Sing prison where you're being kept. Study it and memorize the places we've marked where you'll have the best chances of escape if you can't get to the main entrance. We've done everything we can, but this prison is more heavily guarded than Green Haven. Even with the blackout, it will be difficult…but not impossible.

We all love you and miss you terribly. Good luck.

Love,
All of Us

Filled with an overwhelming and wholly unexpected sense of hope, Andy read the letter several more times. She assembled the Glock and loaded the magazine before taping it securely under her bed. Then she donned the gloves and mask and carefully applied the acid to the lock on the door to her cell. The smell from the chemical reaction was intense, but Andy knew she was safe from detection this late in the day.

She studied both sides of the map before folding it within the letter and slid both papers beneath her pathetic little pillow. Then she taped the mask, gloves, key, flashlight, baton, and the bottle of acid underneath her bed. Finally, she put on the watch and concealed it beneath the cuff of her sweatshirt, the same sweatshirt she'd been wearing since that day at Green Haven. Forty days of sweat and body dander had made it stiff and odorous.

Then, she vomited in her toilet.

* * *

The wound hadn't healed properly. The risk of infection had been averted, but his range of motion was significantly reduced. Ben could barely lift his arm horizontally without feeling a sharp twinge of pain.

He was still inside the closet on the eightieth floor of the Empire State Building. By now his eyes were accustomed to the darkness, but the rest of his body was aching and restless. Today he was shaking more than usual and the urge to vomit was acute. It was always like this after the high wore off, but just when the symptoms became almost unbearable, the door would open and the needle would enter his vein. Then the euphoria would come and everything would be perfect for a few hours. He would lie on the floor, though sometimes it felt like he was lying on the ceiling looking down or lying on the wall hanging sideways.

Today when the needle stuck him in the left forearm, he thought of Andy and looked up at the ceiling just before the Fixer closed the door and the light disappeared. He wondered if she was still above him or if she had been moved somewhere else entirely. During the brief moments of sobriety before the withdrawal symptoms paralyzed him, his memory would taunt him with images of their one night together by the fireplace. He would remember the feel of her skin beneath his fingers, the smell of her wet hair, and the sound of her stifled cries the moment he had entered her. He wouldn't cry, but his eyes would well up as the mental ache over the loss of her existence in his life overpowered him. But then physical pain would set in and the craving for the heroin would begin again.

Sean's revenge was horrific, but each time the drug coursed through Ben's veins, he became oblivious to it.

* * *

08 December 2021

Day fifty-one.

She checked her watch when she woke up that morning. She'd worn it every day since Susan's visit. Time was of little consequence in prison but today it was imperative.

Around four in the afternoon, the guards delivered what she hoped would be her last meal in the cursed place: salty vegetable soup and soggy canned pears. Andy grudgingly ate everything on her plate. She would need her strength.

After pushing her empty tray between the bars and into the barren hallway, she set the alarm on her watch for five-thirty before lying down for a brief nap. An hour later, she awoke with a jolt. It was time to get ready. With the car key and the baton tucked safely into her front and back jeans pockets, she double-checked the Glock and chambered a round. Then she read over the map of the prison one more time. With the gun in her right hand and the flashlight in her left, she sat on the edge of the bed—and waited.

The cellblock was quiet. Even the usual hushed noises of guards and prisoners seemed to have faded into silence. Or maybe it was just the ringing in her ears.

At exactly one minute after six o'clock, darkness enveloped the entire prison. Seconds later, shouts of chaos and confusion filled the air.

Andy stood up and approached her prison bars. She gave the door a heavy shake and the latch loosened a bit but not enough. She turned on the flashlight and pointed the beam toward the bed to suppress its intensity from view by the guards before giving the door a hard kick with the bottom of her shoe. The corroded latch gave way and the door swung open. She stepped into the hallway and ran.

Scurrying like a cat, Andy followed the bouncing beam of light as she passed several prisoners in their cells. Wild yells and whistles erupted as she flew by, but the sounds barely registered to her senses. She took a right turn and then a left and ran into two guards coming from the opposite direction. She raised the beam of the flashlight to their eyes, temporarily blinding them, and when she approached, she stopped and gave the one to her right a sharp elbow to the ear, disabling him. She then gave the guard on her left a sideways kick to his knee in the same manner as she had opened her cell door. The guard's leg buckled, and he collapsed to the ground in excruciating pain. Though the gun was still in her right hand, Andy's inherent compassion prevented her from needlessly shooting anyone.

In the dark, the prison was an impossible maze to navigate, but she had memorized every turn. When she stumbled across two more guards, she quickly immobilized them with the help of the baton, all the while maintaining her focus on the prison map in her mind.

When she reached the prison's main entry, the chaos stemming from the loss of power enabled her to blend in with the commotion of disoriented guards bumping into one another, and without any further obstacles, she squeezed beyond the last door and emerged into the night.

The cold air hit her lungs and invigorated her body. The Hudson River was a mere hundred yards to the west, and the moisture in the air was instantly perceptible. It was the first fresh breath Andy had knowingly inhaled in weeks. The sky was crisp and clear, and the light from the waxing crescent moon was enough to illuminate her final path.

Her brain extinguished the interior prison map and shifted attention to the exterior map. She raced through the narrow parking lot to the footbridge that crossed over the train tracks running north and south outside the prison compound. Once on the other side of the footbridge, she headed south along the tracks for almost a mile. The buildings and trees on her right faded away until there was just a thin strip of dirt between the tracks and the river.

Though weak from nearly two months of incarceration and insufficient food and water, the knowledge that she was no longer living for just herself propelled her forward as she hopped between the tracks. She stared down at the wooden ties in order to sustain her footing until she passed the old Scarborough Post Office on her left and a tiny parking lot squeezed between the train tracks and the river on her right. The lot was empty except for a red SUV sitting alone in the dark.

Andy hopped off the tracks and ran toward the vehicle, out of breath, and reached into her pocket to retrieve the key. Half a minute later, she was steering the SUV east across a small bridge that ran over the train tracks. She drove aimlessly for a few minutes to distance herself from the prison. She pulled over along a quiet residential street, opened the glove compartment, and retrieved three different maps and a short handwritten note. After reading the note, she poured over the maps and spotted her final destination, marked with a red "X" on the third map. The location surprised her.

In the back of the car, she found the food and water beneath a winter coat, a hat, and gloves. Also in the trunk were three five-gallon cans filled with gasoline. Now armed with warmth and sustenance, Andy read over the maps once more and determined her route.

An hour and two bottles of water later, Andy pulled off the highway and into a strip mall with a 7-Eleven and a drugstore. She went inside the dark 7-Eleven first to use the bathroom, but as she passed the near-empty shelves, she abruptly stopped and stepped back outside. The drugstore was just a few storefronts away, and she headed in that direction. Once inside, she scoured the shelves with her flashlight. Her bladder was about to burst, but she did her best to ignore the intense discomfort until she found what she was looking for.

On the second-to-last shelf, she found the right location but the shelf was empty. Desperate, she got down on all fours and flashed the light under the shelf. To her surprise, not one but two boxes of what she wanted had fallen underneath. After removing her gloves, she pressed her cheek against the dirty carpet and strained her left arm under the shelf until her fingertips barely brushed the first box. With her insides screaming for relief, Andy freed the box and strained once more for the second, and just as she thought she was going to wet her pants, her hand achieved a precarious hold on the second box. With a grunt, she finally secured it and scrambled to her feet.

The bathroom door of the drugstore was locked and there was no time to find the key. Andy ran back outside and turned on the SUV's ignition. After flicking on the headlights, she glanced once at her surroundings before squatting down in front of the vehicle. Her bare hands struggled in the cold to open the two boxes. Inside each

were two sticks wrapped in plastic. After tearing apart the plastic from each stick, Andy gathered all four exposed sticks in her left hand and yanked her filthy jeans and underwear down around her ankles with her right.

Though air chilled her bare skin, the urge to relieve her bladder was far greater. After adjusting her position, she carefully aimed the stream of urine on each stick before tossing them aside on the ground. After pulling her pants back on, she paced around the parking lot and waited.

As the minutes ticked by, Andy grabbed one of the empty boxes and read over the instructions on the back. She then picked up the first stick.

The pregnancy indicator in the middle displayed an unmistakable symbol.

Epilogue

04 January 2022

With an average of a quarter million vehicles crossing between Virginia and Maryland daily, the Woodrow Wilson Bridge was once a traffic nightmare for residents of the Washington DC Metropolitan area. More than a mile long, the bridge spanned the Potomac River at the southern section of the Capitol Beltway.

Riding a motorcycle, Chad's was the only moving vehicle in sight as he headed east from Virginia into Maryland. The rusted-out skeletons of dozens of abandoned cars, trucks, and SUVs still littered the highway in both directions of the bridge; permanent reminders of a past that would never return.

Chad zoomed ahead for a few more miles beyond the bridge as a cold, winter rain pelted his helmet and jacket. He exited the Beltway and made his way onto Andrews Air Force Base. After parking his bike out of the rain within a particular hangar, he walked beneath the canopy before stopping directly in front of a UH-1N Iroquois twin-engine helicopter. Daunting in size and scope, the helicopter stood in the same position as it had for over six years, seemingly frozen in time. As he stared up at the impressive machine, a rare emotion stirred in Chad: fear.

The aircraft seemed to be taunting him, daring him or anyone who gazed at it to give it a spin.

C'mon, hop in! Push a few buttons…it'll be fun!

Without realizing it, Chad took a step backward. He'd never flown in an airplane before, let alone a helicopter.

The sound of an approaching vehicle pulled Chad's attention away, and he glanced at his watch.

Five minutes early.

Resorting to habit, Chad reached into his back pocket and pulled out his knife. He began flipping it back and forth between his hands as three people exited the SUV and approached.

Two were boys, Brandon and Calvin, each around sixteen or seventeen, both Infantry officers reassigned to Chad in DC, and both frustrated by their current situation and rank. Chad's painstaking observance of the pair over the past few months led him to conclude that their loyalty to Sean was dangling by a very thin thread.

The third person was a tough-looking girl of about the same age. She had short, dark hair and wide brown eyes, and she seemed to wear a permanent smirk.

"You Megan?" Chad asked as the girl drew closer.

The girl gave a half-hearted nod as she chomped away on a piece of gum. "Yeah, that's me."

She didn't look at Chad, or anything else except the helicopter towering before her. She walked around it slowly, touching a few rivets and joints here and there, all the while smacking away at her gum.

"It's not in terrible shape, but it'll take some time to fix," she declared after completing a lap. "I should have it running again in…I dunno, a month. Two, at most."

Chad raised his eyebrows skeptically. "A month? You better not be fucking with me."

"Maybe two," she quickly repeated before turning back to the aircraft. "You got someone who can fly this thing?"

Chad looked at the two boys, one of whom nodded. "Let me worry about that."

Megan shrugged. "Whatever, but I can't be a hundred percent sure that everything's working without a goddamned pilot. Got it?"

Chad took a deep breath. She was right, but instead of relenting, he forced a smile across his face.

"This is one of Sean's highest priorities right now, so let's just get it done fast."

The game was just beginning.

Coming Soon…

The Fractured Road

Part II: North and South

P*rologue*

25 October 2024

Despite the unseasonably warm autumn sun, the woman walked swiftly and with her arms crossed over her chest to fight her chill. The lightweight jacket hugging her shoulders would have been sufficient for most others in such weather, but her waifish frame made her particularly susceptible to the cold.

Heading east along *Rue de Rivoli*, she avoided eye-contact with several passersby while marching alongside the *Jardin des Tuileries.* She stopped upon reaching the northern Richelieu entrance of the *Musée du Louvre*, thereby avoiding the main entrance at the famous glass Pyramid, which by now was in utter shambles. Broken shards of glass still littered the ground surrounding I.M. Pei's controversial masterpiece, to the great distress of the young woman. Her father had taken her to Paris three times before the age of twelve, and the Louvre was always the highlight of each trip. That and the warm *pain au chocolat* for breakfast each morning.

After descending inside the museum, she walked past the empty Starbucks and the bookstore containing every book imaginable detailing the thousands of works of art assimilated into the museum over the centuries. Once beyond the main entry assembly on the bottom floor, she ascended the frozen escalator and headed into the heart of the Denon Wing.

The museum was empty and dark, with only light from the windows providing any illumination. Unbeknownst to the woman, the humid and musty air was gradually damaging every priceless painting she passed. She stopped for a moment at the *Mona Lisa*, and using her flashlight, she studied the world's most famous painting from a mere foot away. It had, like most of the artwork in the museum, survived the wrath of vandals over the last nine years. The city itself may have been in the worst shape since the end of the Second World War, but Parisian survivors still respected the treasures inside the museum, if not those on the outside.

Breaking away from Da Vinci's masterpiece, the woman took a turn to her right and entered Room 76 before taking an immediate left into Room 77, the signs on the wall guiding her to the correct location. Once inside, she wandered to the fifth painting on the left and stopped. Light from the vast ceiling window enabled her to clearly see the expressions of the figures portrayed in Delacroix's *Liberty Leading the People*. Her eyes fixed themselves upon the dominant female figure representing "Liberty" and holding the French Tricolour, and her thoughts drifted as she took a seat on the nearby bench in the middle of the immense room.

After staring blankly at the painting for another moment, she reached into the beautiful Chanel bag she had found within the basement of Galeries Lafayette a few days earlier, miraculously still encased in its original packaging, and retrieved a compact mirror. A quick glance at her reflection was unsatisfying. Despite her twenty-two years, she lamented her weary appearance. The last few years had taken their toll on her complexion. And then there was her nose, no longer straight and perfect.

With a frustrated sigh, the woman snapped the compact shut and thrust it into her bag with disgust. She chastised herself sharply under her breath as footsteps approached.

"Nataliya?"

The sound of her name and its subsequent echo were startling. Drawing in a quick breath, she turned sharply to her left and spotted a young man in his late-teens or early twenties.

"Yes?"

Nataliya rose to her feet as the stranger drew closer. Shorter than she with mousy-brown hair and an unremarkable face, his clothes were tattered but well-fitted to his thin frame.

"*Je m'appelle Christophe,*" the stranger said quickly with a hand to his chest before gesturing to the bench. "*S'il vous plaît, asseyez-vous.*"

Nataliya's eyes narrowed.

"I don't speak French."

"I don't speak *russe.*"

And so with their language barrier clearly established, they both took a seat and began to converse in their only common language: English. Nataliya's English was better than Christophe's, but she understood him clearly.

"So you are wanting to find your…*frère*…"

Christophe snapped his fingers in frustration over forgetting the word.

"My brother?" Nataliya supplied. "Yes. I assumed that was already explained to you."

"It was. I am just making certain."

"Well? Where can I find him?" Nataliya said with growing impatience.

Christophe's eyes narrowed.

"You are worried about him?"

"He's my brother," was Nataliya's detached response. "Now let's get this over with. I paid for this information weeks ago."

Sensing that another word would only further provoke her anger, Christophe reached into the back pocket of his jeans and retrieved a folded piece of paper. He calmly handed it over.

"What's this?" Nataliya demanded as she began unfolding the paper.

"It is where you will find your brother," was all Christophe said as he rose from the bench. "*Bonne chance.*"

Following a nod of farewell, Christophe turned and left. Yet another encounter with a random stranger that Nataliya would never see again.

Returning her attention back to the paper, she squinted at the words before employing a pair of reading glasses that she was now forced to use almost daily.

On the paper was a hand-drawn map with words scribbled in French, but the drawing itself was mercifully clear. Still, Nataliya's face quickly fell. The location indicated with a small circle on the map was hundreds of kilometers away, and one could argue, not even on the continent. Worse, it was somewhere she'd never heard of.

Underneath the map was scribbled a single name: Chad Heinrich.

Acknowledgements

First, I would like to thank my friend JB for his remarkable dedication to helping me edit the final drafts of this book prior to its publication. Thanks to his efforts, readers will be able to enjoy this book without stumbling over typos (we think we caught them all—fingers crossed!), grammatical errors, and "awkward" wording and dialogue. You're the best, JB!

I'd like to thank Amanda Day for her terrific work on my author photo. Despite being severely camera-shy, this is one picture that I'm happy to show to the world.

Finally, I wish to thank my parents, David and Nancy, for all their support, particularly during these last eighteen months. Without their love and encouragement, this book would've never become a reality. I love you both very much.

About the author

Born between two record-breaking blizzards in the suburbs of Boston, Britt Holewinski spent her formative years moving from city to city, always taking her active imagination with her. One fateful night during high school, seventeen-year-old Britt suffered a particularly vivid nightmare after watching a film version of William Golding's "Lord of the Flies". Upon awakening, the idea of a world controlled by teenagers inspired Britt to begin writing. Following an additional seventeen years of college, graduate school, 'grown-up' work, and self-admitted procrastination, the first book of "The Fractured Road" Trilogy was completed.

A lover of running, Britt gets her best inspiration while attempting to maintain a nine-minute mile pace. When not pounding the trails in Arlington, Virginia, she loves wine tasting, both in her home state and around the world. Britt's favorite varietal is Malbec, though a good bottle from Châteauneuf-du-Pape is hard to beat.

To learn more, visit: www.brittholewinski.com